SOARING

➤ WITH ⬅

VULTURES

By Dan Kelly

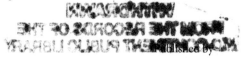

Published by

Dan Kelly
www.dankellykc.com

Printed by The Covington Group, Kansas City, Missouri

ISBN: 978-0-9991875-0-0

*Cover photos: Sallie Warner Nutter Botsford with Sam Nutter, top, and
Colonel William A. Warner*

ACKNOWLEDGMENTS

I would like to thank the following for their assistance in the research and production of "Soaring with Vultures":

Doug Weaver, Scott Couturier, and Anne Stanton of Mission Point Press; copy editor Liz Garcia; John Audley and Randy Lackey of the Covington Group; the staffs at the State Historical Society of Missouri in Columbia, at the Lafayette County and Pettis County courthouses, at the Sedalia Public Library, and at the Missouri State Archives in Jefferson City; my family members whose assistance was invaluable; and especially to Georgette Stanley Page, who provided documents and photos from her family history as well as her unwavering support.

WRITER'S NOTE

All the characters mentioned by name in this book were real people, and all the major events really occurred. Other details are the product of poetic license.

I have interspersed sections of fiction with sections of fact, presenting them in a way that enables the reader to recognize which is which and to never be left wondering, "Did that really happen?"

PART

I

A MISSOURI MARRIAGE

Colonel William A. Warner

September 28, 1866

The wind whistled past Leslie Warner's face as he pushed his chestnut gelding at a gallop over a narrow trail through oak, chestnut, and pine trees. It was early autumn, his favorite time of year. The sky was blue and the air was crisp.

Leslie didn't know where he was going, but he was riding as hard as he could to get there.

The twelve-year-old had grown to love riding his horse in the countryside when he was a young boy in Kentucky, before the war started. From the Warners' new home in Lafayette County, Missouri, he could venture any direction and explore endless places he'd never seen before.

One or more of his sisters usually accompanied him on rides, but on this morning Leslie was alone. He had left the breakfast table and gone to the stable to saddle his gelding without telling anyone what he was doing.

As he headed south, Leslie vaguely wondered how long it would take to ride all the way back to Kentucky.

It felt good to be on his own, Leslie thought, taking on a new adventure that would lead to who knew what. Perhaps he would even encounter some of the bushwhackers who were said to hide out in these woods.

Leslie was riding through rough country. The thought occurred to him that he might have trouble finding his way back home, but he figured if he got lost he could simply head north and would eventually reach the Missouri River. From there he was confident he could get home.

He pushed on.

After Leslie had ridden about forty-five minutes, the trail widened and showed more wear. Leslie surmised he was nearing a populated area, so he slowed his gelding to a walk. He reckoned he still was heading south because the sun was on his left, but he had no idea whether he was about to encounter a village or a farm or an encampment of bushwhackers.

Just as he imagined himself sauntering into a swarm of gun-toting bad guys and trying to explain what he was doing alone in this remote area, he heard a noise. A fawn, he thought, mewing for its mother. No, it was a moan. And it sounded human.

Then a grunt. That was definitely human.

Leslie stopped and listened. More moans, more grunts. The noises were coming from about twenty-five feet ahead of him, just off the trail it seemed.

He nudged his gelding forward—slowly, quietly—two steps, then two more. A parked carriage came into view, and then he saw the source of the moans and grunts.

A man and a woman were sprawled on the ground, and the man was on top of the woman. Leslie wasn't sure what to make of this scene. They weren't kissing, as, slyly watching from a distance, he had seen his older sisters do with beaus on occasion.

Nor did they appear to be fighting. The woman seemed to be in no distress. Leslie saw no fear in her face. In fact, she was smiling as she exhaled intermittent moans. Her reddened face was round and somewhat puffy, her hair a scraggly mess. Leslie figured she was older than any of his sisters and younger than his mother, probably about thirty.

"Howdy, folks," he exclaimed.

The man jumped to his feet, and the woman scrambled up behind him. Both glared at Leslie.

"What the hell ya doin', sneakin' up on people that way?" the man spit out.

He was big and powerfully built, with a nose that reminded Leslie of a ripe turnip, and was dressed in a plaid shirt and dungarees that he pulled up by the waistband as he stood. He did not look welcoming, Leslie thought.

"Sorry if I surprised ya," he said from atop his gelding. "I was out ridin' and heard some noises. Just wanted to make sure there weren't no trouble."

"As you can plainly see, we're fine," the man said. "The noises you heard was just the two of us playin' a little game we sometimes enjoy."

"Whatever you two was playin' at, it looked like you was winnin'," Leslie said earnestly.

"I reckon I was at that," the man said with a smile.

"What kinda game is it? Can three play?"

"Well, this game is best with just two people," the man said, again smiling. The round-faced woman laughed.

"This is a family game," she said as she dusted off her skirt. "He's my brother."

"Yeah, she's my *favorite* sister," the man said. "We play as often as we can."

"I got five sisters," Leslie said. "Any chance of ya teachin' me your game?"

"That might be fun," the woman said as she surveyed Leslie from head to toe and took several steps toward him. "You're kinda cute."

Blushing, Leslie now wondered whether the game these two were playing was meant to involve twelve-year-old boys.

"Oh, well . . . I guess . . . maybe you really want to be alone. Sorry I interrupted you and your brother. I best be goin' now."

He turned his gelding to the north and took off at a gallop.

The War

Leslie's full name was Leslie Combs Warner, after his mother's father, General Leslie Combs.

General Combs was a significant figure in Kentucky history. He had been a hero in the War of 1812 before becoming a politician. He was a close friend of former U.S. Senator and Secretary of State Henry Clay. His father, Benjamin Combs, had been a captain under George Washington during the Revolutionary War.

Leslie's father also was something of a war hero.

William A. Warner—despite being a slave owner—enlisted in the Union army after the Civil War began. He was commissioned as a colonel in October 1861 and was given command of the Eighteenth Regiment Kentucky Infantry the following February.

His regiment's assignment was to guard railroads in north-central Kentucky, but it was thrust into the thick of things in August 1862. Its first significant action was at the Battle of Richmond, Kentucky.

Union forces there were routed. The Eighteenth Regiment suffered significant losses, and almost all the men who weren't killed or wounded were captured.

Colonel William A. Warner was wounded *and* captured.

No less than *The New York Times* reported that Warner had been killed in action.

In the battle fought near Richmond, yesterday, as near as can be ascertained, the National force was between 8,000 and 9,000, under command of Gen. NELSON. They drove the rebels back until about 4 o'clock in the afternoon, when the rebels were largely reinforced, and crossed the Kentucky river, capturing nearly all our artillery, and routed our men.

The rebel force is estimated at from 15,000 to 20,000. The National loss is reported at 150 to 200 killed and wounded. The rebel loss is not known, but is said to be heavy. Gen. NELSON was wounded slightly. Col. WARNER, of the Eighteenth Kentucky, and Col. TOPPING, of the Seventy-first Indiana, are reported killed.

—*The New York Times, September 1, 1862*

Well, you can't believe everything you read in newspapers.

The *Times*, however, can be forgiven.

General Charles Cruft, who commanded the Second Brigade at the Battle of Richmond on August 29 and 30, 1862, said in his official report: "Colonel Warner, Lieutenant-Colonel Landrum, and Major Bracht, of the Eighteenth Kentucky, exhibited proper courage and daring. The former, I regret to say, is reported mortally wounded."

General Cruft's words were likely based on the report he received on the Eighteenth Kentucky's action at Richmond from Major Frederick G. Bracht, who served under Warner. The Eighteenth Kentucky had suffered by far the most casualties of the Union regiments that fought at Richmond, with 32 killed and 107 wounded, according to Cruft's report.

Major Bracht wrote that "a terrible fire was poured into us from the foe in front, screened and concealed by a fence and thick brush. Before we were yet formed considerable numbers of each company had bit the dust and many more were groaning with ghastly wounds . . . and to make our position more terrible and untenable a severe cross-fire was opened upon us from the corn field on our left and from a still hidden foe."

They were forced to retreat, he said, adding that his horse as well as the horses of Colonel Warner and Lieutenant-Colonel John J. Landrum were shot out from under them, and that Landrum was wounded in the face. Major Bracht continued:

"Colonel Warner and myself mounted fresh horses and succeeded, with the assistance of Lieutenant Robbins, acting adjutant, and company officers, in collecting together about 300 of our men for the second conflict, in which we took position on the right. . . . Finally, however, by a flank movement, the enemy in overwhelming numbers passed around a corn field and made a precipitate rush upon our line in front, while they outflanked us in the woods and subjected the right of our line to another severe cross-fire, by which means they quickly turned our right, threw it in confusion, and produced another unavoidable retreat, in which Colonel Warner received a mortal wound through his chest.

". . . Lieutenant Robbins and Captain Fisk had taken Colonel Warner off the field, whence he was sent in an ambulance to Richmond."

Warner's wound wasn't mortal, but the hospital in Richmond is where he would have been taken prisoner. The custom early in the war, however, was for prisoners of war to be paroled and sent home unharmed.

We know a few other details about Warner's service in the Union army. He evidently had been active earlier in 1862 arresting men he suspected of being sympathetic to the Confederates. He could do so under the provisions of the Conspiracies Act of 1861 and the Treason Act of 1862.

According to newspaper reports of the time, among those Warner or his men arrested were Richard Stowers, who had been a director of the Kentucky Central Railroad, and General Lucius Desha, a member of the state legislature.

Warner might have been perceived as a bit overzealous in his pursuit of possible traitors. Kentucky was, like Missouri, a border state, and thousands of Confederate sympathizers in both states considered the Union soldiers an occupying force.

In western Missouri, the harsh actions of Union soldiers led by the likes of Jim Lane (looted and burned Osceola; burned the courthouse and homes in Papinville), James Montgomery (burned the Butler town square, including churches and the courthouse), and Charles "Doc" Jennison (looted Harrisonville; looted and burned Pleasant Hill) helped spawn gangs of men who were compelled to fight back—including the notorious William Quantrill, Cole Younger, and "Bloody Bill" Anderson.

Warner didn't go as far as Lane, Montgomery, and Jennison, whose men terrorized Missouri towns. But he had at least one significant detractor.

On May 14, 1862, William A. Dudley, the quartermaster general of Kentucky, wrote to John Jordan Crittenden, a former U.S. attorney general and Kentucky governor who was then a member of the U.S. House of Representatives, complaining of "unlawful arrests" by Warner.

The letter is included in Crittenden's papers, which are contained in the Library of Congress.

Dudley wrote:

Col. Warner (of one of our Kentucky regiments) is here in command of a detachment. He is daily arresting men without warrant, and sending them off to Camp Chase in this without even the form of a trial. He refuses to obey the writ of Habeas Corpus . . . unless it suits his pleasure, and as I am credibly informed declares his intention to arrest and imprison every man who expresses a sympathy for the South. . . .

Since the advent of Col. Warner, discontent is daily increasing. No man feels safe who has ever been known as a 'Southern Rights' man. . . .

There are gentlemen here who express great satisfaction at what they are pleased to term the 'energetic conduct' of Col. Warner and seem to think that his is the true course to quell a rebellious spirit in the people. You know that so far from such being the fact there is nothing so well calculated to defeat the end we angle to have in view—the restoration of harmony to our country. The presence of arms may compel temporary submission but no people who have been free will long tolerate a tyranny so monstrous and so degrading.

It's worth noting that Dudley was not a "Southern Rights" man. He was a horse breeder and banker who was, like Crittenden, a Unionist. In 1861, he had sought neutrality for Kentucky.

As it turned out, the state was split but far from neutral.

* * *

After the Battle of Richmond, Warner's Eighteenth Kentucky regiment participated in several other campaigns, including the Battle of Chickamauga in September 1863 and Sherman's March to the Sea in 1864. But as far as can be surmised from official and unofficial records, it did so without Warner.

We know he was given a disability discharge in December 1863. We also know that he hadn't regained command of the 18th Regiment in July 1863 because of a letter from his father-in-law to Major General William S. Rosencrans, in which General Leslie Combs urged Warner's return to action.

My Dear Sir,

I am much gratified to tell you that the hole through my son-in-law Col. Warner has grown up sufficiently to enable him to take command again of his veteran rgt. (the 18th KY) which distinguished itself, so signally, in the Battle at Richmond—before Nelson reached the field. You may remember that he had two horses shot under him & was himself shot thru the breast, within an inch of the heart, on that occasion & reported "killed."

I think you will find him a good soldier with a reliable rgt.

Very truly

Leslie Combs

General Combs's appeal evidently fell on deaf ears.

The Union Regiments of Kentucky: Published Under the Auspices of the Union Soldiers and Sailors Monument Association in 1897 indicated that Colonel H.K. Milward commanded the Eighteenth Kentucky from January 20, 1863, until the regiment was mustered out at Louisville on July 18, 1865.

A final newspaper report involving Warner's military career was in the form of a letter that Warner himself wrote two months before his disability discharge in December 1863. It confirms he wasn't in command of the Eighteenth Kentucky then, and it also describes the bushwhackers operating in northern Kentucky at that point of the war.

Warner wrote, in part:

I have just returned from the funeral of Maj. A. G. Wileman, of the 18th Kentucky, who was foully murdered and robbed in this county on Monday night last. He had only returned on furlough, on Friday last. He was wounded at the battle of Chickamauga River. . . .

He was sitting in his house between 6 and 7 o'clock P.M.; with four of his neighbors, three gentlemen and one lady and his wife, when the murderers entered with pistol in hand presented, demanding money and person. They represented themselves as belonging to Breckenridge's Command, and said their forces had taken Falmouth and they had been sent for him. He refused positively to let them have his money, which they did not get, but they got near two hundred dollars from two of the gentlemen present.

They then took him out and carried him about a mile and a half from his house, and there stripped him of all his clothing, with the exception of his boots and shirt, shot him through the head, the ball entering the left temple and powder-burning his wounded arm, his chin mashed down and jaw broken. After murdering him, they dragged him down a branch some thirty steps and left him dying on his face, his shirt over his head, being dragged by his feet.

. . . This is the beginning of a terrible state of affairs in this part of the State, and a stop must be put to it. If I only had my trusting Old Eighteenth here, we would soon quiet the Northern half of the state, as have done theretofore. There is great excitement here, and well there might be—We have several returned Morgan men here that will have to take their washing further South. They are made heroes of and nursed as pinks of perfection, whose hands a short time ago were red with the blood of their fellow citizens, riding their stolen horses, and are allowed to settle down quietly amongst us until a fresh opportunity offers for them to commence their hellish work again.

The Major left a wife and three children to mourn his sad fate.

Yours truly, W. A. Warner

—Western Citizen newspaper of Paris, Kentucky,

October 8, 1863

* * *

Like William A. Warner, the town of Lexington, Missouri, also had emerged from the Civil War wounded.

Sitting on the bluffs above the Missouri River in Lafayette County, about forty miles east of Kansas City, Lexington was the largest city west of St. Louis in the 1830s and at that time was the commercial center of western Missouri.

It was populated mostly by settlers from Virginia, Tennessee, and especially Kentucky. They named it after the city in that state and built large, stately homes like the ones they had left behind.

As did the South, Lexington and Lafayette County relied on a slave-based economy. The 1860 census showed the county had 6,374 slaves, nearly one-third of the county's overall population and the most slaves of any county in Missouri.

It is hardly surprising, then, that residents of the area, part of what was known as Little Dixie, mostly supported the Confederacy during the Civil War. Two significant battles were fought in Lexington, and the Rebels most certainly were the home team.

General Sterling Price, a former governor of Missouri, led the Confederates to victory in both battles. But the fighting, the dissolution of slavery, and the neglect caused by the years of war left Lexington a shell of its former grandiose self.

Worse still, in Lafayette County, the hostilities didn't totally end. At least not in 1865, or even in 1866.

Bands of bushwhackers—the most famous being William Quantrill and Bloody Bill Anderson—had terrorized western Missouri during the war (they occasionally visited Kansas, too). They sympathized with the Confederate cause, but they weren't regular members of the Southern army. So when General Robert E. Lee surrendered at Appomattox, they had no real motivation to give up their weapons.

Some nonetheless turned themselves into government authorities, and many received complete amnesty, despite having committed atrocities that would make a twenty-first-century serial killer blush.

But others, Frank and Jesse James among them, kept right on doing what they did best—bushwhacking.

Lafayette County became one of their primary hangouts, and they had free rein there in late 1865 as well as most of 1866. Their misdeeds were regular fodder for the Lexington newspapers.

A COWARDLY ACT.

We learn Jim Anderson, the celebrated bushwhacker, who boasts of having never given himself up to the Federal authorities, and who is a brother of that cruel monster Bill Anderson, of Centralia notoriety, is showing his pluck by beating poor negroes whenever occasion offers, because they are free.

This dirty wretch has not the manliness to attack those who have made the negro free, but sates his villainous greed by injuring the helpless; for instance last week he rode into town and seeing a negro walking on the sidewalk rode his horse in ahead of him, drew his pistol and compelled the poor darkey to take the street, amid curses, jeers and other indignities heaped upon him.

The scoundrel is having considerable rope just now, but he'll reach the end soon and HANG THERE.

—Missouri Valley Register, of Lexington, January 18, 1866

STILL WAVING.

A gentleman from the eastern part of the county informs us that the bushwhackers at Waverly are still waving their weapons with defiance in that quarter. A man (German by birth) was assailed on the street about a week ago, after nightfall, while on the way home from work, by two ex-bushwhackers and robbed of fifty dollars and ordered to say nothing about it or they would see him again.

He however mentioned the fact to some parties, and he was waited on a few days after by two or three worthy's who formerly belonged to Quantrel's gang, drawing their pistols and accusing him of reporting that they were the men who robbed him, he begging them not to kill him. They then caught him by the hair and dragged him down stairs and began abusing him, when some citizens interfered, and he made his escape through a corn field back of the town, and came to this city.

If this is the return these men intend making the Union men and the government for the kindness and mercy extended them, the sooner it is "played out" the better.

—Missouri Valley Register, of Lexington, January 25, 1866

ANOTHER OUTRAGE.

Last week we are informed that two or three ex-bushwhackers, on leaving town and near the fair ground, met a negro and drawing their pistols, made the negro kneel down as a target, they then went off some distance and were preparing to shoot him, when some one coming along the road saved the negro, and these valiant cowardly assassins rode off, waving their pistols and shouting for Jeff Davis.

We advise these men to lay off their pistols, sober down and go to work, or their days will not be long in the land.

—Missouri Valley Register, of Lexington, February 1, 1866

COLORED SOLDIER SHOT BY A BUSHWHACKER.

Last Sunday, while the steamer Fanny Ogden was at the Waverly Landing, a colored soldier, who had been discharged from the Federal army, returning to his home somewhere above this place, went ashore, when a returned bushwhacker by the name of James, rode to him and asked him where he got those soldier clothes.

He answered "in the Federal army." He was asked if he had been a Federal soldier; he answered he had.

James then shot at him three times, one ball passing through his chest, supposed to be a mortal wound. The soldier was then carried on board. He had his family with him.

—Missouri Valley Register, of Lexington, March 15, 1866

In March 1866, the James brothers hadn't yet made their names known among the public. So this cold-blooded killer named James could have been Jesse or Frank or somebody else; the newspaper never further identified the killer.

In any case, this incident was a prime example of the violent times in Lafayette County. In fact, it might have been the most violent and bloody 640 square miles in the country at the time.

Yet that is precisely where William A. Warner had decided to move his family.

October 2, 1866

The day was filled with hope.

Hope for Sallie Warner, who was getting married on this sunny afternoon and was looking forward to starting a family. Hope for her family, because she was marrying one of the wealthiest men in the county. And hope for Leslie Warner, Sallie's younger brother, because he spotted a rare chance to sneak off with some liquor.

The aroma of wet paint and freshly sawed wood permeated the proceedings.

The Warners' still unfinished house—only the front façade and porch were painted; workers would get to the other three sides next week—faced east and sat atop a hill. Not a big hill, but enough of an incline to make the structure the dominant feature of the surrounding landscape. Behind it and to one side were dense trees that grew nearly uninterrupted for two miles north to the Missouri River.

It was a grand setting for a house. And a wedding.

A swarm of people filled the grounds in front of the house, and Leslie didn't know but a few of them. They were mostly townsfolk from Lexington, he supposed.

Leslie never saw such a fuss in all his days. His sister Mary was the maid of honor and wore a fancy floral-themed dress. So did Maggie, their oldest sister, and a bunch of other girls, all bridesmaids, who lined up beside Sallie during the ceremony.

The man Sallie had just married, Sam Nutter, and some of his friends were dressed in fancy suits on the other side of the preacher.

Sam had given Leslie his first drink. It was a winter ago, and Leslie liked how it warmed him up. The taste almost made him sick, but that didn't prevent him from being determined to drink more liquor, if only because his mother told him it was something he should never do.

He'd had just one glass that day last winter, and since then he would sneak a sip now and again. He'd never been truly drunk.

On this fine October day, nobody was drunk. Yet.

But there was a lot of liquor sitting on the table in front of Leslie.

"Leslie Warner, what are you doing?"

It was Mary. She was tall and thin but stood straight and held her shoulders back as she walked. With flowing blonde hair, large green eyes, full lips, and perfect skin, Mary was without doubt the prettiest female Leslie had ever seen.

At sixteen, she still usually acted like a young girl. Sallie was eighteen, and she was more serious minded. When Leslie said something funny to Mary, she laughed long and loud. If he said something funny to Sallie, she'd say, "That's quite amusing, Leslie," while making a face.

Leslie figured it was Sallie's fault the family had moved from Pendleton County, Kentucky, to Missouri. She had been visiting Missouri regularly before she got engaged to Sam.

The Warners had lived in Lafayette County, near the town of Dover, almost a year now, and Leslie still didn't like it much. The landscape wasn't all that much different from Kentucky, and the house was certainly nice enough. The problem was, Leslie didn't have any friends.

There were few close neighbors, and most of the folks who did live within hollerin' distance weren't eager to be nice to the Warners. His mother told Leslie it was because his father had been a Union colonel, and almost everybody in these parts hated the Union during the war.

Even so, it seemed to Leslie the people in Lafayette County weren't all that friendly to begin with. These Missouri people seemed naturally suspicious of anybody they didn't know and weren't keen on welcoming strangers. As a result, Leslie didn't know any boys his age, so he spent most of his time with his sisters. Five altogether: three of them older than him and two younger. No brothers.

Leslie liked his sisters, but they could be a nuisance at times.

Like when Leslie was up to no good.

"Whadya think I'm doing?" Leslie said to Mary as he turned away from the table.

"Well, it looks as if you're planning to thieve a bottle of whiskey."

Drat, Leslie thought, realizing he wasn't being as sneaky as he'd hoped. He quickly changed the subject.

"You sure look purdy today," he said.

"Why, thank you, Leslie. I wish I could say the same about you."

She threw her head back and laughed. Leslie merely smiled.

"Ah, Mary, quit funnin' me. I ain't in the mood."

"What's the matter?"

"I've got my worries about Sallie and this marriage. I ain't for sure Sam is all that great a catch for her. I guess I like him, but he don't seem good enough for Sallie."

"Well, it's too late now," Mary said. "In any case, I thought the ceremony was beautiful. I hope to have one just like it someday."

"Good luck with that," Leslie said.

His quest for liquor thwarted, Leslie wandered away from Mary and decided he would check out the visitors to see whether any appeared interesting. He enjoyed observing people and imagining stories about them.

A man with one leg caught his attention.

His stump wiggled this way and that while he sat and talked to other guests. It was almost as if the stump had a mind of its own.

Leslie figured the man had been in his pa's unit during the war. He thought he was sort of lucky to have suffered such an obvious injury. Folks could see that he'd been wounded in the war just by looking at him, and they would naturally feel sympathy for him.

Nobody could tell that his pa had been injured. Almost killed. His scars were under his shirt.

Leslie noticed that Sallie, standing with their mother, was watching the one-legged man, too.

Everybody talked about how beautiful Sallie was, and Leslie had never seen her look so pretty as she did today. She was slightly shorter and heavier than Mary, with darker hair, which she wore in a complicated arrangement atop her head. Her white wedding dress and veil accentuated her large brown eyes.

Leslie sidled closer to Sallie, intending to ask her about the man, but she spoke first.

"Mother, who is that?" she asked, nodding toward the one-legged man.

"Sallie, stand up straight," Georgia Warner said sternly. "You're too pretty a girl to stand slump shouldered like that. It makes you look like an old woman."

"Mother, you know the best way to get me to do something is to tell me to do the exact opposite. Haven't you learned anything in the eighteen years you've raised me? I'll stand any way I want, thank you."

Sallie then turned away and began visiting with other guests.

Many of the men wore uniforms, both blue and gray, as if to brag that they had fought in the war. Sallie's new husband had done no such thing.

Most everybody in Lafayette County knew Sam hadn't fought. Sallie never said whether that bothered her, but she had told Leslie she had other doubts about Sam, indicating that he wasn't as cultured as the boys she knew in Kentucky and that he was too full of himself.

"I don't want to judge Sam too harshly, though," she had told Leslie, "because I don't really know him all that well."

Sallie didn't know Sam's sister Lizzie at all.

Oh, she'd met Lizzie, but the two had rarely spoken to each other. Now they'd be living under the same roof. Lizzie and Sam had been the only occupants of the Nutters' grand family estate for several years, and Lizzie would remain in the house with the new Mr. and Mrs. Sam Nutter.

Leslie saw that Lizzie was standing a few feet behind Sallie, talking to what Leslie figured was a friend of Sam's. The young man looked to be no older than Sallie, which made him quite a lot younger than Lizzie.

Lizzie wasn't married, and she looked to Leslie's eye to be the oldest unmarried woman at these festivities. Almost all the other women wore their hair in buns, but not Lizzie. Her hair was the muddy brown of Missouri River water, and it fell to just above her shoulders. Her eyes were small and narrow, and she blinked constantly when she talked through her thin lips. Unlike her brother, however, she was not plump.

Leslie had joked with Mary that Lizzie looked like she could be a Sunday school teacher. But Lizzie Nutter wasn't a Sunday school teacher. Not hardly.

"How do you plan on pleasurin' my little brother tonight?"

Sallie nearly jumped out of her skin when she heard the words spoken behind her. She turned to see Lizzie, who emitted a laugh that sounded like a lamb bleating for its dinner.

Sallie wasn't laughing, however. She wasn't smiling, either.

"Have you got any recommendations, Lizzie?" she said. "I suppose you must be an expert in the art of copulation, with numerous partners and copious experience. I have very little myself. None, really."

"Oh, Sallie, I was just funnin'," Lizzie said. "I don't want to know what the two of you got planned. To tell the truth, I'm just happy to have another woman around the house again."

"I'm sure you are," Sallie said. "But I hope you realize that I will be the woman of the house. You will be my and Sam's guest, nothing more."

"Why, of course," Lizzie said. "I wouldn't have it any other way."

October 30, 1866

This was just about the most exciting thing ever to happen, Leslie thought. Everybody was talking about the bank robbery in Lexington.

Five men had ridden into town in the middle of the day, gotten off their horses, walked into Mitchell's Bank, pulled their pistols, made the cashier hand over all the money, and then took his gold watch.

They didn't kill anybody, but they sure scared a bunch of folks.

Leslie learned of the bank robbery from his pa, who learned of it from two men riding past their house no more than two hours after the robbery. They said the bushwhackers did it.

The men said a posse followed the bank robbers but couldn't keep up. The two men themselves were headed to Dover to make sure the robbers weren't there, because bushwhackers were known to spend time in Dover. Likely as not, though, the robbers had crossed the river back into Clay County.

Leslie stayed outside all afternoon hoping to see something more, but nothing happened.

"Damnation! If only I'd been in Lexington, I coulda seen a bank robbery," he said.

He wished right quick that he had kept his mouth closed.

The whole family was seated at the dinner table, including Sam and Sallie, which made this a special occasion. But it wasn't Sam and Sallie who caused Leslie to fret his words.

"What kind of language is that for the dinner table?" his mother snapped.

"Sorry, Mother," Leslie said. "But I ain't never seen no bank robbery before."

Oh, oh, that really did it.

Georgia Warner scolded Leslie about the coarse way he talked every chance she got, which was just about every time he said something. She scolded him about plenty of other things, too. In fact, his mother angered more quickly and thoroughly than anybody else Leslie knew. She seemed to have rage inside her all the time, building until it erupted into periodic fury.

"I think Mother ain't happy unless she's mad," Leslie once told Mary.

Georgia Warner was mad now.

"Leslie Warner," she exclaimed, "how many times have I told you that you sound uneducated when you talk like that? You know better than to say 'ain't never seen no bank robbery.' You've learned proper grammar, and I want you to start using it."

Leslie knew she was right, of course. He had learned all about good grammar.

It was just that he didn't like to use it. He thought it sounded unnatural.

"I talk the way most folks around here talk," he responded. "People who use good grammar sound like they think they're better than everybody else. Besides, what difference does it make? As long as folks know what I'm saying when I say something, who cares if it ain't exactly the Queen's English?"

That drew a glare from his mother that he felt down to his toes.

Leslie stayed quiet the rest of the meal. But as soon as everybody had finished eating and had gone to various parts of the house, he found Sam alone on the porch with his hound dog, Jo Shelby.

He figured Sam might know more about the bank robbery.

He did.

"It likely was Arch Clement and his boys," Sam said as he patted Jo Shelby on the head. "They done robbed the bank in Liberty a few months back, too. The humorous-most part of it is that Dave Poole led the posse that rode after 'em outta Lexington. That's like sendin' a wolf to track down the coyote what raided your chicken coop. Dave Poole knew exactly where them boys was ridin' off to, and he made sure the posse didn't catch 'em."

Leslie knew about Clement and Poole from stories he'd heard and newspapers he'd read. They were among the most notorious bushwhackers during the war, but Poole surrendered in Lexington after the fighting ended and now lived there, more or less peaceably, while Clement was still out in the woods with a bunch of other bushwhackers, raising a ruckus every chance he got.

"How do you know so much about the robbery?" Leslie asked Sam.

"I know some of them boys. Not the ones that done the bank robbery, but some of the others. I got boys workin' for me who rode with the likes of Clement and Poole during the war. They turned themselves in and got amnesty, just like Dave Poole."

"So, do you know Dave Poole?"

"Oh, I drink with him some. He don't seem so bad now, but I heared he done some evil things during the war. I heared he cut off fingers and ears and noses and worse, and he scalped more than a few blue bellies. At Centralia, he done some of the worst things to men anybody ever done."

"I surely would like to meet a legendary bad guy like Dave Poole," Leslie said. "He reminds me of the villains in my dime novels. Can you make my acquaintance with him some time?"

"Maybe you can meet up with me next time I go to Lexington. I'll be ridin' in for the election. I can even arrange for you to vote, if you've a desire to. Course, you'd have to vote the way we want you to. I happen to know there's gonna be more than a few boys in town to scare off folks who don't plan on votin' our way."

"Sounds good to me," Leslie said.

November 6, 1866

The Warners' farm was some twelve miles east of Lexington, which made for a mostly unexciting existence for Leslie Warner.

For entertainment, he enjoyed reading about the daring deeds and lively action in Beadle's Dime Novels, even though his mother said he should read books by Victor Hugo or Charles Dickens, whoever they were. Elsewise, there wasn't much for Leslie to do to pass the time other than finding new ways to avoid the chores his mother insisted on giving him.

Accordingly, he took advantage of every chance he got to go somewhere else. Anywhere else.

Going to Lexington was the best. He could always count on seeing something interesting there. It had rich folks and poor folks, former slaves (lots of them), and former Rebs (even more), and the bushwhackers. They ruled the town.

They were definitely ruling the streets on Election Day when Leslie arrived in town with his father.

Sam had told Leslie to inform the men outside the courthouse who he was, and they'd let him vote.

"What men?" Leslie had asked.

"You'll know 'em when you see 'em."

Sure enough, it wasn't hard to tell who was running the show at the courthouse, where folks were gathered fly-thick to vote. The ones in charge were the ones with guns, and they were shooting them in the air anytime somebody they thought was a Radical (some folks called them Republicans) got too close.

A lot of folks expected Leslie's father to be a Radical since he had been a Union colonel. But Colonel William A. Warner was a Democrat and proud of it.

Colonel Warner walked right past the men with their guns and voted. Then he went off to do other business in town. He told Leslie to stay out of trouble.

Not likely.

Leslie circled back to the courthouse at about the time Sam said he would be there.

The courthouse in Lexington was (and still is) an impressive white building standing two stories tall and occupying most of a square block, topped by a domed clock tower and fronted by four columns. Near the top of the far-left column was a crater where a cannonball had struck it during the 1861 Battle of Lexington.

The courthouse, which had been built in 1847, reminded Leslie of home. Fact was, a lot of Lexington reminded Leslie of Kentucky, with its grand houses like the ones back home. The Lexington courthouse was just about the grandest building he'd ever laid his eyes on.

Leslie didn't see Sam. He wanted to wait for his new brother-in-law but knew he didn't have a lot of time before his pa would come looking for him.

He decided to walk right up to the courthouse.

A few potential voters were standing behind posts and around corners, no doubt because they didn't want the bushwhackers to notice them and try to scare them off.

"Them Radicals know better than to try to vote now," a man standing just in front of the courthouse steps said to Leslie.

The man wore two pistols, carried a rifle, and was covered in mud and grime from head to toe. "You ain't one of 'em, is ya?"

"Nah, I'm Leslie Warner," Leslie said, in the best adult voice he could muster. "Sam Nutter said you boys would let me vote."

"You look a mite young to vote, but I ain't gonna stop ya, if you's plannin' on votin' the right way. You are plannin' on votin' the right way, ain't ya?"

"Whatever you say," Leslie said.

"OK then. This might be kinda fun. Come with me."

The man walked up the steps and into the courthouse lobby, approaching a table where two gray-haired men wearing ties sat in tall, straight-backed chairs. Leslie tried to look as old as he could.

"I got a live one for ya," the armed man said. "You best give him a ballot."

The men at the table looked confused. Leslie was tall for his age, but he otherwise had no traits of a grown man.

He pulled his hat down to cover his face as much as he could.

"Are you old enough to vote, young man?" one of the gray-haired men asked.

"Sure he is," Leslie's escort said. "This here is Archie Clement, and he's plenty old enough to vote."

The armed man didn't laugh or smile or anything.

Leslie, meanwhile, was ready to take off running for the door. Lying to vote was one thing; having people think you're Archie Clement was a whole other thing.

The two men at the table weren't buying the Archie Clement story, however. Leslie could tell by the way they looked up and down at him, then at each other. But they didn't say anything, likely figuring they might get shot if they didn't do what they were told.

"Here," one gray-haired man said, shoving a paper at Leslie.

This being the first time Leslie ever voted, he wasn't sure what to do. The paper had a bunch of men's names on it, so he figured they were the candidates. But he didn't know which ones he was supposed to vote for.

He stared at the paper for a few seconds, then looked up.

"You can use that desk over there," one man at the table said.

The armed escort grabbed Leslie's left elbow and directed him toward the desk, where he half-pushed him into a chair.

"Vote for the ones that say Democrat," he said.

That seemed easy enough. Leslie recognized some of the names, including J. M. Poole, who was Dave Poole's brother and was running for sheriff. Seemed like a good candidate to Leslie.

He put marks by all the Democrats, and the armed man grabbed the paper and handed it back to the gray-haired men at the table.

That's when Leslie saw Sam and Jo Shelby. They were standing just inside the courthouse door, and Sam was smiling. Then he started laughing.

"I weren't serious when I said you could vote, Leslie, though I thought it might be interestin' to see you try. And, by god, you done it! I reckon you are the youngest boy who ever voted in Lafayette County. Congratulations."

With a sheepish grin, Leslie skedaddled past Sam and Jo Shelby and got out of that courthouse as fast as his legs could carry him. Turns out, Sam hadn't said anything to anybody about Leslie voting. It made the twelve-year-old boy wonder what else he might be able to get away with, if he put his mind to it.

***

Leslie wasn't mad at Sam, even though the prank could have got him in trouble. Fact is, Leslie thought it was funny, too.

The worst part was that Leslie plumb forgot to ask Sam if Dave Poole was around town and if he could meet him. He reckoned the former bushwhacker leader was somewhere near the courthouse for the voting, since his brother was running for sheriff.

Leslie walked up North Street, hoping to find his pa. Shortly, he saw their buckboard parked out front of Mitchell's Bank. He climbed in just as his pa arrived.

Colonel Willliam A. Warner was the tallest man almost everywhere he went, but he was not imposing. He was barely thicker than Leslie and had slumped shoulders, with gray hair and a gray beard framing a thin face.

"What have you been up to, Leslie?" he asked.

"Nothin' much," Leslie said. "Though I did see Sam over at the courthouse."

"What were you doing at the courthouse?"

"Nothin' much. Just watchin' folks."

That was true enough, Leslie figured. It wasn't a lie. He didn't like to lie to his parents. He was no good at it. In addition, he found that avoiding the truth worked better than lying almost every time.

Either avoiding the truth or changing the subject right fast.

"Did that bank have any money left after they was robbed?" he asked.

"Certainly," Colonel Warner said. "The robbers only got away with about two thousand dollars. That's not much."

It seemed to Leslie that his pa did a lot of business in Mitchell's Bank. He went there almost every time they went to town. Leslie had no idea what kind of business and didn't care at that moment, but he wanted to keep the discussion away from what he and Sam were doing at the courthouse.

"Why was ya in the bank, Pa?"

"Just had some business is all."

Leslie's pa wasn't usually a big talker, at least not with him. Leslie was always asking about fighting in the war and getting shot and whatnot. Colonel Warner never told him much.

As his father guided the buckboard east on North Street to begin their trip back home, Leslie figured it was a good time to try again. It was just the two of them, though there was still some commotion in town, with the bushwhackers firing their pistols every few minutes.

"How come you vote the same way as them bushwhackers, Pa? Seems to me you woulda been on opposite sides during the war. Why are you on the same side now?"

His pa stared straight ahead for a bit before answering. Finally he said, "Leslie, it's only politics. I wouldn't say that I'm on the same side as those men. We just support the same things when it comes to politics."

"But, Pa, ain't it true that they hate the Negroes? They've been cajolin' them and a lot worse all over Lafayette County ever since we lived here. You ain't got nothin' against Negroes, have ya?"

"You know I don't, Leslie. We were one of the first families in Pendleton County to release our slaves once the fighting started. And you know how well I treat the Negroes who have worked for us. I think what those renegade bushwhackers are doing is appalling."

"But you still vote for the same candidates?"

"Like I said, it's politics. I just agree more with what the Democrats want to do than what the Republicans want to do. You're too young to understand these things, Leslie."

Ah, that's when he knew he had his chance. Colonel Warner didn't want to talk about politics anymore, so Leslie changed the subject to what he wanted to talk about in the first place.

"Did you encounter any bushwhackers during the war?" he asked.

"They weren't as big a problem in Kentucky as they were here in Missouri. I never encountered any bushwhackers in person, but it was those types of men who murdered my friend, Major Wileman. They took him from his home and murdered him in cold blood. I swore then that if I did meet any of those renegades, I would show them no mercy."

Colonel Warner seemed to be getting hot under his collar now, so Leslie pushed onward.

"Major Wileman got killed after you was wounded, didn't he?"

"That's right. I was back home by then."

"I remember you was in bad shape. Mother weren't sure you was gonna make it. Do you remember gettin' shot?"

"Like it was yesterday," his father said as he stared at the road, reins tight in his hands. "I was on a strange horse—mine had been shot out from under me—and was trying to reorganize the men after we had been overrun by the Rebels. The men fought valiantly, but they were dropping on both sides of me. The ground was red with their blood.

"One moment I was yelling encouragement to the men. The next moment I was lying on that bloodied ground, with my own blood running out of my chest. Captain Fisk and Lieutenant Robbins carried me off the battlefield. I owe those men my life."

"Did you kill any Rebs before they got you?"

"That's not likely. I wasn't doing much shooting. My efforts were focused on my men, keeping them organized and moving forward as much as possible in the face of an overwhelming enemy. Too many of my men died that day. It was the most gruesome experience of my life."

Colonel Warner stopped the horses and turned to look at his son.

"Leslie, I hope you never have to go off to war. Nothing good comes from violence."

The Warners

Georgia (or Georgette) and William Warner had a bunch of kids. That we know. Exactly how many is hard to figure.

Based on the 1870 census, we know of six Warner children: Sallie, twenty; Mary, seventeen; Leslie, sixteen; Ella, seven; Emma, five; and their oldest daughter, Margaret, who by this time was twenty-two and married to Captain W. B. Riggs. (It should be noted that these ages are as they appeared on the census, but in some cases—including Sallie's—they appear to be off by a year or two.)

The 1860 census had included three other Warner children—Debby, then eight; Ann, four; and William, a year and a half—none of whom appeared on any ensuing census listings. "Debby and Willie Warner" share a marker in the Warners' family plot in Lexington (Kentucky) Cemetery, showing both died in 1862. There are no other records on Ann.

The 1880 census shows another child, "Joe. Shelby Warner, 14," a girl who was named after the well-known Confederate general. Records show she was born May 24, 1866, in Kansas City, Missouri, and died there twenty-eight years later. Based on their ages, it is possible that the "Emma" in the 1870 census and "Joe. Shelby" in the 1880 census were the same person. Neither name shows up on any later censuses.

In any case, a bit of addition from all the census information suggests that Georgia and William A. had at least nine children. But even that is likely to be an undercount.

Given the infant mortality rate of the time (about two hundred per one thousand births in 1850, compared with about six per one thousand births now), the Warners could have had other children who didn't survive long enough to be counted in a census. A letter from Georgia to her father in 1850 suggests as much. Georgia mentions "Little Mag," who was her daughter Margaret, and she also says to her father, General Leslie Combs, "My Leslie would be so much company to you."

This 1850 reference could not have been referring to the Leslie who was sixteen in 1870; the math is too far off even for the apparently lax census-answering standards of the time. A more likely conclusion is that the Warners had an earlier son, also named Leslie, who died after Georgia wrote her letter.

***

William A. Warner was the son of a successful and wealthy cabinet and clock maker, Elijah Warner of Lexington, Kentucky. He died when William was still a boy.

In 1840, before the census recorded specifics on wives and children, William A. Warner lived in Edmonson County, Kentucky. His household included five free white persons under twenty years old and one free white person age twenty to forty-nine, with a total of thirty-two free whites and colored slaves, all of which suggests Warner had a young wife and a big operation (with about twenty-five slaves).

The 1850 census showed that Warner had been married to Georgia for about five years, and they had four slaves. William and Georgia were listed as thirty-two and twenty-one years old, respectively, so they would have been about twenty-seven and sixteen when they got married. They were living in Pendleton County in 1850 and had children ages three (Margaret), two (Sallie, although her name was listed as Georgia, for some reason) and zero (Mary).

But also listed were sons John (thirteen) and William (eight).

A bit of research indicated that William A. Warner had headed a previous family before his marriage to Georgia Combs. He was married to Mary Foster in the 1830s, and she was the mother of John and William.

None of the three—Mary Foster and sons John and William—show up in any census after 1850. It is possible Mary Foster died giving birth to William or at some other time before William A. Warner married his second wife, but no records of that exist.

Based on his age, the younger William was born about 1842, three years before his father married Georgia Combs. Both brothers would have been old enough to have fought in the Civil War, and enlistment records show several soldiers with the names John Warner and William Warner. But we can't be sure any of them was the John or William in question.

Bottom line: We don't know what happened to Mary Foster, John Warner, or William Warner.

***

We also don't know why William A. Warner and his family moved to Lafayette County, Missouri, in late 1865, just months after the end of the Civil War.

The move must have seemed odd even at the time. That part of Missouri was hardly the type of place you'd want to raise a family.

One possible explanation for the Warners' relocation in late 1865 was the marriage of daughter Sallie to Sam Nutter.

Sallie was 18 when she married Sam on October 2, 1866, less than a year after the Warners relocated. It was also less than a year after the Warners' oldest daughter, Margaret (or Maggie), had married Captain William Bingley (or Benjamin) Riggs in Pendleton County, Kentucky.

It seems possible, if not likely, that Sallie's wedding had been in the works while the family was still living in Kentucky.

Several relatives of Georgia Warner lived in Carroll County, just north of Lafayette County, so Sallie might have met Sam while she was visiting Missouri at some point. It's also possible the marriage was more or less an arranged merger between a well-to-do Missourian and a Kentuckian with a good family name.

Perhaps William A. Warner uprooted his entire family to support Sallie, with the prospects of a comfortable situation in Lafayette County, thanks to Sam Nutter's wealth.

Perhaps there was another reason.

The move might have been more about Warner feeling the need to get his family out of Kentucky, even if it meant settling in bushwhacker heaven.

For one thing, court records in Kentucky and Missouri show that he had a history of financial problems and that those problems landed him in court frequently.

Shortly after arriving in Missouri, William A. and Georgia Warner became the defendants in a lawsuit filed by John W. Hall in Pendleton County, Kentucky, where they previously lived, over a debt of $265.35.

That suit appears to have been tied to another Pendleton County lawsuit, filed against William A. Warner by William Neff over a debt of $1,273.50, which was resolved in 1866. More on that later.

Three years earlier, in Fayette County (Kentucky) Circuit Court, Elijah Clarke had filed a lawsuit against Warner, claiming Warner had "unlawfully obtained" a diamond breastpin worth $150. Warner returned it after the court ordered him to do so.

And in an 1861 case that was similar—but with a vastly different piece of property in dispute—Warner had been sued in Pendleton County Circuit Court, where the documents remain available and are worth quoting:

"The plaintiff, John E. Chiles, states that he is the owner and entitled to the possession of a female slave, named Fanny, about fifteen years old, and of the value of eight hundred dollars, that the defendant unlawfully detains the slave from the plaintiff's possession, and has unlawfully detained her without right for five days past, and still detains her."

Chiles sought recovery of the slave and $1,600 in damages. Warner's response said he had hired the slave from the plaintiff for $40, having paid him $10 and having agreed in writing to pay him the remainder.

The court ordered Warner to return the slave to Chiles.

After the family relocated to Lafayette County, the financial problems continued.

Warner was listed in the *Missouri Valley Register* in both 1867 and 1869 for being delinquent paying his Lafayette County taxes in the previous years. The 1867 listing showed he owed $56.40 on ten parcels of land totaling about 420 acres. In 1869, he owed $18.69 on 247 acres.

Finally, the Lafayette County records for the November 1867 term of Missouri's Sixth Judicial Circuit indicate William A. and Georgette Warner were the defendants (with General Leslie Combs also named, as "trustee of Georgette A. Warner") in no fewer than four lawsuits.

All accused them of failing to pay for goods or services relating to the construction of their home the previous year.

One was brought by John F. Eneberg, a leading merchant in Lexington who later established the Kansas City Lumber Company, and his partner, Wyley Jennings. Another was by Isaac S. Warner (no relation, as far as we know) and John G. Talbot.

Both suits claimed the Warners had failed to pay for lumber and materials, and both sets of plaintiffs had filed mechanic's liens against the Warners' property.

Accordingly, the court ordered that on May 21, 1868, in front of the courthouse, the sheriff would auction off the Warners' house—"A two-story frame dwelling house, with hip roof and gutter cornice, with two front rooms with hall between them on lower story, and back rooms, and has twelve rooms altogether . . ."—and one acre.

There are no records indicating that the auction was ever completed, but we know the Warners moved out of the house later that summer.

***

Maybe William A. Warner wasn't being dishonest in any of these legal cases. At the very least, though, it's clear he wasn't good with money.

In addition to the tax and lawsuit problems, other facts suggest as much.

One of the earliest times his name appears in an old newspaper was an advertisement in the *Kentucky Gazette* of Lexington in August and September 1840 under the headline "Splendid Farm for Sale."

The farm was "on the east side of the Tates' Creek road, three miles south of Lexington . . . (owned) by Wm. A. Warner, of Lexington. . . . It contains 318 or 320 acres of first rate land, well improved. . . . It has an excellent brick dwelling, with 8 or 9 commodious rooms, Brick Kitchen and smoke house, a cottage . . . good Negro houses . . . carriage house, fine bar, stables. . . ."

The 1850 census listed that his real estate was valued at $3,000, which sounds like a considerable downgrade from the "Splendid Farm" outside Lexington ten years earlier.

The aforementioned letter from Georgia Combs Warner to her father in 1850 also indicates the Warners had fallen on financial hard times.

She wrote: "We went to town yesterday and thought of writing to you of the fix we are in, but hated to trouble you. Since receiving your letter I have concluded to write anyhow. Mr. Warner has had to stop paying his hands on account of having nothing to pay them with. He now owes them. We will be without corn and meat in two or three days. We feed our hands and they eat enormously."

Chances are Georgia's father, General Combs, helped the Warners financially at that time. In any case, by 1860 the census showed their real estate was worth $11,000.

We also know General Combs helped the Warners when they made their move to Missouri.

Lafayette County records show that on September 20, 1865, he paid Charles O. and Anna M. Moore $7,445 on behalf of his daughter and William A. Warner for several parcels of land totaling 531.8 acres. This land almost certainly is where they settled when they moved to Missouri.

This brings us back to that Pendleton County lawsuit against the Warners by William Neff over a debt of $1,273.50.

General Combs again came to the Warners' rescue just after their move to Lafayette County. The Warners evidently had forfeited most of their household goods and farm equipment to Neff to resolve the Pendleton County suit, and Combs bought it all back.

Among the items William A. and Georgia Warner got from General Combs for one dollar were a piano (valued by Combs at $150), two buggies with harnesses for each ($350), two gray mares ($200), four carpets ($85) and dozens of other items, including bacon and lard worth $50.

Even with the return of all their personal property, the Warners evidently still were short of cash.

Lafayette County records from 1866 show that the Warners, with General Combs's permission, sold seventy acres of the land Combs had given them for $2,500. The purchaser was Alexander Mitchell and Co., and the purchase date was August 19, 1866.

Six weeks later, on October 30, 1866, Alexander Mitchell and Co. became part of American folklore when what would become the James-Younger gang robbed the company's bank in Lexington of about $2,000.

December 13, 1866

Colonel William A. Warner wasn't the man he once had been, not since his war injury. He wasn't an invalid by any means, but he couldn't do many things around the farm that he had done before the war.

So, the Warners were lucky to have a neighbor like Frank Allison. Colonel Warner hired him to do work from time to time, and Allison was always willing to help.

Allison watched out for the family, too. For example, he knew Colonel Warner fought for the Union and advised him it probably wasn't in his best interest to ride alone on the roads around Lafayette County.

Since the election, the bushwhackers were getting bolder than ever, Allison said.

"I know these boys," he continued, "and if they knowd you was a Union colonel, they might not take too kindly to it."

Of course, that made Leslie ponder how Frank Allison knew so much about the ruffians who terrified Lafayette County. He determined he would ask him about that sometime. But not with his pa around.

Frank Allison was as fine an example of a man as Leslie had ever seen. He stood almost as tall as Colonel Warner but was much thicker and more powerfully built. Leslie reckoned his age to be about 30 or 35. He had sandy hair that was neatly trimmed compared with most men in these parts, and he was clean shaven. He dressed like a working man, not like a dandy or a gunfighter. Leslie hadn't seen him wear pistols, but he kept a rifle on his horse.

His property was just a short ride down the road from the Warners, and he visited regularly to check if Colonel Warner needed his help with anything.

On this particular day, Colonel Warner told Allison he had business in Lexington and would be obliged if he would come along.

"I'd be happy to ride with you," Allison said.

"That would please me," Colonel Warner said. "And, yes, Leslie, you can come with us."

So Allison, Colonel Warner, and Leslie set off for Lexington. Leslie and his pa rode in a buckboard while Allison rode his gray mare.

They arrived on the Lexington square after an uneventful trip, and Colonel Warner climbed out of the buckboard, saying he had business at the courthouse and the bank.

"Leslie, you stay with Allison here," he said. "And don't get into trouble."

His pa always seemed to be able tell what Leslie was thinking, and he knew Leslie liked to mosey around town, hunting for interesting things to do or see.

But Leslie planned on staying with Frank Allison, anyway. He struck Leslie as a man who could find whatever of interest was going on in town, and he was hoping for a chance to ask Allison what he knew about the bushwhackers.

They'd caused so much trouble in Lexington before the election and on Election Day that the Missouri governor had sent a band of soldiers to try and control things. The soldiers now roamed all over town, though most of them didn't look much like soldiers. They looked rough and ready, more or less how Leslie figured the bushwhackers to look. Most wore dusty blue pants or blue shirts, like you might expect of a soldier. But almost none wore a full uniform.

They walked in the streets in groups of three or four, carrying rifles and wearing sidearms and not looking at all friendly.

That didn't keep Allison from approaching one of the groups in front of the City Hotel.

"Why, Joe Woods, you're just as ugly as last time I seen ya," Allison said to the biggest and meanest-looking one of the bunch. "Don't tell me you've joined up with Major Bacon Montgomery's crew. I guess they don't know who you really are. Or maybe they don't care."

"Keep your mouth shut, Allison," the man said. "Or I'll have to shut it for ya."

"What are ya gonna do, shoot an unarmed man in the middle of the street? Major Montgomery probably wouldn't approve of that, would he?"

"Just stay away from me, Allison. Go on. Get about your business."

At that, Allison smiled a crooked smile at the man he called Joe Woods and walked across North Street toward the Eneberg & Jennings supplies store, which is where he and Leslie were headed in the first place.

Leslie walked close behind Allison, looking over his shoulder at Joe Woods and the other soldiers. He saw Woods march on down the street, then step abruptly to his right to bump purposely into Mr. Keller, who ran a clothing store on North Street.

"Outta my way, you goddamn Teuton."

Leslie had never heard of a Teuton, but his best guess was that it was a bad thing to call the foreigners who mostly lived outside Lexington and talked English that was hard to understand. Mr. Keller was one of them.

Joe Woods bumped Mr. Keller so hard the storekeeper fell to the ground, but Mr. Keller said nothing. He just got up, dusted himself off, and ambled toward his store.

Woods sneered as he continued down the street, leading the other soldiers.

Leslie and Allison went into the supplies store, where Allison bought some nails.

"You can't never have too many nails," he said.

"I ain't never owned a nail," Leslie said. "But Pa done loaned me a few. Course, he made me hammer 'em into something as soon as he loaned 'em to me."

***

As the two headed out the door, a commotion erupted right in front of them. A whole outfit of rough men galloped down North Street—there must have been a hundred of them, and all were wearing guns. And not just one or two guns. Leslie saw one man with at least six sidearms thrust in his belt.

A little man rode out ahead of the bunch. He didn't appear nearly as tall as Leslie, and he didn't look much older.

He nodded at Allison as he rode past.

"Who's that?" Leslie asked.

"That's Archie Clement," Allison said.

Leslie, of course, knew the name. And he knew that if this was the real Archie Clement, the men riding behind him were undoubtedly bushwhackers. By the looks of them, just about every bushwhacker in Missouri must have been riding down North Street—Leslie recognized two or three of them as troublemakers he'd seen on Election Day.

Leslie thought it was fortuitous to have Frank Allison at his side this day.

"What's goin' on?" he asked.

"I ain't sure," Allison said. "This could mean big trouble."

Clement stopped the group in front of the courthouse, where the raggedy riders were greeted by a man in full military uniform and by several other soldiers who looked more official than the men Leslie saw earlier on the streets.

"That's Major Bacon Montgomery," Allison said. "I think I know what's goin' on now. Archie and the boys are here to register for the state militia. Course, they're doin' it as a joke."

As far as Leslie could see, there was nothing funny about it. Clement and Major Montgomery talked only briefly. Then all the bushwhackers dismounted and stood in a loosely formed line while holding onto their horses. The man at the front signed something a soldier handed him, then the next man in line did the same thing. And then the next, and so on.

They all signed whatever it was they were signing before remounting their horses.

"We don't want trouble today," Major Montgomery said to a good many of the bushwhackers.

And there wasn't any trouble.

After the thirty minutes or so it took all the bushwhackers to sign, they turned around and rode peacefully out of town.

"I don't believe it," Allison said to Leslie. "It ain't possible they came all the way into Lexington just for that. Come with me."

Leslie followed Allison as he walked across North Street and headed for the City Hotel. That's where Leslie's folks usually stayed when they came to town and spent the overnight, and he'd stayed there more than once himself.

Allison went into the saloon area, stopped, and surveyed the men inside. They were seated at various tables, one of which seemed to be the center of attention.

At that table sat a not very big man, thin, with long, dark hair and a trimmed mustache and beard to match. He wore neat, dark clothing and a flat-topped, wide-brimmed black hat. He held a glass—containing liquor, Leslie guessed—in his right hand and a cigar in his left.

He smiled when he saw Frank Allison.

"How do, Captain Poole," Allison said. "I figured I'd find you here. I guess you knowd about what just happened out by the courthouse. I bet you got a good laugh out of that."

"You're damn certain I did," the man said.

Leslie knew when Allison began speaking to him that this man was Dave Poole, the notorious bushwhacker leader.

"Is this your boy?" he asked Allison.

"Nah, he's a neighbor boy. I do some work for his pa from time to time."

"Whereabouts you livin'?"

"Out Dover way, just like always."

Allison then sat down, and Leslie wondered what he should do. He knew that his mother would kill him if she knew where he was and that his pa might already be looking for them. Frank Allison didn't seem worried about Leslie's plight, however.

Leslie decided to stand to the side of Allison, where he had a good view of Dave Poole.

"I thought maybe they was gonna rob the bank again," Allison said. "But I guess they wouldn't need so many men if that was what they had in mind. Little Archie always did have his own way of thinkin' about things. Don't make no sense to me to put on such a big show just for a joke."

"That's Archie for ya," Poole said. "I kinda hate to say it, but I think he learned a good many of his tricks from me. Hard to believe he's in charge now. He was no more than fifteen or sixteen when he first joined up with us. He sure growd up in a hurry. Said he was gonna join me for a drink after they finished registerin' for the militia, but he ain't showed up yet."

Leslie was getting uneasy, not knowing if his pa was looking for them. But he wasn't about to walk out on a chance to hear Dave Poole hold court. Leslie had heard all sorts of talk about the bad things he'd done to Union soldiers at Centralia and to the Germans in Lafayette County, and he wanted to find out if they were true.

He wasn't planning on asking, however.

Just then, the door to the saloon swung open, and who strode through but the little man Leslie saw earlier on the street, Archie Clement. He had five pistols tucked into his belt.

Another man, who stood a full head taller than Archie, was with him. The man had a scraggly beard to match his long black hair, which was topped by a tattered black hat. The two walked to where Frank Allison and Dave Poole sat. Pulling over two chairs from a neighboring table, they sat down.

"Captain Poole, it's an honor to have you buy me a drink," Clement said.

"Archie, the pleasure is truly mine," Poole said. "You remember Allison here, don't ya?"

"Of course. I saw him on the street earlier. I guess you're staying out of trouble, Frank? You look like you fit right in here with the fine folks of Lafayette County."

"I try," Allison said. "These are my people, after all. I was glad to see you didn't shoot nobody when you and the boys rode into town. You outnumbered them soldiers. You coulda turned it into a bloodbath."

"Never. That was just for fun," Clement said.

The barkeeper brought a bottle and two glasses, setting them on the table in front of Clement and his scraggly haired friend. Clement filled both glasses, and the two of them made quick work of downing the liquor. Leslie thought if he drank liquor that fast it would knock the breath clean out of him.

Clement pointed the bottle at Allison.

"No thanks, Arch, I ain't drinkin' today," he said. "I'm kinda on a job."

"Have it your way," Clement said, then poured two more glasses full.

They drank those two just as fast.

Leslie was still to the side of Allison, but he had backed up several steps and was now standing with his back against a wall. His eyes were fixed on the little bushwhacker, who just then noticed Leslie for the first time.

"What do you find so fascinatin', boy?" Clement asked with a bit of a growl. "Ain't you never seen a man drink whiskey before?"

"Well, I . . ." Leslie mumbled as he felt his face turn red, his stomach tightening into knots. "You're Arch Clement. I know all about ya. I just can't believe you're right here in front of me."

"Better in front of you than behind you," Dave Poole said, causing the entire group to laugh.

"I guess my reputation precedes me," Clement said. "Do I live up to your expectations, boy?"

"Truth is, I guess you're shorter than I suspected you was," Leslie said.

The laughing subsided, replaced by silence.

"It don't take a tall man to pull a trigger," Clement said. "How old are you, boy?"

"Twelve."

"You're tall for your age, ain't ya?"

"I guess I am."

"You must be near a half-foot taller than me. Walk over here so we can see."

Leslie hesitated, then took a step toward Clement.

He was in mid-stride of a second step when Clement disappeared from in front of him. Frank Allison had risen to his feet and slid in front of Leslie.

"I guess we've had enough fun with the boy, Archie," Allison said. "He's a friend of mine."

"I didn't know, Frank," Clement said. "You know I wouldn't have done him no harm."

"I don't suppose you woulda," Allison said.

He turned toward Leslie and motioned him to resume his position by the wall. "We'll be leavin' directly," he whispered, then sat back down.

"Well, Arch, have you been stayin' outta trouble?" Dave Poole asked.

"I think you know the answer to that," Clement said. "Fact is, though, trouble has been hard to find since Election Day. We've got a few projects in the works. You ain't lookin' for a little work, are ya?"

"No thanks," Poole said. "I'm a respectable businessman now, ya know."

Every man at the table, including Frank Allison, laughed at that comment.

"Well, we got plenty of good boys, anyhow," Clement said. "But we'd welcome your talents if you change your mind."

Just then, three men strode into the saloon, making for the bar. They were among the men in town who were dressed vaguely like soldiers. When they reached the bar, they turned and looked right at Archie Clement.

"We don't want no trouble," one of them said. "In fact, we want to buy you boys a drink."

"I got no problem with that," Poole said.

Clement, meanwhile, didn't say a word. He studied the three men, then surveyed the room and the entrance to the saloon. He looked somewhat nervous, which wasn't the case a few seconds earlier. Frank Allison was looking uneasy himself.

Leslie had no idea what was happening, but he reckoned it wasn't a good time to ask questions. So he didn't.

"Barkeep, bring a bottle," one newcomer said. "And three glasses."

The man filled the glasses on the bar for himself and his two partners, then turned toward the table where Frank Allison sat with Dave Poole and Archie Clement. He began to pour liquor into their glasses.

He was tipping the bottle toward Clement's glass when Little Archie jumped to his feet, quick as lightning, pulling two pistols from his belt.

But he didn't point them at the man with the bottle.

Three more men dressed like would-be soldiers had burst into the saloon. One of them yelled, "Surrender!" Then a man at the bar hollered, "Goddamnit, Wood, what the hell are ya doin'? We was gonna take him peaceably."

Clement fired in the direction of the saloon door.

Leslie dove to the floor, and Frank Allison dropped on top of him.

Leslie couldn't see anything, but he heard shots being blasted every which way in the saloon. But just for a few seconds.

Then Leslie heard the shooting move outside to the street.

Allison got off Leslie, who rose to his knees and looked around.

Dave Poole was still in his seat, but Archie Clement, his companion, and the six would-be soldiers were gone.

Leslie scrambled to his feet, and that's when the frights hit him. His legs got all shaky, and his stomach churned. The gunplay had started so suddenly he didn't have time to get scared, but he was good and scared now.

Yet he still wanted to see what was going on. Leslie went with some trepidation to a window and looked out.

Little Archie was on a horse, firing off shots, while men on both sides of the street and in windows and on roofs shot at him. He rode down North Street a good thirty yards, shooting and getting shot all the way, before he finally fell from his horse.

The men in blue gathered around Little Archie, and Leslie saw him still trying to cock a pistol with his teeth. Words were exchanged, but Leslie was too far away to hear what was said.

That was the end of Little Archie Clement.

***

That was almost the end of Leslie Warner, too, Leslie thought, though he gathered his wits soon after Clement met his demise. He reckoned his pa would most definitely be looking for him now and would be fretting about his well-being.

Leslie hoped he'd be fretting enough to forget to get mad at his only son.

"Let's get out of here," Frank Allison said.

They left the City Hotel saloon and approached the townsfolk who were crowding the sidewalk, gawking at the commotion in the street and chattering like baby birds.

"He don't look so tough now," one man said. "Not with twenty-five or thirty holes in him."

"He had it comin'," another said. "He weren't no good no how. I guess that will be the end of such trouble in these streets."

Leslie and Allison must have fit in with those folks, because when Colonel Warner arrived perhaps a minute later he didn't ask where they had been or what they'd been doing.

"Did you see what happened here?" he asked Allison.

"We didn't see everything, but we seen enough," he said.

"Who is that man the soldiers killed?"

"Archie Clement. He was wanted on more than one warrant," Allison said. "He headed the band that likely robbed the bank."

"Leslie, see what happens to men who cause trouble?"

Leslie wasn't sure what his pa was getting at, seeing as how he was too young to have robbed a bank. But he figured his father was suggesting Leslie also would meet a bloody demise if he ever caused too much difficulty.

In any circumstance, Leslie didn't want his pa asking any more about what he and Frank Allison had seen or done. He didn't want to lie to him, but he certainly wasn't about to tell the truth.

"I ain't been causin' no trouble, Pa," Leslie said. "I stayed with Mr. Allison the whole time you was gone."

"Glad to hear it," Colonel Warner said. "I'm done with my business here. Do you have anything you need to do before we head home, Allison?"

"As a matter of fact, I got some supplies I need to pick up. I was hopin' I could borrow the boy to help me collect them and, if you don't mind, we could transport them home on your buckboard. If that's no problem."

"We'd be happy to help," Colonel Warner said. "Leslie, you go with Allison there. I'll follow you with the buckboard and Allison's horse."

It didn't take a genius to figure out that Frank Allison had something on his mind other than supplies. He and Leslie had already visited the supplies store, and he hadn't said anything about needing to pick up more things.

Sure enough, as soon as they got out of the range of Colonel Warner's ears, Allison put his hand on Leslie's shoulder and started talking in a soft, low voice Leslie had never heard him use before.

"Boy, you best not tell your folks where we was today and what happened," he said. "I'm darn sure they wouldn't be happy about it. We best keep it between the two of us."

"I weren't planning on sayin' nothin', Mr. Allison," Leslie said. "You can count on me to stay quiet. I reckon there's more to your story than Pa and Mother know, but they'll never hear a word of it from me. I reckon you musta rode with Dave Poole and Archie Clement and those boys during the war. Is that right, Mr. Allison?"

"Yeah, but let's don't talk about that now, boy," he said. "I ain't proud of what I done in those days. Those goddamn Kansans came into Missouri and started all the trouble. They burned Osceola and killed innocent Missourians. Still, them sumbitches didn't deserve to die the way we done 'em in Lawrence."

With that, Allison grabbed a bag of flour and motioned for Leslie to pick up a bushel of potatoes, and they rejoined Pa at the buckboard.

December 14, 1866

Leslie woke up early after lying awake most of the night thinking about what had happened in town. It was the most exciting thing he'd ever witnessed, but the most terrifying, too.

Seeing a man get killed was different than he expected. The dime novels made killings seem so simple. They didn't describe the noise or the dirt or the blood or the stillness of the dead body after the killing was done.

It was something Leslie wouldn't soon forget.

Arch Clement was a bad man, he reckoned, but he didn't deserve to die like that. Nobody did.

Thoughts of the famed bushwhacker's bloody death almost made Leslie forget about the previous day's other development—learning that his neighbor Frank Allison had ridden alongside the likes of Clement and Dave Poole.

That meant Leslie actually knew a bushwhacker, or at least a former one.

He wondered how many men Allison had killed, whether he had been involved in the bank robberies and other mischief the bushwhackers had gotten into since the war, and whether his pa or anybody else knew about Allison's past.

It was all very exciting.

Leslie was dying to tell somebody about all he'd seen. He wanted to tell Mary, but he couldn't take the chance his mother and pa might find out. So he decided to keep quiet about it and went downstairs to eat breakfast.

His mother was waiting for him.

"What's this I hear about you seeing a killing in Lexington, Leslie Warner?" Georgia Warner demanded.

Drat. She was the last person he wanted to talk to about it.

Leslie knew she had no idea he saw a lot more than the killing, but she still made him uneasy. She always did. His mother had a way of making him feel like he'd done something bad even when he hadn't.

"Yes, Mother, it was appalling," Leslie said, hoping that's what she wanted to hear.

She tilted her head and smiled.

"I'm sure it was," she said. "I just hope you weren't traumatized too much."

"No, ma'am. I was traumatized just the right amount."

She laughed, and that was the last time the killing of Archie Clement was mentioned in the Warners' house.

December 25, 1866

Leslie rushed to Mary's room as soon as he woke up.

Actually, it wasn't just Mary's room. She shared it with their little sister Ella. The baby slept in Mother and Pa's bedroom.

Leslie figured he was lucky. As the only boy, he'd gotten a room to himself.

Anyway, Mary and Leslie always hurried downstairs together on Christmas morning.

Leslie was so eager to get downstairs that he pretty near flew to Mary's room. He pushed the door open, ready to greet Mary with "Merry Christmas, let's get goin'," but was stopped dead in his tracks.

He couldn't believe what he was seeing right in front of him.

Mary was standing with her back to Leslie, and she was wearing only her underdrawers. Leslie was looking right at her, though he barely got a glimpse of anything before she hastily wrapped a blanket around herself.

"Leslie, get out of here!" she screamed. She had never yelled at Leslie like that.

He stumbled backward as he yanked the door shut and ran back to his room, where he threw himself on his bed and tried to figure out what had just happened. He'd never seen a near-naked girl before, and Mary was the prettiest girl he knew.

Fact is, he didn't really see anything of interest except Mary's bare back. Still, he felt guilty.

But why? Leslie didn't go in there planning to see Mary without her clothes. For all he knew, both girls were still fast asleep. He reckoned he hadn't really done anything all that wrong.

The worst part was having Mary mad at him. Leslie hated having people mad at him, especially people he liked as much as he liked Mary. He didn't know what he would say to her next time he saw her.

Before he could figure out what to do, Mary charged through the open door of his room and stood over him, hands on hips. She was now fully dressed.

"Leslie, you can't just come barging into our bedroom. You have to knock first," she said. She wasn't yelling, but her voice quivered as she spoke. "I am so angry with you now. Only a husband is allowed to see a woman in that state. You have violated me."

Leslie couldn't look her in the face, and he didn't want to look at her other parts, so he stared down at the bed.

"I'm sorry," he mumbled. "But it's Christmas, and we always go downstairs together, and I was excited, and I just wanted to see you . . . but with your clothes on. I'll knock from now on."

"You better," she said. "Now, the question is what the proper punishment should be. There's no need for Mother and Pa to know what you did, but I can't let you get away without suffering consequences for your action."

Sudden like, Leslie had an idea. "To make things even, I could . . ."

"Don't you finish that sentence, Leslie Warner. I have no desire to see you without your clothes on."

How'd she know what he planned to say?

In any case, Leslie was mostly relieved, because he had no great desire to show Mary (nor anybody else) what his scrawny body looked like.

"I know what we'll do," Mary continued. "You'll take over my chores for the next two weeks. In exchange, I won't say anything to Mother and Pa about your little indiscretion. Agreed?"

"Agreed," Leslie said.

"Good. Now let's get on downstairs."

Mary turned and strode out the door, and Leslie scrambled off the bed to follow her, embarrassment almost forgotten.

Downstairs, their parents sat in chairs across from the family Christmas tree, an eight-foot cedar Leslie had cut from the property between the house and the Missouri River and which he had helped decorate with simple, homemade ornaments. Leslie loved the cedar fragrance, which melded with the aromas of the oak logs burning in the fireplace and the bacon sizzling in the kitchen.

Wrapping paper covered the floor, as Ella was already inspecting her presents. Everybody said, "Merry Christmas," and before long they all opened their goodies.

***

Sallie and Sam arrived shortly, with Lizzie and Jo Shelby, of course.

Nobody was talking when their carriage drew up in front of the house, and they surely didn't have the look of Christmas joy about them. Even Jo Shelby wasn't his usual friendly self.

It was gray and bitter cold, though there was no snow on the ground. Leslie had been hoping for snow, because he hadn't seen a white Christmas since he was a young'un in Kentucky. He thought maybe, as cold as it was, it might snow later in the day.

Sallie jumped down from the carriage with no help from Sam.

"I'll not have you touch me when you're in this condition," she said to her husband as she scurried into the house.

"Runnin' to Mother, I suspect," Sam said as he watched her go.

He climbed clumsily out of the carriage, then offered Lizzie a helping hand. She also hurried into the house, though not as fast as Sallie. That left just Leslie and Sam and Jo Shelby outside.

"Something wrong with Sallie?" Leslie asked.

He was close enough to smell Sam, who reeked of liquor even worse than usual. He kept his left hand on the big back wheel of the carriage, and he still seemed to struggle to hold his body upright.

"Ain't there always?" he said. "Don't matter none. How's my favorite Warner doin' on this fine Christmas morn'?"

"Ain't Sallie your favorite Warner?" Leslie replied.

"She ain't no Warner now," Sam said. "She's a Nutter. She's mine now."

He then turned his attention to Jo Shelby, who was still in the carriage.

Sam said to the dog, "Does my big boy want to get down?" Then in a higher voice, "Does my big boy want to get down?"

Leslie laughed.

"Sam, that dog ain't gonna answer no matter how many times you ask him," he said.

Sam laughed, too. Reaching, he lifted Jo Shelby from the carriage and placed him on the ground. He patted his head, scratched his ears, rubbed his belly and patted his head again.

"Jo Shelby, you are the best dog in the world," he said.

At that point, Leslie noticed his mother standing at the door.

"You know you aren't bringing that beast into the house," she said. "I don't care how cold it is. You can put him in the barn."

"That barn ain't hardly any warmer than it is out here," Sam said. "If Jo Shelby can't go in the house, I ain't goin' in, neither. I'll spend the day with him in the barn."

Sam was serious, too.

He stumbled a few steps toward the barn, with Jo Shelby trotting close beside him. Leslie saw Sam reach with his right hand inside his jacket, hunting for the pocket where he kept his liquor. He didn't pull anything out, though, just kept wobbling toward the barn.

"Fine with me," Georgia Warner said. "We don't allow drunks in the house, either."

Sam didn't turn around.

"Fine with me, too," he called over his shoulder.

***

Sam stayed in the barn all day, just like he'd said he would. Leslie checked on him once, saw he was asleep in the hay with Jo Shelby beside him, and went back into the warm house.

Nobody inside even asked about him. Truth be told, nobody said much of anything all day.

Around sunset, a knock sounded on the front door.

"Leslie, go let Sam in," Georgia Warner said. "But make sure he doesn't have that dog with him."

Sure enough, Leslie opened the door to reveal Sam shivering in front of him. He was alone.

"I found Jo Shelby a nice spot amid the hay," he said. "I reckon he'll be OK. I for one am freezing my fingers and toes off. Dinner ain't been ate yet, has it?"

Leslie stood aside and held the door for Sam to enter. He walked considerably sturdier than earlier. Evidently, the sleep had done him some good.

"We was just gettin' ready to sit down for dinner," Leslie said.

Most everybody stayed quiet during the meal, especially Sam. He didn't say a thing. Sallie talked only a bit about how good the food was and other such things, and she never once looked at her husband.

Even Lizzie, whom Leslie had come to expect to provide some entertaining words, talked only when she was responding to polite conversational questions from Georgia Warner.

It seemed like the longest Christmas dinner Leslie'd ever experienced.

The mood afterward didn't improve much, and Leslie and the kids went upstairs without their mother even telling them to.

The drama with Sam and the silent dinner had made Leslie forget for a while about what happened that morning, when he'd burst upon Mary in her room. After he climbed into bed, however, thoughts of his near-naked sister started bouncing around in his head again.

Leslie decided it wasn't such a bad thing to have seen.

January 11, 1867

"What's incest?" Leslie Warner asked his sister Sallie.

He was visiting her and Sam, which he'd done occasionally since they got married. He liked spending time at their place, and he also liked getting away from home. Leslie thought nothing was more boring than being at home.

It was most of a morning's ride from the Warners' house near Dover to Sam and Sallie's, which was some eight miles west of Lexington, near Wellington.

Sam had a nice place. The house was even bigger than the Warners', and he had more land, too. He'd gotten it when his father died, just before the war started. His mother died a year before that.

Sam grew up in the house with a bunch of sisters, just like Leslie, but now it was just Sam and Lizzie.

And Sallie, of course.

Georgia and Colonel Warner didn't mind Leslie spending time there. In fact, his father seemed to want him there as much as possible and always asked about things Leslie saw while he was there. Leslie figured his pa didn't trust Sam much.

He couldn't blame his pa. He'd seen a lot of stuff at Sam's that didn't go on at the Warners' house, that's for sure. Drinking and guns, mostly. And cursing, too. But he didn't tell his pa about those things. If his mother found out about all that went on at Sam and Sallie's, she might forbid him from going there.

"Why in the world would you ask me about incest?" Sallie said, looking at Leslie like he was their Grandpa Warner back from the grave.

"Well, I told Mary I wanted us to be lovers when we was old enough, and she said we couldn't. She said that would be incest 'cause she's my sister.

"So what's incest?"

Sallie fidgeted a good minute before she answered.

"That's when one family member marries another family member. It isn't allowed," she said.

"Why not?"

It just didn't make sense to Leslie. Family members live together all the time, he thought. What difference is it if they were married, too?

"It just isn't allowed," Sallie said. "Leslie, this really isn't something you should be asking about. Mary was right—you won't be marrying your sister."

"But I ain't never gonna meet a girl I like better than Mary."

"Leslie, you need to stop saying things like that. And you need to stop thinking that way about Mary."

Discomfited, Sallie rose and left the room, but Leslie saw Lizzie standing in the hallway. She was grinning, so he reckoned she had heard what he'd asked his sister.

"Lizzie, can you tell me about incest?"

Lizzie proceeded to explain that it wasn't solely about marriage but was when one family member had sexual relations with another family member.

"But the family members have to be blood related for it to be incest," she said. "It would be incest if you had sexual relations with your sister or if your pa had sexual relations with your sister."

"What about aunts and uncles and cousins and such?" Leslie asked. "Seems like that should be allowed."

"Well, cousins are mostly allowed, but not aunts and uncles. And it's not incest if a man and woman related only by marriage have sexual relations. So it would be fine if I had sexual relations with you, 'cause we ain't related by blood, only by marriage.

"Leslie, would you like to have sexual relations with me?"

She's teasing, Leslie thought.

In any regard, he could feel his whole body getting hot and his mouth going dry. He liked Lizzie, but she was more than twice as old as him, even older than Sam. Leslie reckoned she wasn't much younger than his mother. *That* was a scary thought.

But the bigger quandary he faced was that he wasn't exactly sure what sexual relations involved, and he didn't want to tell that to Lizzie. Oh, he knew bits and parts about sexual relations, mostly that they somehow involved a man's bits and a woman's parts. But he wasn't sure how everything fit together.

"Well, I don't know . . . I guess I wouldn't mind having sexual relations with ya," Leslie finally blurted out.

Lizzie laughed her lamb-bleating laugh and put her right hand on Leslie's left shoulder. She leaned in and kissed him on the cheek.

"You are so sweet, Leslie Warner," she said. "I wish you was ten years older."

He did the math right quick and figured that would make him twenty-two years old, which would still leave him some ten years younger than Lizzie.

"What difference would that make?" he asked her.

"Well, then we could be lovers, and people wouldn't think nothin' of it."

"So it ain't a problem that Mary is four years older than me?" he asked.

"No, you and Mary are blood related. That's incest. That ain't allowed. Course, if you don't get caught, that's another matter. It's like anything else. It ain't so bad unless you get caught doin' it."

That wasn't exactly the Golden Rule as Leslie learned it.

He figured incest would be an easy thing not to get caught doing, so maybe it wasn't all that bad. Not like stealing or killing or lying.

He wondered whether there might be people he knew, maybe even members of his own family, who were having incest and not getting caught doing it. He wondered if Sam and Lizzie themselves were having incest.

"Lizzie, did you and Sam ever incest with each other?" he asked.

"Well, Leslie, that's the kind of thing a lady don't discuss."

February 12, 1867

"When are you going to do something about this, Mr. Warner?" Georgia Warner screeched at her husband. "I'm tired of being made to look the fool."

Leslie wasn't sure what his mother was talking about, but he figured he'd soon find out. He was in the front room, and his parents were in the kitchen, so Leslie could hear what they were saying. They had no idea he was listening.

His mother was fairly shrieking at this point.

"You will be the very death of me, I swear. Sometimes I believe you are a total idiot. I don't know why I married you and brought you into our family. You are unable or unwilling to do anything I want you to do."

"If you had paid those men when the work on the house was finished, they wouldn't have had reason to file these suits against us," Colonel Warner said. "But you insisted that we not pay them because you weren't happy with their work."

"I didn't pay them because we didn't have enough money to pay them, and that is your responsibility," Georgia howled. "I said I wasn't happy with their work only so that people wouldn't know how broke we are. You simply are unable to provide for this family.

Thank goodness for Father. If not for him, we'd be living on the streets of Lexington."

That was news to Leslie. He thought they had plenty of money.

"You know I hate to keep asking General Combs for help," Colonel Warner said.

"Well, Mr. Warner, we wouldn't have to ask General Combs for help if you displayed the slightest aptitude for farming, not to mention taking better care of the money we *do* have," Leslie's mother bellowed. "You are such a disappointment to me."

"You know I've never been much of a farmer. I don't think the good Lord intended me to be a man of the earth. In any case, I'm somewhat old to be converted now. What about Sam's money? That was the idea behind this marriage, after all, wasn't it? It isn't as if we wanted him to be a part of our family."

Georgia Warner sneered, although she finally lowered the tone of her voice to something close to a normal conversational volume.

"The idea was that Sam would want to be part of this family and would want to help support it," she said. "It would be wonderful if he offered us aid, but he obviously has other ideas. I can envision no scenario in which we would request financial help from Sam."

Colonel Warner thought for a few seconds, then said, "There must be another way to get Sam's money."

March 25, 1867

It was about one hour past sunset when Leslie looked out his bedroom window and saw the intruders. Two men on mounts, galloping away from the paddock area, leading four horses. Four of the Warners' best horses, Leslie reckoned.

"Pa!" he called as he ran out of his room and leapt down the stairs three at a time. "Pa, there's men stealin' our horses!"

"Leslie, what in tarnation are you yelling about?" Georgia Warner cried as she emerged into the hallway from the bedroom. "What's that about horses?"

Leslie ignored his mother, striding past her to find his pa in the sitting room.

"I just seen 'em out my window," he said, a bit calmer now. "Two men ridin' off with our horses. We can catch 'em if we leave now."

Colonel Warner was sitting with Captain William Littlejohn, a frequent visitor. They had served together during the war, and, like the Warners, Capt. Littlejohn had moved to Lafayette County after the fighting ended. He lived not far from Sallie and Sam.

Colonel Warner stood up sharply at Leslie's pronouncement.

"Leslie, slow down now," he said. "Tell me exactly what you saw."

"Like I said, I seen two men ridin' off with four of our horses."

"This just happened?"

"Not two minutes ago."

"What direction were they riding?"

"They was headin' east."

"How fast were they riding?"

"At a full gallop."

"Were they armed?"

"It was too dark to see."

"Fine," Colonel Warner said. "No sense in contacting the sheriff. It would be hours before he could get on their trail, and he's probably a friend of theirs, anyway. Our best plan of action is to track them tonight to see where they're headed, then decide how to deal with them when we find out.

"Captain Littlejohn, would you like to join us?"

"Yes, sir, I wouldn't miss it for anything," the visitor said.

Captain Littlejohn, who was now standing beside Colonel Warner, didn't seem much like a soldier to Leslie. He was several inches shorter than Colonel Warner and on the plump side, with a balding head and spectacles. He was dressed in dungarees and a green wool shirt.

"I'm glad they took off east," Colonel Warner said. "That means they'll be riding past Allison's place. He's just the man we need. I believe you have met him, Captain?"

"Yes, sir," Captain Littlejohn said. "He's a bit rough around the edges but seems a good man."

Captain Littlejohn wasn't at all rough around the edges. Leslie had never seen him when he wasn't clean shaven and neatly dressed. He carried an air of confidence about him.

"Leslie, you go out to the paddock and figure out which horses they took," Colonel Warner said. "We need to be able to identify them. See if anything else is missing while you're out there. Be sure to note if any saddles were taken. Now go."

Leslie hurried out the door, amazed by how calm and organized his pa was acting. He was totally in charge. Leslie had never seen him like that.

After checking the paddock, Leslie went through the tool and carriage house. He was pretty sure nothing was missing except the four horses. One thing was certain—the thieves knew which horses to take. But that would make them easy to trail, too, because all the Warners' best horses had specialized shoeing.

Leslie ran back to the house to report in.

Colonel Warner, who had changed into riding clothes and his old Union hat, was carrying a 12-gauge shotgun he kept locked in a cabinet in the hall. As far as Leslie knew, the shotgun hadn't been out of the cabinet since the family moved to Missouri.

"Leslie, you'll come with us," he said. "But if we catch up with these thieves, you'll ride back. I expect we can retrieve the horses without any shooting, but these men likely are desperate, and I won't take a chance on your being injured."

"Should I take my huntin' rifle?" Leslie asked.

"Yes, but don't load it. I don't want you shooting one of us by accident."

Georgia Warner was watching all of this and didn't say a word. Meanwhile, Captain Littlejohn maintained a serious gaze on his old friend, nodding and following a step or two behind Colonel Warner wherever he walked.

As he strode out the door with the 12-gauge folded over his left arm, Colonel Warner said, "These thieves picked the wrong man to steal from."

***

Fortunately, Leslie thought, it wasn't too cold. Snow had fallen a few days earlier but had melted, though the ground remained soft.

He figured he, his father and Captain Littlejohn were about twenty minutes behind the thieves when they left home, yet they weren't riding particularly fast. Colonel Warner didn't seem to be in a hurry.

The three reached Frank Allison's place within about ten minutes, and Allison was eager to join the group. He said he had heard horses ride past but didn't think anything of them. Horsemen went past his house on a regular basis.

He now seemed angry, though.

"Them sumbitches oughta be strung up," he said to Colonel Warner as he strapped on two pistols. Leslie had never seen him carry pistols.

Colonel Warner was interested in what Allison might know about the men involved in the robbery.

"Allison, would you reckon these thieves are from among the bushwhackers? They appear to know what they're doing. They certainly knew which horses they wanted, and the bushwhackers are always in need of good horseflesh."

"More than likely they are bushwhackers," Allison agreed. "They likely scouted out your place in recent days and devised a plan. Probably thought your house was an easy mark, what with all the girls and women around, and figured you wasn't the sort to put up a fight. They don't like to leave much to chance."

"They took off east and are still heading that direction, but wouldn't you expect them to turn north and west?" Colonel Warner asked. "Don't these bushwhackers generally head back to Clay County to hide out?"

"That's right, Colonel," Allison said. "I can't imagine they'll head east for long."

"Exactly what I thought. In that case, I propose we head north and see if we can't give them a little surprise before they get to the river. Where's the most likely place for them to cross?"

"I know of two or three places, Colonel," Allison said. "But if they want to cross the river as soon as possible, there's one place they'd most likely go."

"You and I will ride there," Colonel Warner said. "Captain Littlejohn, you and Leslie remain on their trail. And pick up your pace now. See if you can't get within their hearing distance by the time they reach the river. I want them to know they are being followed, if possible. That will make our greeting all the more a surprise.

"There are only two of them, and they are leading four horses. If we catch them just right, they will either have to let the horses go or will have a good deal of difficulty organizing themselves for a fight."

"Yes, sir," Captain Littlejohn said.

"Yes, Colonel," Frank Allison said.

"Sounds good to me, Pa," Leslie said.

"Now, Captain Littlejohn, under no circumstances will you put Leslie in harm's way," Colonel Warner said. "If that means we must let these scoundrels go, then that's what we will do. Is that acceptable to you?"

"Yes, sir."

The group galloped off to the east, but within about a mile, Colonel Warner and Frank Allison turned onto a trail north, leaving Leslie and Captain Littlejohn following the thieves' tracks to the east. The trail cut through thick woods.

The bandits were easy to track but were still a far piece ahead. Captain Littlejohn kept a steady pace, fast enough to make good time but not so fast as to tire the horses too quickly.

Leslie's racing mind finally slowed enough that he realized this was maybe the most exciting adventure of his lifetime. He felt fear mixed with anticipation, like a soldier galloping through the dark toward an uncertain fate.

He smiled, the silence broken only by the sound of horse hooves clacking along the ground, as he inhaled the aroma of the pine trees on both sides of the trail.

Leslie had a serious desire to ask Captain Littlejohn about his pa and the war, but they were riding too fast to carry on a conversation. They stopped to water the horses, though, and Leslie had a quick opening.

"So, Captain Littejohn, how long did you serve with Pa?" he asked, as they led their mounts to a stream beside the road.

"Right from the start, when the Eighteenth Kentucky mustered in Cynthiana," he said, "until Colonel Warner got shot at Richmond. I thought he was killed. He fought bravely. He was the best officer I served under. Hasn't Colonel Warner told you about his service during the war?"

"Not much," Leslie said. "He don't seem to want to discuss it much."

"Can't say I blame him," Captain Littlejohn said. "Richmond was the worst fightin' the Eighteenth saw. Those of us not killed or wounded were lucky.

"We best be movin' on, now," he said, seemingly eager to end the conversation. "I reckon we still have a lot of ground to make up."

The two mounted and took off again. Within twenty minutes, they saw that the horse thieves had turned onto a trail leading north, just as Colonel Warner said they would.

The farther Leslie and Captain Littlejohn rode, the hillier and rockier the trail got. They were in thick woods the whole way.

They continued riding hard for what seemed to Leslie to be hours, though it likely wasn't more than forty minutes. He couldn't be sure where they were because he had never ridden this far from the farm, but he figured they must be nearing the river.

Sudden like, Captain Littlejohn stopped, and Leslie with him, just as they reached the crest of a hill where the trail curved sharply to the left.

Then Leslie saw what Captain Littlejohn had seen.

Two men on horseback flanked the trail, with rifles aimed right at their pursuers. Leslie saw four familiar horses tied to trees.

He'd never been in the crosshairs of a rifle before, and the experience was every bit as unnerving as he'd imagined it to be. He was frozen, unable to do more than stare at the barrel of that rifle.

"We been waitin' for you boys," the smaller but meaner-looking thief said. He had a nasty scar across his right cheek. "Never thought you'd get here."

"What do you gents want?" Captain Littlejohn asked. "My boy and me are just out for a ride."

"Right," the smaller thief said through a sneer. "You always go for rides at midnight? Or is this a special occasion?"

"I don't reckon we need to answer your questions," Captain Littlejohn said. "Now, if you gents don't mind, we'll be riding on through."

"I do mind," the thief said. "In fact, I'm afeared we're gonna have to shoot you boys. We can't have no witnesses, after all. And two more horses would make our little visit to Lafayette County all the more worthwhile."

"He's just a boy," Captain Littlejohn said. "Let him go. He can't cause you any harm."

"He's carryin' a rifle, ain't he?" the thief said. "Now, both of you, drop your weapons."

Leslie was tempted to tell the man his hunting rifle wasn't even loaded, but instead he threw it to the ground beside the trail.

Captain Littlejohn slid his pistol from his belt and dropped it, then slowly pulled his rifle from its sheath, raised it to chest level and threw it down. When it hit the ground, it fired.

Boom!

The gunshot reverberated through the trees, where the only other noises at this hour had been frogs croaking.

The shot didn't hit anybody, but the two horse thieves nearly jumped out of their saddles. Leslie, too.

"Sorry, gents, I don't handle firearms much," Captain Littlejohn said with a sly smile.

"You sorry excuse for a man, we oughtta shoot you both right now," the small thief said.

"I ain't gonna shoot no boy," his partner said.

He was a hulking man, but he was kind looking.

"I ain't never killed no children nor no women, and I ain't startin' now. We don't need to kill 'em nohow. Long as we got their horses and their guns, they ain't gonna cause no problems."

Normally, Leslie might have disputed being included among children, but he figured that wouldn't be wise, given his predicament. He kept his eyes on Captain Littlejohn.

"Your cohort is correct," he told the chief thief. "What harm could we possibly cause? Just take our horses and . . ."

Captain Littlejohn stopped in midsentence, and Leslie looked past him and past the two thieves and saw why.

Colonel Warner and Frank Allison had ridden up behind the pair of bandits, and Allison had two pistols drawn.

The thieves turned to face them, and Captain Littlejohn leapt off his horse and grabbed up his rifle, all in one smooth motion. He pointed it at the thief who had been doing most of the talking.

It appeared Colonel Warner's posse had caught themselves a couple of horse thieves.

"You boys have my horses," Colonel Warner said. "We've got you outgunned. Why don't you just lay down your weapons?"

"I'd just as soon shoot 'em," Allison said.

"I thought that was you when I first seen you two, Allison," the smaller thief with the scar said. "Now I knowd it's you. What are you doin' with these soft horns? We ain't got no reason nor no inclination to tangle with you."

"Put down your guns," Colonel Warner said.

"I don't think so," the thief said.

Everybody had a gun aimed at somebody else, except Leslie. He was still frozen on his horse, with his unloaded hunting rifle lying on the side of the trail.

Nobody said a thing for a few seconds.

Finally, Colonel Warner said, "Surrender peaceably and come with us to Lexington, and nobody will get hurt."

"I say we shoot 'em now," Allison said.

"You could do that," the smaller thief said. "You'd likely get both of us, no problem. But before my body hit the ground, I'd put a bullet in the boy's head."

He turned in his saddle and pointed his rifle at Leslie.

"And you ain't takin' us into Lexington alive, that's for certain," he said.

For the first time since Leslie told his pa about the horse thievery hours ago, Colonel Warner appeared flustered.

"Well . . ." he started, "we'll just have to . . . if you just give back the horses . . ."

"If you let us take the horses," Frank Allison said, "I won't kill you. At least not now. Your other choices are to ride out with the horses, in which case we'll send the boy back home, track you down as far as it takes, and I'll kill ya both. Or we can shoot it out now, in which case I'll kill ya both now."

That last choice didn't appeal much to Leslie, considering it likely would mean his bloody demise. But he reckoned Frank Allison knew what he was doing.

"How do you want to do this?" he asked the thieves.

"Take the horses," the smaller thief said. "We can thieve some other soft horn's horses."

"Whadya think, Colonel . . . Mr. Warner? Do we let these sumbitches go?" Allison asked.

"Yes," Colonel Warner said. "Whatever it takes to keep Leslie safe."

Allison kept his pistols leveled at the thieves while Captain Littlejohn quickly untied the four horses.

"You two get on back to your friends, now," Allison told the thieves. "Go."

The would-be thieves galloped madly away while Leslie and the others watched them go. They stared down the trail for a good minute, until they heard the sounds of horses no more.

"Allison, I thank you," Colonel Warner said. "You saved my son's life."

"Colonel, no man can save another man's life," Frank Allison said. "All he can do is postpone his death."

May 2, 1867

This was the first warm day of the spring. The sky was a deep blue, and there wasn't a cloud to be seen or a breeze to be felt. The rising sun was just peeking through his window when Leslie hurried to the girls' room. He knocked this time, and Mary knew right quick who it was and what he wanted.

"Yes, Leslie, it's a beautiful day for a ride," she said as she opened the door. "And, yes, Leslie, I want to go with you. But I have to get ready first. I'll see you at breakfast."

Leslie figured to get outside as quickly as possible. No breakfast needed. But if he had to wait for Mary to get ready and to eat, he reckoned it was worth the delay.

He and Mary had been getting along as well as could be expected since he saw her nearly naked on Christmas. Leslie had felt a bit uncomfortable around her for a few days, but he got over that feeling soon enough. She acted like she always did.

Leslie would admit it didn't seem altogether the same, though. Once you've seen somebody without their clothes, there's no taking that back. No way you can ever look at them the same again. It happened regular when he was talking to Mary that his thoughts wandered to that time he saw her bare back and shoulders.

But she didn't know that, and he wasn't about to say anything to her about it.

Seeing as how Mary was going to be awhile, Leslie wasn't in a rush to get downstairs for breakfast. He knew no matter how long he took, he'd be ready before Mary was.

He decided to read from one of his Beadle's Dime Novels before moseying downstairs. He read them most nights before going to sleep and every other opportunity that presented itself, and he'd just got a new edition.

So he plopped down on his bed and began following the adventures of Ned Starling in the wild country of Arkansas in 1835.

About three pages into the tale, Ned was about to tangle with a gang of bad guys when, next thing Leslie knew, Ned Starling was nowhere to be found. It was Leslie who was there in the woods, and he wasn't on a horse. Worse yet, he wasn't wearing any clothes. The bad guys were rushing at him, and all he had on were his boots and a belt holding a pistol.

Scared doesn't begin to describe what he was feeling.

Funny thing was, Leslie was more worried about being naked than tangling with the bad guys. He counted five, all dressed in black, all holding pistols and all astride black horses thundering right at him. Leslie realized all five men were identical, down to their black mustaches and dark, beady eyes.

He didn't know what he'd done to deserve it, but they were definitely out for his blood.

Leslie tried to hide behind a tree, but it was just a sapling and wasn't nearly wide enough to cover him. Meanwhile, the bad guys kept coming toward him. He pulled his pistol out of his belt and pointed it. But he didn't shoot. He couldn't shoot. Hard as he tried, he wasn't able to pull the trigger.

"Go ahead and kill me!" Leslie hollered.

"Who wants to kill you?"

It was Mary.

Leslie jumped awake and looked down to make sure he had clothes on.

"Oh, I guess I falled asleep and was dreamin'," he said. "Five bad guys were out to get me."

He didn't mention the naked part.

"I guess I saved you, then," Mary said.

"I guess you did. Thanks."

"I'm ready for breakfast. How 'bout you?"

"I'm starvin'," Leslie said, even though he wasn't all that hungry. He just wanted to get as far away from that dream as he could.

Mary was dressed nicer than was usual when she went riding. She wore a crisp yellow dress and a blue bonnet, which made Leslie wonder if she planned on going riding at all.

She started down the stairs.

"Why are you wearin' that dress?" Leslie asked.

She stopped midway down and said, "I thought we would take the buggy into Dover instead of riding today. I have some things I want to do there."

Leslie wasn't too keen on that idea. Dover wasn't much of a town. It lay about two miles north of the Warners' farm, and they went there for church and school and such, not for fun.

"I had my heart set on a ride today," Leslie said.

The sister and brother were downstairs by then, within earshot of their mother, who was in the kitchen.

"Mother, you don't mind if Leslie and I go to Dover today, do you?" Mary said.

"Why, no, but what do you have planned there?" Georgia Warner asked.

"Nothing much," Mary said. "I just want to go for a drive in the buggy on this beautiful day, and Dover is as good a place to go as anywhere. I thought we might go down to the river afterward."

"Leslie has agreed to go with you?"

"Yes. Tell her, Leslie."

"Well," he said, "point of fact is I thought we was gonna go ridin', but I guess I'll drive the buggy."

Leslie still wasn't sure what Mary had in her mind. She'd never wanted to drive to Dover before.

"Be home in time for supper," their mother said.

So, after breakfast, off the brother and sister went.

On the ride to Dover, Mary talked and talked about silly things, such as the pretty weather, the lovely trees, and how nice Leslie was for coming with her.

"May is the most misunderstood month, don't you think?" she said. "It's not summer yet, but it doesn't seem like spring either."

Mary gushed about the bloodroot blooming along the woody trail, explaining enthusiastically that the beautiful white wildflowers open in the sunlight but close at night and survive only one or two days. She said the plant got its name because it produces a reddish-orange sap that Indians used for dyes and as medicine.

"I think bloodroot is my favorite flower in the world," she said.

Leslie had never heard Mary ramble on like this. She wasn't her usual self, he thought. He and Mary typically talked to each other real easily. He felt safe telling her things he couldn't tell anybody else.

Now, though, Leslie surmised she was holding something in and was talking just to be talking.

"Are you mad at me, Mary?" he finally said.

"No. Why do you ask?"

"It seems to me you're actin' peculiar today."

"Well," she said, somewhat reluctantly, "if you must know, I lied to Mother. I do have a reason for driving to Dover, but I didn't want to tell her. She would have forbade me from going."

"Huh? But why didn't you let me know?"

"I didn't want to tell you, either, Leslie, because you might not have wanted to drive with me, and then Mother would have forbidden me from going alone. The fact is, the Plattenburg boys are expecting to see me in Dover today."

The Plattenburgs were the fanciest family in Dover, and Harvey and John Plattenburg were the fanciest boys in Dover, though both were closer to Sallie's age than Mary's. Their little brother George was Leslie's age.

All Leslie knew about Harvey and John was that they rode with General Jo Shelby's Fifth Cavalry Rebel regiment during the war, and now they pranced about Dover like they were Jeff Davis and Robert E. Lee themselves.

Leslie yanked the reins to halt the gelding that was pulling the buggy and turned to look at Mary.

She was right. He likely would have refused to drive her to Dover if he had known the whole story.

"I reckon if you had your druthers, I wouldn't be no part of this trip, neither," Leslie said.

It wasn't too late to turn back, he thought. He figured he could go back home and take a ride by himself, but he didn't want to make Mary mad at him.

They were almost to Dover, anyway.

Leslie gave the reins a shake, and they drove on in that direction.

He didn't say anything the rest of the trip. Neither did Mary.

Once in Dover, they pulled up in front of the livery, which was on the same side of the street as the bank and the dry goods store. On the opposite side was the hotel, with a saloon and a small restaurant attached. That was about all there was to the hamlet, other than the school and church, which both stood at the far edge of town.

The only folks active in Dover appeared to be two old men sitting outside the hotel and some ladies furtively coming and going from the dry goods store.

"Let's walk to the store," Mary said.

The store, it turned out, was where Harvey and John Plattenburg worked. They were both there. Harvey was behind the counter, and John was busy stocking the shelves. Or maybe John was behind the counter, and Harvey was busy stocking the shelves. Truth be told, Leslie didn't know one Plattenburg from another.

Didn't rightly care which was which, anyhow.

"Welcome, Miss Warner," the Plattenburg behind the counter said. He appeared a bit shorter than the Plattenburg stocking shelves, but otherwise the two looked pretty much the same—about six feet tall, sandy hair, neatly dressed, and very clean looking. Neither was wearing a hat.

"Hello, Harvey Plattenburg," Mary said.

"Good day, Miss Warner," the Plattenburg stocking shelves said.

"Hello, John Plattenburg," Mary said.

Nobody seemed to care much about Leslie, even though he was standing directly between Mary and the shelf-stocking Plattenburg. He thought about introducing himself to the Plattenburg boys, but seeing as how all he really wanted to do was get out of that store as quickly as possible, he figured silence was the most prudent way to go.

Leslie walked around the store looking at things, acting as if he might be shopping, while Mary and the Plattenburgs continued their silly conversation.

"You look positively lovely today, Miss Warner. Not that you don't always look lovely," one Plattenburg said.

"After all, you are the loveliest girl in Lafayette County," the other Plattenburg said.

"Well, I don't know about that," Mary said.

They all giggled.

"Do you have any plans for the summer?" one Plattenburg said.

"We will be vacationing back east," the other Plattenburg said.

"No, we're planning to stay in beautiful Lafayette County this summer," Mary said.

They all giggled again.

"Is that a new dress?" one Plattenburg asked.

"Yes, it's quite becoming on you," the other Plattenburg added.

"Oh, this old thing?" Mary said. "I've had it forever."

Even more giggling.

"The blue of your bonnet perfectly matches the blue of your eyes," one Plattenburg said.

"And the yellow of your dress matches . . ."

"Your teeth," Leslie blurted out.

He couldn't take the silliness any longer.

Both Plattenburgs finally and abruptly noticed Leslie was there. They didn't say a word, however.

"Mary, ain't it about time to go?" he said to his sister. "This ain't no way to spend such a pretty day."

She looked at Leslie with anger in her eyes.

After a few seconds, Harvey Plattenburg stepped around the counter and went right up to Leslie. He stood no more than three feet in front of him, but he directed his conversation to Mary.

"Who is this human broomstick, and why does he have such animosity toward the English language?" he asked.

Leslie wasn't sure exactly what he meant by that second part, but he reckoned it was an insult.

"Leslie is my younger brother," Mary said. "He was kind enough to drive me to town today."

"Well, perhaps he should be kind enough to keep his mouth closed around his superiors," Harvey Plattenburg said.

"Or perhaps he should go down the street and play in the sandbox," John Plattenburg said.

Leslie got hot with anger all over, and he took a step toward the closest Plattenburg.

"The fact that you both still play in the sandbox don't mean I do," he said.

Now both Plattenburgs were definitely noticing him, though he figured there was no way they would assault him, not when they were trying to woo Mary.

"Just 'cause you fought with Jo Shelby don't make you nothin' special," Leslie continued. "As I recall, you Rebs come home with your tails twixt your legs."

Leslie reckoned he had pushed the Plattenburgs about as far as he could, but they both seemed more confused than angry.

"That's quite enough, Leslie," Mary said sternly. "Why don't you wait for me in the buggy?"

Leslie spun around and trudged out of the store. He was hoping Mary would follow him, but she didn't.

He jumped into the buggy, where he sat and contemplated what he might do to further antagonize the Plattenburg boys. Nothing much came to mind, other than shooting them, and he didn't have a gun.

After a few minutes, Mary still was in the store, so Leslie slid to the ground and began walking down the street. It wasn't long before there was no more street to walk down, so he turned around.

As he did, he saw Mary coming out of the store, bidding a giggly good-bye to the two Plattenburgs. They helped her into the buggy, a task she'd done by herself hundreds of times before.

Leslie walked slowly to the buggy and jumped in, grabbing the reins and giving them a lively shake. The gelding burst into a trot, and Mary bounced so high she grabbed his right arm to steady herself.

"Guess we'll see you boys around," Leslie hollered over his shoulder.

At the edge of town, he slowed the gelding. He didn't say anything, though, and neither did Mary. They didn't talk for a good five minutes.

Finally, Mary grabbed his right arm again.

"Leslie, listen to me," she said. "I think you are the best little brother a girl could have. But you are my little brother, not my beau."

"I know that," he said.

"Do you still want to drive down to the river?" she asked.

"I reckon not," he said.

And they drove on home in silence.

May 10, 1867

Happy birthday, Leslie Warner.

It wasn't a big deal to turn thirteen years old, Leslie thought, but he for sure felt older than he had on his last birthday. Since then, he'd seen a girl almost naked. He'd voted. He'd seen a man killed. And he'd nearly got killed himself.

If the next year tops that, Leslie thought, he might not be around when he celebrated his fourteenth birthday.

Fact is, he'd been pondering his future of late. That's something he never did much before.

He wondered where he'd be when he was fully grown and what he'd be doing with himself. As the only boy in the family, he might someday take over the farm from his pa, but that didn't appeal to him much.

Nor did the life of a banker or shopkeeper or any other occupation that calls for a person to be civil to folks who don't much deserve it.

He'd decided he probably didn't want to be an outlaw, either. He was pretty sure he wasn't cut out for that bushwhacker kind of life.

At this point, he had no idea what he wanted to become.

"Whadya think I ought to do when I grow up, Sallie?" he asked.

She, Leslie, and their father were in the stable. Sallie groomed a horse while Leslie and her father did other chores. She had been staying with her family for a few days, as had been her wont in recent weeks since learning she was going to have a baby.

"I think you would be a fine lawyer," she said. "You've got a good mind, and you're always asking questions."

"I ain't never thought of that," Leslie said. "Don't that require extra schoolin'? You know I ain't big on schoolin'."

"You could manage," Sallie said. "It would be worth it. When you're a lawyer, you can go anywhere you'd like to practice your profession. You wouldn't have to be stuck on a farm for the rest of your life."

"And what's wrong with farms?" Colonel Warner interjected. He had been listening to his children's conversation from a few feet away. "I've lived on farms nearly my entire life. No matter what your mother thinks of my farming skills, I can't imagine living anywhere but on a farm."

"That's you, Pa," Sallie said. "That's not me. I've decided I don't like farm life."

"You probably shouldn't have married a farmer, then," Colonel Warner said.

"Sometimes I wish I hadn't," Sallie said, then covered her mouth with her hands. "Oh, I shouldn't have said that. But the truth is, Sam Nutter is a pig."

"Sallie, that's not fair," Colonel Warner said with a smile. "Pigs are fine animals."

"I'm serious," Sallie said. "He drinks all the time and has those dirty men in the house. He rarely wants anything to do with me, except when he forces himself on me."

That got Colonel Warner's attention. Sallie might have been married to Sam, but she was still her pa's little girl.

"What do you mean?" he asked.

"One time, he came into the bedroom long after I'd gone to sleep, smelling of alcohol, and forced himself on me. He didn't say a word. I woke up with him on top of me and had to push him off so I could get out of bed. I fetched a frying pan and clanked him on the head to make certain he knew that was not acceptable behavior."

"Has he been acting this way even while you're with child?" Colonel Warner asked angrily.

"Well, he still drinks to excess," Sallie said. "He does whatever he wants when he's drunk, and that's most of the time. But I'm fairly certain he won't be interrupting my slumber with his amorous advances again."

"I think it's time I have a discussion with Sam Nutter," Colonel Warner said.

"No, Pa," Sallie said. "It isn't anything I can't handle. I know how to deal with Sam."

The Nutters

So what was Sam Nutter doing in the years before marrying Sallie Warner?

We can't be sure, but we know that he almost certainly hadn't been a soldier.

U.S. Civil War draft registration records in 1863 listed Nutter as Class I, meaning he was subject to military duty.

But Nutter's name doesn't appear on any roll of soldiers on either side of the conflict. It does appear, however, on a considerably less-heroic roll.

In March 1863, the Missouri Legislature passed "An Act to provide for the Payment and Support of the Enrolled Militia Forces of the State of Missouri," which created a "commutation tax in lieu of personal service."

In essence, men could pay their way out of the militia.

The tax amounted to $30 plus one percent of a man's property valuation.

According to the assessment rolls for Lafayette County available at the Missouri State Archives, Nutter paid $30 in 1863 and $30.50 in 1864 to maintain his exemption from militia duty. That indicated he had no property in 1863 and property worth $50 in 1864.

It is possible that Sam Nutter fought guerrilla style alongside the likes of Quantrill and Anderson during the Civil War. But if that were the case, why would he have bothered to pay the commutation tax? He would have spent most of his time hiding in the trees and brush, trying to avoid the very people he was paying $30 a year not to serve.

So, chances are Sam Nutter was not a combatant of any type during the war.

***

Sam had been the only son of Walter and Elizabeth Nutter.

The Nutters were among Lafayette County's wealthiest residents, as reflected by the 1860 census: Walter Nutter estimated his real estate was worth $30,000, which wouldn't have counted the value of the twenty-six slaves he said he owned.

So Sam, at age twenty-two or twenty-three, would have been loaded after he inherited his father's Lafayette County house and farm when Walter Nutter died January 13, 1865. (Elizabeth Nutter had died in 1858.)

Sam had five sisters, including the wonderfully named Cinderella, but only Elizabeth was still living at home when her father died. She received some land in his will but no house, and she continued living in the family home with Sam.

Just the two of them, it appears.

Elizabeth A. Nutter, known as Lizzie, was five years older than her brother Sam.

Or maybe she was two years older. Or maybe she was actually younger than her younger brother.

It's hard to tell.

In the 1850 census, Sam was listed as being ten and Lizzie fifteen—making their birth years about 1840 and 1835, respectively. But over the ensuing fifty years, Lizzie aged only thirty-seven years—if we are to believe the census reports. She was listed as twenty in 1860, thirty-eight in 1880 and fifty-two in 1900.

The 1910 census listed her as having been born in 1843, making her sixty-seven. So the years were finally beginning to catch up with her.

The final statement on Lizzie's age is on her headstone in Lexington's Machpelah Cemetery, where she is buried near her parents (with no Sam to be found). It says she was born October 19, 1837 (eleven years earlier than she listed in the 1900 census), and died January 31, 1916.

Assuming that headstone birth date to be the most nearly accurate of those mentioned here, she was three to five years older than Sam.

None of this would matter all that much, except that Lizzie Nutter became an important character in the drama that would involve her brother, Sam, her brother's wife, Sallie, and Sallie's father, William A. Warner.

In effect, when Sallie Warner, at the age of eighteen, married Sam Nutter on October 2, 1866, she also married Lizzie Nutter. It proved to be a rocky relationship all the way around.

May 28, 1867

"Leslie, I can't begin to tell you how happy I am you are staying with us," Sallie said, as she stroked the head of her favorite cat. "Me, too," Leslie said. "Truth be told, I'm more than happy. I'm as excited as a hog in a fresh pen of slop."

Leslie had arrived that morning with a burlap bag full of clothes to spend the summer at Sallie and Sam's big house.

He wanted to stay at Sallie and Sam's mostly because he figured he could get away with almost anything there, without his mother knowing about it. Sam not only let him do whatever he wanted, he encouraged behaviors that would get Leslie walloped at home. Drinking, for one. And cussing. He had acquired a considerable new vocabulary from Sam.

Of course, he hadn't told his mother that.

What he had told her was this:

"I surely miss Sallie, and I'd like to see her more often. And what with her gonna have a baby, she likely could use help with some chores over there. That's an awful big house. So I was thinkin' maybe I could spend time over there this summer. She said she would love my company."

"Why, Leslie, that certainly is a loving and generous attitude on your part," Georgia Warner said. "Your interest in visiting Sallie wouldn't have anything to do with the mischief you could get into over there, would it?"

"No, ma'am," Leslie lied. "Course not. You know you can trust me."

He didn't know for certain that his mother trusted him, but she did agree to let him go.

Mary said their mother and pa were worried about Sallie's well-being and figured Leslie could keep an eye on her and keep them informed about what went on in Sam's house. Leslie had no problem with that.

Shortly after Leslie arrived, Sallie walked with him to what was to be his new room. She sat on the bed with her cat while Leslie emptied his burlap bag and placed his things in the bottom two drawers of a dresser.

"You aren't here to spy on me for Mother and Pa are you, Leslie?" Sallie said.

"Not really," Leslie said. "Though they do worry about ya."

"Well, I'm a grown woman now. I can manage on my own, despite the trying situation I'm in. Sam and Lizzie are always siding up against me, always agreeing with one another and disagreeing with me, treating me like an outsider. In that regard, I am happy to have you here to give me some family support."

"Whadya mean by family support?" Leslie asked. "Ain't you and Sam part of the same family?"

Sallie sighed. "I suppose, but sometimes it doesn't seem that way. Sam and Lizzie mostly want to keep doing things the way they've always done them, with no consideration for me or my feelings. I feel like I don't belong in my own home. But then, this doesn't even seem like my home at times.

"Sam spends more time with his ruffian friends than he does with me, always drinking and carousing. I've told him I don't like having them around here, and that I certainly won't allow them in the house after the baby is born."

"You ain't been married all that long," Leslie said. "Things could change."

"My fear is that they'll change for the worse, not for the better," Sallie said. "The baby will be here in a few months, and I don't know how Sam will handle that. He's drunk most of the time, and I fear what he'll be like around the baby. Truth be told, I wish there wasn't going to be a baby."

Leslie's eyes widened.

"But you like babies, don't ya?" he said.

"I love babies," Sallie said. "I just don't think I want to have one."

"But ain't havin' babies part of being married?"

"It doesn't have to be. A husband and wife can be married without having children. They just have to be careful."

"Whadya mean by that?" Leslie said.

Sallie frowned at him. "Leslie, do you know how babies are made?"

"Sort of. Two people lay together, and then the baby comes."

"Well, there's a little more to it than that. Maybe I'm not the best person to explain it to you, but the fact is two people don't always have a baby when they lay together. And people don't have to lay together when they're married. You also realize that not all people who lay together are married, don't you?"

"Yes, I guess. What exactly happens when a man lays with a woman?" Leslie asked. "And why do men always want to do it so bad?"

"I think that's a question for you to ask Pa," Sallie said.

"Ah, Pa ain't gonna tell me nothin'. Sallie, how did you learn what to do?"

"Mother told me just before the wedding. She said it's absolutely awful, and I must say this is one of the rare times I agree with her. It *is* awful. At least with Sam it is."

"I guess I won't be asking Sam how to do it then," Leslie said.

"I think that's a good idea."

"But I gotta learn from somebody."

"Don't worry," Sallie said. "You'll figure it out. Men always seem to figure it out."

Leslie wanted to know more, but he had something else he wanted to ask Sallie.

"How are you and Lizzie gettin' along?" he asked.

Sallie scowled.

"We're not. I avoid her as much as possible. If she wasn't Sam's sister I would have nothing to do with her. She is not a lady by any means."

"I enjoy being around Lizzie," Leslie said. "I reckoned the four of us—me, you, Sam, and Lizzie—might have some fun times together this summer."

"Not likely," Sallie said. "I'm certain Mother wouldn't approve of you having fun the way Sam and Lizzie have fun."

"You ain't planning on tellin' Mother nothin' about what I do here, are you, Sallie?" Leslie asked cagily. "I figured you was on my side."

"Your secrets are safe with me, Leslie. As long as you don't kill somebody or do something else egregious."

June 2, 1867

Sam barged into Leslie's room with Jo Shelby right at his side.
"Leslie Warner, I need your advice on somethin'," Sam exclaimed.

Leslie thought, Drat, he's fixin' to ask something about Sallie.

He dreaded that conversation, figuring nothing good could come of it. He wasn't about to tell Sam the true facts of anything Sallie had told him, and he didn't want to lie because he figured he was about the worst liar in the world.

"Sam, I'm kinda busy," Leslie lied. He hadn't been busy since he'd got to Sallie and Sam's.

"Won't take but a minute of your time," Sam said. "I wanna ask you about your pa."

"I reckon I got time for that."

"What can I do to make him like me?"

Truth was, Sam couldn't do much of anything to make Colonel Warner like him, short of turning himself into a corpse and leaving his entire estate to Sallie.

Time to try another lie.

"Pa likes you more than most," Leslie said. "He just don't show it sometimes."

"No, he don't like me at all. I can tell. I ain't all that stupid. Your pa ain't never said a kind word to me. Fact is, he like to never say no words to me at all. Is it 'cause I paid my way outta the war? But if that's so, why did he give his blessing for me to marry Sallie? I'm thinkin' it's somethin' else."

"You oughtta talk to Sallie about this," Leslie said.

"She says I'm worryin' about nothin'. Says it don't matter what your pa thinks. But it does to me. So whadya think I should do?"

"Well, Sam," Leslie started, "you might try drinkin' less. Pa don't approve much of drinkin'. You don't have to quit altogether, just cut down on your consumption some, 'specially around my family."

"Leslie, you know good and well I ain't gonna do that. What else ya got?"

"Mother," Leslie said. "She might be your answer. She don't hate you too bad. If you get her on your side, I reckon Pa might go along with her."

"But I don't care much for your mother. I don't want nothin' to do with her."

"Sam, you ain't makin' this easy. You say you want to fix the situation, but you ain't willin' to do nothin' that might fix it. If you truly want to get Pa to like you, you're gonna have to do somethin'."

"I know that," Sam said. "That's why I'm talkin' to you in the first place. But you don't have no good suggestions, far as I can see. How 'bout I give your pa some money? I heard he could use some money."

"I reckon that's true enough," Leslie said. "But I ain't sure, Sam. It seems to me Pa would like more money, but I ain't sure he wants it from you. He don't like you much."

"You just said he likes me fine."

"I was lyin'. He don't like you at all."

"OK, now that we got that cleared up, what am I s'posed to do?"

Leslie thought for a few seconds.

"You know, Sam," he said, "Sallie is the reason you're in this family. Maybe she's the only person who needs to like ya. Maybe it don't matter that Pa don't like ya."

"That may be true enough. But I ain't sure Sallie likes me all that much, neither. I gotta say, I'm beginnin' to wonder if this marriage weren't a bad idea all along."

"I reckon it's too late now," Leslie said.

"I reckon so," Sam replied.

June 11, 1867

The more time Leslie spent at Sallie and Sam's, the more time he spent with Lizzie Nutter. And the more time he spent with Lizzie, the more he liked spending time with her.

She didn't talk like anybody else he knew. He couldn't make sense of some of her talkings, but he enjoyed hearing them.

Lizzie visited Leslie in his room on regular occasions. She hopped right on the bed with him, and they talked. There hadn't been a single question Leslie asked that she hadn't given a straight answer.

She once said, "I like my men like I like my drinks—tall, strong, and stupid."

Lizzie then said, "Of the three, you qualify only on the first count. But given time, you could become my ideal man."

Then she laughed that loud, bleating laugh of hers.

This day, Leslie asked her about babies, what with Sallie expecting to have one. He avoided the topic of how they were made, however.

"Why do folks think babies are so special?" he asked Lizzie. "We've had one baby or another in the house ever since I can remember, and they all seem pretty much the same. Seems to me, everybody was a baby once, so they ain't nothin' special."

"Leslie, you are wise beyond your years," Lizzie said, putting her hand on his left arm. "I agree completely. I find nothin' special about babies, neither; nor their parents, for that matter. Folks are always sayin' babies are wonderful, but they don't think most grown-ups are none too wonderful, so when does all that wonderfulness go away?"

"I ain't never thought of it quite like that," Leslie said.

Lizzie was right up against him now.

"What's even worse is the way women act like they're the only person who matters just because they have a baby," she said. "They think they're the queen of Siam just because they have an infant at their teat. It don't take no special talent to have a baby. Anybody can do it."

"You ain't had a baby, have ya, Lizzie?" Leslie said.

"Not by a long shot. And I ain't plannin' on havin' one, neither. I think havin' a child is the selfishest thing a person can do. People want to create another human being so they can have little versions of themselves. Or they want a boy or girl to work the farm, or whatever. They ain't doin' the world no favor by addin' another human. There's plenty enough already."

Leslie had never heard a person express such thoughts. He wasn't certain what to think.

But Lizzie wasn't finished.

She sat up on the bed and looked right in his eyes.

"Leslie, I know Sallie is your sister and all, but she ain't no different than all the others. Everybody thinks Sallie is perfect. She ain't hardly. They haven't seen her of a mornin'. And she sure don't know how to keep Sam satisfied."

"Lizzie, you shouldn't say such things about Sallie," Leslie said. "I know the two of you don't get along, but she's my sister. And she's your brother's wife. We're all part of the same family."

"It don't seem so to me," Lizzie said. "Leslie, you know I'm fond of you, but I truly wish Sam never married Sallie."

June 18, 1867

L eslie and John, a Negro who worked for Sam, were about halfway between Lexington and the Warners' home near Dover.

They were headed there from Sallie and Sam's place. Georgia and William A. Warner wanted their son to come home for the big to-do planned to celebrate General Jo Shelby's return to Missouri.

Of course, Leslie wasn't going to miss that, no way.

He had never met General Shelby, but he'd heard a good many stories about him. About how he whupped the Kansans on the border before he became a hero for the Rebels; about how he led his Rebel cavalry soldiers all across Missouri during the war; about how he refused to surrender, even after General Lee did, and took his army to Mexico.

The war had been over for two years, and he was just now coming back from Mexico.

Colonel Warner knew Jo Shelby's family in Kentucky and knew the general himself before they both became soldiers. In fact, he named the Warners' youngest child after him, even though she was a girl—Joe (short for Josephine) Shelby Warner.

Folks said General Shelby had been the wealthiest man in western Missouri before the war. He'd had a plantation just like the ones in

Kentucky, not far from where the Warners lived now. But he lost everything during the war.

He was going to start over back in Missouri, and Colonel Warner was throwing a welcoming party for him tomorrow. Sam and Sallie weren't planning to come until the next day, but Leslie was needed to help set up for the big celebration.

He was more than happy to make the trip with John in Sam's buckboard.

John, who also would help prepare for the party, had grown up as a slave on the Nutters' estate, working in the fields while Sam lived in the big house.

The two must have been about the same age, but John had the look of a much older man. He had soft, tired eyes and walked slow and with a limp. His clothes were ragged but always clean.

Leslie liked John. He was straightforward, and smart, too.

The two had left at first light and had passed through Lexington, which was near halfway on the trip from Sam's to the Warners' house, a journey that generally took most of a morning. Little was going on in Lexington, as early as it was, so they had no reason to dally there, and they were making good time.

John held the reins loose while the workhorse ambled along the road, pulling the buckboard behind him.

"John, you knowd Sam when he was a boy. What was he like?" Leslie said.

"Trouble. Nothin' but trouble," John said. "Mr. Sam and me had right fun together, but I done got more than one whuppin' 'cause of him. He'd be sent to his room, and I got a whuppin'. Mr. Sam was a sneaky child, always seekin' out mischief and usually findin' it. I spent a good amount of time with him, till I got old enough to work the fields."

"What was it like bein' a slave? We had a slave family when I was a young'un in Kentucky. Two boys and a girl, all of 'em older than me, and I didn't never play with 'em. Mother and Pa said that weren't proper."

"Things be different in Missouri," John said. "What be proper in Kentucky don't matter much here. Never did. Them Nutters generly treated me and the others as fair as could be 'spected."

"Why did you stay? Couldn't you have run off?" Leslie asked.

"Where could I go? Wasn't no darkies in Missouri 'ceptin slave darkies. More than one slave run away, got hisself caught, and wound up sent away from his family to who knows where. Weren't worth it. I stayed. Coulda been worse. Lot worse."

"Why are you stayin' now?"

"Mr. Sam still needs me," John said. "He'd be lost iffin I left. He don't always make the best decisions, ya know. Besides, he puts a roof over my head, whiskey in my gullet, and a few dollars in my pocket."

John was looking at the road as he held the reins and talked. He not once looked directly at Leslie, which resulted in him seeing the trouble before Leslie did.

Ahead, straddling the road, were three of the orneriest-looking, dirtiest rapscallions Leslie ever saw. They were on horseback, and all three wore beards and Union blue shirts.

But Leslie knew right quick they weren't soldiers.

As John and Leslie approached, they positioned their horses in front and beside the buckboard, so John had no choice but to stop. Leslie was scared.

John didn't say a thing and didn't move.

The smallest of the dirty rapscallions was closest to John—close enough he could reach out and touch him, and he did just that. He slapped the hat off John's head, then smacked him soundly on the back of his skull.

Then he pulled out his pistol.

"Get out of the buckboard, nigger," he said.

John did as he said.

"Now run."

John limped a few steps, barely faster than a walk, down the road back toward Lexington.

"Run, I said."

The small, dirty man shot at the ground near John's feet. Then the other two dirty men started shooting.

John's pace picked up, though he dragged his left leg as he hobbled away as best he could.

They kept shooting, and John kept hobbling.

Leslie knew he had to do something, so he finally yelled, "Stop. Stop now or you'll be sorry!"

Of course, he didn't know how he might go about making the three dirty, well-armed men sorry. But it didn't matter. They ignored him.

Leslie thought about jumping down from the buckboard and running to John's side, but the shooting guns discouraged him from that option.

Finally, the first shooter ran out of bullets and stopped to reload. John was about fifty yards back down the road by then.

As Leslie watched John's retreat, he saw a carriage trundling toward them with two men in it. It was his pa, accompanied by a man Leslie didn't recognize.

The shooting stopped abruptly.

The carriage pulled to a halt just after passing John, so it shielded him from the dirty men. The passenger said something to Colonel Warner, and they drove slowly forward, toward where Leslie sat in the buckboard and the three dirty men sat immobile on their horses.

Suddenly, before anybody could say or do anything, the men turned and galloped back in the direction they'd come from.

The man with Colonel Warner laughed so loud it echoed through the woods.

"Perhaps they recognized me," he said as his mirth subsided. "Likely so," Colonel Warner said. Then he looked at his son. "Leslie, are you all right?"

"Yes, Pa. Thanks to you."

Colonel Warner turned. "John, are you injured?" he asked.

"No, sir," John said. "I'm obliged to you and mighty happy you happened along."

"As am I," Colonel Warner said.

Then he turned to the man in the carriage with him. "This is what you've been missing for the past two years, Jo."

Jo! It was General Jo Shelby in the flesh. He wasn't wearing a uniform, but he looked just as Leslie imagined he would—tall, straight, with a dark beard and darker eyes. And confident. He looked like he was the man in charge, and he knew it.

"General Shelby, this is my son, Leslie," Colonel Warner said.

"Pleased to meet you, son."

"Pleased to meet you, sir. I reckon you're happy to be home."

"We'll see about that," General Shelby responded.

With that, John clambered into the buckboard, and they all headed to the Warners' farm.

June 19, 1867

So many people wanted to celebrate General Jo Shelby's return that buggies, carriages, and buckboards lined the road to the Warners' farm as far as the eye could see, in both directions. Must have been hundreds of them.

General Shelby had spent the previous night in Leslie's room while Leslie slept downstairs on the floor. Naturally, Leslie had a good many questions he wanted to ask, but it became clear that he wasn't going to find himself alone with the Confederate general. Too many adults around.

The best Leslie could do was watch. And listen.

Leslie was bursting with pride that the great man was in his house. It was almost like having a hero from one of his Beadle's Dime Novels walk into their living room. The only fly in the ointment was that he was a Rebel. But Leslie could overlook that for now.

The house and yard area looked much as it had for Sam and Sallie's wedding, except even more people were in attendance.

General Shelby was the center of attention, of course. One man after another heartily shook his hand as the general moved among the visitors.

He didn't say much, until two men approached General Shelby and embraced him, one after the other. They clearly knew the general better than most anybody else at the party.

General Shelby put his right arm around one man's shoulders and his left arm around the other man, and guided them to an area beside the house, where they found some privacy. The three talked there for a good long while, looking serious one moment and laughing together the next.

Leslie couldn't hear what they were saying, but he employed his powers of deduction to decide the two men had served under the general but hadn't gone to Mexico with him. The warm greeting told him they knew one another well but hadn't talked in quite a spell. They looked to be catching up on old times.

In any regard, Leslie concluded that the two men with General Shelby were likely the most interesting visitors at this to-do, and he reckoned he would keep his eye on them as the day proceeded.

They noticed Leslie, too.

In fact, not ten minutes later, the two men made their way to where Leslie was standing. He was talking with his sister Mary at the time.

"Howdy, young feller," one of the men said.

Up close, Leslie could see he had cold, piercing blue eyes that made the boy think the stranger could see right through him. He was smiling. The other man wasn't.

"You look like you might belong here," the first man said. "This is a mighty fine house. I understand it is the property of Colonel Warner, formerly of the Union army. You wouldn't be the son we've heard so much about, would ya?"

"I would," Leslie said. "I'm Leslie Warner. This here is my sister Mary."

"Mary Warner, you are a vision like no other," the man with the piercing eyes said. "I'm pleased to make your acquaintance."

The stranger didn't give his name, and Leslie noticed his companion seemed uncomfortable with the conversation. He nudged his talkative cohort with his shoulder and nodded his head, as if to signify they should walk away.

The talkative man looked younger than the other, probably no older than twenty, but both were fairly tall and very strong looking. Both wore nice clothes and expensive-looking hats. Both had fancy pistols on their hips.

"Leslie Warner, what can you tell me about yourself?" the talkative one asked.

"I ain't all that interestin'," Leslie said. "We moved here from Kentucky a while back, and I ain't sure I like Missouri."

"Give it time," the man said. "Missouri is the grandest state in the Union. Your family couldn't have chosen a better spot. My brother here and I are from Clay County, but we're fond of Lafayette County, as well. We visit here regular."

That's when it struck Leslie like a bolt of lightning. He had seen these two men before, in Lexington. They'd ridden with Archie Clement that day the little bushwhacker got shot and killed in the street.

Before Leslie considered the wisdom of it, he excitedly blurted out, "You rode with Arch Clement the day he got killed. I was there and saw it happen. You must be bushwhackers."

The silent man finally spoke.

"I believe you are mistaken," he said. "We're simple businessmen from Clay County who served with General Shelby and came to pay our respects."

"I might be mistaken," Leslie said. "But I'm fairly certain I ain't."

"So, you actually saw Archie Clement get murdered?" the younger, more talkative man said as the other man turned away.

"True enough. I was in the City Hotel saloon with Frank Allison and Dave Poole when the whole ruckus started. Almost got killed, myself."

"What are you saying, Leslie Warner?"

It was Mary.

Leslie had plumb forgot she was there. He hadn't told her (nor anybody else) about the events of that day, as he had promised Frank Allison. Now he had more to worry about than the possibility of two likely bushwhackers resenting the fact that he knew they were likely bushwhackers.

"It's true, I swear it is, Mary. But you can't tell nobody," Leslie said.

Mary looked at him, then looked at the two men.

"Please forgive him, gentlemen," she said. "My younger brother has a vivid imagination. This no doubt was a dream of Leslie's, or perhaps a scene from one of his favorite dime novels."

"That ain't so, Mary. It really happened, and I saw it."

"Even if you did, you would be wise not to boast about it to strangers."

"Ah, Mary. I ain't boastin'. I'm just talkin' to these fellas. You won't say nothin' to Mother and Pa, will ya?"

"Leslie, you know you've always been able to trust me."

Mary then turned and walked silently away.

"Well, Leslie, I truly am delighted you weren't killed that fateful day," the talkative man said. "Can you tell me who fired the shot that killed young Archie Clement?"

"There was so many men shootin' and so many bullets hittin' him that nobody could say who killed him and who didn't," Leslie said. "All I know is it was somebody wearin' blue."

"No doubt," the man said. "It must have been an appalling sight."

The quieter man nudged him again.

"It was more excitin' than appallin'," Leslie said.

To his surprise, the talkative man flashed a smile. "It's been a pleasure talking with you, Leslie Warner. My brother and I best be moving along now. I hope to see you and Mary again sometime. Good luck to you."

He turned and followed the other man, who was already walking briskly across the yard.

Leslie feared that would be the last he saw of the bushwhacking brothers, but it wasn't.

No sooner did they stride off than Leslie saw Sam and Sallie with Mary across the way, and Sam was vocalizing loudly. Leslie moved closer.

Sam was directing his loudness at Sallie.

"I won't have my wife talkin' about me to her sister behind my back," he bellowed. "You shan't do it. I'll do whatever it takes to keep you from doing it."

He stepped closer to Sallie and shoved his face up next to his wife's.

Mary tried to step between them.

"Sallie didn't say anything about you," she said. "We weren't even talking about you."

Sam turned from Sallie and toward Mary.

"You mind your own matters," he said, raising his right hand.

His hand, which was opened as if ready to swat a fly, was just rising above his shoulder when it stopped abruptly. It stopped because it disappeared into another, larger hand, which grabbed it deftly from behind.

It was the talkative man with the piercing blue eyes, and he wasn't smiling now.

"You weren't thinking of striking the lovely Mary Warner, were you, sir?" he said. "That would be a grievous mistake."

Still behind Sam, he kept a grip on Sam's hand and twisted the arm behind Sam's back. Sam's face turned red as a ripe tomato as he struggled to free himself, to no avail.

"This is not your affair," he said, at about half the volume with which he'd been addressing Sallie and Mary.

"Perhaps not," the man said. "But at this point that hardly matters. I'll not allow you to physically attack this lovely young woman. I'll release you only if you swear that you will not do so."

"I won't. I wasn't gonna hit Mary. I ain't never struck a woman."

"That is true, sir," Sallie said forcefully. "Sam Nutter is a drunk and quite often disagreeable, but he has never struck me. I appreciate your concern in this matter, but further violence is not merited."

With that, the man shoved Sam and let loose of his hand and arm. Sam spun around to face him.

His face quickly lost its red color; in fact, it lost all its color.

"Oh, I didn't know it was you," he said.

"So, you know who I am. I presume, then, that I won't have to further avail myself in the defense of these women."

"Suffice it to say," Sam said.

***

Leslie didn't see the two strangers the rest of the day. He figured they left soon after the commotion with Sam.

He saw Sam alone with a glass in his hand about an hour later.

"I ain't in a talkative mood, Leslie," he said.

"That ain't no problem, Sam," Leslie said. "I just have a single question. Who was that man you had the dustup with?"

"Don't know his first name for certain," Sam said. "Just know his last name is James and he rode with Arch Clement."

Leslie knew that last fact, of course.

"The man he was with is his brother," Leslie said. "And the two of them seemed right close with General Shelby. I'm fairly certain they're both bushwhackers."

"That being the case, their names don't matter much," Sam said. "All that matters is they ain't the kind of men a person should trifle with."

Sam raised the glass to his mouth and poured all its contents down his throat.

If he wasn't drunk yet, he was well on his way.

July 1, 1867

"Kansas City," Sam shouted. "We're goin' to Kansas City."

They were all at the dinner table, Sallie and Sam and Lizzie and Leslie, and Sam was excited. Probably as excited as Leslie had seen him since before the wedding.

"Let's go to Kansas City for the Independence holiday. The circus is gonna be there, and we can do some shoppin' and some dancin' and maybe even a bit of drinkin'. I ain't been to Kansas City since I don't know when."

"Sounds like fun," Lizzie said.

"I think I might enjoy a trip," Sallie said. "I haven't been outside of Lafayette County since learning I was with child. And I know Leslie is always champing at the bit for a new experience."

"That's true enough," Leslie said.

"Sallie, do you think you should travel in your condition?" Lizzie said. "It's dangerous. Them bushwhackers been harassin' folks again, 'specially between here and Kansas City."

She turned toward her brother.

"Maybe just the three of us should go, Sam. You, me, and Leslie."

"And leave Sallie home alone?" Sam said. "No. That ain't a good idea. If we take a couple of the boys, I think it would be safe for all of us. How 'bout that?"

"I s'pose if you want to put your expectin' wife in harm's way, that's your decision," Lizzie said. "Long as we go to Kansas City, that's all I really care about."

"Do I have a say in this?" Sallie asked. "Does it matter what I think about my safety and the safety of my baby?"

"Course it does, Sallie," Sam said. "If ya don't wanna go, I won't make ya."

"But I do want to go," Sallie said.

"Then it's settled," Sam said. "We're goin' to Kansas City."

July 4, 1867

Leslie had never seen an Indian before. For that matter, he had never seen a cow running wild in a city street, either.

It was a day of firsts in Kansas City for the young visitor from Lafayette County.

He had made the trip west with Sallie, Sam, and Lizzie—plus two of Sam's hired hands, and Jo Shelby, too—one day earlier, a Wednesday, and they planned to remain through Saturday. Leslie and Sam and the women had checked into the new Sheridan Hotel at Fifth and Wyandotte, and Sam's hired hands had gone off on their own.

The cow thing was how the day started.

Leslie was barely awake when he looked out his second-floor hotel room window to see whether anything interesting was happening in the street below. He never would have figured on this.

A cow charged down the street, past the front of the Sheridan, with several men in hot pursuit. The bovine stopped, pawed at the ground, then spun and charged back up the street in the opposite direction.

The beast didn't appear to be in a good mood.

She ran full out, and appeared to be targeting one of the men who had been chasing her. Then she veered off and headed toward a bystander taking in the spectacle. The bystander darted to the side just in time, and the cow changed directions again, heading once more away from the men pursuing her.

Leslie was enjoying the impromptu rodeo, wondering whether this kind of thing happened every day in Kansas City or whether it might be something special for the Fourth of July.

But then a gunshot rang out. The cow immediately dropped.

That was the end of the show.

Well, Leslie thought, at least this is a good story to tell the others when they wake up.

Just as was the case at Sallie and Sam's house pretty much every morning since he arrived earlier in the summer, he was awake before everybody else—even though it was past 8:30.

He figured that Sallie and Lizzie wouldn't be ready to hit the town for at least an hour and that Sam would be sleeping off his previous night's overindulgence. Leslie decided he didn't want to waste any more time cooped up in his room waiting for them.

He headed down to the streets of Kansas City on his own.

Leslie hadn't been to a real city since the Warners lived in Kentucky and visited Louisville on occasion. Louisville was far bigger than Kansas City, but Kansas City was growing like crazy.

Those trips to Louisville weren't all that memorable for Leslie; he'd just been a boy who tagged along with his parents wherever they went.

Now he was thirteen and alone in Kansas City, the gateway to the West.

As several men pulled the dead cow's carcass down dusty Wyandotte Street, Leslie walked briskly in the opposite direction. He didn't know where he was going, but he wanted to get there as soon as he could.

He had read that Kansas City was a wide-open town, with gambling parlors, drinking establishments, and brothel houses galore. He wasn't planning on patronizing any of those places; he just wanted to soak up the atmosphere.

Leslie walked down Fifth Street for several blocks. Off to his left, between buildings and at street crossings, he could see the beginnings of a bridge that was being built over the Missouri River. He stopped and looked in wonder at the enormous project.

After traversing a few more hilly blocks, Leslie saw an area bustling with activity.

This was different from anything he'd seen in Louisville. Many of the men appeared to be cowboys, just as they were pictured in his dime novels, with big, wide-brimmed hats, colorful shirts, and dirty pants and boots.

Men were coming and going in all directions, stopping here and there to trade goods from the backs of buckboards or entering and leaving places of business.

That's when Leslie saw his first Indian. Several of them, actually. They were right there with the cowboys, trading beads and other items.

Leslie had read and heard plenty about Indians, and everything he read and heard suggested he should be frightened of them. But he saw no reason to be scared of these Indians in the streets of Kansas City. Nobody else seemed scared.

He wanted to talk to them, to ask them questions, but as best as he could tell, they weren't doing any talking. Just a lot of nodding and head shaking as they traded with the cowboys and townsfolk.

With nothing to trade and no way to ask his questions, Leslie just stared. He stood about twenty feet away and watched the Indians for a good five minutes. He was mesmerized.

These were real, live Indians who no doubt lived on the plains, shot arrows with bows, and rode ponies with no saddles. They wore buffalo-skin clothing and moccasins. Their dark faces were framed by long, black hair.

One of the Indians returned Leslie's stare, looking him straight in the eyes. Leslie didn't turn away. The supposed savage didn't scare him a bit. In fact, Leslie thought he recognized sorrow in the man's eyes.

The Indian returned to his bead-and-trinket trading, and Leslie finally moved along.

He saw plenty more interesting things, including a man lying in an alley who Leslie figured was drunk but might have been dead, for all he could tell; women who had painted faces and uncovered legs prancing about in broad daylight; Dapper Dans dressed all in black, coming and going from storefronts; and folks who were carrying placards promoting Lake's Circus.

On one street corner, he encountered a group of odd young men, all dressed in similar gray costumes, their heads topped by little caps.

"Howdy, boys," Leslie greeted them. "I ain't never been to Kansas City before. Can you tell where I might find somethin' interestin' to see or do?"

"You can come with us," one of the men said. He sported the grandest mustache Leslie had ever seen. It spread well beyond the width of the man's face and appeared to have its own wings.

"We're the Antelopes, and we're gonna play a baseball game this afternoon. You might enjoy that."

Leslie had heard a bit about baseball. He knew there had even been a few games played in Lexington, though he'd never seen one.

"Antelopes? Why are you the Antelopes?" he asked.

"That's just the name we've given our team," one of the baseballers said. "Antelopes are graceful creatures, and so are we."

"Oh," Leslie said, still not fully understanding. "Wish I could watch you boys play your game of baseball, but we got plans for this afternoon. Goin' to the circus."

"Guarantee you our game will be more excitin' than any damn circus," the man with the grand mustache said. "We will put on a marvelous display. I personally expect to win the silver badge for best batting and best scorer. Maybe for most fly catches, too."

Now Leslie wondered if these men were foreigners talking some strange language.

The grandly mustachioed man could see his confusion.

"Why don't you come with us down to the ball field?" he said. "We've gotta get the field ready and practice our skills before game time. You can see how baseball is played for yourself. If you want, you can even try it. No charge. And you'll still have plenty of time to go to your silly circus."

"Sounds like it might be fun," Leslie said.

So he walked with the oddly dressed men a few blocks to an open field, where Leslie saw another group of similarly oddly dressed men. Some were swinging sticks. Others were throwing and catching hard-looking balls with their bare hands.

"What's your name, young man?" the mustache man asked.

"Leslie Warner. I come from Lafayette County."

"Well, Leslie Warner from Lafayette County, pick up one of those bats over there."

The man pointed at the polished sticks Leslie had noticed. He grabbed one, and his new friend showed him how to grip it with both hands at one end and to rest the stick on his right shoulder.

"Now step over there beside home base, and I'll pitch the ball. Your goal is to swing the bat and hit the pitched ball."

"That don't sound too difficult," Leslie said.

"It just might be more difficult than you imagine," the mustache man said.

Standing about sixty feet directly in front of Leslie, he proceeded to hurl the ball. It was flying directly at Leslie's head—or so he thought—and instead of trying to hit the ball, he dove to the ground to prevent it from hitting *him*.

"Strike one!" he heard as he gathered himself. He also heard lots of laughing.

Leslie stood, and the mustache man walked to him, put his arm on Leslie's shoulder, and said in a kindly tone, "Leslie, you can't be afraid of the ball if you plan on hitting it. Let's try again. This time, force yourself to remain upright. I won't hit you with the ball, I promise."

The man returned to his spot sixty feet away and hurled the ball again. Leslie stayed on his feet and swung the stick violently from his shoulder in an effort to smite the ball, his body spinning as he did so. The stick failed to make contact with the ball, however, and the spinning caused him to lose his balance. He wound up on the ground again.

"Strike two!"

"Better," the mustache man said. "Let's try again. This time, instead of swinging so hard, you should concentrate on the ball and making the bat collide with it."

"I'm ready," Leslie said, after dusting himself off again.

He gripped the stick as tightly as he could and stared at the mustache man, waiting for him to throw the ball. When he did, Leslie took a deep breath and focused on the ball as it floated toward him. It seemed to be approaching slower this time.

Leslie waited until it was just in front of him, then swung the stick—firmly but not violently—at the ball. And the stick went flying, almost hitting the mustache man. The ball, meanwhile, remained unsmitten for the third time.

"Strike three! You're out."

"I guess I won't be playing for the Antelopes anytime soon," Leslie said.

"Don't feel bad, Leslie," the mustache man said. "The same thing happened to most of us the first time we tried. This game of baseball takes a lot of practice."

"As much as I like you fellows, I don't think baseball is for me," Leslie said. "Seems boring. I surely doubt that it will ever catch on."

"Perhaps, perhaps not," the mustache man said. "All I know is that we enjoy playing it."

"Well, good luck to y'all," Leslie said.

***

The circus scheduled three shows for July 4, and everybody—Leslie, Sam, Sallie, and Lizzie—agreed they would go to the third show of the day.

"The last show is always the best," Sam said.

"How do ya know that?" Leslie asked.

"I just do."

"Sam, if you really knew all the things that you think you know, you'd be a whole lot smarter than you actually are," Lizzie said, laughing.

Sam laughed, too.

"I reckon I know enough to get by," he said.

Given her condition, Sallie wasn't up for a long walk, so all four rode in Sam's carriage to the circus grounds. Jo Shelby faithfully followed after them the whole way.

Sweat rolled down Sam's face as he guided the carriage, and Leslie was plenty uncomfortable, himself. It had been sunny and hot all day, but now the heat intensified as clouds lined the horizon, and the early-evening air was thick with humidity.

Leslie wasn't sure what to expect at the circus, other than seeing clowns and a variety of animals.

Before Leslie and the others made their way into the big circus tent, they stopped at a smaller tent. Three small boys in ragged clothes lay side by side on the ground just behind the canvas, lifting the fabric to peak underneath at the strange sights, which included a midget, a fat woman, a man with no arms and a bearded lady.

Inside the smaller tent, visitors tittered and pointed at the humans on display, calling them freaks. Sam and Lizzie seemed to enjoy the show, too. But not Sallie.

"I'll wait for y'all outside," she said to the others.

"Wait, I wanna get out of here, too," Leslie said.

The brother and sister quickly walked to the exit.

"Thanks, Leslie," Sallie said. "I found that disgusting. Those people are human beings, not wild animals."

Leslie nodded. He was beginning to wonder whether he would enjoy the circus if this was what it was like.

But the performances inside the big tent were different. They dazzled Leslie.

The grandstand was filled to overflowing, with many folks standing on the ground in areas beside the wooden seats. Leslie sat with Sallie on his left and Sam on his right—Lizzie was on the other side of Sam, who had Jo Shelby at his feet. The proceedings began with a grand entry of horseback riders, acrobats, jugglers, camels, elephants, and clowns, while a brass band played.

"Have you ever seen such a big beast?" Leslie asked of no one in particular. "That elephant is the size of four sows."

He then heard a distant rumble of thunder. A few minutes later, while a pretty woman stood atop a horse galloping around the ring, a louder clap of thunder sounded.

The woman and horse gave way to jugglers and acrobats, who performed tricks that stupefied Leslie.

"It musta taken 'em years to learn how to do these things," he said to Sallie.

"Most of the performers have been with the circus since they were children," Sallie said. "They've been raised in the circus. It's a way of life for them, just like farming is for most folks."

"I guess I ain't never gonna be an acrobat, then," Leslie said.

After the jugglers and acrobats, several clowns entertained the crowd with their antics. Then it was time for the tightrope act.

Before it began, however, thunder exploded so loud it sounded as if the storm was directly over the tent. The wind started whipping at the heavy canvas, and rain began beating down on the big top, wildly drumming overhead.

It was blowing and raining so hard Leslie couldn't hear the brass band playing, if it still was. As the performers huddled in the ring, the people in the grandstand mostly stayed where they were.

"Should we get outta here?" Lizzie shouted.

"Better off in here," Sam shouted back. "At least we're dry."

Leslie looked upward, watching the canvas sag as low spots filled with rain water. He heard the wind whipping outside at a stronger and stronger clip.

Eventually, the tall wooden post holding up the center of the tent began to teeter. It was only a matter of seconds before Leslie could see that the entire structure was collapsing.

He turned to Sam and hollered, "We best get outta here."

Sam said nothing. He placed one hand against Lizzie's back and began ushering her toward the aisle, gripping a piece of twine he had tied around Jo Shelby's neck with his other hand. He barged through the crowd, shoving people out of his way.

Leslie took Sallie's right hand in his left hand and pulled her toward him. He tried to catch up with Sam, Lizzie, and Jo Shelby, but too many others in the crowd were in the way.

By then, the center post was nearly parallel to the ground, as were all the other posts, but the canvas remained high enough that people had room to maneuver. Nobody was trapped, and, as best as Leslie could see, nobody was hurt.

It took a few minutes for Leslie to lead Sallie down the grandstand, out the exit, and into the open, where the rain still beat down but the lightning and wind had abated. He saw Sam, Lizzie, and Jo Shelby standing beside the carriage.

"That was excitin'," Sam said. "Least it cooled things down."

Sallie was hot, though.

"What were you thinking, Sam Nutter?" she yelled. "You ran out and left behind your wife, soon to be the mother of your child. Thank goodness for Leslie."

"You're fine, ain't ya?" Sam said. "Besides, I had my hands full takin' care of Lizzie and Jo Shelby."

"I guess that says it all," Sallie said. "Lizzie and Jo Shelby come first."

"Well, they was with me before you was," Sam said.

July 22, 1867

Sallie wasn't smiling much these days, Leslie thought, and she wasn't much fun to be around.

Truth be told, Sallie never had been the most frolicky female in the world. Or even in the family. That would be Mary. But Sallie was a sourpuss of late. She was beginning to remind Leslie uncomfortably of his mother.

Her seriousness had made Leslie's summer with her and Sam considerably less enjoyable than he had envisioned. He was spending much of his time alone, which was exactly what he'd have done if he had stayed home in the first place.

Sam took him to town once in a while, and Leslie got to see him get drunk and make a general fool of himself. And Lizzie was nice to Leslie, regularly asking questions about his private thoughts and frequently touching his shoulders and rubbing his back and such.

But the four of them—Sallie, Sam, Lizzie, and Leslie—almost never did anything together after their trip to Kansas City. Sam was mostly busy drinking and carousing with his ruffian friends, sometimes taking Lizzie with him. Sallie wanted no part of that behavior, and Leslie was compelled to stay with his sister much of the time.

Even Jo Shelby was doing little more than moping around all day. So Leslie asked Sallie about it.

"Sallie, why ain't you no fun no more?" The brother and sister were on their way to Lexington, where Sallie said she wanted to shop for clothes. Sam didn't want to come. Lizzie stayed with him, of course.

"What do you mean, Leslie?"

"I mean you ain't no fun," he said, as he drove Sam's finest carriage east toward Lexington. "We never do nothin' fun together, which was the main reason I came to spend time here."

"I thought it was to help me because I'm expecting a child."

"Oh, that, too. But I figured there would be more fun involved."

"Well, I think you've come to the wrong place at the wrong time for that. I'll be having a child in a few months, and that is all that concerns me now."

Leslie let that sink in for a while.

"That don't explain everything," Leslie said. "It seems to me you and Sam don't even try to have no fun. Least ways not together. You always are doing one thing, he's always doing something else."

"Well, Leslie, a good many things happen in a marriage that only the two persons involved can know about."

"Like what?"

"Suffice it to say that I no longer believe Sam Nutter is the man I thought he was before we married."

Sam was fat before he married Sallie, and he was still fat. He was also drunk most of the time before he married Sallie, and he was still drunk most of the time.

"He seems like the same Sam to me," Leslie said as he gripped the reins loosely.

"As I said, you know very little of what happens behind closed doors in our house. If you knew, you would agree with me. Sam simply is not the husband I hoped he would be."

Leslie wasn't exactly sure what Sallie was getting at, but it made him curious.

"Sallie, you might feel better if you got things off your chest."

"You might be right. But you know Mother. I can't talk to her. Nobody can. I'm afraid Father has too many other things on his mind. I don't want to bother him with my troubles. Who else is there?"

"What about Lizzie?" Leslie said.

Sallie laughed.

"Lizzie is the last person I would ever talk to. She is almost as big a part of my problems as Sam is. My life would be much easier if Lizzie wasn't around. But I don't suppose she's going anywhere."

"Why does Lizzie still live here, anyway?" Leslie said. "Shouldn't she be married and off livin' with some other man by now?"

"I don't suppose many men want anything to do with Lizzie Nutter," Sallie said.

"I sorta like her."

"Leslie, one thing you should know is that Lizzie can't be trusted. The way she acts around you, all sweet and caring, is not her normal behavior. She wants something from you, though I'm not certain what. It might be that she simply wants you to like her. Or . . . it might be something more sinister."

"Like what?"

"She might want to rob you of your virtue."

That didn't sound so sinister to Leslie, though losing his virtue to Lizzie Nutter wasn't exactly how he envisioned losing his virtue.

"Well, if you don't want to talk to Mother or Pa or Lizzie, you know I'm a good listener," he said.

"Yes, you are, Leslie. But I'm not certain a twelve-year-old boy is the appropriate confessor for a young woman with marital difficulties."

"First of all, I'm thirteen now. And second of all, you ain't got nobody else. You said so yourself."

Sallie sighed and looked straight ahead into the distance, then turned back toward Leslie.

"Well, you can't say anything to anybody if I tell you. Do you promise, Leslie?"

"No need for me to promise. I ain't got nobody to tell if I wanted to."

Sallie gathered her thoughts and proceeded to unburden her soul to her younger brother sitting beside her.

"If I were to be honest, I would admit I never should have married Sam," she said. "I always knew what kind of man he was, that he drank to excess and cared more about having a good time than anything else. I was hoping marriage would change him. It did, but not for the better.

"To Sam, I'm nothing more than another possession, it seems. He wants to control everything I do, yet at the same time he rarely shows that he even cares about me. It's almost as if once we were married he no longer felt he needed to please me or even show any interest in me. Except for when he wanted to fornicate. He most certainly was interested in me for that."

Sallie had never said the word "fornicate" before, as far as Leslie knew.

"But here of late, Sam has rarely even had interest in me for fornication. As you have seen, he ignores me most of the time. He's gone most evenings, to who knows where, and when he is at home he rarely pays me any mind. He has more interest in Lizzie, Jo Shelby, and his drunken friends.

"I guess I should be pleased he no longer forces himself on me. But ours just isn't the marriage I always dreamed of."

"Sam don't hit you, does he?" Leslie asked. "I ain't never seen him even slap you."

"That much is fact," Sallie said. "I was telling the truth when the man grabbed Sam at the party for General Shelby. He has never struck me. However, there is more that goes into a good marriage than an absence of violence. I've never seen him strike Jo Shelby, either, but I've seen him show that dog more affection than he ever shows me. Lizzie, too. I honestly believe he would be married to Lizzie if he could be. I've told him that, and he didn't deny it. It would not surprise me if those two have an unnatural relationship. Who knows what they might be doing this very minute while they are alone together in that house?"

The carriage was approaching Lexington at this point, and Leslie was approaching the point of disbelief. He never thought Sallie would say the things she was saying, much less say them to him.

His mind was all scrambled with thoughts, but he couldn't put them into words.

Neither talked for a few minutes. Finally, Sallie grabbed Leslie's right arm tight with both hands as he held the reins.

"Leslie, I don't know why I told you those things," she said. "I guess I feel I can trust you."

"There ain't nobody you can trust more than me," he said. "I ain't gonna say nothin' to nobody, but I'm wonderin' if I can do anything to help. I hate to see you so sorry-faced all the time. You think maybe you should come back home, at least for a while?"

"No. I am not going to run away from my problems. I still have hope that Sam and I can work through things."

When they reached Lexington, Sallie didn't talk anymore about her problems. She spent much of the day trying on dresses, hats, and shoes. She took most of them home and put them all on Sam's account.

August 15, 1867

It was a day to remember for Leslie Warner.

He went into Lexington alone with Sam—not even Jo Shelby made the trip with them. They had left the farm late in the afternoon, when it was about as hot as it had been all summer. Leslie was hoping they were going somewhere with plenty of shade.

"I got somethin' special planned," Sam said.

Every trip to Lexington with Sam seemed to involve liquor. He was either buying it—by the gallon, to take home—or drinking it. Or both. So, Leslie naturally figured liquor would be involved on this visit to Lexington.

He was wrong.

Sam had only one thing planned, and it had nothing to do with liquor.

"We're gonna visit my favorite gal," he said.

He and Leslie were side by side in Sam's buckboard, more than a mile into their trip, when he made this revelation. Leslie was stunned.

Sam had never mentioned his "favorite gal" before, though he did talk about having spent time with Lexington saloon girls before he married Sallie.

"Are you sayin' what I think you're sayin'?" Leslie asked.

"I just might be," Sam said. "My gal will put a smile on your face, that's for darn certain. I think you'll like her. You ain't never been with a woman before, have ya?"

"No," Leslie said. "I am only thirteen, ya know."

"I forget sometimes," Sam said. "You seem older for some reason. Anyhow, you're old enough. It don't even matter if ya don't know what to do. She'll take care of you. She's an uprighteous person.

"Gals who make their livin' on their backs are about the only women a feller can trust. They know what you want, and they're willin' to give it to you, no questions asked and no complainin' about it before or afterward. And I guaran-damn-tee ya you won't be complainin' none."

Leslie had more than occasionally thought about being with a woman, and he was intrigued at the prospect. He wasn't expecting it to happen this soon, or this way, however.

"What's her name? Is she pretty? Does she know we're comin'? I mean, does she know you're bringin' me? How much does it cost? I ain't got much money, ya know."

"Slow down there, Romeo," Sam said. "You ain't gotta worry about payin'. I'll take care of that. All the rest don't matter."

By this time, excitement was overtaking Leslie, making it hard to think straight. One day later, he wouldn't even remember the rest of the ride into Lexington.

But there they were, in a dark room above one of the saloons, standing inside the door, facing a woman in her undergarments. It was still hot as blazes, but Leslie didn't care.

The woman was sitting on the edge of the bed, with her legs dangling over the side and her feet barely touching the floor.

She wasn't pretty, but she wasn't ugly, either. She wasn't young, nor was she old. She reminded Leslie of Lizzie Nutter, mainly because of her brown eyes, though she appeared a bit younger than Lizzie and was somewhat more attractive. Her straight yellow hair reached just to her shoulders, and she had short legs and was thick around the middle. She was looking directly at Leslie.

"What do we have here, Sam?" she said. "Did you bring me a present?"

"Lizzie, this is Leslie," Sam said.

"You're Lizzie, too?" Leslie said excitedly. "That's Sam's sister's name."

"Ain't that a coincidence?" she said.

Leslie got the feeling she already knew about Sam's sister and her name.

"Sam, you should have told me you were gonna bring a boy. I would have arranged for one of the other girls. Maybe one closer to his age."

"No, Lizzie, ain't no other girl would do. You are perfect in every way. Don't you think so, Leslie?"

"I don't know about perfect," Leslie said. "But I reckon she's close enough."

"She's all yours," Sam said. Then he left the room, chuckling.

Lizzie rose from the bed and walked to Leslie, who stood frozen in place, unable to move or speak. She took his hand and led him to the bed, where she began unbuttoning his shirt. Then his pants. Then his underdrawers.

Leslie lay on his back while Lizzie, still wearing her undergarments, maneuvered herself on top of him. She rolled onto her side, pulling Leslie with her, then onto her back, making sure Leslie remained positioned just right.

Leslie was so excited he thought he would explode.

"Just relax, Leslie," Lizzie said. "Let me do all the work."

Less than a minute later, it was over.

Leslie put his clothes back on, said "Thank you, ma'am," left the room, and hurried downstairs. Sam was sitting in a chair at the bottom of the stairs.

"Gracious, Leslie, you know we wasn't payin' by the hour, don't ya? We don't get no discount for finishin' in less than five minutes."

"I reckon I took all the time I needed," Leslie said. "Weren't nothin' left to do. Lizzie said I done real good for my first time."

"Was it everything you expected it to be?"

"Well, not really. But I guess I was expectin' somethin' altogether different than what it actually turned out to be. It's more complicated than I figured."

"That's a good thing to learn early," Sam said. "Ain't nothin' between a man and a woman that ain't more complicated than it oughtta be. I just hope you enjoyed yourself."

"That's for sure," Leslie said. "Can't wait to do it again."

"Sorry, Leslie, this was a one-time offer. Consider it a going-away present. You'll be headin' back home soon, and I wanted you to have somethin' to remember your summer by."

"I reckon I owe you a debt of gratitude then, Sam."

They walked out to the buckboard and climbed in.

"We best be gettin' back home," Sam said. "Dinner will be waitin'."

Leslie felt somewhat light-headed as Sam guided the buckboard west along the bumpy trail toward his farm. The sun was dropping near the tree-filled horizon in front of them, though the air remained stifling.

"Look there to the north," Sam said, pointing.

Leslie turned his gaze to the right and saw a slew of large birds soaring gracefully in the blue sky, high above the trees and stone outcroppings encroaching on the Missouri River. He counted five birds, then saw another join the group. Not one was flapping its wings. They were all floating on air as they darted up and down, this way and that.

"That's a beautiful sight," Leslie said. "I'd be tempted to say they was eagles, but I know better. Vultures are my most favorite birds. I wish I could fly up there with 'em."

"I ain't sure you'd like their diet," Sam joked. "Vultures are disgusting."

"Just 'cause they're ugly and they eat dead critters don't make 'em disgusting," Leslie said. "They serve a purpose in the world. Vultures clean up the mess other animals and us humans leave behind."

"I'll take an eagle any day. They're honorable birds."

"You know, eagles eat dead critters sometimes, too," Leslie responded. "Course, they get most of their food by stealin' it from other birds. There ain't nothin' honorable about that. I seen young eagles fly with vultures before, but they don't last long. The vultures don't want nothin' to do with 'em."

"Leslie, you'd really rather fly with vultures than with eagles?"

"That's for certain. I think I'd be a right good vulture."

Sam shook his head.

It was hard to think about eating dinner right then, but Leslie's appetite returned by the time they reached Sallie and Sam's place. Sitting across from Lizzie Nutter and next to Sallie, he ate like a vulture.

August 18, 1867

"Well, the prodigal son has returned," Georgia Warner said as Leslie, with his burlap bag filled with clothes slung over his shoulder, stepped through the door of the Warners' fine house.

Leslie knew his Bible verses pretty well, so he recognized his mother's reference to the prodigal son. But he didn't think he qualified. After all, his intention always was to return home at the end of the summer, and his parents knew right where he was the whole time he was gone.

Well, not the whole time. Leslie hoped they would *never* know what he was doing a good part of the time he was staying with Sallie and Sam.

"How is Sallie doing?" his mother asked. "We haven't seen her in weeks."

Leslie, after talking with Sallie, had decided he wouldn't tell their parents how strained her marriage had become. He and Sallie figured nothing good could come of telling them, and with the baby due in a couple of months, Sallie's situation would soon change, anyway.

"I reckon she's fine," Leslie said. "Don't ya wanna know how I'm doing? I am your only son, ya know."

"Yes, I know," his mother said. "That's one reason I don't worry about you as much as I worry about my daughters. You're old enough to take care of yourself, for the most part. But if you insist. . . . How are you doing, Leslie? How was your summer with your sister?"

"OK, I guess," Leslie said. "Not real excitin'. I didn't get in no trouble or nothin', if that's what you wanna know."

"At least you have no visible wounds," Colonel William A. Warner said. Leslie's father had just walked in from outside. "Welcome home, son."

"Thanks, Pa," Leslie said. "It's good to be home."

Leslie wasn't lying. As much as he wanted to get away from home in May, he was just as happy to be back in August. Though he had some good times at Sallie and Sam's, he was worn down from dealing with the drama and tension there.

"Your room awaits you," his father said.

"So do your chores," his mother added. "I'm sure your sisters will gladly return them to you."

Ugggh. That made Leslie remember one of the reasons he'd been so eager to get away from home for the summer. He had grown fond of having no chores to do.

Before Leslie could turn to head upstairs to his room, his little sister Ella scurried up to him and hugged him around his waist. Just behind her was a smiling Mary.

"We *are* glad you're home, and not just because of your chores," Mary said. "I missed my little brother, and Ella and little Jo missed their big brother."

Truth be told, Leslie missed them, as well. He felt like an only child at Sallie and Sam's, likely because he was the only child there, though he hated to think of himself as a child.

"I reckon I missed you girls, too," he said. "But right now I'm hungry. Ain't it about dinnertime?"

His mother smiled and said, "Never fear. We were waiting for you." The family then adjourned to the dining room for the best meal Leslie had had in months.

***

Leslie heard a knock on his bedroom door. Then, "Leslie, it's me, Mary. I want to talk to you."

"Come on in," he said.

He was sitting on his bed, and Mary stopped just inside the doorway.

Leslie hadn't felt the same about Mary since their trip to Dover, when she tricked him into taking her to see the Plattenburg boys. She seemed older to him now, but he still considered Mary his favorite sister, and he liked it when she visited him in his room.

"I know why you're here," he said. "You wanna know about Sallie and Sam. Well, I ain't gonna talk about Sallie and Sam. Sallie don't want Mother and Pa to know about her and Sam."

"Well, if everything was good, she wouldn't care if Mother and Pa knew about it," Mary said. "So that means everything isn't good. If everything isn't good, there must be something bad. Did Sallie tell you not to speak to *me* about it?"

"No," Leslie said, reluctantly. "But if you knew that Sallie weren't happy, you might tell Mother and Pa that she weren't happy. So I ain't gonna tell ya nothin'."

"That's fine," Mary said. "I wouldn't want you to betray Sallie's trust, though I doubt she was very frank with her little brother about her real thoughts and feelings."

"Oh, she was frank as frank can be," Leslie said. "She told me things I couldn't believe my ears was hearing. But I ain't gonna tell ya none of it."

"I can't force you to talk," Mary said. "But I always thought we shared everything. You know you can trust me."

She was now sitting on the bed beside Leslie.

"I trust ya," he said. "It's just that I promised Sallie I wouldn't say nothin' to nobody."

"Don't you think she would want me to know what is going on in her life?" Mary asked. "I am her closest sister, after all."

"If that's the case, she'll tell ya next time she sees ya," Leslie said. "You ain't gettin' me to tell ya anything."

"Fine, have it your way."

"You ain't mad at me, are you, Mary?"

"No, Leslie," she said. "In fact, I'm kind of proud of you. You are an even better brother than I thought you were."

"There's somethin' else I want to tell you, Mary. But you can't tell nobody about this, neither."

"I promise. What is it?"

"Sam took me to town, and . . ." Leslie hesitated. "We went to a saloon, and he bought me . . ."

Mary interrupted as she rose from the bed. "Sam buys you whiskey. Don't worry. As disgusting as liquor is, I don't think any less of you."

Before Leslie could gather his wits to say anything else, Mary had turned and walked from the room.

August 19, 1867

This was it, Leslie thought.

His father said at breakfast that he wanted to see Leslie, alone, later that morning. He told Leslie to find him in the barn at 9 a.m.

Leslie didn't ask him why. He figured his pa had found out about something bad he'd done. He guessed it involved his summer with Sam and Sallie, but it might have been something earlier, like when he voted or when he was in the saloon with Frank Allison and all hell broke loose.

Whatever it was, Leslie was ready to admit to everything and say how sorry he was. No reason to lie. He was a lousy liar. Besides, his pa would be more likely to forgive him if he admitted to his bad deed than if he tried to lie when his pa already knew the truth.

Colonel Warner rarely disciplined Leslie, or any of his children for that matter. Georgia was the disciplinarian of the two.

When Leslie did things he knew he shouldn't, he was afraid his mother would find out, because he would incur her wrath. On the other hand, he didn't want his father to find out, because he might be disappointed in his only son.

Leslie went to the barn to face the music.

"Howdy, Pa," he said.

Colonel Warner stood next to a buckboard, trying to look as if he was working on it, although Leslie had never seen him fix anything in his life. Every time his father tried to do any kind of repair work, he made the problem worse. Or he wound up hurting himself. Or both.

"Hello, Leslie," he said. "I guess I haven't told you how happy I am that you've returned home. We all missed you."

"Thanks, Pa."

"Now, I guess you know why I want to talk to you."

No, Leslie thought, I don't. But he didn't say that.

"You know how I worry about Sallie," his father continued. "And I know you must have seen and heard some things this summer. Now, I'm not asking you to betray any confidences you might have with Sallie or even with Sam. But it's important you realize that my only concern is with Sallie's welfare. If there is any chance she is in danger there at Sam's, I want to know about it."

"She ain't in no danger that I can see," Leslie said. He was looking at the buckboard, not at his father. "She ain't much happy, but she ain't in no danger."

His father gently grabbed Leslie by his shoulders and turned Leslie's body toward him, so they were looking straight at each other.

"Why do you say she isn't happy? Did she tell you that?"

Leslie was beginning to feel like he was backed into the corner of a barn stall with a bull blocking his path. He had told Sallie he wouldn't talk of these things with their parents. But he never *promised* Sallie he wouldn't. He reckoned there was a difference between saying and promising.

"Well," he started, "she don't want me talkin' about it. She says she can handle the situation on her own. But if you was to ask me if I thought she could be happier, I'd have to say yes. But she ain't afraid of Sam causin' her no physical harm."

"He doesn't strike her?"

"I never seen it, and she said he don't."

"Is he still drinking too much?"

"Every day and night, more or less."

"Does he bother Sallie when he's drunk?"

"He mostly ignores her. He mostly ignores her all the time."

"Did you see any other reasons for Sallie to be unhappy?"

"She thinks their marriage ain't turned out the way she hoped. She don't much like Lizzie Nutter, either, and she sure don't like living in the same house with her."

"Does Lizzie mistreat Sallie?"

"No, that ain't the problem. It's more that Lizzie and Sam kinda team up to ignore Sallie. Sallie said Sam would marry Lizzie if he could. They spend a lot of time alone together."

Colonel Warner's expression darkened. "I'm beginning to get the picture," he said. "I appreciate you telling me these things, Leslie. I must say, it's not as bad as I feared in some ways but worse than I could have imagined in others."

"You won't tell Sallie what I said, will ya, Pa?" Leslie asked.

"I can't promise you that, Leslie. Your mother and I are going to have to talk to Sallie, and she'll know where I learned these things. But you did the right thing by talking to me, I guarantee you that."

"What about Sam?" Leslie asked. "He don't have to know I snitched on him, does he?"

"Don't worry about Sam," Colonel Warner said. "I'll take care of him."

PART

II

DIVORCE AND ANIMUS

Sallie Warner Nutter

Introduction

Divorce was rare in the United States in the post-Civil War period, although not as rare as in most other countries.

A Report on Marriage and Divorce in the United States, 1867 to 1886 by Carroll Davidson Wright, who was the nation's commissioner of labor, provides a detailed analysis of divorce in the late nineteenth century. It indicated there were 9,937 divorces in the United States in 1867, compared with 130 in England and Wales, 190 in Switzerland, and 2,181 in France.

The report stated that 362 divorces were granted in Missouri in 1867 and 387 in 1868, with two-thirds being granted to wives in both years.

Lafayette County, with a population of more than twenty thousand, saw three divorces in 1867 and four in 1868.

If only murders were so rare in Lafayette County.

The most common reason by far for divorces, both in Missouri and in the nation as a whole, was desertion. In Missouri, a spouse had to be absent from the household for a year before that could be the reason cited in a divorce petition. Adultery and cruelty were the other most common claims in divorce proceedings.

Wright painted a colorful and graphic picture of married life during the period in a section of his report that listed causes for which divorces were granted. Among many others, he gave the following examples:

Plaintiff alleges that defendant does not wash himself, thereby inflicting on plaintiff great mental anguish.

Defendant does not speak to plaintiff for months at a time, thereby making life a burden.

Plaintiff says that the defendant, her husband, is also her uncle, being the brother of her father; that she was but fourteen years of age at the time of marriage; all of which so preys on her mind that she sues for divorce on ground of cruelty.

Plaintiff was married twenty-seven years; defendant then said to her, 'You are old and worn out; I do not want you any longer;' which remark caused plaintiff mental anguish.

Defendant made plaintiff climb a ladder to drive nails in the wood shed; not liking the way she drove the nails, he lassoed her on coming down from the ladder, tied her fast to the gate post, then stuck sticks and straws in her nose and ears, gouged his knuckles in her eyes, and said he 'wanted to see if she was Dutch.' On untying her he threw or shoved her into a nest of bees; all of which sorely grieved her body and mind.

Defendant sharpened an axe, saying he meant to chop off this plaintiff's head, and he did knock out two of her front teeth.

Defendant threatened to eat out plaintiff's heart and drink her blood; complained because plaintiff bought him $1 shirts. On one occasion at dinner-table he thrust a fork through her hand, pinning it to the table.

Defendant would compel plaintiff and their daughter to sit up all night, and would not allow a fire.

"Defendant cut off my bangs by force."

"My husband would never cut his toe-nails, and I was scratched very severely every night, especially as he was very restless." (From plaintiff's testimony.)

Defendant pinched plaintiff's nose until it became red, thereby causing her mortification and anguish.

The writing in these divorce proceedings makes you wonder whether the newspapermen of the day made extra cash moonlighting as writers of legal briefs.

***

Sallie Warner Nutter filed for divorce on April 9, 1868, and on April 13, Sam Nutter was served with a summons to appear in court. The divorce was to be heard during the May term of the Lafayette County Circuit Court.

The details of the case are laid out in records that are still available in the Lafayette County Courthouse.

All of the Nutters's divorce documents were handwritten in mostly legible longhand. On rare occasions, a word is impossible to decipher, so this account condenses the sentences in which those words appear.

Missing words or not, none of what Sallie Warner Nutter said leaves room for misinterpretation.

It should be noted that Sam responded to all her claims, point by point, and denied them all.

One more item worth noting is that Sallie's name wasn't the only one on the divorce petition. The document actually read: "Sallie W. Nutter by her next friend William A. Warner."

In her petition, Sallie wasted no time getting to the dirt. After saying "That she has conducted herself towards her said husband as a dutifully and affectionate wife," she listed the reasons for her action:

She further states that her said husband has in various ways violated his marital vows.

That he has been for the last year just preceding the commencement of this suit an habitual drunkard and habitually addicted to drunkenness for more than one year past.

That he has offered to the Plaintiff such indignities as to render her condition in living with him intolerable and assigns the following array of other indignities, outrages and wrongs.

First he has kept in the house with the Plaintiff his sister Lizzie A. Nutter well knowing that said sister was a woman of bad repute, addicted to habitual intoxication from the use of spirits, morphine and opium, and also a thief and addicted to habitual stealing whenever opportunity presented itself.

And said defendant well knowing that his said sister was a drunkard and thief as aforementioned has compelled the Plaintiff to associate with her and live in the same house with her and has insisted on the Plaintiff aiding her in stealing and concealing stolen articles. And has insisted that Plaintiff should also steal, saying persons who would not steal were fools. . . .

And . . . defendant has told her she should continue to live with his said sister and to treat her kindly and say nothing of her offences and that he intended always to keep her in the house. And refused to refrain from drinking and stealing himself.

And the sister of said defendant when drinking has threatened to take Plaintiff's life, which threats were well known to the defendant as well as her depraved morals and dreadful passions. And he has still persisted in compelling the Plaintiff to wait on her and let her live as a member of the family.

And told Plaintiff she could go if she wanted but that he could not and would not part with his said sister and that he would kill any persons that had her arrested or disclosed her crimes. And has also told Plaintiff of crimes which the defendant had been guilty of and said nobody suspected him of stealing, that he could steal as much as he pleased. And has persisted in stealing chickens and bringing them home and wanted Plaintiff to use them and has in various other ways insisted on the Plaintiff joining with and aiding him and his said sister in crimes abhorrent to the Plaintiff's sense of justice and right. . . .

Said defendant has also insisted upon and importuned the Plaintiff to join with him and his sister in these drunken orgies, all of which is so repulsive to Plaintiff's sense of right and propriety as to render her utterly miserable in living amidst such associations.

Plaintiff further states that she has reason to believe and does believe and charge that the defendant has been frequently guilty of the crime of incest and adultery with said sister. She further charges that her life is not safe in living in the house with her and that said defendant well knows the fact and persists in keeping her and shows an utter disregard for the safety and happiness of the Plaintiff and her child.

Of course, Sam said none of this—including the charge of incest—was true.

Much of his documented response consisted of his saying "Defendant denies . . ." followed by Sallie's accusations, word for word.

But he did feel compelled to explain further when it came to some of the accusations about him and Lizzie:

Defendant further answering states that his sister, Lizzie A. Nutter, is an orphan, having neither father nor mother living, and is and has ever been unmarried. That the lands inherited by her from her father adjoins the lands of defendant inherited by him from his father, and on which defendant resides in Lafayette County, Missouri. That said

Lizzie A. Nutter has no dwelling house on her lands, and that she at the time of the marriage of plaintiff and defendant, lived and resided at the house and home of defendant, being the old homestead of the family, as plaintiff well knew at the time of their marriage.

. . . And that defendant gave his said sister a home in his house, and allowed her to be and remain there as a fraternal duty, as he properly and lawfully should and might do.

And so it was that sometime after the marriage of plaintiff and defendant, the defendant having discerned that peaks, whims and petty differences have, as is not unusual among ladies, grown up between plaintiff and his said sister, though trivial in their nature, yet for the sake of harmony in his family and in deference to the prejudices and whims of plaintiff and to give time for the abatement of the same, under the advice of defendant, his said sister went from home and visited the city of Saint Louis and friends there, and remained most of her time away from the home of defendant, up to about the time when plaintiff deserted and left the house and home of defendant.

At this point, Sam Nutter's response talked of how Sallie packed her bags and left. He said that, on about April 1, Sallie "commenced secretly and clandestinely and without the knowledge of defendant removing her trunks and effects to the house of a neighbor."

Then, on April 5:

Plaintiff without any reasonable cause or excuse, in company with her parents and sister, deserted defendant and his house and home, taking with her not only her wearing apparel and effects which had been given to her by defendant but also taking with her a large amount of other property and effects of defendant, including table and silverware, tumblers, spoons, forks, knives, plates, etc., and also the sum of about five hundred dollars in money, the property of defendant, which had been deposited for safekeeping in the trunk of plaintiff. And that plaintiff has ever since without reasonable cause or excuse remained absent and away from defendant and his house and home and has and still keeps and retains the money and the property of defendant so taken away by her.

You'll notice that Sam mentioned that Sallie took tumblers, spoons, and forks, but he left out one fairly important item that Sallie also took—their baby girl, Georgie.

Sallie had given birth November 15, 1867, so Georgie was less than five months old when Sallie moved out.

Sam said later in his response that he was "lawfully entitled to the custody and control of his said child, and is able, ready, willing, and desirous to properly support, train and educate the same."

For all of Sallie's actions, Sam blamed not Sallie but her parents, saying that she acted "through the persuasions, undue influence, scheming, and machinations of her parents and especially of her said father and next friend in this suit, William A. Warner."

Sallie filed a short response to Sam's response, in which she emphasized that all of her charges were true. She also stated that "since the session of this court, defendant has approached her several times without this affiant's approbations, and made overtures for this affiant to return and live with him, conveying to her at the time that the charges in her petition for divorce were true, and he was sorry for them."

She concluded by saying "that she never can and never will, believing and knowing that defendant has committed the crimes alleged against him in her petition, ever live with him or be to him a wife again, that this is her firm determination, and that she has made it uninfluenced by others but upon the conviction that it is her duty to do so."

The Lafayette County Courthouse records include several other documents on the case, among them one from Sam that said Sallie "expressed to defendant her desire and willingness to return to and live with defendant as his wife" but that she hadn't done so because of pressure from her parents.

Sam also claimed that his property was worth no more than $18,000 to $20,000, which Sallie denied in her response.

The answer by Sallie to Sam's allegations also read:

. . . And plaintiff feeling and believing that her life was in danger and all her feelings of right and duty revolting at the thought of remaining with such a great criminal, and amidst such scenes of vice and immorality and raising her little daughter amidst associations that must tend to contaminate and debase her, prompted by a sense of duty to herself and child and for just cause the plaintiff did on the 5th day of April 1868 leave the house of the defendant and go to her father's and take with her her child and such articles as belonged to them. . . .

. . . That plaintiff was compelled to leave for the causes set forth in her petition. And states that said causes are all true and that not one half of crimes, wrongs and outrages on the part of the defendant are set forth in said petition. That many of them are of such a terrible character that she shrinks from their statement. So revolting are they to all the better factions of human nature, and of such obscene and immoral character, that it is difficult to believe that any person could be so depraved and which render it impossible for the plaintiff to live with him without bringing degradation, dishonor and shame upon herself.

Sallie filed a motion for alimony and maintenance, and, on May 23, 1868, the court ordered Sam to give her $250 in three installments.

***

It is impossible to know how much Sallie fabricated or exaggerated in her allegations. But there is evidence that Sam Nutter was doing at least some of what she claimed he did.

The Lafayette County Courthouse holds records that suggest Sam probably was the drunk Sallie claimed and that he likely was vindictive against his soon-to-be ex-wife.

In the court's probate records are page after page of bills Sam Nutter had accumulated but hadn't paid. Most confirmed his affinity for libations, showing he had purchased more than seventeen gallons of whiskey from February to October 1868.

Sam's sister Lizzie might have made some of these purchases, and she almost certainly helped him drink some of the whiskey. Remember, Lizzie had lived with Sam before and during his marriage to Sallie, and the two remained together in their father's house after Sallie moved out and filed for divorce in April 1868.

We can only imagine what went on in that house in the summer of 1868. But given the accusations Sallie made in her divorce petition plus the amount of whiskey that we know was on hand, the Nutter siblings probably weren't spending their time reading the Bible.

The only thing we know for sure is that Sam took an extreme step to try to keep his property from going to Sallie in the divorce.

Records in the Lafayette County Recorder of Deeds office show that on July 30, 1868, Sam Nutter sold more than 580 acres, which must have included the family house, for $13,000. The buyer was his sister Lizzie.

Of course, Lizzie didn't have $13,000.

And she certainly didn't have $17,000, which was the total amount on the bill of sale, which also included much of Sam's personal property.

It didn't take long for the Nutters's financial house of cards to fall apart.

Sallie Nutter filed a lawsuit, as did three other sets of plaintiffs, and, by virtue of a writ of attachment issued by the clerk of the circuit court, Lafayette County sheriff Thomas Adamson announced in a legal advertisement in the *Missouri Valley Register* that he would auction the Nutters's property on November 17, 1868.

The ad ran on October 22, 1868, which was to become a very important date in this saga.

April 14, 1868

Sam Nutter was drunk. Nothing unusual about that. Sam was mad, too, though, and that was not part of his usual demeanor.

Everyone who knew Sam considered him a jovial sort of fellow, quick with a smile and a laugh. He wasn't prone to anger, not even when he was three sheets to the wind, and that was a lot of days and almost every night.

Sam might have been a drunk, but he was a mostly happy drunk. Not now, though.

"Goddamnit, I ain't gonna take this standin' up," Sam said to his sister Lizzie. "If them Warners want a fight, they got themselves one. If they think ol' Sam Nutter is just gonna crawl in a hole and go away, they are as wrong as rain. I'm gonna fight 'em all the way, goddamn 'em."

"You know I'm always on your side, Sam," Lizzie said. "They can't say such things about us. Half them things ain't even entirely true. Who do they think they are?"

Darkness had started to envelope the Nutters's homestead as the brother and sister sat in the living room of the big house where they had grown up. Alone except for each other, they sipped bourbon from glasses, and a gallon jug of the stuff sat on a table between them.

Also on the table was a copy of the divorce petition that Sam's wife, Sallie, had filed a few days earlier. A few days before that, she had packed up most of her things, grabbed her daughter, Georgie, and left the big house in a carriage driven by her father, Colonel William A. Warner.

"Sallie can't divorce me," Sam said. "I didn't do nothin' to deserve such maltreatment. She's my wife, goddamnit, and she'll stay my wife until I say elsewise."

"What are you gonna do about it, Sam?" Lizzie said. "Are you gonna show you've got a backbone for a change? You're always talkin' about what you're gonna do, but then you never do it. These people have smeared the Nutter family name, and as the only Nutter male, it's your duty to gain retribution."

"Whadya want me to do? Shoot the whole damn bunch of 'em, Sallie included? I ain't got nothin' against Sallie. Fact is, I still want her to be my wife. I ain't gonna give her up easy. I ain't gonna let her divorce me just like that. I don't know nobody who's ever been divorced, and I ain't about to become the first."

"You ain't gonna make a fool of yourself and go crawlin' on your hands and knees to beg for forgiveness, are you, Sam?" Lizzie asked.

Sam scowled. "Well . . . what do you have in mind?"

"I ain't exactly sure what would be the best response, but give me time. I'll come up with somethin'."

May 2, 1868

"Tonight's the night, boys. We got us a Union colonel to visit."

Sam Nutter was the unlikely leader of a small band of ruffians, but a leader he was, nonetheless. At least that's what he had convinced himself.

Sam had let it be known several days earlier that he needed some men willing to do whatever he told them to do (for a price, of course), and four showed up. All of them were now armed with pistols, although two kept their guns hidden under long white coats. All four were unpleasant looking and grimy, and their clothes were even grimier.

Sam figured they were bushwhackers, maybe even some of Bill Quantrill's old gang who had been riding on the wrong side of the law since the war ended.

They certainly looked the part, and that was just what Sam wanted. He had gathered them at his house as part of his grand plan to scare Colonel William A. Warner into withdrawing his daughter's divorce proceedings.

Well, it wasn't exactly a grand plan. It was more like a rough idea.

Sam figured he and his ornery-looking companions would roust Colonel Warner and talk some sense into him. Sam was convinced that Colonel Warner was behind the divorce and that Sallie, if left to her own devices, would return to him.

The idea originated with Sam's sister Lizzie, although she wanted Sam and his ruffians to do more than frighten Colonel Warner.

"I think that man at least deserves to be shot," she said. "Maybe killed."

Lizzie had explained her thinking to Sam a few days earlier, and Sam was ready to go along with it. But when Sam told John, his Negro worker and former slave, what he was thinking of doing, John looked dour and shook his head.

"Mister Sam, that ain't much of a plan," John said. "If you truly want Miss Sallie to come back to you, you likely don't want to wound or kill her father. Ladies generly don't favor men who done shot their fathers."

"You might have a point there, John," Sam said.

So, he adjusted his thinking.

"We ain't gonna kill him," Sam told the men, as they shared a jug of whiskey on Sam's front porch. "But I ain't opposed to a warning shot or two, if that's what it takes to persuade him to think twice about following through with this divorce."

It hadn't occurred to Sam that his four ruffians might not do exactly as he told them; that they might, in fact, kill the former Union colonel of their own accord. After all, these men would have frothed at the idea of killing a Union colonel during the war.

Sam knew that Colonel Warner—along with his wife, Georgia, and Sallie—was in Lexington this very evening, staying at the City Hotel. He knew this because he had his very own spy in the Warners' house.

He and Leslie Warner had grown close after Sam married Sallie. He genuinely liked Leslie, and Leslie liked him. They were, in fact, friends, and Sam had few acquaintances he could call friends.

Sam had talked with Leslie twice since the boy's sister had moved back home and filed for divorce. He had run into Leslie in Lexington and had arranged for an on-the-sly meeting with him in the woods near the Warners' farm a few days later.

"I want to stay married to Sallie," Sam told Leslie.

"I want that, too, I guess," Leslie said. "What can I do to help?"

"Just keep me up to date on things." And with that, Sam had his spy.

Of course, he didn't tell Leslie what he was planning to do.

Sam figured he had his chance to confront Colonel Warner while he was staying at the City Hotel. He reckoned he and his companions would enter the hotel, find Colonel Warner, scare him a bit, and be on their way.

That's not how it worked out.

First, Sam and his boys didn't even leave for Lexington until well after dark. They did, after all, have to finish that jug of whiskey.

Upon arriving in town, Sam realized he needed to get Colonel Warner on his own, away from his daughter and wife. He didn't want to see Sallie, because he thought the sight of her might cause him to back down from his plan. He didn't want Georgia around, because he was just plain scared of her.

By this time, Sam had correctly surmised, Sallie and her parents had adjourned to their rooms in the City Hotel, which sat directly across from the courthouse.

Rather than barging into the hotel with his men, Sam wrote a note to Colonel Warner, saying he wanted to see him, and sent one of his boys into the hotel with it. He waited outside with the other three, sharing sips from a newly opened bottle of whiskey.

His messenger returned a few minutes later.

"I seen Warner in his room, Room Seven it is, and gave him the note," the man said. "He said, 'To hell with Sam Nutter. I've got nothing to say to him.' He said he weren't gonna leave his room."

Sam said nothing. He just stormed into the hotel lobby, with his four new friends following him, and stomped up to the front desk.

"I demand to see Colonel Warner," Sam said to the man behind the desk, hotel owner John Cather. Sam knew Cather, because he frequently stayed at his hotel, and Sam liked the man.

"John, he done me wrong, the things he said about me and Lizzie in them divorce papers. Why, he called me a thief and even suggested that me and my sister engaged in carnal encounters. I won't stand for it. We ain't gonna hurt him. I just want to make certain he knows I ain't happy."

"If that's all you have in mind, why did you bring these men with you?" Cather asked. "I can't let you go up to his room, Sam. I will protect Colonel Warner as long as he is in my house."

"John, you know we could overwhelm you, and the Warners, for that matter, too," Sam said. "Just go tell Colonel Warner to show his face to me like a man, and nobody will get hurt."

Cather didn't back down. He had known Sam for years and recognized him as a pleasant (if usually drunk) man who never tended to violence.

"Sorry, Sam," he said. "I can't do that. I will protect the man as long as he is in my house."

Sam's companions were getting restless.

"We could persuade this gent, if you'd like, Sam," one of them said.

"No, we won't do any harm to John Cather," Sam said, in a defeated tone. "Let's go."

With that, Sam walked from the hotel hobby through the entry into the hotel's saloon. He had a scowl on his face as he sat at a table, but he remained silent as he tried to figure out his next step.

If he and his little gang forced their way into the Warners' hotel room, he not only would have to face Sallie and her mother, but he likely would also have to endure their screams for help.

And he surely didn't want Sallie to be hurt in any way.

His four cohorts were talking among themselves at the bar, and Sam could tell they were growing impatient with him.

"Sam, are we goin' after this man or not?" one ruffian asked. "We ain't got all night. We know what room this colonel is in. This can all be over in a few minutes."

Sam responded loudly, wanting all the men in the saloon to hear him: "Colonel William A. Warner is a sonofabitch and a liar who done me a grave injustice. I ain't gonna let him get away with what he's done. He is a scoundrel of the worst order. He shall pay. I shall see to it. But now, it's time for drinking. Bartender, a bottle for me and my friends."

For Sam, drinking liquor was almost always the best way to resolve a problem. After an hour, he couldn't remember why he'd come to town in the first place. After another hour, he bid his four new friends farewell and stumbled out of the saloon to his horse.

He actually fell asleep for part of the ride home.

***

By the time Sam reached the farm, he had sobered up slightly. He was surprised to see the big house's first floor glowing with light. He was even more surprised to see two figures on the porch as he approached.

They were Lizzie and John, his Negro worker.

"What are you two doing awake at this ungodly hour?" Sam slurred.

He dismounted slowly, maintaining his balance by keeping a hold of the saddle horn. He wondered why neither Lizzie nor John said anything. Then he saw that they weren't alone on the porch.

At their feet was a mass of fur that Sam recognized as Jo Shelby, his faithful hound dog.

Blood covered his torso and much of the porch. Jo Shelby wasn't moving.

Sam sprang up the two steps to the porch, fell to his knees, and lifted the dog against his chest.

"No, no, no," Sam wailed. "Jo Shelby's dead, ain't he? What happened?"

"Sam, somebody done shot Jo Shelby," John said. "He was layin' outside the barn this evening, waitin' for you to return, like always. But then he wandered off. I heard a shot maybe two hours ago. Didn't think nothin' of it, but then Jo Shelby come back from the woods, strugglin' to walk and all bloodied. I carried him to the porch, but he succumbed. Stopped breathin' altogether."

"Sam, I know how you loved that dog," Lizzie said. "I'm surely sorry."

"Do . . . you . . . know . . ." Sam had a lump in his throat and tears forming in the corners of his eyes and could barely get the words out, "who . . . done . . . it?"

"I didn't see nobody," John said. "Miss Lizzie, she was alone in the house, asleep I presume."

"I saw nothin' and nobody, Sam," Lizzie said.

Sam noticed that John's shirt and pants, the only clothes he ever wore, were smeared with Jo Shelby's blood.

"Thank you, John, I appreciate what you done," Sam said, struggling to regain his composure.

"You want me to bury Jo Shelby out by the trees, Mr. Sam?" John asked.

"No. I'll take care of it. I want to be alone with him. I'd appreciate your fetchin' a shovel, though."

Sam was still on his knees, with the dead dog cradled in his arms. He felt as if he didn't have the strength to stand, so he stayed in that position while Lizzie returned to the house and John walked toward the barn.

Sam held Jo Shelby for ten minutes before standing as he maintained a tight grip on the dog's body. He managed to get to his feet and carry Jo Shelby to the edge of the woods. He gently laid his friend on the dirt near where John had left the shovel.

As Sam dug, he thought of how faithful a friend Jo Shelby had been. How he had always been there for him. No matter how low Sam felt on a given day, Jo Shelby was always there to cheer him up.

Tears were streaming down Sam's face.

But then he started thinking about who might have shot Jo Shelby. And why.

His sadness gradually turned into anger.

Colonel Warner, goddamn him, he done this, Sam thought.

Sam realized it likely wasn't Colonel Warner himself, knowing as he did that the Warners were in Lexington on this evening, but he figured it would have been no problem for him to have arranged for somebody else to do the deed.

That Allison feller who lives near the Warners likely done it, he thought.

After Sam carefully lowered Jo Shelby into the hole and covered him with dirt, he tamped down the soil atop the new grave and said a prayer out loud.

"Jo Shelby, you was the best dog a man could ever have asked for. You gave me more happiness than any other creature in my life. I tried to give you as good a life as I could, and I hope you was happy. I know you have gone to a better place. And I promise I will avenge your killing. Amen."

May 3, 1868

If nothing else, Sam figured his foray into Lexington had succeeded in one regard. It convinced him he needed to get some pistols. Why hire guns when he could carry his own?

He would need them for his planned vengeance against Colonel William A. Warner, who he now was convinced was out to ruin him in any way he could.

"I ain't done with that sonofabitch," Sam said to Lizzie.

They were alone at the dining table, as usual, eating some eggs and grits. It was early morning, at least for Sam. About 9:30. Lizzie hadn't asked a question or even said a word, but she knew whom her brother was talking about.

"I guess I'm just gonna have to go kill one of his critters. A colt or a gelding; it don't matter to me. Maybe one of each."

Now Lizzie was confused.

"Why kill one the Warners' animals? Why not shoot the man himself?"

"He killed Jo Shelby, so I'm gonna kill one of his critters."

"Whadya mean he killed Jo Shelby? How'd you arrive at that conclusion?"

"I done realized it last night when I was burying Jo Shelby. It seems obvious to me that sonofabitch done it. He's out to get me, I just know it."

"But, Sam, you know he was in Lexington last night, same as you. No way could he have shot Jo Shelby."

"Maybe not, but he could have had somebody do it for him."

"Don't make sense to me, Sam," Lizzie said. "I betcha John would agree with me. He might even have some insight into who really done the deed. He mighta heard or seen somethin' last night."

"Have you seen John today?" Sam asked.

"He's out in the barn, like he always is of a mornin'."

Sam pushed his chair away from the table, stood, and walked through the kitchen and living room, out the front door, and across the yard to the barn. Slipping inside, he found John mucking out a horse stall.

"John, I gotta question for ya," he said. "You know anything about who killed Jo Shelby?"

"Not directly," the black man said, unwavering in his task. "But I got a notion or two about who done it."

"It was that sonofabitch Warner, weren't it?" Sam said. "He's the only man who got it out for me."

"That may be so, Mister Sam, but I doubt he done it. Ya know Jo Shelby been visitin' the neighbors' chicken coops, don't ya? Likely as not, that's what got Jo Shelby shot. Colonel Warner didn't have no call to kill a dog."

"I don't know," Sam said. "I still reckon that sonofabitch is to blame. Even if he didn't pull the trigger or hire the man who pulled the trigger, he's to blame. If he hadn't angered me so much that I was compelled to leave the farm to roust him in Lexington, Jo Shelby wouldn't have wandered off like he did."

"Blame the man all you want, Mister Sam," John said. "But that ain't gonna get you Miss Sallie back."

"I know Sallie better than you do, John. And I reckon she'd gladly return here if it wasn't for her father's undue influence over her. He has poisoned her against me."

"So what ya got planned now?" John asked. "Your excursion last night don't seem to have done no good."

"First thing, I'm gettin' me some pistols. Then I'll be ready for anything."

"Now, Mister Sam, pistols ain't gonna get ya nothin' but more trouble."

"That sounds good to me. I ain't afraid of no trouble."

May 17, 1868

For most people in Lafayette County, it was very early on a Sunday morning. For Sam Nutter, it was very late on a Saturday night.

So late the sun was about to come up.

But Sam hadn't been to bed yet. He hadn't even made it home.

Sam had acquired his pistols, two navy Colt revolvers that he now kept strapped on his person whenever he was away from the farm. He made a special trip to Kansas City to buy them. They were his prize possessions.

He wore them on his hips as he rode toward home, his mount walking so slowly that on each step Sam wondered whether he was coming to a stop. It had been a long night of riding, and both man and horse were worn out.

Sam's big farmhouse was barely a mile away now. He was riding alone, but not really.

His sister Lizzie was no more than four hundred yards behind him on the road, which was not a road at all. It was a little-traveled backwoods trail through mostly private lands that required occasional stops to open and then close gates.

They were riding west on the trail, which traversed much of Lafayette County while avoiding Lexington.

Sam and Lizzie had figured this was the smart route to take, considering the clandestine nature of their overnight adventure. They had hoped to make it home without being seen.

But Sam had heard what he suspected was a man on horseback ahead, so he told Lizzie to stay put while he rode on to check things out.

Sam was hoping he would find that it was only a deer, and he kept listening for it to scurry into the undergrowth. If it was indeed a person, he hoped it would be a passing stranger who didn't know him.

Instead, Sam's heart sank when the morning mist parted to reveal his neighbor William Littlejohn astride a horse standing at a crossing that Sam knew led to Littlejohn's house. He watched as Sam approached.

"How goes it, neighbor?" Littlejohn asked, somewhat warily.

Sam managed a smile, even though William Littlejohn was probably the last person Sam wanted to see on this trail.

Littlejohn not only recognized Sam, he was a close friend of Sam's sworn enemy, Colonel William A. Warner. Sam knew the two had served together in Kentucky during the war, Littlejohn having been a captain under Colonel Warner's command.

"Top of the mornin'," Sam said. He left it at that, because he knew what the next question would be if this conversation continued.

It did.

"What brings you out at this hour? You must have laid out last night."

Sam had sobered up by this point, but even that consideration didn't help his thought process much.

He knew for sure he couldn't tell the truth. Other than that, he scratched his brain to come up with something that made at least some sense. That wasn't simple, especially given the fact that he didn't know whether Lizzie might come riding into their conversation at any moment.

"Just out for a ride," Sam said. "I hope your family is well."

"Yes, all is well," Littlejohn said. "And yours?"

"Good as can be expected. Wish I could converse further, but I best be gettin' back home now. Good day to ya."

"Good day to you," Littlejohn said.

Sam nudged his mount, and they continued along the trail toward home. His mind raced with the possibilities of what would happen next.

He would reach the house in a few minutes, but what of Lizzie? Sam hoped she'd seen from a distance that Littlejohn was on the trail and would wait until he was out of sight before she continued.

If Littlejohn encountered Lizzie on this obscure path early in the morning just moments after meeting Sam, who everyone in Lafayette County knew hadn't seen a sober sunrise in years, he would no doubt figure something was amiss.

And if he then heard that the cistern at the home of Colonel William A. Warner had been laced with poison just hours before, well, it wouldn't take a Pinkerton detective to solve that mystery.

***

Sam didn't get off his horse when he reached home. He turned the head of his mount back toward whence he'd come and sat waiting. He hoped it would be a long wait, thinking that would indicate Lizzie had avoided Littlejohn.

But Lizzie rode up within a few minutes.

"Goddamnit, Lizzie, you rode right into that man, didn't ya?" Sam snorted. "What did you say to him?"

"Nothin'. Just hello and good-bye. Didn't even stop. You've been frettin' like a schoolgirl, ain't ya?"

"That's the good gospel truth. Littlejohn must already be suspicious about our activities this morning. If he hears about the poisoned cistern at the Warners, he'll know we done it."

"He can't *know* we done it," Lizzie said. "He can only *figure* we done it. Nobody can know for certain 'cause nobody saw us actually do anything."

"Saw *you* do it, I guess you mean," Sam said. "I told you I didn't want no part of this particular scheme. It don't make no sense to poison the whole bunch of Warners when I got no quarrel with but one of 'em. I just hope that neither Leslie nor Sallie was the first to drink from that cistern this morning. I weren't about to let you ride over there alone, but that don't mean I like what ya done."

"I told ya, Sam, it ain't gonna kill 'em," Lizzie said. "Just make 'em sickly. Likely as not, they won't even realize that cistern was poisoned by a person. They'll figure a dead critter of some sort got in there. We got nothin' to be afraid of."

June 12, 1868

"Sam, I don't want nothin' to do with you no more," Leslie Warner said.

This was the first time Colonel Warner's only son had seen his brother-in-law in more than a month. Sam encountered Leslie outside Pigott's bookstore in Lexington, where Sam knew the fourteen-year-old liked to spend time.

Sam had no use for books. He just happened to be walking past Pigott's when Leslie walked out.

"What's gotten into you, Leslie?" Sam asked. As usual, he was wearing a bowler hat on his head and his navy pistols on his hips, giving him the look of a well-heeled dandy. "I ain't done nothin' to raise your ire."

"Other than tryin' to kill everybody in our family, ya mean?" Leslie responded. "We know you poisoned our cistern."

"I did no such thing," Sam said. "Leslie, I swear on your mother's grave, I weren't the person who done it."

Technically, he wasn't lying, but Leslie was having none of it.

"Captain Littlejohn said he saw you out on the trail, headin' back from our house early of a Sunday morning following the Saturday night on which the cistern was poisoned. The sheriff said that ain't proof you done the deed, but it was enough to satisfy Mother and Pa. Are you sayin' that it was merely a coincidence that Captain Littlejohn seen you early that mornin'?"

"I don't know about no coincidence, but I can in good conscience say I didn't poison your cistern," Sam said. "Leslie, you know I wouldn't do nothin' that might harm you. Or Sallie, for that matter. I already done lost Jo Shelby, ya know. I ain't eager to suffer no more losses in my life. The two of you still mean something to me. I for certain ain't gonna try to kill ya."

"I didn't know Jo Shelby died," Leslie said. "What happened?"

"He got shot," Sam said. "More than a month ago now."

"I am truly sorry, Sam. I know how much he meant to you. I liked him, too. But I still ain't convinced you wasn't involved in poisoning me and mine. Maybe you didn't do the deed yourself, but I reckon you know who did."

Sam looked away from Leslie and got kind of fidgety with his feet, turning this way and that before taking a step on the sidewalk toward the street. Then he turned back toward Leslie.

"Ya know, your father had no call to instigate this divorce against me," he said. "If he'd just left well enough alone, everything woulda been fine. None of these things woulda happened. I wish he woulda just minded his own business and left me and Sallie alone."

Sam then walked briskly away down the sidewalk, turning into the first saloon he came to.

June 27, 1868

Sam was drinking in his big house. Alone. Sitting at the dining table in midafternoon, he was reflecting on his situation.

Things weren't going well in his life, and none of his attempts at changing the course of events had succeeded.

The rousting of Colonel Warner in Lexington had been a failure, and Lizzie's cistern poisoning accomplished nothing.

Meanwhile, the divorce proceedings continued to wear on him. The court had ordered Sam to pay Sallie $750, even though the case hadn't yet reached the habeas corpus stage.

Enough, Sam thought. Time to get serious. Time to make sure those Warners knew he meant business.

He trudged out of the house toward the barn.

"John, get two horses saddled," he bellowed at his black worker. "You're comin' with me."

"Whadya got in mind, Mister Sam?" John asked as he grabbed a saddle and plopped it on a chestnut gelding.

"We're gonna pay Colonel Warner a little visit. Grab some rat poison from the tack room. Better collect a shotgun, too."

"Mister Sam, I don't like the sound of this here," John said. "Sounds to me like you is goin' to go out lookin' for trouble that you don't need to find."

"Trouble is what I plan to cause," Sam said. "I want Warner to know that Sam Nutter ain't to be trifled with. I want him to rue the day he filed those divorce papers. I want him to learn proper respect and fear for me."

John had both horses ready to go now. But *he* wasn't ready to go.

"I ain't for sure I want to be a part of this here activity," he said. "Whadya gonna do with rat poison, anyhow, Mister Sam?"

"You just let me worry about that," Sam said. "I know what I'm doin'. Don't worry, we ain't gonna kill nobody. No humans, anyhow."

John helped his tubby, half-drunk boss mount his horse, then neatly climbed aboard his own steed. The mare he rode also belonged to Sam, but she as good as belonged to John. He'd cared for her as long as she'd been on Sam's farm, and nobody but John rode her.

The two men headed east on the familiar trail toward Lexington. Sam wasn't taking the back way this time, as he and Lizzie had a few weeks earlier. He and John would ride right through Lexington on the main road, then on to the Warners' farm.

Sam hadn't done much planning for this excursion. He figured he and John would arrive at the Warners' shortly after dark and cause whatever mayhem they could. Hopefully, without being seen on the premises. If somebody saw them on the road, that wouldn't be proof of anything.

And, for a change, things happened just as Sam had hoped.

When the two men arrived at the Warners', they tied their mounts to trees where they couldn't be seen and surveyed the situation.

Clouds covered the moon, so it was exceptionally dark. They could barely make out several horses in a paddock forty yards or so away from their position at the edge of the trees. Sam pointed at them, squatted, and began creeping toward the paddock's outer fence. John followed, also squatting and creeping.

After both men maneuvered through the board fencing to enter the paddock, Sam slid a rope over the head of a gray mare, then pointed to a gray colt drowsing at her side. John didn't need to put a rope on the colt; the little guy trundled after his mother as Sam led her to the gate, which John held open.

The horses remained silent, not a whinny to be heard.

Sam led the mare just a few yards, to the edge of a disused well that was covered only by two planks. After pulling off the planks, he grabbed the colt around his neck, sliced his throat with a knife and pushed him into the opening and down into the depths. The mare whinnied loudly and thrashed about in Sam's grip. Pulling out the rat poison, he forced open the panicked horse's mouth and poured as much as he could down her gullet.

Then he ran for the woods.

John said nothing. He didn't have time. The entire episode lasted less than a minute.

But he ran for the woods, too.

He and Sam returned to their horses, mounted, and headed back west.

***

"Mister Sam, I want nothin' more to do with your vengeance against the Warners," John said as they rode in the dark toward Lexington. "Was a time I'd do anything for you. But not now. Not this. You ain't tryin' to win back Miss Sallie no more. You just wanna punish her pa.

"Those horses didn't do nothin' to deserve what you done. That was just plain mean spirited, and I don't want no more part of it."

Sam Nutter stared straight ahead as he rode. He didn't change his expression as his hired hand and childhood friend addressed him in a way he never had before.

"You done changed, Mr. Sam," John continued. "You always loved critters, and you never woulda killed no horses before."

Sam remained a silent figure on his mount.

Neither man spoke as they rode through Lexington and on west, toward Sam's farm.

Finally, a full thirty minutes after John had last spoke, Sam responded.

"You're right, John, I have changed," he said. "Between Sallie movin' out, Jo Shelby gettin' killed, and all the misery this divorce has heaped on me, ain't no way I could help but change. Ain't nothin' good in my life no more. I guess I just want to share my misery as much as possible with the man who mostly brought it on me.

"I ain't done yet. Colonel Warner ain't seen the last of me."

July 2, 1868

It was one thing to read the accusations the Warners had made about him in the divorce papers filed in Lafayette County Circuit Court.

But now Sam had to listen to them in person.

Lawyers had gathered Sam and Sallie and a good many other witnesses in Lexington for a hearing on a writ of habeas corpus, filed by Sallie in an attempt to force Sam to pay child support for little Georgie.

Sam wasn't much of a father; even he admitted that.

Georgie had been born November 15, so she wasn't even eight months old. Sam hadn't seen her in three months, since Sallie moved out April 5, and he rarely thought of her.

He didn't feel anything like a father, and he had no problem with Sallie keeping Georgie. But he didn't see why he should have to pay her to do it. The Warners were the ones who wanted this divorce. Besides, Sam had already been ordered to pay Sallie $750 for her support. Why should he have to give her any more?

Now, Sam had to listen in court as Sallie and her family recounted what an awful person he was, in an attempt to convince a judge that Sam should provide financial support for this child, whom he barely knew.

He heard about how he was a drunk and a thief and how he had an incestuous relationship with his sister. He sat silent in the courtroom through it all, but inside he was boiling. By the time the hearing ended, the anger that had been building for months had reached an all-out rage.

He said nothing in his defense. His lawyer had told him that wouldn't be prudent, given that Sam was half-drunk and fully infuriated.

"I don't care no more," he said to his sister Lizzie on the carriage ride home. "They can't do no more to me than they already done. It don't matter how much of my money they take. I reckon I'm gonna get my money's worth."

"Whadya mean by that?" Lizzie asked.

"I'm gonna kill at least one Warner. I reckon I can kill me another one or two, if need be."

"Sam, you know I hate them self-righteous people as much as you do, and I want Colonel Warner dead, too. But I don't think killin' him is the smart thing to do right now. Everybody will know you done it. You'll get hung for sure."

"Like I said, I don't care no more. You always told me I needed to stand up for myself, that I let people take advantage of my good nature. Well, I ain't got no good nature no more, and I plan on standing up for myself. If I get hung, I get hung. If I let them get away with this, I might as well be dead, anyhow."

July 5, 1868

"The end is at hand," Sam said.

Knowing John would want no part of this, Sam had rounded up another hired hand—a man who had worked for him only a few weeks. In truth, he wasn't much more than a boy, and he certainly wasn't much of a gun hand. But Sam figured it didn't matter.

He had his two navy revolvers, and that was enough.

"You won't have to kill nobody," he told the hired hand. "I just need ya to stay at my side and watch my back."

The sun was setting behind them as they rode purposefully out of the lot in front of Sam's barn. He and his cohort headed east on the trail, their mounts moving at a comfortable trot while sweat rolled down Sam's face, neck, and back. It was a steamy summer evening, and the heat magnified Sam's anger.

He finally had decided he would kill William A. Warner. His mind was made up. As he urged on his mount, he dwelled on thoughts of Sallie's sudden departure in the company of her father and on the Warners' castigations in court.

When the pair arrived at the Warners' farm near Dover, the sun had set. However, a nearly full moon was on the rise, shining so bright Sam knew it would be difficult to sneak all the way to the house without being seen.

He and his cohort lurked in the woods some forty yards from the paddock and house, just as he and John had done barely a week earlier. As before, they tied their horses to trees out of sight of anyone in the house.

Unlike the previous week, Sam wasn't sneaking this time. He led his cohort boldly toward the barn, figuring they would be spotted, which would draw out Colonel Warner as the only man in the house. He hoped a gunfight would ensue.

But they reached the tool and carriage house without being noticed.

Sam told his worker to grab whatever tack he could carry and haul it back to their horses. Sam picked up a carriage wheel, slung it over his shoulder, and marched back to the woods.

He made it all the way back, again without being noticed. Cursing, Sam dropped the carriage wheel near the saddles and harness his partner had laid on the ground. Figuring he needed something more obvious to roust his prey from the safety of the house, he decided he would go right up to the front door and knock on it.

Sam walked toward the house, with his partner just to his left and behind him. They didn't get far before Sam noticed a commotion, visible through a second-floor window.

He stopped about thirty yards from the house, but nobody emerged from the front door. Realizing he would be an easy target if somebody aimed a rifle from that second-floor window, which could result in him getting killed without even firing a shot, Sam again retreated to the woods, with his partner in tow.

"I wanna get Warner to come outside," Sam said.

He decided to return, alone, to the open area. He figured it was bright enough out that he would be recognized and that if Warner was any kind of man he would leave the house to confront him. Then he would kill Warner with one of his navy Colts.

If somebody took a shot at him from the house, he would return fire and hope for the best.

But nobody in the house did anything. So Sam stood and waited. And waited some more. He waited until he started getting bored. Finally, in frustration, he turned and started to return to his partner in the woods, muttering profanities. He had taken only two steps when he heard a man's voice calling from the house.

"Sam Nutter, I know that's you," the voice said. "Stop where you are, or I'll shoot."

Sam recognized it as Colonel Warner, but he was calling from the second-floor window. Sam couldn't see him, so he had no target to shoot at. He decided to keep walking toward the trees.

"Stop, or I'll shoot!" Colonel Warner hollered again.

Sam spun, took hasty aim at the window, and shot. Then shot twice more. Then he ran, not terribly fast but as quickly as his stubby body would go, toward the tree line.

He heard three shots from the house echo off the barn and trees, but no bullets struck him.

Sam was breathing heavily and his heart was hammering when he finally reached the woods. He had never been shot at before, and it wasn't something he enjoyed.

Worse, he was pretty sure his own sloppy shots hadn't hit their target. He just hoped a bullet hadn't struck Sallie.

All in all, Sam figured this was another wholesale failure on his part to exact the revenge he wanted on Colonel William A. Warner.

July 8, 1868

S

am avoided Lexington for a couple of days after the shoot-out at the Warners', so he still didn't know whether his shots had damaged anything other than the house.

He was half-expecting a visit from the Lafayette County sheriff with an arrest warrant. But nothing.

He decided he might be in the clear.

"I'm runnin' low on liquor, so I'm goin' into town," he said to Lizzie. "Be good if you'd come with me; make things look as normal as possible."

Sam had told Lizzie all the details of his shoot-out with Colonel Warner, and she figured Sam could get away with it if he played his cards right.

"Them Warners don't know for certain it was you, 'cause you never answered when he called your name," she said. "And you was too far from the house for them to see your face in the dark. It was good you left behind the tack you took. Nobody saw you on the road there or back. If anybody accuses you, all you have to do is say you was at home that night. I'll back your story."

So, with Lizzie at his side, Sam drove the carriage into Lexington as the midsummer sun beat radiantly down on them. He was wearing his pistols on his hips, as usual.

Sam entered the store of Young and Green to pick up a gallon of his favorite beverage, telling the proprietor to add the amount to his tab. That was no problem. Sam Nutter's credit was good at every business in Lexington.

He returned to Lizzie, who was waiting in the carriage.

"Let's get dinner, Sam," Lizzie said. "It's too damn hot to stay out in this sun any longer. I'm about to melt."

"Sounds good to me," Sam said, reaching to help Lizzie from the carriage.

They stepped onto the sidewalk and walked east up North Street, away from the courthouse.

"Hey, Sam," a voice called from behind.

Sam reached awkwardly for a pistol with his right hand as he turned. Seeing a familiar and unthreatening face, he casually lifted his right hand away from the weapon and instead pointed his index finger.

"Oughtn't sneak up on a man, Phares," Sam said.

"I was doing no such thing," Deputy Sheriff Phares E. Hammond said. "I was merely trying to attract your attention."

"Well, you done that, all right. You're lucky I didn't shoot."

"I'd say *you're* lucky you didn't shoot," the deputy said, "'cause you most likely woulda missed me, and I woulda returned fire. Why are you so nervous with that pistol, anyway? Think somebody might be after you? Did you do something to provoke somebody?"

"Not in the least," Sam said.

"Are you sure, Sam? I hear tell you mighta paid a visit to your in-laws over near Dover. The way I hear it, you mighta fired that very pistol into the Warners' house, and mighta come very close to plugging your own soon-to-be ex-wife. Did I hear wrong, Sam?"

"I reckon you did," Sam said. "I ain't been nowhere near that house. When did this supposed shooting take place, anyhow?"

"Three nights ago," Hammond said. "The Warners swear it was you who shot at their house. Only reason we ain't arrested you is because they got no proof it was really you. Turns out nobody got a good look at your face. Guess that's lucky for you, too, Sam."

"They didn't get a good look at my face 'cause it weren't my face," Sam said. "I told ya I wasn't there."

"Be that as it may, I got no reason to doubt the Warners' story," Hammond said. "But I also ain't got enough proof to haul you off to jail. On the other hand, you might consider this a warning against doing any such nonsense again. You might not be so lucky next time."

Sam didn't respond. He also avoided looking the deputy in the eyes, turning his head this way and that as Hammond spoke before finally fixing his gaze on the ground in front of him.

"Sam couldn't a done no shooting that night," Lizzie blurted out. "He was home with me that night."

"I'm sure he was," Hammond said. "Be that as it may, there ain't nothin' I can do about it, anyway. However, you might be interested to know that any future foray to the Warners' house likely will end badly for the person who endeavors to make it. I have it on good authority that the Warners have hired their neighbor Frank Allison to serve as a protector. You're familiar with Frank Allison, ain't ya, Sam?"

"I know his reputation," Sam said.

"Then you know any future visitor to the Warners' house better come in the light of day and with his hands clearly visible, or he might wind up in Machpelah Cemetery. That's where your folks are buried, ain't it, Sam?"

"I understand what you're sayin', Phares," Sam said. "I guess you made your point. Can my sister and me move along now? We got things to do."

"So do I, Sam," Hammond said. "I guess I best be on my way. Good day to you, Miss Nutter."

"Good day, Deputy," Lizzie replied.

***

"Whadya gonna do now, Sam?" Lizzie asked her brother as they dined at the City Hotel. "You ain't fool enough to tangle with Frank Allison, I hope. I heard he killed more men than Bloody Bill himself during the war. He ain't a man to be trifled with."

"I know that," Sam said. "I ain't plannin' on it."

"You best resign yourself to the fact that you ain't gonna stop this divorce through force," Lizzie said. "Or any other way, for that matter."

"Maybe so, but I still ain't gonna give up without a fight," Sam said. "I can't let Colonel Warner get away with doin' this to me. And I sure ain't givin' that family my property in the divorce settlement. I'd sooner give it to a stranger."

"You might be on to something with that, Sam," Lizzie said.

"Give my property to a stranger, ya mean? Who ya got in mind?"

"Not to a stranger. To me. Course, you'd have to sell it to me, to make it all legal. But the Warners can't take somethin' from you if you don't own it."

"By god, Lizzie, that's a right good idea."

August 2, 1868

S am was pretty proud of himself.

"Them Warners are in for a surprise when they try to take everything I got and find out I ain't got nothin' to take," he said.

He smiled as he sat at the dinner table in the house that was now technically his sister's. The sale of Sam's house, land, and almost everything else was legally recorded at the Lafayette County Recorder of Deeds office.

Rarely had a man who had lost everything been so happy about it.

The records claimed Lizzie paid him $17,000 for his 580 acres, his house, and most of his other property, but that wasn't altogether truthful. In fact, it wasn't truthful at all.

Lizzie hadn't paid him a penny.

"We outsmarted 'em, Sam," Lizzie said. "You won't have to give 'em nothin' in the divorce. We can go right on livin' like we always done."

"Hold up, now. You know I love ya, Lizzie, but I ain't done with them Warners yet," Sam said. "Not by a long shot. Maybe I can't catch Colonel Warner unawares at his house, but that Allison can't be at his side all the time. I still might get a chance to gun him down. Meantime, I reckon there are other ways to ruin the man. Sallie told me a few family secrets about their time in Kentucky."

"What kind of family secrets?" Lizzie asked.

"You know he was married once before, long before he ever met Sallie's mother, and had two boys," Sam said. "Well, Sallie said ain't nobody knows what happened to the first Mrs. Warner. She more or less disappeared just around the time Colonel Warner met the woman who became the second Mrs. Warner, who happened to be the daughter of one of the wealthiest men in Kentucky."

"You think Colonel Warner did something to her?" Lizzie asked.

"Looks mighty suspicious to me. Sallie said her father faced considerable legal troubles in Kentucky, too. She figured that was part of the reason the family moved to Missouri. In any regard, it seems Colonel Warner has a past that might be worth lookin' into."

"Maybe we can get the newspaper to write a story that might embarrass the upstanding Colonel Warner," Lizzie said. "The *Caucasian* might enjoy taking down a former Union colonel."

August 8, 1868

Sam didn't know much about newspapering, so he didn't understand why the man at the *Caucasian*, William Musgrove Jr., refused to write a story about Colonel William A. Warner's past.

"You've got no facts, just suppositions and assertions," Musgrove said. "As much as I'd like to write about a Union scoundrel, you've given me no basis for a newspaper story."

"To my mind, suppositions and assertions are plenty good enough," Sam said. "The man is a rascal, and you oughtta write that."

"It simply isn't enough. We have journalistic standards here at the *Caucasian*. If you were to bring me actual proof, I might change my mind."

"Proof?" Sam said.

"Yes, written records of the man's transgressions and firsthand accounts of illegal activities, not just reports of his personal peccadilloes."

Sam didn't know a peccadillo from an armadillo, but he got the idea.

"Sam, you simply don't have enough facts for me to write a story," Musgrove said. "But perhaps I have an alternative. There is nothing preventing you from publishing your *own* story. You can say anything you want, and we can print it in pamphlet form for you to distribute."

"You mean it don't have to be altogether true?" Sam asked.

"Legally, nobody can prevent you from publishing whatever you want to write," Musgrove said. "Of course, if you libel your subject, you could face legal consequences. But those would occur only after publication."

Sam figured he had nothing more to lose, since the Warners were already trying to get it all in the divorce case. Besides, he no longer owned much of anything. Everything was safely in Lizzie's name now.

He decided that if the Warners could lie about him in the divorce papers, which all of Lafayette County could read, then he could lie about *them* in a pamphlet for all of Lafayette County to read.

"I'll be back," Sam said to Musgrove. "Meantime, I got me some writin' to do."

August 17, 1868

S am decided he didn't like being a writer.

It wasn't the writing itself he loathed as much as the sitting at a desk and focusing on a single task for any length of time. After five or ten minutes, he inevitably surrendered to the urge to stand up and do something else.

Anything else.

Writing just didn't come naturally for him. Fortunately for him, his sister Lizzie loved it.

"Sam, can we say Colonel Warner killed his first wife, even though we don't know for certain that he did?" Lizzie asked as she held a pencil poised above a piece of paper.

The brother and sister sat at the table in their dining room. A bottle of whiskey and two glasses rested on the table between them.

"Damn for sure we can," Sam said. "The man at the *Caucasian* said we can write anything we want."

He downed a long gulp of whiskey.

"So we could say he had intercourse with women other than his wife, even with his own daughters?" Lizzie asked.

"We could if we wanted," Sam said. "But I ain't sure that's somethin' we want to say. I don't want to say nothin' that will reflect bad on Sallie. We should just attack Warner. And that wife of his."

"Why don't we say she's a thief and a drunk, just like they said about you?" Lizzie said. "Or maybe that she was the one who done intercourse with somebody else. Can you imagine that woman doing intercourse with anybody?"

Lizzie laughed her bleating-lamb laugh, and Sam laughed, too.

It was perhaps the first time there had been any laughter in the big, old house since Sallie had packed up and left five months earlier.

It felt good, Sam thought.

"You're onto somethin' there, Sis," he said. "If they can make up things about us, we can sure make up things about them."

"How about this?" Lizzie said.

She started writing and reciting at the same time: "Georgia Warner, the daughter of General Leslie Combs and the wife of Colonel William A. Warner, is knowd to have enjoyed sexual encounters with many of the gentlemen of Pendleton County in Kentucky, where she earned a reputation as a harlot in the years the family lived there. She was also knowd as a thief."

"Good," Sam said.

Lizzie continued:

"Mrs. Warner stole many of the items that now inhabit the family house in Lafayette County, including dishware, jewelry, linens, and candlesticks. She done so by presuming to buy these items on credit and taking them home but never paying for them. When questioned about the items, she claims that she did indeed pay for them and that the storekeeper was lying.

"Mrs. Warner done this many times while living in Kentucky. She then moved the stolen items with her family to Missouri, where she is beyond the grasp of Kentucky law."

"I like it," Sam said. "What about the husband?"

Lizzie grinned, wrote, and recited again:

"Colonel William A. Warner was knowd to have ordered the killing of Confederate prisoners his men took into custody during the war. Many of the men he killed was not even a soldier but a mere Southern sympathizer who Warner ordered captured. He done this many times.

"Warner also ordered his men to burn to the ground the houses of several men he suspected of sympathizing with the Southern cause. This was done in Pendleton and surrounding counties early in the war.

"Perhaps most damning, Colonel Warner commanded a unit made up completely of Negro soldiers."

"I like that last part," Sam said, through gales of laughter. "What about his first wife? Let's say he done her in."

"Colonel Warner was married once before," Lizzie said as she wrote. "She gave birth to two children he fathered, both boys. Those who knowd the family at that time said Mr. Warner (this was before he served in the war and therefore wasn't yet a colonel) physically beat his first wife on a regular basis, even when she was with child. He finally took the beatings too far and fractured his wife's skull with one of his blows. She was dead on the spot."

"Excellent," Sam said. "I've a desire to accuse the man of incest, as he did me in the divorce papers, but not with his daughters. He must have a sister somewhere, but I ain't sure."

"Well, ain't nobody around here gonna know if he has a sister or not. . . .

"During his time in Kentucky before the war, Mr. Warner had occasion to lay with his own sister on multiple occasions. This was before he was married, but he was a full-growd man and knowd what he done was wrong."

Lizzie looked up.

"Think we need more details on his incest, Sam?"

"Ain't much more to say on that account," Sam said.

"What about your visit to Kentucky before the wedding? You said you talked to some folks who knowd Colonel Warner there. Anything we can use?"

"Nothin' that's true. But we're free to fabricate some details. I talked to his son-in-law, Captain Riggs. He might be a source for some sordid fabrications."

"I got it," Lizzie said, picking up the pencil and resuming her recitation:

"Captain Benjamin Riggs—Warner's son-in-law—said that those in Kentucky despised Warner and his wife and that any marriage to his daughter would have been doomed from the start. He said they had made life miserable for him and would make life miserable for any man who married into the family."

"Well, we've got a good start," Sam said. "With a little more work, it'll be ready to show the *Caucasian* man."

August 26, 1868

William Musgrove Jr. of the *Caucasian* hesitated to help Sam further than printing his pamphlet, knowing that the false accusations against Colonel Warner were libelous. However, he figured that he wouldn't be held accountable so long as his name didn't appear on the publication. Plus, he couldn't resist taking a former Union colonel down a peg or two.

When he saw the writing Sam put before him in the cluttered *Caucasian* office—dry and grammatically challenged as it was—his creative juices got to flowing.

"Sam, you must make this more personal to pique the reader's interest," he said. "You should describe your trip to Kentucky in detail."

Musgrove wrote for about three minutes, then began reading aloud:

"When I was first married, I went upon a tour to Kentucky, where I had a chance of knowing how Warner stood in the eyes of the community there, and it did not take me long to discover that he was regarded by almost everyone as a great scoundrel, even by his own relatives."

Musgrove stopped reciting and transcribed for a few minutes, then said, "If we put this part in the words of this Captain Riggs, it might sound more authoritative. How about . . .

"'Mrs. Warner,' he said 'is no better than he is. She is a perfect Jezebel and can make more mischief in a neighborhood than any woman I ever saw; but let her get a spite at you once, and she'll follow you to the devil in her vindictiveness.'"

Sam was impressed.

"Sir, you are a master," he said. "Can you work the same magic with the rest of my words?"

"It would be my pleasure," Musgrove said. "Return this afternoon, and I'll have a finished product. If you approve it, we can print it in a day or so."

***

When Sam retrieved the edited version at the *Caucasian* office a couple hours later, he had his worker John with him. Sam wanted John to see the pamphlet, hoping for the former slave's approval.

John had never learned to read, so Sam read aloud from the pages as his black worker drove Sam's carriage on the road back to the Nutter farm.

He said nothing until Sam finished.

"Is you serious about printin' this for public consumption, Mr. Sam?" John asked.

"Serious as a judge," Sam said.

"Well, I reckon you know what you be gettin' yourself into. No man gonna swallow that without chokin' some, and you be the one he choked. This ain't gonna get you nothin' but more trouble."

"Trouble is what I'm after. If Colonel Warner comes for me seekin' retribution, I'll be ready for him. Me and my navy Colts."

"You might have your Colts at your side, but you ain't gonna have me," John said, after a long moment's silence. "I want no part of this here."

"I ain't expectin' you to fight for me, John," Sam said. "I can handle that rascal by myself."

"Mr. Sam, I ain't talkin' about not fightin' for you. I mean to say I will leave your farm and family if you follow through with this here. They's all lies, and you know it. Them Warners don't deserve this. I stayed by your side through your trips to their house and all the mischief you done there, but no more. You likely as not gonna start a war with them Warners, and more than one person is likely to get killed. No thank you."

John stared straight ahead, and Sam could tell he was serious.

"If that's how it's gotta be, that's how it's gotta be," Sam said. "You know I don't want you to leave, John. We been together since we was boys. But I'm gonna do this, with you or without you."

"It's gonna be without me then, Mr. Sam," John said.

Neither man talked again until they reached the farm.

"I'll be gone in the mornin'," John said.

Then he climbed from the carriage and ambled toward his room in the barn.

Sam's throat grew tight, and he couldn't force any words through it. He sat on the carriage and darn near cried.

He'd lost Sallie, and then he'd lost Jo Shelby, and now he was losing John. He had very little left in his life except Lizzie. And all of it was one man's fault.

Colonel William A. Warner. Goddamn him.

September 12, 1868

"Lizzie, I'm goin' to town. You wanna come?" Sam asked his sister.

"Are you gonna pass out more of them damn pamphlets?" Lizzie responded. "I must say, you are dedicated to their distribution. I should think every citizen in Lexington has seen one by now."

"Don't forget Carrollton," Sam said. "That coward Warner thought he could get away from me by moving his family across the river, but I reckon I showed him there's no escaping the clutches of Sam Nutter. I had a right good time in Carrollton. Those folks up there didn't know what kind of man they'd got in their midst.

"In any event, I still have a fistful of pamphlets. No reason to waste 'em. You're welcome to accompany me into Lexington."

"I ain't got no interest in standing in the streets of Lexington and passing out pamphlets," Lizzie said. "You're likely gonna spend time in a saloon or two, anyhow. You go now, on your own. I'll be fine here at home."

Truth be told, Sam was beginning to weary of his pamphlet project, too. He had thought their dissemination would draw Colonel Warner into a gunfight, one that inevitably would end with Sam sending a bullet into the chest of his nemesis.

But now he wondered if that day would ever come. Sam didn't know what else he could do to provoke Warner.

So off to Lexington he rode.

Sam figured he'd lost a lot of drinking time to these pamphlets. In fact, he reckoned his first duty today in Lexington ought to be drinking instead of pamphleteering.

So he headed straight into the City Hotel saloon when he reached town.

After ordering a whiskey, he settled in at a table and pulled up a chair next to Henry Flint. Sam had given Flint, a well-respected man in Lexington, one of his pamphlets a few days earlier.

"Have you perused the pamphlet, Henry?" Sam asked.

"I have," Flint said.

"Well? Whadya think?"

"I don't know Colonel Warner or his family, but if they are as evil and vile as you say, they are certainly a blight on this country," Flint said. "So, how much of what you claim is actually true?"

"Every word of it," Sam said.

"Your pamphlet doesn't offer much in the way of proof. If they are guilty of these things, how have they escaped the arm of the law?"

"They had the influence of General Leslie Combs on their side in Kentucky," Sam said. "He ain't in Missouri, though. It's time that scoundrel paid for his sins."

"What do you propose?" Flint asked.

Sam put his hands on his two navy revolvers.

"Damn him," Sam said. "If he can shoot before I can, he is welcome."

"Well, Sam, I hope you know what you're doing," Flint said. "I like you. I'd hate to see you get hurt. Or worse."

"Ain't no way that'll happen," Sam assured him with a cockeyed grin.

Flint left the table, and his chair was quickly filled by George Mountjoy, whom Sam considered a friend. Of course, their friendship consisted entirely of buying each other rounds and discussing their troubles in the various saloons of Lexington.

Like Sam, Mountjoy enjoyed imbibing, although not to the extent that Sam did.

Like Flint, Mountjoy had the respect of most of Lexington's residents.

He'd already told Sam his opinion of the pamphlet, and that included some hearty laughter. Mountjoy knew Colonel Warner fairly well, so he was aware that very little of what the pamphlet said was true. He found it amusing that Sam had the gall to say such things, however.

"Sam, you passin' out them lies again?" Mountjoy asked as he drew near to the table.

"Not yet," Sam said. "I thought I'd enjoy a drink first."

"You picked the right place to do that," Mountjoy said. "I guess you ain't had your showdown with Warner yet?"

"The day is fast approachin', I reckon. That is, if Warner ain't too damned a coward. I'm ready for him anytime. I saw the man in Carrollton when I circulated my pamphlets there, but he steered clear of me."

"He'd be a fool to confront you and your Colts," Mountjoy said. "He don't typically wear guns. Fact is, I ain't ever seen him armed at all."

Sam had never seen Colonel Warner armed, either. But he knew his father-in-law owned a shotgun and figured he would bring it to any showdown he might ultimately have with Sam.

"You ain't gonna shoot him if he ain't armed, are you?" Mountjoy asked.

"No," Sam said. "Only a coward shoots an unarmed man."

***

Sam returned home, drunk, after about three hours in multiple saloons. He didn't distribute a single pamphlet.

October 1, 1868

Sam was in a rare good mood. He had grown weary of worrying about the fate of his family farm, which he still feared he could lose in the divorce settlement with Sallie. And he was worn down by his ongoing efforts to gain vengeance against Sallie's father.

But today, he was almost able to forget all that.

The weather was gorgeous, a bright sun and brilliant blue sky nearly blinding him when he stepped out of the house. The cool of autumn had pushed out the heat of summer, and the air was so fresh Sam took in as much as he could gulp down in a single breath.

On a day like this, Sam saddled his horse almost by instinct and hit the trail to Lexington. He had no real plans, other than to enjoy the ride and a few drinks afterward.

Sam figured it was nearly a perfect day.

Then it got even better.

As Sam rode into Lexington, he saw a familiar figure walking along the pavement, dime novel in hand.

"Leslie Warner, I can't believe my eyes," Sam shouted. "It's really you. What in good heaven's name are you doin' here? I knowd your family moved up to Carroll County. Did you finally come to your senses and move out of your parents' house? If so, you're welcome to stay at my place."

Leslie didn't return Sam's enthusiastic greeting. He kept walking while Sam rode alongside.

"Leave me be, Sam," he said. "I want nothin' to do with you. The things you done to my family and said about my folks, I got nothin' but dislike for you now. You leave me be."

"Aw, Leslie, I ain't hurt nobody, least of all you," Sam said. "I would never do nothin' to hurt you."

"But you done plenty to hurt Pa and Mother," Leslie said. "You killed our colt, shot at our house, stole our tack. Then you wrote all those lies. It ain't right, and I don't want nothin' to do with you, unless it's to shoot you, myself."

"You ain't gonna shoot me, Leslie," Sam said. "I got these two navy Colts to make sure of that. Besides, we're friends."

"We ain't friends no more. And the only reason I ain't gonna shoot you is 'cause I ain't got no gun."

"Well, what are you doin' in Lexington alone, anyhow?" Sam asked, halting his mount as Leslie stopped on the sidewalk and turned toward him.

"I ain't run away from home, if that's what you think. I rode here to make our entries in the Lexington fair. We still plan on comin' down to it."

Sam had forgotten about the Lexington fair. It was the biggest event in town every year, and it was only about a week away. Sam loved the fair when he was a boy.

"So, will the whole family be comin' to Lexington, includin' Sallie?" Sam asked.

"I expect she'll be here," Leslie said, "though I don't know for certain. Pa and Mother and Mary and me are comin', I know that."

"Does Sallie ever talk about me?"

"Yeah, but you don't wanna know what she says when she does. She ain't no more fond of you than I am."

"Ya know, Leslie, we were good friends not so long ago," Sam said in a pained tone. "You ain't forgot that summer you spent with us, have you? You ain't forgot the fun I arranged for you with Miss Lizzie, have you? I'd hate to think we ain't friends no more."

"Sam, there ain't no way we can still be friends," Leslie said. "Not after all you said and done."

"I ain't done or said nothin' to nobody in quite a spell. Truth be told, I've lost some of my enthusiasm for gettin' vengeance against your pa. What if I was to apologize? Like I said, I ain't really hurt nobody. Do you think Sallie would forgive me?"

Before this moment, Sam hadn't remotely thought about ending his campaign against the Warners. Or about apologizing. The words just kind of came out of his mouth.

"Whadya mean, apologize?" Leslie asked.

"I'll say I'm sorry for what I done and promise not to do nothin' else against your family," Sam said.

"What about the divorce? What about when the judge says you gotta give Sallie your farm? You still won't do nothin' then?"

"All I gotta say is good luck with that. I reckon I'll be OK. I just wanna put all this nastiness behind us."

Leslie frowned. "I ain't sure I believe you, Sam," he said.

Sam wasn't sure he believed himself. But the words sounded good when they came out of his mouth, and at least part of what he said was true.

He *was* growing tired of all the nastiness. "I admit I ain't never gonna forgive your pa for what he said about me in the divorce papers," Sam said. "But . . . I reckon maybe it's time me and Lizzie got on with our lives."

"Well, you do what you gotta do, Sam," Leslie said. "All I know is that people have been tellin' Pa you've been braggin' you're gonna kill him first chance you get. That don't sound like no apology I ever heard before."

"I was drunk when I said them things," Sam said.

"So you didn't mean them?"

"I ain't sayin' that. I guess I meant them at the time. But right now, where we stand right here, I'm tellin' you I ain't got no plans to kill your pa. Unless he tries to kill me first, of course."

"That don't mean much, as far as I'm concerned," Leslie said. "I guess I'll tell Pa what you said, but I don't think it will change anything.

"I best be gettin' on to the fair office now, Sam. I still gotta ride home today."

"It was good to see you, Leslie," Sam said. "You give Sallie my best."

He watched as Leslie walked down the sidewalk. Sam then turned and headed toward the City Hotel saloon. He had some thinking to do.

PART

III

SHOWDOWN IN LEXINGTON

Sam Nutter

October 21, 1868

A mist fell over the Warners' family carriage as it splashed down the road to Lexington.

The black carriage was covered by a fabric top, which kept the four people riding inside relatively dry. The rain had pounded down earlier in the day, but now it came in faint, intermittent waves. The midafternoon temperature was in the lower sixties, so the occupants were not unduly uncomfortable for the long drive from Carroll County.

Colonel William A. Warner held the reins in front, with his son Leslie beside him. Seated behind them were Leslie's sister Mary and his mother, Georgia Warner.

Leslie was excited about going to the Lexington fair, which was one of the local highlights every year. But he was also concerned about the possibility of trouble. He had told his father of his encounter with Sam Nutter a week earlier, making it clear he didn't trust that Sam was truly interested in making amends with the Warners.

Neither did Colonel Warner. That's why Sallie had remained at home with her and Sam's daughter, Georgie.

It also was why Colonel Warner's 12-gauge shotgun was lying, loaded, between Leslie and his father.

"Pa, do you reckon Sam would really try somethin' in town, especially with so many people there for the fair?" Leslie asked.

"I don't know, but I will be ready if he does," Colonel Warner said, hands tightening on the reins. "I don't plan on letting him do anything else to harm or threaten the family. I have had my fill of Sam Nutter."

A voice from the backseat said, "He ought to be shot for what he said in that pamphlet."

It was Georgia Warner. As always, she sounded cross.

"And, Mr. Warner, can you please make a better effort to avoid these nasty puddles? I'm tempted to think you drive through them on purpose, as rough as this ride has been."

Colonel Warner stared straight ahead, emitting a sound that was between a sigh and a grunt. Then he turned and smiled at Leslie.

"I'll wager you can't wait to be married," he said, softly enough that the passengers in the back couldn't hear.

Leslie laughed. It wasn't often that his father made him laugh, and it felt good.

"Sam wasn't so bad when him and Sallie first got married," Leslie said. "I liked him. But I guess marriage changes a man."

"I fear that wasn't the problem in his case," Colonel Warner said. "I'm not certain Sam Nutter was ever a quality man. The truth is, we likely never should have allowed him to marry into our family. I suppose that was my mistake."

"Of course, it was your mistake. I certainly never wanted him to marry into our family."

It was the voice from the back again.

"Sam Nutter has been a bane on this family," Georgia Warner continued. "I should have thought you would have done something about him by now."

"What would you have me do?" Colonel Warner asked calmly, again while keeping his eyes fixed straight ahead.

"I don't know. Something to get rid of the man. We divorced him, and that only made things worse. We moved to Carroll County, and he followed us there with his notorious pamphlet. I just wish to be rid of him!"

"Perhaps you will get your wish," Colonel Warner said, almost to himself.

Leslie looked up at his father's eyes as he spoke those words. He saw a resolute determination he had witnessed in his father only once before—the night a year and a half earlier when two men rode off with four of the Warners' horses. He remembered Colonel Warner swiftly taking control of the situation, tracking down the thieves and recovering the horses. Leslie thought at the time that maybe it was his father's experience during the war that enabled him to not only remain calm in such a situation but to take charge.

With a shiver, he wondered whether the soldier in Colonel Warner was again stirring, this time with darker intentions than chasing horse thieves.

"Have you got somethin' planned, Pa?" Leslie asked.

"No. No actual plan," Colonel Warner said. "But if it's a showdown Sam Nutter wants, it's a showdown he'll get. I will not back down."

"Ain't that takin' a chance, what with him havin' those navy pistols? It ain't gonna be easy to get the drop on him. How do you propose to get close enough to use that shotgun?"

"That's what I'd like to know, Mr. Warner," Georgia Warner piped in. "You need to have a plan. Otherwise you're likely to get yourself killed, leaving me a widow with all these children. I'll not have you do that to me."

Mary smiled and said, "None of us want that. That would make Leslie the man of the house."

"That ain't funny, Mary," Leslie said.

"Hush, the two of you," Georgia Warner said. "I'd still like an answer from your father. I want to know what he plans to do to rid us of Sam Nutter."

"I will not discuss this with you, Mrs. Warner," Colonel Warner said sternly. "I don't need you to tell me how to handle this kind of business. I didn't need your input when I commanded the Old Eighteenth at Richmond, and I don't need it now. I'll tell you when the task is completed. Nothing more."

Mary and Leslie sat silently stunned. Neither had ever heard their father speak to their mother in such a defiant tone.

"Well, do what you must," Georgia Warner said. "But don't blame me if it all goes badly."

October 22, 1868

7:30 a.m.

Leslie Warner usually slept as long as he could at home, which generally was as late as his mother would let him get away with. But he wasn't at home today, and he couldn't wait to get out of bed.

The family was staying at the City Hotel, a place Leslie loved.

Now that the Warners lived in Carroll County, the trip to Lexington was a bigger deal than ever, even though it was only about twenty-five miles farther than when they lived near Dover. Now they had to cross the Missouri River.

Making things even more exciting for Leslie was that the fair was under way. Lexington was flooded with interesting people and things to do.

So, Leslie was the first family member to arise and see what Lexington had to offer. He dressed hastily and ran down the steps to the ground floor of the hotel, making it out onto the street in a matter of seconds.

The fairgrounds were quite a ways outside of town, but nothing there interested Leslie all that much, anyway. Not at this hour of day. If he wanted to look at livestock and farm produce, he could have stayed home.

Downtown Lexington, on the other hand, was awash with folks who mesmerized young Leslie.

Dave Poole had moved to Texas, and most of the other former bushwhackers were keeping a much lower profile than they had in late 1866, when Leslie saw Little Archie Clement get killed. As a result, violence and murder weren't as rampant in Lexington as they had been two years earlier.

However, there still were plenty of ornery-looking men, sinful-looking women, and mournful-looking Negroes. Leslie also saw strangers. Lots of strangers.

He could tell they were from out of town because they wore cleaner clothes—though not necessarily new or fancy duds—than Lexington's usual townsfolk, and they wandered around looking and pointing at things.

This is the big city to some people, Leslie thought.

He had no real strategy for his morning. He figured he had an hour or so before the rest of the family would be up, dressed, and looking to get breakfast. Later, he was supposed to take his sister Mary and his cousin Mary to the fairgrounds. That was fine with him. He liked to spend time with pretty girls, and he knew the two Marys would attract a lot of attention at the fair.

For now, Leslie looked up and down North Street, seeking anything that might grab his attention.

The streets were still muddy from all the rain, and they were dotted with puddles.

It was mostly men out at this hour, and nothing much was going on just outside the hotel. So he walked down the sidewalk on North Street toward the river, then turned the corner onto Laurel Street, where many established businesses operated.

Leslie walked past several of them, then stopped to take in the entire panorama, when he felt a tap on his shoulder from behind. The surprise caused him to stumble as he turned to see who it was.

"What's wrong, Leslie, you gotta case of the frights?"

Frank Allison was smiling at him.

Allison had been a neighbor and a regular visitor to the Warners' place when they lived near Dover, but Leslie hadn't seen him since the family moved to Carroll County a few months earlier.

"No, I ain't got no case of the frights. You just startled me is all," Leslie said, relieved. "I wasn't expectin' to run into nobody I knew, but I'm always pleased to see you, Mr. Allison. What brings you to Lexington, the fair or business?"

"A bit of both," said Allison, who as usual impressed Leslie with his pure manliness. He was carrying a rifle on this day.

"We sure do miss havin' you as a neighbor," Leslie said. "We ain't got nobody interestin' livin' nearby us up in Carroll County. It's a mostly boring place to live."

"I reckon your pa is just fine with boring after the events of this summer," Allison said. "That Nutter fella has been a nuisance of the worst sort. He hasn't made himself a threat to you in your new home, has he?"

"Nah, not really," Leslie said. "I guess you seen the pamphlet he wrote. He was up in Carrollton distributin' it last month, but nothin' came of it. We ain't seen him in weeks. Well, that ain't exactly true. I seen him barely a week ago, right here in Lexington. I told him I'd like to kill him myself, if only I had a gun."

"He didn't threaten you, did he?" Allison asked.

"No. Sam is fond of me. He always says I'm his favorite Warner. In fact, he told me he might like to end his hostileness and apologize to our whole family."

"Did you believe him?"

"Not entirely," Leslie said, "though he seemed sincere at the time. That's the thing about Sam. He can be sincere about somethin' one day, then turn around and be sincere about the exact opposite thing the next."

"He's likely to be here at the fair this week, ya know," Allison said. "Your pa knows that, don't he?"

"I reckon he does, but he ain't talked to me much about it. He does have his shotgun with him, though."

"I ain't sure how much good that'll do him if Nutter confronts him with those Colts he's always wearin'. But I guess it's better than nothin'. Does Nutter know your pa is in town?"

"Fact is, I mighta let it slip when I seen Sam here last week that we'd be here for the fair," Leslie said. "I guess maybe I shouldn't have said nothin', but I did."

"Well, maybe I oughtta talk to your pa today," Allison said. "Do you know where I can find him?"

"Sure. He's still in the City Hotel, as far as I know. Probably about time for him to get breakfast, I reckon. We can go over there if you want."

"Let's do just that," Allison said.

Leslie reversed course and walked back toward the hotel with the impressive Mr. Allison at his side.

When they reached the lobby of the City Hotel, Leslie asked the proprietor, John Cather, if Colonel and Mrs. Warner had come downstairs yet. Cather said they had not, so Leslie led Allison up to their room.

He knocked and waited for a reply.

"Who is it?" he heard his mother say.

"Mother, it's me, Leslie, and I got Mr. Allison with me. Is Pa here?"

Less than two seconds later, the door opened, and Colonel Warner filled the doorway, a wide smile on his face.

"By good god, it is you, Allison," he said as he reached to shake hands. "You are one Lafayette County citizen I surely have missed since our relocation to Carroll County. Come on in."

"Colonel, I think it best we find a private spot to talk," Allison said. "Can we go downstairs and get ourselves a table?"

"I was just headed that way," Colonel Warner said. Then he turned toward the room. "Mrs. Warner, is it agreeable to you to meet up with us downstairs after a while?"

"Fine," Georgia Warner said. "Wait for me before eating, though."

Leslie remained quiet and followed the two men through the hall and down the stairs. He planned to tag along and listen to whatever they said, and he figured his pa was less likely to shush him away if he was as nearly invisible as possible.

He was surprised when he heard what his father said as they reached the lobby.

"I'd like for Leslie to be a part of this," Colonel Warner said. "I think he can help us."

"What exactly are you talking about, Colonel?" Allison said.

"Nutter, of course," Colonel Warner said. "I reckon there's a good chance he'll try to kill me today."

9:30 a.m.

As usual, Sam and Lizzie Nutter were alone in the big house. The brother and sister didn't have many visitors anymore.

It had been raining for days, and it seemed the sun hadn't shown itself in weeks. The roads and trails had turned into quagmires. On this day, however, there was no rain, and there were even a few small breaks in the clouds.

"Sam, why are you mopin' around like a lost puppy?" Lizzie asked.

"I reckon I *feel* like a lost puppy," Sam said. "I reckon I ain't got no reason to live no more. Ma and Pa are gone, and Sallie left, and John, and Jo Shelby. And I told you about Leslie, how he says he ain't my friend no more.

"It seems I ain't got a friend in the world. I think even the girls in Lexington don't want nothin' to do with me no more. They still lay with me, but they don't seem to enjoy it."

"You've got me, Sam," Lizzie said. "You've always got me."

"True enough," Sam said. "And I appreciate that. But it ain't enough, Lizzie. You are my sister, after all. I reckon it's all my fault. I guess Colonel Warner turned me sour on folks. For a bit there, I couldn't think of nothin' but killin' that man. It made me lose track of what's really important, I guess. I still want him dead, but it ain't my mission in life no more. I need somethin' else."

"Whadya got in mind, Sam?" Lizzie asked.

"Ya know, I got a daughter I ain't seen in months. Ain't no reason she shouldn't be part of my life. I ain't never felt like a father, but that's what I am, I guess. I don't reckon the Warners can keep me from seein' my own daughter."

"Ah, Sam, you ain't no more a father than I am a mother," Lizzie said. "You ain't thinkin' straight. You don't want nothin' to do with that little girl, whether you realize it or not. That's just askin' for more trouble."

"Maybe you're right, Lizzie, but it's somethin' I wanna do," Sam said. "I've made up my mind. Ya know, the Warners are at the fair. I can approach them in Lexington this very day."

"Sam, that ain't a good idea," Lizzie said. "You've been braggin' to all and sundry that you're gonna kill the man the next time you see him. Now you say you just want to talk? Colonel Warner ain't likely to be in a talkin' mood."

"Well, he's been avoidin' a confrontation with me for weeks," Sam said. "He ain't likely to be lookin' for one now. I told Leslie I wanted to apologize to his folks, that I didn't want no more trouble. If I approach him peaceably, there won't be no trouble."

"If the man sees you wearin' them navy Colts, he won't think you're bein' peaceable," Lizzie pointed out. "And you ain't been to town without them things since you got 'em."

"I'll leave 'em here, then," Sam said. "That's what I'll do. Everybody will know I'm bein' peaceable if I ain't wearin' my Colts. I'll leave 'em right where they are now, on the bureau."

Sam patted the pair of pistols and turned toward the door.

"You are comin' with me to the fair, ain't ya, Lizzie?" he said.

"Yes, Sam," she said. "And I'm takin' my own little pistol, just in case."

"Well, let's be on our way, then. Time's a wastin'. I'll hook up the carriage. Meet me outside the front door in five minutes."

Fifteen minutes later, the brother and sister were on the road to Lexington.

11 a.m.

Leslie looked at the endless pens of horses and cows and pigs and goats as he walked with the two Marys at the fairgrounds, but his mind was in Lexington. He normally would have amused himself by chatting with the girls and looking at the people, but the fair's goings-on did not engage Leslie's interest on this day.

The fairgrounds were bustling with wagons, carriages, and folks both on horseback and on foot, all making great efforts to dodge the puddles and mud. Leslie, Mary, and Mary had left their carriage in a relatively dry spot in a field south of the fairgrounds and were viewing the displays and exhibits.

Meanwhile, many of the young men—and some not so young— were not so subtly keeping tabs on the two pretty girls at Leslie's side. They were drawing more attention than a prize-winning sow.

Leslie figured nobody even saw he was there. All eyes were on the Marys, and that was just fine with him. He had a couple hours to figure out a way to sneak away from the fairgrounds and return to town with as few people as possible noticing his absence. The more invisible he seemed, the better.

Leslie just wished he could get on with the plan right now. The waiting made it hard for him to think about anything else. He wasn't saying much, either.

"Leslie, you're being uncharacteristically mute," his sister Mary said. "If I know you, you've got something on your mind."

"Nothin' I'm gonna share with you," Leslie said. "I suspect you'll know soon enough what's occupyin' my thoughts."

"Oh, now you've piqued my interest," Mary teased. "What could possibly be so captivating that you've virtually ignored all these wonderful animals? You have been positively distracted this morning."

Leslie thought briefly about telling Mary what was going on, but his pa had been very clear: "Say nothing to anybody." Leslie figured Mary didn't really count as anybody, but he decided to keep the plan to himself.

Besides, he most certainly didn't want his cousin Mary to hear anything. She was a gossip of the worst sort and no doubt would blather the details to anyone willing to listen.

"I can't say nothin'," Leslie said to his sister. "It's just somethin' involvin' us menfolk."

Both Marys laughed at that, though Leslie wasn't sure why.

When the laughing subsided, his sister Mary said, "Well, I guess it's just lucky we have a man like you to protect us today."

It turned out, Mary was right.

Not ten minutes later, as Leslie and his pretty companions made their way—three abreast, with his sister Mary in the middle—toward a tent housing jams, jellies, tomatoes, tobacco, pickles, pies, and assorted other baked goods, their path was blocked by two young men. Boys, really, not much older than Leslie.

Both were smiling, and both were a fair number of teeth short of a complete set.

Leslie figured they were brothers because both were small—much shorter than Leslie and not much thicker—and both dressed similar to Kentucky hill folks Leslie had encountered. They wore dungarees that appeared relatively clean but were marked by worn spots and holes, and their boots looked to have the thickness of a kerchief. Both were shirtless and hatless.

"Howdy," one said, his gaze fixed on Mary, Leslie's sister. He stepped directly up to her, forcing her to jump back to keep some distance between them.

The stranger turned slightly to his right, pushing his face toward Cousin Mary.

"Well, then, howdy to you, instead," he said.

Leslie's cousin Mary jumped out of his way, too. That left the girls standing side by side, with Leslie between them and the young stranger.

"Who are you?" he said to Leslie, who was overcome by the odor emanating from the man's body and, worse still, his mouth.

"My name's Leslie Warner, and these here are my sister and my cousin," Leslie said. "It's been a pleasure meetin' you, but we'd like to walk past you, if you don't mind."

Although Leslie didn't feel threatened by the two young men, they definitely made him uncomfortable. He wanted to get far away from them, but he wasn't about to leave the Marys to fend for themselves.

He tried to keep himself positioned between the strangers and the girls.

"We're just tryin' to be neighborly," the stranger said. "My brother don't talk much, but he ain't nobody to be scared of. Me neither. It's just that we ain't never seen such pretty girls before. Can we kiss ya?"

He was looking at Cousin Mary when he said it, but Sister Mary was the one who'd finally had enough.

"You boys aren't going to kiss anybody," she said. "Now if you don't mind, we'll be on our way."

With that, she grasped her cousin's right hand with her left hand and forged ahead, nudging Leslie from behind. The three proceeded forward, moving as a unit.

The two strangers put up no resistance, each turning to create a path for Leslie and the Marys to pass.

"Nice meetin' ya," Leslie said.

After the three were several yards past the prurient strangers, Leslie's sister Mary stopped, and the other two followed suit.

"Leslie, you did very well back there," she said. "Maybe you are getting to be a man, after all."

"Oh, that weren't nothin'," Leslie said.

He and the Marys spent some fifteen minutes in the food-and-produce tent before deciding to check out the stables. As proud Kentuckians, Leslie and Mary considered themselves experts on horses, and they were eager to inspect the stock and share their knowledge with Cousin Mary, who had grown up in Missouri.

Of course, all three wanted to see the young colts more than anything else.

"They are so cute when they're little," Cousin Mary said. "They just make a person smile."

Leslie and the Marys were standing in front of a stall containing a particularly rambunctious filly, who likely had only recently been weaned away from her mother. She was an elegant chestnut, with three white socks, a narrow blaze on her forehead and a matching stripe on her nose.

"She's a beauty," Leslie said. "Likely bred in Kentucky."

He turned to his left to visit the neighboring stall, where he saw a black man brushing a trembling colt. Leslie recognized the man immediately.

"John, what the devil are you doin' here?" Leslie asked. "I know Sam don't have no horses this fine."

John turned slowly and smiled.

"Why, Mr. Leslie, if you ain't a sight for sore eyes. You musta grown a half foot since I last seen ya," John said.

"It ain't been all that long, John," Leslie said. "Less than a year, I reckon. Since before the divorce and all. Are you still workin' for Sam?"

"No, Mr. Leslie, I ain't. Left him about a month back and found myself a new job. I just couldn't abide his nastiness no longer. He turned mighty sour after your sister left him and took the young'un.

"I expected he mighta killed your pa or elsewise got hisself killed by now. I ain't heard that either occurrence has happened yet. But that was the fate he seemed to be headed toward, and I didn't want no part of it."

"I reckon you was right," Leslie said. "But last time I seen Sam, he claimed he was a changed man. Said he didn't want no more nastiness with my family. I didn't believe him for a minute, though. I think . . ."

"We best be moving on, Leslie," he heard his sister Mary say.

Leslie had pretty much forgotten about the Marys, who were standing silently at his side. Both had encountered John in his role as Sam's worker, but neither had ever spoken to him.

"You girls go on," Leslie said. "I'll catch up with you later."

Leslie wanted to talk further with John. Also, he realized this might be his best chance to separate himself from the Marys, which was part of the plan his father had devised.

He was to sneak back into town, while drawing as little attention as possible to himself. Then he was to track down Sam, if he was in Lexington, and inform his father of his whereabouts and intentions.

Colonel Warner had said he "would take care of it from there." He'd also told Frank Allison he wanted him to remain nearby, in case Sam brought some of his ruffian friends with him.

Leslie figured his father planned to confront Sam, likely to try to talk some sense into him. But he wasn't sure. He knew for certain he didn't want Sam to kill his father or, for that matter, his father to kill Sam. He just wanted to do whatever he could to help his father handle the situation.

The Marys continued down the aisle between horse stalls, chatting but not looking back. Leslie returned his attention to John.

"John, do you think Sam is still aimin' to kill my pa?" he asked.

"I can't say for sure," John said. "A year ago, I'd a said there weren't no possibility of Mr. Sam wantin' to kill nobody. But a month ago, he was a different Mr. Sam. So full of hate, 'specially for your pa. I just ain't for sure."

"Well, I ain't neither, but he ain't gonna get the chance, if I can help it," Leslie said.

"Whadya mean by that?" John asked.

"I can't tell ya that. It's a secret. And the fact is, I need to be on my way into town to take care of my end of it. So I'll bid you farewell now."

"You take care, Mr. Leslie," John said. "And keep Mr. Sam out of trouble, if you can."

2 p.m.

"I've got some business to take care of before we head out to the fairgrounds," Sam said to Lizzie, as he stopped the carriage on North Street.

Sam felt odd. He wasn't wearing his pistols, and he wasn't drunk. He wasn't even drinking.

"Whadya expect me to do while you're gone?" Lizzie asked.

"Whatever you want. I won't be long."

"Please don't be. I'd like to get to the fair before everything shuts down."

Sam walked across the muddy street toward Mitchell's Bank, where he needed to take care of his business. But he couldn't resist a detour to the City Hotel, where he heard laughing and loud voices coming from the saloon.

When he walked inside, all the tables were occupied, so he found a spot at the bar and slid between two men he didn't know.

He ordered a whiskey and gulped it down. Then he ordered a second whiskey.

Before he could raise his glass, he felt a hand on his shoulder and heard a familiar voice.

"Sam, are you buyin' today?" It was George Mountjoy, one of his favorite drinking buddies.

"Not for you, I ain't," Sam said. "I ain't got time for more than a drink or two. Lizzie's waitin' for me outside."

"That never stopped you before," Mountjoy said, winking.

"Yeah, well, we're headin' out to the fairgrounds directly," Sam said.

Suddenly, Mountjoy stepped back to arm's length and inspected Sam from head to toe and back up again.

"Oh, my god, I thought somethin' was off with you," he said. "Sam, you ain't wearin' your trusty navy Colts. Did you leave 'em in the buggy for some reason?"

"Nah, I left 'em at home," Sam said. "I don't need 'em today."

"How do you know that? What if you run into trouble? Or into Colonel Warner?"

"I ain't got no interest in findin' trouble today. As for Colonel William Warner, well, I guess you could say I ain't sure I still have foul intentions toward him. I think I've put that nastiness behind me."

"You say that now, Sam, but I know you," Mountjoy said. "You might feel different tomorrow. Or after another drink."

"Maybe," Sam said. "But for now, I'm just peaceable Sam Nutter. I plan on makin' amends with the Warners this very day at the fair. Ya know, I've got a daughter who lives with them Warners, and she carries my name. I think I might want to be a part of her life."

"That don't sound like you at all, Sam. But if that's what you wanna do, I guess it's better than spendin' all your energy tryin' to kill the man. Lot less likely to get you killed, too."

2:45 p.m.

Leslie approached Lexington from behind.

Rather than driving the carriage down North Street, he entered town on Franklin and circled down Laurel, to the livery operated by Benjamin Fish.

The Warners were regular customers of Fish's, and Leslie was usually responsible for dropping off and picking up the family's carriage or buckboard, so he was familiar with the crusty old man.

"How goes it there, young Leslie?" the livery operator greeted him.

Leslie was not particularly fond of Fish, who more than once had tried to overcharge him. Fish said on each occasion that he was bad at math, but Leslie wasn't so sure.

"I'll likely be leavin' the rig for only a short while," Leslie said. "I just want to keep it out of sight."

"And why is that?" Fish asked.

Leslie wasn't about to spill the beans.

"Because I don't want nobody to see it," he said.

"Well, I figured that," Fish said. "Why don't you want nobody to see it?"

"That ain't none of your business. Can you do it or not?"

"I reckon I might be able to . . . if there's somethin' extra in it for me."

"I'll pay you your usual rate," Leslie said. "And if that ain't good enough, I'll go elsewheres."

"Ain't no need for that," Fish said. "I'm a businessman, ya know. I'm just tryin' to take care of business."

"Your business ain't no concern to me. Speakin' of which, have you seen Sam Nutter today?"

"Well, here again you're askin' me to go above and beyond my duty. What is that information worth to ya?"

"It's worth exactly the same as you keepin' my rig out of sight. Nothin'. But if you don't want our business no more, that's fine with me. I reckon Pa can take his buckboard elsewheres from now on."

"Ah, ain't no reason to get belligerent," Fish said. "I was just havin' a little fun with ya."

"I ain't in the mood for no fun," Leslie said. "Have you seen Sam or not?"

"Well, it just so happens I *have* seen Sam Nutter. Him and his sister come to town no more than an hour ago."

"Do you know their whereabouts now?"

"You know as well as I do that Sam Nutter is most likely in a saloon," Fish said. "Beyond that, I ain't got a clue. Maybe you oughtta just go look for him on your own."

"I'll do just that," Leslie said.

He left the livery by its back door and slipped out through an alleyway. Stopping in a shadow, he peered out onto the bustle of Laurel Street. Seeing no familiar faces, Leslie proceeded down the sidewalk toward North Street, walking briskly.

Again, he stayed in the shadows, keeping one eye locked on the street. It was filled with horses, carriages, and people. He surveyed one side of the street, then the other, then back to the first, neck craning.

Finally, near the bank, he noticed a carriage with Lizzie Nutter sitting in it. No sign of Sam, though.

At this point, Leslie had a decision to make. He could keep an eye on the carriage, figuring Sam would return to it sooner or later. He could approach the carriage and ask Lizzie where Sam was. Or, he could avoid the carriage and Lizzie altogether and keep looking for Sam on his own.

Leslie ruled out the first option straightaway, because he had no desire to stand around and do nothing for who knew how long.

As for the second option, he always enjoyed talking to Lizzie, and he hadn't had a chance to do so for several months. But he figured it likely wasn't a good idea to let Lizzie know he was looking for Sam; she would want to know why, and he wouldn't be able to tell her. Then she likely would get suspicious, and in that case who knew what she might do? Besides, Leslie no longer trusted Lizzie, given that she probably had been a participant in many of Sam's summer shenanigans.

So avoid the carriage it was.

Leslie figured North Street was busy enough that he could move about largely unnoticed, especially with so many out-of-towners on hand for the fair. He decided to simply walk about as he always did and not worry about keeping in the shadows. He wasn't going to find Sam by standing in alleyways and skulking around corners, after all.

Leslie knew the likeliest place for Sam was the City Hotel saloon, so he headed in that direction. As he dodged puddles in the street, he got to thinking. He couldn't just walk into the saloon to see whether Sam was there. He was fourteen, after all, and, tall as he was, he couldn't pass for a typical customer.

When he got to the sidewalk, he turned away from the City Hotel instead of toward it. He needed to ponder some more.

He slipped into Pigott's bookstore, deciding it would be a good place to plan his next move. The little shop was his favorite haunt in Lexington. He could pick up just about any book or magazine and learn something new.

Leslie's favorites were the weekly and monthly publications that came from the East Coast. They made him think people there were smarter than these Missouri folks, or even Kentuckians.

Leslie knelt to get a better view, eyeballing a few publications before picking up an issue of the *Galaxy*. It had been printed earlier that year, in February, but Leslie hadn't seen it yet. He thumbed through the pages, waiting for something to grab his attention.

MEMORANDA
General Washington's Negro Body-Servant
A BIOGRAPHICAL SKETCH.

That sounded interesting. And it was by a writer Leslie had heard of, although he never had read anything by him.

Mark Twain.

He started reading: "The stirring part of this celebrated colored man's life properly began with his death—that is to say, the notable features of his biography begin with the first time he died."

Leslie laughed out loud. He wondered whether this man had actually died more than once.

He continued reading for several minutes, so involved in the story that everything else floated out of his brain. No thoughts of his father or Sam, or anything.

But then . . .

"Leslie Warner, what are you doing here?" he heard.

Startled, Leslie dropped the magazine, jumped to his feet, and turned toward the voice.

It was his mother.

"You're supposed to be at the fair with your sister and your cousin," she said sternly.

Leslie was so startled and dismayed he got dizzy, and his heart began racing. Georgia Warner was the last person he expected to see. Or wanted to see.

"Uh, I am at the fair," he said. "I mean, I was at the fair. I just had to come pick up something."

"What in this bookstore could you possibly need so desperately that you made a special trip into town to get it?" his mother asked.

"Well, you see, Mary wanted me . . ."

"Stop right there, Leslie Warner," she said, fixing him with an iron glare. "I know what you're up to. Your father told me everything that is going on. And I must say, it is about time he did something about Sam Nutter, though I wish he hadn't gotten you involved.

"Now, I'll repeat my initial question. What are you doing here?"

"Well, if Pa already told you most of it . . . I'm almost certain Sam is in the City Hotel saloon, but I ain't for sure. I can't go in there to find out—I know you wouldn't like that—so I come in here to figure out what to do next. Then, I saw this magazine with this article, and I started readin' it," Leslie said.

"Fine," Georgia Warner said. "Now take a breath. You still have a job to do. Your father is waiting for word on whether Sam is in town. He's been pacing in that hotel room all day, with that shotgun folded over his arm."

"You mean, he's upstairs at the City Hotel while Sam likely is downstairs in the saloon?" Leslie asked. "That ain't a good predicament."

"No, I don't suppose it is. Perhaps our best plan of action now is to inform your father of the situation and let him decide what to do."

"I'll go to the room, if ya want," Leslie said.

"Fine, but go in the back way, and make sure Sam doesn't see you," Georgia Warner said. "And, Leslie, be as careful as possible. I would never forgive myself if I allowed you to be a part of this and you were injured . . . or worse. You are my only surviving son, and I love you dearly."

She reached out and pulled Leslie against her body in an awkward embrace, briefly resting her head on his shoulder.

Georgia Warner then backed away and walked briskly toward the door and out to the sidewalk, where she turned left, away from the City Hotel.

Leslie, dazed by the entire encounter with his mother, followed her to the door. But he turned right.

3:25 p.m.

Sam stumbled slightly as he stepped down from the sidewalk outside the saloon. When he regained his balance, he looked down North Street to where he had left Lizzie and the carriage.

He saw the carriage, but Lizzie wasn't in it.

Sam wasn't surprised; he'd been in the saloon far more than the few minutes he'd told his sister to expect. But he also knew that Lizzie knew him well enough to understand that a few minutes likely would lead to quite a few minutes more.

She would be in one of the shops down the street, no doubt.

He still had business in Mitchell's Bank, so he turned in that direction. To his surprise, he saw Lizzie sauntering toward him, a package tucked tightly under her left arm.

"It's about time," she said. "I gave up waitin' on ya, musta been twenty-five minutes ago. Now, let's get out to the fairgrounds."

"Still gotta go to the bank," Sam said. "Won't be but a few minutes."

"Sounds familiar. Ya know, it ain't safe for a lady to be alone in these streets, 'specially not with all the strangers in town."

"Thank goodness you ain't no lady," Sam said, laughing.

Lizzie laughed, too.

"Well, I got my little pistol, just in case."

"I don't suspect you'll need that," Sam said. "I'm the one who oughtta be armed. I ain't so sure it was altogether smart to leave my Colts at home. I feel kinda naked without 'em."

"You want to take my pistol?" Lizzie asked. "Just in case, I mean."

"Nah," Sam said. "It wouldn't do no good. That thing couldn't kill a one-eyed, three-legged squirrel. I'll meet you back here at the carriage after I'm done in the bank."

3:40 p.m.

Leslie still hadn't seen Sam with his own eyes, but he didn't hesitate when his father asked.

"Yes, Sam's in town," he said. "I ain't sure where, though. I thought maybe he was in the saloon, but I can't say for certain. I looked all over town."

Colonel William A. Warner was uneasy, just as his wife had said, pacing in the hotel room. His shotgun was leaning against the bed.

"You've done your job, Leslie, and I'm thankful," Colonel Warner said. "Now you should return to the fairgrounds. I don't want you involved any further."

"Yes, Pa, if you say so," Leslie said. "What are you gonna do?"

"Well, I plan to take the offensive. I don't want Sam to get the drop on me. Not in the saloon; it must be on the street. I need a clean shot, and I don't want to hit any innocents with buckshot."

"You mean you're gonna shoot Sam, unprovoked? You ain't plannin' on confrontin' him? You're just gonna shoot him?"

"Yes. I would stand no chance in a gunfight. Are you all right with that?"

"I . . . guess. If that's how it's gotta be. How do you plan on meetin' up with Sam in the street?" Leslie asked.

"I'll just have to wait for him," Colonel Warner said, pacing faster. "I'll position myself in a place where I can see him leaving the saloon. I'll need to be close enough that I can be accurate with my shotgun. That will be a challenge, because if he sees me before I'm close enough to fire, he's liable to shoot me dead. Is Sam any good with those pistols?"

"I ain't never seen him shoot," Leslie said. "He likes to say he's good with 'em, but you know Sam. He likes to say a lot of things. I reckon he don't have to be too good if you can't get close enough to hit him with the shotgun. Even then, you'll have just your two loads, and he'll have his twelve."

"Yes, Leslie, I know the math," Colonel Warner said. "And I know what I'm doing is probably foolhardy. But a man must protect his family. At some point, he must take a stand. I've reached that point with Sam Nutter. I can't allow him to threaten your mother and your sisters any further.

"I realize chances are good that Sam will shoot me," he continued soberly, "maybe even kill me. I've been shot before, and I survived. I can survive again. If I don't, well, I'll have died protecting my family. That's all I can do. That's what I must do.

"If death turns out to be my fate, Sam will have won. At that point, I can only hope Sam will have sated his anger and will do no more harm to the family. You'll be the man of the house, Leslie, and I expect you to do what you must to protect your mother and sisters. I hope you won't be bent on vengeance and risk getting yourself killed as well. The women would then be on their own, and we can't have that. We simply can't. You will have to make peace with Sam, whatever it takes."

"Ah, Pa, you ain't gonna get killed," Leslie said.

"How can you be sure of that?" Colonel Warner asked.

"I just know, that's all."

"Needless to say, I hope you're right," Colonel Warner said through a sigh. "In any case, I want you to go back to the fairgrounds now. I'll be going out the back way from the hotel, so I don't risk running into Sam downstairs. I hope to see you this evening."

3:50 p.m.

Sam finished his business in Mitchell's Bank and headed toward the door. He was eager to get to the fairgrounds, where he could relax, drink, and visit.

He also hoped he might encounter the Warners there. Sam hadn't seen any of them in town, so he figured they were at the fairgrounds, and he very much wanted to let them know he no longer harbored hostile feelings toward them. Or, at least tell them he wasn't planning on acting on those feelings any further.

Sam reflexively fingered his hips, where he had grown accustomed to feeling his pistols, before he reached the door. He smiled, remembering he had left them at home, and proceeded outside.

3:55 p.m.

No way Leslie was going back to the fairgrounds. At least not yet.

He reckoned his pa knew as much, so Leslie figured he wasn't really disobeying him. Still, he didn't want his father to see him, so he resolved to stay out of sight as best he could.

He wanted to see whatever was going to happen, and the street in front of the City Hotel seemed the most likely venue. Colonel Warner almost certainly would be concealed somewhere close by the saloon, waiting for Sam to come out.

Leslie decided to position himself across the street, among a clump of trees that stood on the north side of the courthouse. Since that spot was more or less on the way from the hotel to old man Fish's stable, where he had left the carriage, he wouldn't have to be sneaky getting there.

It took Leslie about two minutes to reach the trees, duck behind one of them, and stake out his position.

He peered back across North Street. He didn't see his father, but he did see another interested party.

Frank Allison. He was in an alley, leaning against a building with rifle in hand.

Leslie was glad to see Allison was at the ready. If Sam had some of his ruffian friends with him, his father wouldn't stand a chance by himself. And if Sam fired his pistols before his father could fire his shotgun, well, maybe Allison could either rescue or avenge Colonel Warner.

Continuing to scan the street, Leslie noticed Sam's carriage now was parked in front of the bank, with Lizzie still sitting in it. He knew Sam had to be nearby.

He was right.

Sam emerged from the bank. He hadn't been in the saloon, after all.

Leslie was surprised by that. But he had an even bigger shock.

Sam wasn't wearing his pistols.

Leslie felt sick to his stomach. This wasn't part of the plan. Nobody even considered the possibility that Sam wouldn't have his pistols.

His father would be committing cold-blooded murder if he shot an unarmed man. Of course, Leslie figured his father wouldn't purposely shoot an unarmed man. Not even Sam.

But, Leslie thought, his father might not see that Sam was unarmed until it was too late.

On the other hand, Leslie thought, at least his father wouldn't die this day.

"Look out," someone hollered. "Get back!"

Before Leslie could figure out who was yelling, he heard a loud boom and recognized immediately it was a shotgun blast. He saw Sam fall to the ground, then saw his father about forty feet away, near the door to Pigott's bookstore, smoke coiling from the left-hand barrel of his shotgun.

Leslie froze.

Most everybody else on the street started running. Some toward Sam, a few toward Colonel Warner, most away from the scene.

The first person to reach his father was the deputy sheriff, Phares Hammond. He grabbed the shotgun from Colonel Warner.

Townsfolk surrounded Sam, a couple of them inspecting him for signs of life. There was a collective shaking of heads.

Lizzie Nutter jumped from the carriage, ran to her brother, and knelt beside him. She howled, unleashing a sound unlike any Leslie had ever heard. The mournful wail filled the town as it echoed off the buildings for nearly a minute.

Finally, Leslie took several steps away from his spot in the trees and toward the scene of the shooting. He didn't know what he was going to do or say, but he figured he had to do or say something.

Before he reached the street, he felt someone holding him back by his right shoulder.

"Leslie, you best be gettin' outta here," a voice said. It was Frank Allison.

"Nothin' good can come from you getting' involved with this situation now," he continued. "You ain't supposed to be here, and you can still say you wasn't here if you get out of town now. You go back to the fairgrounds, you hear?"

"What's gonna happen to Pa?" Leslie asked.

"I don't rightly know, but I presume the deputy will take him to the jail," Allison said. "He shot a man, after all. Evidently killed him. And it looks like Sam Nutter was unarmed. That's a problem. Did you know he was unarmed?"

"Not until he walked out of the bank," Leslie said. "I woulda told Pa if I knowd. I reckon Pa didn't see that Sam wasn't wearin' his pistols until it was too late."

"It don't matter now," Allison said. "The deed is done."

Leslie looked back down the street. He saw that Sam's body had been moved to the sidewalk, while Lizzie, now holding a small pistol, stood beside her brother's corpse, accepting comfort from a man Leslie didn't recognize.

He saw the deputy leading his father into the bookstore. The crowd that had gathered was beginning to disperse.

"I guess I'll do as you say," Leslie said.

He turned and, walking quickly with his eyes down, headed toward the livery stable.

The Aftermath

THE MOB SPIRIT.

Killing of S.W. Nutter—

Samuel W. Nutter, of this county, was shot and killed by Col. Wm. A. Warner, in the streets of this city, on Thursday afternoon last. The weapon used was a gun, loaded with buckshot, and the fatal shot was fired as Mr. Nutter was getting into his buggy to go home. Col. Warner is in jail, and we refrain from giving any particulars, further than to remark that the matter grew out of family trouble. There was nothing of politics about it, both being democrats.

—Weekly Caucasian, October 24, 1868

That was the extent of the *Caucasian's* reporting after the incident, although it also printed the verdict of a coroner's jury that concluded: "Samuel W. Nutter came to his death by a gun shot wound, fired by William A. Warner, on the 22nd day of October in the city of Lexington."

Just another killing in Lexington, or so it seemed to the *Caucasian.*

It was hardly that. The story of the former Union colonel murdering his son-in-law was picked up and printed by several publications in the state as well as by at least one out-of-state publication—the *New York Times.* The *Times* actually reprinted the St. Joseph *Daily Morning Herald's* version of events, which included a few more details than the *Caucasian's.*

But only the *Missouri Valley Register of Lexington* captured the full drama . . . and then some.

TERRIBLE TRAGEDY.

A Father-in-law shoots his son-in-law in the street.

On last Thursday our city was startled by a terrible tragedy which was enacted in our streets. Col. Wm. A. Warner, formerly a Colonel of the 18th Kentucky U.S. Vols., shot and killed Samuel W. Nutter.

Some two years ago Nutter married the daughter of Warner. From some cause unknown to us, the match proved to be an unhappy one.

A few months ago Mrs. Nutter returned to her father's house near Dover, and began a suit for divorce. In her bill she charged her husband with theft, incest, and other crimes. Both parties being wealthy, and of unquestionable standing in society, the case caused considerable gossip. Mr. Nutter published a pamphlet concerning the divorce case, in which he charged Col. Warner with murder, theft, arson, &c., &c., and was nearly as severe towards Mrs. Warner.

On Thursday last Col. Warner and Mr. Nutter were both in attendance at the fair. In the evening both came into the city. Mr. Nutter had his sister in the buggy with him. He drove to Pigott's book store, and got out for a moment, leaving his sister in the buggy. Col. Warner seeing him go in, passed down on the sidewalk to within about forty feet of the door, carrying a double barreled shot gun under his arm. When within the distance above named, Nutter stepped out of the store on his way to the buggy. Warner raised his gun and fired at him filling his breast with buckshot and killing him instantly. His sister, frantic with grief and terror, and besmeared with her brother's blood, was an object of universal sympathy.

Deputy Sheriff Hammonds saw Warner approaching, and knowing of the difficulty, suspected his object, and ran after him, but unfortunately was but a second or two too late to prevent the fatal shot. He immediately arrested Col. Warner and confined him in jail. The Colonel made no effort to escape, but expressed his willingness to abide by the law.

We do not presume to judge this matter. Let him have a speedy and impartial trial by a jury of his peers, and we will be satisfied with the result. Both the deceased and the prisoner have many warm friends. Let them join in preventing injustice.

—Missouri Valley Register, October 29, 1868

In Western movies, the bad guy kills somebody, goes on trial a couple days later, and gets his neck stretched the week after that. Unless, of course, his gang breaks him out of jail first.

This wasn't a Western movie.

The first thing to remember are the particulars of Missouri's circuit court system. It was called that for a reason. The judge was responsible for a large geographic area, which he (never a she in those days) covered by traveling a regular circuit. During sessions lasting a week or so, he heard all the cases accumulated over the previous months.

Lafayette County was part of Missouri's Sixth Judicial Circuit, which also included Jackson, Cass, Johnson, Pettis, and Henry counties. Chan Townsley was the new circuit judge, having been elected November 3, 1868.

On November 28, 1868, William A. Warner got his first day in court for killing Samuel Nutter. During that session, the court handled four murder cases. Two defendants were tried and acquitted, and two—including Warner—saw their cases continued.

It begins to look like human life is pretty cheap in Lafayette county. The two cases tried were vigorously prosecuted, why they were released we are unable to say.
                                    —*Missouri Valley Register*, December 3, 1868

Despite the circumstances and the many eyewitnesses, Warner pleaded not guilty. He was ordered to return to jail, where he evidently remained for more than a year.

***

After the killing, men of all ranks lined up to support Warner. Their names appeared in and at the bottom of letters published in the two Lexington newspapers in December 1868.

The testimonies on behalf of Warner appeared in space that normally was used for paid legal advertisements.

The letters provide the best record of what Sam Nutter wrote in his notorious pamphlet, which he published shortly before he was killed.

They included several denials of claims that Warner commanded a Negro regiment during the Civil War—evidently, most folks in Kentucky and Missouri considered that a bad thing—and that he had mistreated Confederate prisoners.

Moreover, they included two passages from the pamphlet.

Captain W. B. Riggs, Warner's son-in-law, and Mary Mitchell, Warner's sister-in-law, each wrote a letter supporting Warner and denying charges in the pamphlet. Both included passages from the pamphlet as part of their denials.

So, here are the actual words of Sam Nutter:

When I was first married, I went upon a tour to Kentucky, where I had a chance of knowing how Warner stood in the eyes of the community there, and it did not take me long to find out that he was regarded by almost every one as a great scoundrel, even by his own relatives; and Capt. Benjamin Riggs—Warner's son-in-law—"told my fortune" to a letter. It was about this way: Said he, "Nutter, if you don't get away from old Warner and his wife they will keep up a perfect hell in your family all the time, and render you miserable with your wife, as they have tried to cause me to be with mine; and as sure as God they will bring about a separation and divorce if you allow them to come about you or hold intercourse with your wife. Mrs. Warner," he said "is no better than he is. She is a perfect Jezebel, and can make more mischief in a neighborhood than any woman I ever saw; but let her get a spite at you once, and she'll follow you to the devil in her vindictiveness. I have thought that was her particular mission on earth to make people miserable in her atmosphere, wherever she went, and Warner cannot live in Kentucky or anywhere else long at a time. Honest men cannot and will not tolerate him; and now let me tell you," he said, "and you remember it; you will not live with your wife two years unless you close your doors against Warner and the shrew known as his wife."

. . . It may not here be out of place to relate a circumstance concerning a defenceless widow lady, who is the sister-in-law of Warner, and whom, on account of some spite he had against her, caused her arrest and incarceration on the charge that she was a rebel. The circumstance occurred during the war; and is very characteristic of Warner, when he is placed in a position where he can serve a relative, after his peculiar manner. This lady, Mrs. Mary Mitchell, daughter of General Combs, left Lexington on the cars bound for Cincinnati, to make some purchases; and this "bostis humani generis"—Warner—telegraphed to the Provost Marshal, in Cincinnati, to have her arrested and thrown in jail, which was done.

When General Combs "found it out," he went to Cincinnati, and procured her release at once.

Writing of Nutter's version of the facts, Captain Riggs said in a published letter, ". . . no such conversation EVER TOOK PLACE BETWEEN US, and how he could have the audacity to have uttered SUCH INFAMOUS FALSEHOODS is beyond my comprehension."

He went on to call Nutter "a vile calumniator and liar" who "richly deserved hanging for his villainous conduct towards his wife and her family."

And he provided this anecdote about Nutter:

I was satisfied as to his character in a few hours after I met him in Kentucky; he was under the influence of liquor from the time he arrived until he left; and the friends of his wife felt greatly distressed for her. He even went so far as to attempt to swindle a poor drayman out of the poor pittance of one dollar, for hauling his baggage from the hotel to the railroad depot, saying he would dodge him by going into the ladies' car, but was prevented by the brakesman because he was smoking.

Finally, Riggs addressed what he said were Nutter's claims that Warner had been forced to move from Kentucky because he was unpopular.

. . . I will merely state that Colonel Warner, just before leaving the state, received UNANIMOUS VOTE of the Pendleton county delegation (democratic) at Covington and Falmouth, for STATE SENATOR. He would hardly have had such a compliment from the citizens of his own county, if he was the man Nutter describes him to be. I can further state that Colonel Warner never had command of a negro soldier, or negro troops, and that he always opposed their being put in the service, except as servants and teamsters.

Mary Mitchell's printed letter was addressed to Warner. At one point, she described Nutter as a "miserable man."

I am very sorry that Mr. Nutter should have made use of my name in any way in his UNTRUTHFUL and scurrilous pamphlet.

. . . I would rather been put in FORTY PRISONS than that he should have presumed to have noticed my arrest as he has done.

In the first place, the FACTS which he pretends to give are FALSE. I was not thrown into jail, as Nutter asserts, but was treated by the Chief of Police and the Mayor of Cincinnati with the utmost kindness, and after being detained one day, was allowed to leave for Baltimore on the evening train.

My father did not find it necessary to go to Cincinnati, as I was released even before he knew I was arrested.

. . . My arrest was not on account of any SPITE, as is represented by Nutter. What he says of me is so UTTERLY FALSE, I am quite certain everything he says is equally without foundation.

The words of Captain Riggs and Mary Mitchell were near the bottom of the letters printed in the *Missouri Valley Register*. Warner himself wrote a letter that appeared above them. It is interesting to note that he makes no mention of killing Sam Nutter, instead focusing on denials of Nutter's accusations.

TO THE PUBLIC
Lexington, Mo., Dec. 22, 1868
M. L. DeMotte, Editor, Register

Dear Sir:—I have been urged by my friends to publish a few of the letters and certificates I have in my possession that go to disprove charges recently published against my family and myself.

I do it reluctantly, but as there are some persons who are disposed to believe the infamous charges true, I yield to the judgment of my friends. You will find enclosed the certificate of my son-in-law, Captain W. B. Riggs, which explains itself, you will also find one from Mrs. Mary Mitchell and copy of a letter I received from General Jno. W. Finnell, who was Adjutant General of Kentucky during the war, and Attorney General under Governor Crittenden.

I would say also, that I now have in my possession certificates from the best citizens of this or any other county DISPROVING in the most unqualified terms EVERY CHARGE made against my family or self, in the pamphlet published as above stated under the title of "Justice, Mercy and Truth vs. Fraud, Theft and Intrigue, in five letters, by Saml. W. Nutter."

Yours Respectfully,

Wm. A. Warner

—Missouri Valley Register, December 24, 1868

***

A letter from General Joseph O. "Jo" Shelby followed Warner's.

Shelby had been one of the richest men in Missouri in the 1850s, when he ran a large hemp operation and owned several steamboats after relocating from Kentucky to Lafayette County.

He also had been one of the leaders of the pro-slavery Missourians who fought and killed free-state Kansans during the 1850s Border War over the Kansas Territory's entry into the Union under the Kansas-Nebraska Act.

During the Civil War, he recruited hundreds of men to the Confederate cause, rose from the rank of captain to general, and became famous for leading the so-called Iron Brigade on a 1,500-mile raid through Missouri.

When the war officially ended, Shelby refused to surrender and led hundreds of his men into Mexico, where they offered their services to Emperor Maximilian. He returned to Missouri when Maximilian was overthrown.

All of this made Jo Shelby a Confederate hero and the most famous man in Lafayette County, where he returned in June 1867. He would later become known as a good friend of Frank and Jesse James, even testifying (in a drunken stupor, it was reported) at Frank's 1883 murder trial in Gallatin.

But the Civil War also had left Shelby broke.

He not only had spent his own money to recruit and outfit soldiers for the Confederacy but had also abandoned his Lafayette County estate after Yankee arsonists burned the home and outbuildings.

By the time he returned to Missouri in 1867, he was starting over. In fact, a legal advertisement declared his bankruptcy in the *Missouri Valley Register* of Lexington in November 1868, just days after William A. Warner shot and killed Sam Nutter.

So why was Shelby writing a letter to show his support of Warner, a former Union colonel?

Like Warner, Shelby was born and spent most of his youth in Lexington, Kentucky, although it is unclear how long the two men lived there at the same time. Shelby, who was thirteen years younger, moved to Lafayette County, Missouri, when he was twenty-one. By then, Warner was working on his second marriage and living in Pendleton County, Kentucky.

Both men were from wealthy families. Both lived in the Dover area of Lafayette County in 1868. But they must have had a relationship before that.

In 1866, when William A. Warner and his wife, Georgia, had their final child shortly after moving to Missouri, they named the girl "Joe. Shelby Warner," according to the 1880 census.

In his letter of support, Shelby said the other published missives vindicated Warner "from those charges which made him commander of a negro regiment during the war, and wantonly cruel to Confederate prisoners."

Shelby went on to say he was "interested in the matter only so far as I desire to see the law vindicated, and a trial by jury awarded to all, and as a simple matter of justice to Col. Warner, whom I have known from my youth up, and who, though opposed to me during the war, never sullied the uniform of a soldier by the harshness of a politician."

***

Another published letter was from J. G. Chinn, who was the mayor of Lexington, Kentucky, but had been the mayor of Lexington, Missouri, some twenty years earlier. Chinn's letter was addressed to Warner:

"I feel it my duty unsolicited by you, to state that I knew you well as Colonel of a Federal regiment; and believe the community were favorably impressed with your gentlemanly bearing as an officer; and I never did hear of your commanding a negro regiment, or treating any Confederate soldiers or citizens in an improper manner; and I believe all such representations as the above without the least foundation."

Similar testimony came in a letter from E. Kirby Smith, who had been a Confederate general. In fact, he had led the victorious Rebel troops against Warner's Union soldiers at the Battle of Richmond.

Smith said, in part:

. . . It gives me great pleasure to testify to the gallant behavior of Col. W. A. Warner at the battle of Richmond, Kentucky, when he was severely wounded and taken prisoner. He commanded a REGIMENT OF KENTUCKIANS. There were NO NEGRO troops opposed to us at the battle of Richmond. Colonel Warner's treatment to our people was in acceptance with his DUTY AS A FEDERAL OFFICER AND A GENTLEMAN.

Two other letters came from Pendleton County and Harrison County, both in Kentucky, and each bore the names of many of its area's leading citizens.

The letter from Pendleton County said it was signed by forty-two men— twenty-seven who had been Confederates and fifteen who had been Unionists.

It said Warner ". . . was well known in this part of the State as a brave and gallant soldier, and good citizen." Among the men whose names appeared below the letter from Harrison County were two judges, two lawyers, a sheriff, a state senator, and Lucius Desha, the former general whom Warner's men had arrested during the Civil War.

It read in part:

It has been represented to us that Col. Wm. A. Warner is charged with having commanded a negro Regiment during the late war of rebellion, and that he was intolerant and oppressive to non-combatants.

As an act of justice to Col. Warner, we state that the reports above are unfounded and untrue; he commanded the 18th Kentucky Vol. Infantry Regiment, which was composed of white soldiers, and his deportment was that of a SOLDIER AND A GENTLEMAN. WE STATE WHAT WE KNOW.

★★★

Sam Nutter was dead, but he didn't stop causing problems for his widow, Sallie, and her family.

In fact, he bequeathed a mess.

When he died, he left a slew of unpaid bills that are still on record in the Lafayette County Courthouse as part of his probate process. They suggest he had quite a taste for the high life—whiskey in particular.

An account with Young and Green shows that from February to August 1868 Nutter made thirteen purchases of whiskey—totaling three gallons, seven quarts, and five pints—for which he owed $27.50.

That seems to be a lot of whiskey for any person to drink in six months, but Nutter also left an account with P. O. Patterson that included purchases from March to July 1868 of three gallons, one half-gallon, one quart, one-and-a-half pints, and five bottles of whiskey.

But that's still not all.

Nutter's account with Friedrich Lehmann and Son included four purchases of whiskey in October 1868: one gallon each on October 2, 4, and 12, and, finally, a five-gallon purchase on October 17.

A bigger problem than unpaid liquor tabs, however, was the status of Nutter's estate.

Remember, he was going through a divorce when he was killed by the father of the woman who was divorcing him.

Typically, a widow gets control of her late husband's estate, but in this case?

There also was the matter of the scheduled sheriff's sale of Nutter's property. This came about because of the suits brought against Sam after he attempted to sell almost everything he owned to his sister Lizzie for a phantom $17,000. The sheriff's sale was scheduled to be held just weeks after Nutter's killing.

Sam Nutter almost certainly was trying to keep his property from going to Sallie in the divorce proceedings.

It was clear that his sister hadn't paid him $17,000, so all the people to whom he owed money, including his widow, had to salvage whatever they could from Nutter's estate.

With Nutter's death, the sale of his property was postponed, and it was left to Moses Chapman, public administrator for Lafayette County, to sort out the mess. It would involve roughly a dozen lawsuits, most of them filed against Chapman as administrator of Nutter's estate, or against Lizzie Nutter.

Chapman issued annual statements of the estate, showing that he procured $7,242.90 from the sale of Nutter's real estate and personal property in 1869 and 1870. Included in Chapman's annual statements were four payments to Sallie, totaling $1,000.

That didn't keep Sallie from joining the lawsuit frenzy of 1869–1871, which must have kept her and her family plenty busy while they waited for William A. Warner's impending murder trial.

On December 2, 1868, Sallie filed a suit in the Court of Common Pleas for Lafayette County, attempting to void the deed of Sam's July sale to Lizzie.

In Lizzie's response of February 1869, she said she had purchased her brother's property for $17,000 but didn't know what had subsequently happened to the money. She admitted she had some of Sam's personal belongings and would turn them over to the estate's administrator. She also claimed Sallie took many items that belonged to Sam, including two lamps and a music box, when Sallie left the Nutter house and filed for divorce in April 1868.

The final flurry of legal activity occurred in early January 1871, when Chapman confirmed in probate court the two sales of much of Sam Nutter's real estate for $7,010.

Chapman ultimately paid off most of Sam Nutter's debts by April 1874. But the estate wasn't fully resolved until November 1881, when a "Final Settlement" notice signed by Chapman ran in the *Lexington Weekly Intelligencer.*

By that time, many folks probably wondered who Sam Nutter was. He had been dead for thirteen years, after all, and the trial of his killer, William A. Warner, was by then a decade in the past.

***

May 11, 1869, must have been a strange day in the Lafayette County Courthouse. A grand jury returned a true bill in the first-degree murder case of William Warner, and representing the state as circuit attorney was William Warner.

Obviously, not the same guy.

William Warner, Esquire had been a major in the Union army, having served with the Forty-fourth Regiment Wisconsin Volunteer Infantry. He moved to Kansas City after the war and was elected to the circuit attorney's post in November 1868. Warner later became mayor of Kansas City, a U.S. representative, and, finally, a U.S. senator from Missouri.

Despite his in-name-only relationship with the defendant, he showed no apparent mercy. William Warner successfully argued that William Warner should remain in the Lafayette County jail while the case was continued.

Both Warners were back in court in November 1869, when Judge Townsley granted the defense a change of venue to Pettis County, where Sedalia was the county seat.

More good news for the defendant was that Townsley granted Warner bond totaling $30,000, the equivalent of perhaps $500,000 nowadays. The court record reads:

. . . William A. Warner . . . acknowledges himself to owe and stand indebted unto the State of Missouri in the sum of Fifteen Thousand Dollars, and also comes Joseph O. Shelby, George H. Ambrose, John McKinnan and Samuel Downing Jr. as his securities and family and severally acknowledge themselves to owe and stand indebted unto the State of Missouri in a like sum of Fifteen Thousand Dollars . . .

The local heavyweights in Warner's corner included his friend General Jo Shelby and Ambrose, who was presiding judge (now called commissioner) of the Lafayette County Court and president of the Lexington & St. Louis Railroad Company.

No John McKinnan is mentioned in any histories of Lafayette County or in Lexington newspaper articles from that era, but a John McKinnin was buried in Lexington's Machpelah Cemetery in 1883. He might have been a proprietor in the McKinnin & Gratz clothing store in Lexington in the 1860s. In any case, we can't be sure of his relationship to Warner.

Samuel Downing Jr. was the son of Warner's brother-in-law. The younger Downing had been a Confederate soldier, having served under Shelby.

So Warner was out of jail by the end of 1869, but he still had a long wait before going to trial.

In January 1870, a trial date for July 1870 was set, but the case was continued twice more before—finally—the ultimate trial date was set for January 1871. By that time, the state's attorney, William Warner, had been elected mayor of Kansas City.

PART

IV

SIX DAYS IN SEDALIA

James S. Botsford

George Graham Vest

John Finis Philips

Introduction

At some point, Colonel William A. Warner hired a crack team of lawyers, who likely further tested his supporters' deep pockets.

Amos Green was on the case from the start.

He had moved to Lexington after the Civil War from Paris, Illinois, where he had been a leader of the notorious Copperheads, who opposed both the administration of Abraham Lincoln and the war itself. Green had been arrested twice because of his opposition to the administration.

In Lafayette County, he was well known as a friend of the Rebels and was active on the Democrats's behalf during the troubled election of November 1866.

After that election, the Republican-slanted *Missouri Valley Register* described Green as "a lawyer from Paris, Illinois, whose reputation there is that of a dishonest lawyer, a falsifier, a swindler, and a social and political knave. He has been here about two years, and thinks, because he has a little money, that he owns a lot of working men."

So Warner might have been looking for an upgrade.

He certainly found it with George Graham Vest and John Finis Philips.

Vest and Philips had formed a partnership in Sedalia after the war, during which both had built substantial reputations—on opposite sides of the political fence.

Vest had served in the Confederate Congress (the Confederacy admitted Missouri, even though it hadn't seceded from the Union, so the border state was represented in Congress as well as by one of the thirteen stars on the Confederate flag). Philips, meanwhile, had been a colonel in the Union army, having commanded the Seventh Regiment Missouri Volunteer Cavalry. He made his mark in the Kansas City area at the Battle of Westport, where he had led Union troops against, among others, none other than General Joseph O. "Jo" Shelby.

Vest and Philips both went on to have distinguished careers in law and politics, Vest as a U.S. senator for nearly twenty-five years and Philips as a judge and U.S. congressman.

To this day, however, Vest is best known not for his role in the Civil War or in the Senate but for a small case he had tried just weeks before he went to court to defend William A. Warner.

Like the Warner case, it involved a killing. Unlike that case, this victim had four legs.

A foxhound named Old Drum had been killed by a sheep farmer, and the dog's owner sued for damages. A trial was held September 23, 1870, in Warrensburg, where Vest became famous because of his closing argument, known as his "Eulogy on the Dog."

An excerpt:

The best friend a man has in this world may turn against him and become his enemy. His son or daughter that he has reared with loving care may prove ungrateful. Those who are nearest and dearest to us, those whom we trust with our happiness and our good name, may become traitors to their faith. The money that a man has, he may lose. . . . The one absolutely unselfish friend that a man can have in this selfish world, the one that never deserts him and the one that never proves ungrateful or treacherous is his dog. . . .

If fortune drives the master forth an outcast in the world, friendless and homeless, the faithful dog asks no higher privilege than that of accompanying him to guard against danger, to fight against his enemies, and when the last scene of all comes, and death takes the master in its embrace and his body is laid away in the cold ground, no matter if all other friends pursue their way, there by his graveside will the noble dog be found, his head between his paws, his eyes sad but open in alert watchfulness, faithful and true even to death.

Vest won the case, including an appeal to the Missouri Supreme Court, and is credited with coining the phrase "dog is man's best friend." A statue of Old Drum stands in front of the Johnson County Courthouse in Warrensburg.

Vest's notoriety in the Old Drum case probably had nothing to do with his being hired by Warner. More likely, General Leslie Combs just wanted the best legal defense his son-in-law could get, and in that time and place, George Vest and John Philips were the best.

Vest and Philips were assisted by another Sedalia lawyer, James S. Botsford. His role in the trial was limited, however, after President Ulysses

S. Grant appointed him U.S. district attorney for the Western District of Missouri just days before the trial began.

Also defending Warner, according to the court records, was Judge William Walker. He was justice of the Court of Common Pleas in Lafayette County, which would seem to be a conflict of interest. But, hey, who was keeping score in 1871?

Clearly, William A. Warner had a veritable legal dream team on his side.

So why the change of venue from Lafayette County?

The courthouse in Lexington undoubtedly would have been a more dramatic setting. An impressive two-story white Greek Revival structure fronted by four columns, it was built in 1847 and remains in use today.

The Pettis County courthouse in Sedalia was a simple frame building, which had replaced another small courthouse that had been destroyed by fire in 1870. The 1891 *Sedalia Weekly Bazoo* described it as an "old wooden building standing at the corner of Ohio and Fourth streets, on the block where the present courthouse stands." (Pettis County used several other buildings in Sedalia as courthouses before the current one was built in 1925.)

The change of venue had nothing to do with the buildings, of course.

Perhaps a factor was that Sedalia was Judge Townsley's hometown, and the base of operations for Vest and Philips.

Warner's lawyers likely figured they had a better chance of winning in Sedalia.

The case was evidently a much-talked-about affair in and around Lexington and had been even before Sam Nutter got killed. People probably had strong opinions one way or the other, and, considering Warner was a relative newcomer to the area while Nutter had come from a well-established Lafayette County family, the feelings might have slanted Sam's way more than Warner's defense team would have liked.

Perhaps another factor was that Pettis County wasn't a bastion for Southern sympathizers, like Lafayette County. Warner had been a Union colonel, so he was more likely to be held in esteem in Sedalia, a Federal military post during the Civil War.

Another possible factor in the trial's move was that Sedalia and Pettis County didn't have the reputation for bushwhackers and killings and violence that Lexington and Lafayette County did.

It is worth noting, however, that Sedalia had recently seen an incident similar to the Nutter killing.

Like William A. Warner, Joe Woods shot an unarmed man in broad daylight in front of multiple witnesses. Unlike William A. Warner, there was no trial for Joe Woods.

Woods was well known in Sedalia, having come from a respected family. He, however, wasn't so much respected as he was feared.

The History of Pettis County, Missouri, published in 1882, described Woods as "a man of violent temper, strong passions and desperate resolution. He was a man of powerful build; thick and heavy set, and possessed of almost gigantic strength."

Woods had been something of a legend during and just after the Civil War. Going by the name Clingman, he led a group of bushwhackers who terrorized southern Illinois, robbing and killing much as Quantrill's gang did throughout western Missouri. Despite the efforts of authorities in the area, Clingman was never captured.

After returning to Missouri, he became Joe Woods again and briefly worked on the side of law enforcement. Sort of.

In a twist of fate, Woods rode to Lexington with Bacon Montgomery, a Sedalia newspaperman-turned-soldier who led a band of state militia dispatched by Governor Thomas C. Fletcher in an attempt to restore order to the bushwhacker-infested area in late 1866.

Woods played a role in the killing of the bushwhacker leader, Archie Clement, on December 13, 1866. Montgomery sent a few men, including Woods, to apprehend Clement, and a shoot-out resulted that left Clement dead in the streets of downtown Lexington—not far from where Sam Nutter would lie dying less than two years later.

Clement's death left a leadership void among the ruffians that Jesse James filled. It also led to somewhat quieter days in Lexington, although Woods and other members of the occupying militia committed outrages of their own before they withdrew in February 1867.

Woods returned to Sedalia and evidently assumed a role as something of the town bully. That didn't last long, either.

On a cold Saturday morning in late March 1867, Woods was drinking heavily.

He got into an argument with some men in the saloon of Joseph Geimer, who it should be noted was a German (Germans were almost as unpopular with bushwhackers as were Negroes). The argument led to violence, and Woods roughed up several men, cutting one with a knife.

Geimer wasn't in the saloon at the time, but he encountered Woods in the street a bit later and expressed displeasure at the trouble Woods had caused in his establishment.

That didn't sit well with Woods, who proceeded to shoot the German— in the back, by most accounts—and then ran off.

Sedalia police officers were able to capture Woods, placing him in an old log building that served as the town jail. Late that night, townsfolk angry that Woods had killed Geimer overwhelmed a deputy, forced their way into the jail, and dragged Woods into the muddy streets.

His naked body was found hanging from the archway over the entrance to a lumberyard the next morning, a Sunday. It was the first lynching in Sedalia's history. A coroner's jury decided that Woods had been killed by "parties unknown," and that was that.

After this, the first and the last session of the court of Judge Lynch, the town was more quiet; there were fewer deeds of violence; less disposition to carry or draw deadly weapons; and, though mob law is the most dangerous thing that can exist in a free country, this act seemed to have a decided and unmistakably beneficial influence upon the whole community.
—The History of Pettis County, Missouri, 1882

If the folks in Sedalia had lynched Woods for a cold-blooded killing, you had to wonder what they might have in store for William A. Warner. A jury would be selected from among them, and its members would hold the fate of Warner in their hands.

What would that fate be? A hanging? Could be. This was a first-degree murder charge, after all.

Prison time? That must have seemed possible.

Or maybe an acquittal?

But on what grounds?

Warner's lawyers clearly couldn't argue that he hadn't shot Sam Nutter. There were too many witnesses for that defense to fly.

Self-defense also didn't appear to be a possible defense. Nutter had been unarmed.

Just about the only thing Warner's lawyers could argue was that Nutter deserved to die, and that Warner was justified in killing him. Even with no apparent provocation. Even with Nutter unarmed.

***

When the Warner murder trial came to town, Sedalia was something of a boomtown.

After getting a city charter in 1864, Sedalia, which is about fifty-five miles southeast of Lexington, had become the Pettis County seat in 1865. It was a railroad hub, and, in fact, a Lexington-to-Sedalia line was in the works. It was finished in 1871, but not until after the Warner trial had concluded.

New buildings, including several nice hotels and two opera houses, were going up at a rapid pace along Ohio Avenue and in what is now the downtown area, and the most prosperous residents were building fine homes farther south on Broadway. In fact, Chan Townsley, the judge in the Warner trial, built the first brick residence on Broadway, in 1867.

Brick buildings became all the rage a few years later, after fires had destroyed many of the new wood-frame buildings in 1867 and 1868 and three times from 1870 to early 1871. In 1871 alone, twenty-two brick buildings were built on Ohio Avenue.

Because of its status as a rail hub, Sedalia was also a cattle town, with cowboys leading herds to the town's stockyards.

Given its military history and its railroad and cattle connections, it shouldn't be surprising that Sedalia was also a haven for gambling and prostitution. Both activities were illegal, but both thrived in the Sedalia of the early 1870s.

The Sedalia *Democrat* in April 1872 carried a report from the city marshal noting that over the previous twelve months the city had made twenty-seven arrests for gambling, thirteen arrests for keeping a bawdy house, and forty-six arrests for being "found in a house of ill-fame."

Seven women among Sedalia's population of some 4,500 even identified themselves as prostitutes in the 1870 census.

Sedalia was well known for its red-light district well into the twentieth century. In 1877, the *St. Louis Post-Dispatch* called the town the "Sodom and Gomorrah of Missouri."

The undisputed queen of the red-light district was Lizzie Cook, who operated with the tacit approval of city authorities.

The Sedalia *Democrat* reported in 1871 that Lizzie had been fined $20 in police court for "running a bawdy house." Meanwhile, six men were fined $3 or $5 for being "found in a bawdy house," and two women were fined $10 for the same offense.

Three weeks later, Lizzie was fined $20 again, and three other women were fined $10.

The fines amounted to a monthly fee, and Lizzie operated her house without much official interference for nearly a decade.

That doesn't mean there weren't incidents.

At one point, Lizzie called her establishment the Junction Hotel, and the *Democrat* newspaper complained not about her business but about its name:

. . . We allude to the sign over Col. Lizzie Cook's bawdy house— the 'Junction Hotel.' This sign should be taken down—peaceably or forcibly, as it decoys many decent people within this den of prostitutes. Strangers visiting our city, who do not know the character of the entertainments dispensed at this bagnio, are liable to stop at this brothel. In truth some have already mistaken it for a Hotel, and have applied for board and lodging thereat.

It is but a few days since a gentleman visited our city for the first time, and seeing the sign of this mock Hotel, very naturally asked for supper and lodging. The head Jezabel [sic], Col. Lizzie Cook, told him he could get a certain kind of 'lodging,' but could get nothing to eat. He asked for the landlord, when she told him that the Hotel was kept by women. Light broke upon him—he gathered his velise [sic] and beat a hasty retreat.

. . . We certainly hope that the Mayor, Marshal and City Council will devise some prompt measure to abate this nuisance, as their right to do so cannot be controverted.
—*Weekly Democrat*, May 15, 1873

The next week, the *Democrat* showed the power of the press, writing:

Col. Lizzie Cook has taken down her Hotel sign. This is well, and we applaud the Colonel for her discretion; but she has only done a small part of her duty, and while we claim no right, either on the score of personal friendship, or long or intimate acquaintance, to advise her, we nevertheless venture to suggest that she take down her house and thus save others from the trouble.
—*Weekly Democrat*, May 22, 1873

The *Democrat* wasn't that powerful. Lizzie Cook ran houses in Sedalia for an additional six years or so.

In fact, she was so bold as to file suit in 1874 against the town marshal, William Inch, seeking $2,500 for damages he caused when he broke down her door and tore her clothes while attempting to apprehend some men inside.

***

Lizzie Cook and others like her would have been operating fairly openly in Sedalia when the Warner trial was held.

Of course, since they were women, prostitutes weren't eligible to serve on juries—or even to vote, for that matter—so they would have no direct effect on the trial.

The men of Sedalia would decide Warner's fate.

Potential jurors in Sedalia would have been less likely to have heard about the Nutter killing than folks in Lafayette County. At least, that would have been the case when the trial was moved there on a change of venue in 1869.

The word must have been out by the time lawyers gave their opening arguments January 25, 1871, however, because the courtroom was packed and the press was out in force.

Sedalia had three newspapers in 1871. The *Sedalia Weekly Times* was published at the time, according to *The History of Pettis County, Missouri*, but no editions exist today.

Also according to *The History of Pettis County, Missouri*, the *Democrat* had started publishing a daily edition less than two weeks before the start of William A. Warner's trial, but records of the *Daily Democrat* exist on microfilm only starting with December 19, 1871.

Fortunately, the *Democrat* also published a weekly edition. The *Weekly Democrat* and the *Daily Bazoo* (which also printed a weekly edition) committed extensive space to the trial. Both were four-page broadsheet publications.

A typical local news story was perhaps one-half column in length. Some major stories might be up to two columns in length. The *Daily Bazoo* committed more than fourteen columns to the Warner trial over five days of coverage, from Wednesday, January 25, through Tuesday, January 31.

It is worth noting that the *Bazoo* ran details of the trial, for the most part, on the day after they occurred. In two editions, Wednesday, January 25, and Friday, January 27, the newspaper even included trial details that had happened that morning.

Given the typesetting requirements of the day—each letter of metal type individually selected and put into place before the hand-cranked printer could produce a single page—the *Bazoo's* editors likely worked nearly round the clock to produce their evening publication.

On the day it covered the conclusion of the trial, Tuesday, January 31, the *Bazoo* also ran the following note: "Last evening we were compelled to print nearly a double edition of our daily to supply the demand for extra papers. We had issued nearly a double edition also for the weekly Bazoo and find that now about exhausted."

The *Weekly Democrat* committed nearly twelve columns to the Warner trial, but they didn't appear until its editions of February 2 and 9, 1871.

That's still a lot of coverage, especially since neither the victim nor the accused had any ties to Sedalia or Pettis County.

The 1891 *Sedalia Weekly Bazoo* account, with twenty years of perspective, summarized it thusly:

"Probably no trial ever had in Pettis county attracted the widespread attention as did the trial of the state vs. Col. W. A. Warner, for the killing of his son-in-law, Sam. W. Nutter, at Lexington, Mo., on October 22, 1868. . . . The old box court house was filled by the people. The owls, bats, cockroaches and tramps were given a vacation."

January 24, 1871

If he had it to do all over again, Leslie Warner thought, he would have shot Sam Nutter himself.

He'd mulled it over a lot in the past two years, ultimately figuring that would have been the best outcome. His pa wouldn't be on trial for murder, and he likely wouldn't be, either. He had only been fourteen at the time. They wouldn't have put a fourteen-year-old on trial for murder, he thought, and they surely wouldn't hang one.

Unfortunately, that's not how things had turned out.

Colonel William A. Warner was, in fact, on trial for murder. Leslie fretted for his father and the possibility that he might be convicted, might even be sentenced to hang. But he also found the entire experience enthralling.

One of his father's lawyers, James Botsford, had spent a great deal of time at the Warners' house in Carrollton over the previous months. The young lawyer was assisting the more established George Vest and John Philips and had talked to just about everybody in the family, although he seemed to spend most of his time with Sallie.

Leslie thought he was sweet on the Widow Nutter, as Leslie had taken to calling her. Sallie hated that nickname.

"If you call me that one more time, Leslie Warner, I'll never speak to you again," Sallie would say.

As for himself, Leslie had told Mr. Botsford everything he knew about Sam Nutter, Sallie, his father, and the day Colonel Warner shot Sam Nutter dead.

"I reckon I know more about this killing than anybody," he had told the lawyer.

"I reckon you do," Mr. Botsford had said. "Maybe you know too much."

Leslie wasn't sure what that meant at first, but now that the trial was beginning he thought he understood.

His father wasn't going to testify, and neither was he—if his pa's lawyers could manage it. They said Leslie could become the prosecution's star witness if he was put on the stand.

Fortunately, the circuit attorney had never interviewed Leslie. He had talked to Sallie and Mary, but not to Leslie.

Turns out, it was probably a good thing Leslie had kept a low profile that deadly October day in Lexington.

Mr. Botsford wanted it to stay that way. He said he and Colonel Warner's other lawyers thought it best for Leslie stay at home during the trial.

Not likely, Leslie had thought. He was sixteen now, not far from turning seventeen, and had put most childhood things behind him. He had even started using proper grammar, as his mother had so long desired. He now thought it had been silly for him to willfully sound so ignorant.

The months after Sam's killing had made him grow up quick. With his father in jail much of the time, Leslie was the only male in the house.

Leslie figured he was a man now. As such, he had to be in Sedalia for the trial.

***

Colonel Warner and his lawyers were in the courthouse for the second day of jury selection.

Leslie had arrived in Sedalia in the afternoon.

It didn't require much sneaking to get there. He had been the only family member left in the Warners' house in Carrollton, since his younger sisters and Sallie's daughter, Georgie, were staying with their Great Aunt Margaret at her Carrollton home.

So, he simply climbed aboard a horse and rode south through the snow.

One of the fiercest winter storms in years had hit west-central Missouri ten days earlier, leaving a foot of snow across the area and four-foot drifts in some places. Special crews were hired to clear railroad tracks.

The weather had remained cold enough that nearly all the snow remained.

Not even a blanket of white could make Sedalia look pretty to Leslie, however.

There weren't any big, old buildings like there were in Lexington. In fact, one section of downtown consisted of little more than charred embers, the result of a fire on New Year's Day.

Leslie thought Sedalia wasn't much of a town, but it did seem more like the Wild West he had read so much about in his dime novels than did Lexington.

Sedalia's streets were populated by rough-looking folk—men who Leslie reckoned were either cowboys or railroad workers.

Leslie also saw quite a few of what he assumed were ladies of ill repute. He enjoyed watching them walk down the boardwalks. Some appeared no older than he was. Inevitably, he started reflecting on the time Sam had taken him to see the lady Lizzie in Lexington. It was the last fun thing he'd done with Sam.

Leslie thought about Sam quite a bit these days. He wished Sallie and Sam had never got divorced, so Sam wouldn't have done the crazy things he did, so his pa wouldn't have had to kill him.

Instead, Colonel Warner was about to face a jury of his peers in Sedalia.

Sallie, Mary, and their parents were staying at the impressive, new Ives House. It was across the railroad tracks from the main part of Sedalia and had survived the most recent fire, though its predecessor, the McKissock House, had burned to the ground in 1867. The Ives House was built on the same site.

Leslie steered clear of the Ives House, of course, because he didn't want to risk being seen by his mother. She would be furious if she knew he was in Sedalia.

But he was determined to see his father's murder trial, no matter what risk it entailed.

Leslie had never done anything quite this daring before. It was the first time he had traveled so far by himself, and he was in a strange town with little money and no promise of meals or overnight lodging.

He figured he would manage somehow.

January 25, 1871

The Trial

The jury had been selected over the first two days of Judge Chan Townsley's session, Monday and Tuesday, January 23–24, 1871.

The 1891 *Sedalia Weekly Bazoo* account said "the whole county was sitted, almost, to secure a jury who had 'not formed or expressed an opinion.'" The twelve lucky men then got to spend a week at the LeRoy House hotel, where they were sequestered for the duration of the trial.

Townsley and circuit attorney J. D. Hines, who had recently taken over the job from the "other" William Warner, also handled the court's other pending cases those first two days. That cleared the docket for the William A. Warner trial to be the sole focus for the next six days. The *Daily Bazoo* of January 25, 1871, described the opening day of the trial:

Our little crib of a Court House was crowded to suffocation this morning, and it was with great difficulty that the attorneys could speak. Quite a number of ladies braved the elements and appeared there, with toilets somewhat mussed, curious to hear every word of 'instructions' and of the plea.

The newspaper said Tilton Davis presented the opening argument for the state and indicated George Vest spoke for the defense.

Mr. Vest, our own townsman—and none know him but to idolize him for his talent and for his generous nature—next spoke for an hour and forty minutes, and such outbursts of eloquence and touching appeals seldom are heard within the walls of our courthouse.

The *Weekly Democrat* called it "one of the most important trials ever held in this County" under the headline:

"THE WARNER MURDER CASE
"Court House Crowded to Excess!
"INTENSE INTEREST MANIFESTED!
"Evidences, Scenes, Incidents, &c. !"

It employed the descriptive prose that marked most newspaper writing of the time:

The defendant William A. Warner is a gentleman of about fifty-five or sixty years of age, and a resident of Carrolton [sic] in this State. He is remarkably prepossessing in appearance, and seated by his Counsel, it were indeed difficult for a casual observer to distinguish between the accused and any of his able defenders. On one side of the Court room were seated day by day the defendant's wife and two daughters, one of the latter being the widow of the deceased Nutter.

They are ladies of culture and refinement, and seem to have the fullest faith in the complete vindication of their husband and parent. At one o'clock on Wednesday, Colonel Hines, the Circuit Attorney, opened the case to the jury on the part of the State and was followed by Judge Walker for the defense. Every available portion of the Court room was occupied, and all present seemed impressed with the solemnity of the occasion.

The daughters in court were Sallie, the widow who was all of twenty years of age, and Mary, who was a year or two younger than Sallie (she was listed as seventeen in the 1870 census).

They clearly made quite an impression on the folks of Sedalia, especially the reporters.

Here's how the 1891 *Sedalia Weekly Bazoo* account described them:

Mrs. Nutter was a pronounced brunette, phenomenal fine figure and was gifted with more than usual conversational powers and endowed with more beauty and comeliness than is fair for one person to possess. . . . Her sister . . . had not quite as commanding figure but was an extremely pretty girl.

The ladies won the wives and daughters of Sedalia and had their sympathy from start to finish.

William A. Warner himself was 53 at the time of the trial.

At such a relatively advanced age and with considerable wealth and standing in society, Warner was a far cry from the usual accused murderer in those days, when men with guns on their hips walked the streets and filled the saloons. In all, he epitomized the idea of the honorable Kentucky colonel.

***

At 1 p.m. Wednesday, January 25, 1871, the prosecution began to present its case.

Pettis County's records provide few details of the proceedings, merely a few sentences each day of the trial indicating that it had occurred. On that first day, the record states little more than the facts of the case and that the jury would be sequestered and should "converse with no one in relation to this cause."

If the court records aren't much help in revealing specifics, the newspaper accounts certainly are. They provide copious and remarkable details of the entire proceedings.

What follows is taken from those accounts, blending the descriptions from the *Bazoo* and *Democrat* into a fairly complete picture of the trial.

In a few instances, the newspaper accounts don't agree on details, such as the spellings of names. The correct information usually could be confirmed and is used here, regardless of what appeared in the *Bazoo* or *Democrat*.

One example is the name of the Lafayette County deputy sheriff, who is "Faris Hamond" in the *Bazoo* and "Farris Hammond" in the *Democrat*. Lexington newspaper accounts called him "Pharez Hammonds." But his tombstone in Odessa, Missouri, reads "Phares E. Hammond," so we'll go with that.

Hammond, in fact, was the trial's first witness.

What better way for circuit attorney Hines to open his case than with a deputy sheriff and Civil War veteran who had witnessed the entire episode?

The shooting occurred at about 4 o'clock on October 22, 1868, a Thursday. There were more folks in Lexington than on a typical Thursday because it was the third day of the Lexington fair, which drew thousands of people. Colonel Warner and much of his family were in Lexington for the fair, and he probably correctly surmised that Sam Nutter would be there for the same reason.

It had rained the previous two days, so the streets of Lexington were muddy. Unlike many towns in those days, however, Lexington had pavement sidewalks outside its downtown businesses, and that was where much of our story's action occurred.

Hammond, who was twenty-nine at the time of the trial, said he passed Warner, who was talking to a Mr. Downing just east of the City Hotel. That likely was Sam Downing, who was married to Warner's wife's sister Margaret, although it might have been one of his sons, Sam or Alfred Downing.

Hammond said he shook hands with Warner, who was carrying a shotgun.

"As I passed Warner the first time, somebody called to Warner and said, 'There he goes,'" Hammond testified. "This was close to the bookstore. It was fifteen minutes after that the shooting took place."

The bookstore, like the City Hotel, was on Lexington's North Street (now Main Street), not far from the majestic courthouse. Both Warner and Hammond evidently were still in the vicinity quite a while later.

Hammond said Nutter came out of the bank or the saloon and was walking to his buggy, where his sister, Lizzie, was waiting. The deputy said he called to Nutter, who then turned around. He said he didn't notice whether Nutter was armed.

"As the deceased turned, the defendant fired. . . . When the shot was fired, the deceased and defendant were about as far apart as across this courthouse."

Warner was near the corner of Laurel Street by the bank when he fired one shot, Hammond said. He immediately took the gun from Warner.

"I laid my hand on Warner's shoulder. He did not move away from the time the shot was fired until I took him."

When cross-examined by the defense, Hammond repeated that he had called to Nutter, that he did not know whether Nutter was armed, and that Warner offered no resistance after the shooting. He added that the other barrel of Warner's shotgun was loaded.

Benjamin Fish, the livery operator, was the only other witness on the first day of the trial. He provided the prosecution with evidence that the killing had been premeditated, although not everyone in court believed Fish's story, as became apparent later in the trial.

Fish said that he not only saw Warner about a half hour before the shooting but that he had seen his son, Leslie, about an hour before that. Leslie Warner was fourteen at the time. Fish said both Warners had come by his stable, which was on Laurel Street about two hundred feet from where the shooting occurred.

"When Warner was at the stable, he asked me if Nutter or Nutter's team was there," Fish testified. "He said, 'I'll kill them both.'"

"Warner was armed with a shotgun. He then left and went north towards Mitchell's Bank."

When the defense lawyers questioned him, Fish said Warner didn't mention any names when he said, "I'll kill them both."

He also said he didn't remember having been a witness at Warner's habeas corpus hearing after his arrest in 1868. But then he changed his story, saying he remembered "being in the courthouse at the time, and suppose I did testify. I have no recollection of what I testified to then."

After Fish's testimony, the court adjourned until Thursday morning.

At that point, the Warner women couldn't have felt good about Colonel Warner's chances. The prosecution had clearly shown he had shot and killed Sam Nutter, and it also had provided evidence of premeditation.

However, the trial was just getting started.

Evening

Leslie saw and heard most of the first day's proceedings from the back of the courtroom, which was so crowded he easily concealed his presence from his parents up front.

He grimaced when he heard old man Fish testify that he had seen both Leslie and his father before the shooting. Most folks in Lexington knew that little of what Fish said was truthful, but these jurors weren't from Lexington. They might actually believe him.

Leslie scurried out the courtroom door as soon as the judge's gavel sounded the end of the day's testimony. So far so good, he thought.

After escaping the cold the previous night in a barn just east of town, Leslie was hoping he could upgrade his accommodations. He was hungry, too. The only food he had brought from home was some jerky and bread, and he already had eaten most of that.

Darkness was descending as he watched the courthouse crowd exit from across the street.

The courthouse was on Ohio Avenue, about three blocks south of Main Street and about four blocks from the Ives House, where the Warners were staying.

Leslie hoped he could catch his sister Mary alone during her walk from the courthouse to the hotel. She would help him, he thought, and would keep quiet about it.

Leslie saw Mary leave the courthouse, but she was walking side by side with Sallie and their mother as dozens of folks along Ohio Avenue watched them pass.

"They're plenty pretty, ain't they?" an unfamiliar man's voice said from beside Leslie.

Leslie nearly jumped out of his boots.

"What? Oh, yeah, I suppose so," he said. Turning, he found himself face to face with what he immediately recognized, both from his garb and his odor, as a cowboy. The man pressed his unshaven face much closer to Leslie's than comfort allowed, his mouth breaking into a gap-toothed grin.

"Why, you're just a boy," the cowboy said. "As tall as you are, from behind I reckoned you were a man."

"Well, I guess I'm as much a man as most," Leslie said. "I don't rightly see that it's any of your business, anyhow."

"No offense intended, young man. I was just trying to make conversation."

"No offense taken," Leslie said.

He had never met a cowboy before, and he wasn't going to let this one get away without asking him a few questions. "Are you a real cowboy?" he asked, quite earnestly.

"I reckon you could say that," the cowboy said. "Though, I must say, I never did like that moniker. I ain't no boy, and most of the critters I deal with ain't cows. They're steers. But I guess 'steerman' just don't have much of a ring to it, does it?"

The cowboy laughed loudly, and Leslie smiled.

"Where are you from?" he asked.

"Down in Texas," the cowboy said. "Can't wait to get back. It's too cold here. What's all this commotion about, anyhow?"

"It's a murder trial," Leslie said. "They're all just leaving the courtroom. This was the first day of testimony. Those two women you were complimenting are the daughters of the man on trial. He was a colonel in the Union army during the war."

"Why, you're just full of information. Are you a newspaperman or somethin'?" the cowboy asked.

Leslie hesitated.

"No . . . I know the family."

"Well, did he do it?"

"Did who do what?"

"Did the man on trial kill the person he's on trial for killin'?"

"Oh, he killed the man, all right," Leslie said. "I saw it."

"You saw the murder?"

"I saw it, but it wasn't murder. The man had it comin'."

"I've knowd a lot of men who had a killin' comin', but it still woulda been murder if I killed 'em," the cowboy said. "What'd this other man do that merited his bein' killed?"

"I don't . . ." Leslie stammered. "He just did."

He wanted to end the conversation before feeling compelled to reveal that Sam Nutter had been unarmed. Or that the man on trial was his own father.

"Well, I hope the trial turns out favorable for you and your friends," the cowboy said, with a grin.

"Thank you, mister," Leslie said.

He decided to move on before he encountered any more inquisitive cowboys.

Leslie walked down Ohio, hoping he might find a place to spend the night. He knew he couldn't afford any of the big hotels in town—he had all of seventy-five cents in his pocket—but he thought he might have enough for someplace better than a barn.

Ohio was lined with newer and nicer buildings, which he passed quickly, making his way to the older part of town on Main.

Once he walked past the burned-out buildings, the action picked up. This was where most of the tippling houses and bawdy houses were located, and the area was filled with noisy men and women.

A lone man approached Leslie.

"Hey, do you know where the Junction Hotel is?" he asked.

"Never heard of it," Leslie responded. "I'm not from here."

"Nobody here is from here," the man said, before hurrying west down Main Street.

Leslie continued no more than twenty feet before another man stopped him.

"Boy, can you direct me to the Junction Hotel?" he asked.

"No. I don't know it," Leslie said, thinking this Junction Hotel might be just the kind of place he was looking for.

So he approached three young men standing outside a saloon.

"Can you boys direct me to the Junction Hotel?" he asked.

All three were eager to help, pointing down the street.

"Just go down a block and around the corner," one said. "Can't miss it."

Sure enough, after walking no more than fifty feet, Leslie turned onto a side street and saw a sign for the Junction Hotel hanging above the entrance to a two-story frame building, sitting between what appeared to be two private homes.

Light shone from all the windows of the establishment, and Leslie heard loud voices coming from within.

He wasn't sure whether he could afford this place, but he intended to find out. Walking up on the porch, he pushed open the front door and stepped inside.

Leslie immediately realized this wasn't like any hotel he'd ever been in. It was as if he had entered a whole different world.

Women. None of them fully clothed. All of them with painted faces.

Many of the women had their arms laced around men, and vice versa, as they leaned against unsightly red wall-papered walls in what Leslie took to be the front parlor. Other women, their bodies covered by nothing more than lacy undergarments, sat on the laps of men. One of the ladies slid off her man's lap, took the man by his hand, and led him to the red-carpeted stairway. They smiled and giggled their way to the second floor.

Leslie felt himself blushing and knew he was staring, but he couldn't help it. This was like nothing he'd ever witnessed.

Sure, he had been with the prostitute Sam had procured for him in Lexington more than three years earlier. But that was just one painted woman.

This was a whole clan.

"My, you're a cute one," a lady said as she approached Leslie. She was one of the less attractive gals in the smoke-filled room, Leslie thought, and one of the oldest, too. "You're young, too. Are you looking to be with your first gal?"

"No," Leslie said. "I've been with my first gal."

"Well, good for you, honey," she said. "What are you looking for, then?"

That was a good question, Leslie thought. He wasn't sure what to say or do next.

He had certainly enjoyed his one experience with a woman and had in fact been wanting an encore for more than three years. But none of the girls he knew back home seemed to be candidates, and there were no bawdy houses in Carrollton. At least, none that he knew about.

In any case, he was in one now. Unfortunately, he had just seventy-five cents on his person.

"Well, I was looking for somewhere to sleep, but I guess I came to the wrong place for that," Leslie said.

"It's a true fact that the men who come here rarely get much sleep," the painted lady said. "But we provide other benefits. Would you be interested in those, perhaps?"

The prostitute put her right hand on the inside of Leslie's left thigh. He flinched.

"Not tonight," he said, backing hastily away from the woman.

As he backed, he collided with another lady of the evening. Stammering, Leslie turned to apologize, only to find to his immense surprise that he recognized the woman.

And she certainly recognized him.

"Why, if it ain't Sam Nutter's little friend!" she exclaimed. "You were the brother-in-law, weren't ya? That would make Sam's killer your father. I ain't sure you're welcome here. Sam was a friend of mine. He didn't deserve to get killed."

"Sam was my friend, too," Leslie said. "Your name is Lizzie, right?"

"That's right. Lizzie Cook. I run this place of business. And it's a first-class operation, not like that place in Lexington where I introduced you to the joys of manhood. I was only there a few months, and that was long enough. I like bein' my own boss.

"Which brings me back to business. Did I overhear you sayin' you stumbled in here looking for a place to sleep? That happens quite a bit nowadays. Guess the sign might confuse some men, but even the confused ones usually leave with a smile on their face."

"Well, I guess I can't afford a smile tonight," Leslie said. "Seventy-five cents is all I got."

"That won't get you far," Lizzie Cook said. "If you were hoping for charity, I'm afraid I got a strict policy against men getting them smiles free of charge. I also have a strict policy against any man spending the whole night here."

"I wasn't expecting to do either," Leslie said.

"Well, as much as I enjoy your company, perhaps you should be on your way, then, eh?"

"Perhaps I should," Leslie said.

He turned and fairly ran back out the front door.

January 26, 1871

Morning

The second night in the frigid barn was worse than the first. Try as he might, Leslie couldn't keep from shivering. His blanket and coat weren't enough protection against the cold, no matter how he positioned himself in the straw.

He considered building a small fire, but he figured being cold was better than roasting in a self-inflicted inferno.

He also was totally out of food now.

This was absolutely the most miserable he'd ever been in his life. The sleepless, hungry, freezing hours dragged on, and Leslie's mind kept revisiting the Junction Hotel and its inhabitants.

He also thought endlessly about returning to the warmth of a real building.

As a diversion, he watched the antics of two black-and-white cats with which he shared the loft. They no doubt earned their lodging in the barn by hunting mice, but now they snuggled. Then they wrestled. Then they cleaned each other, then wrestled some more before finally settling in to resume their snuggling amid the hay.

Leslie envied their camaraderie. He wished he was that close to somebody.

As dawn approached, Leslie made up his mind he would not spend a third night in the barn, even though the resident farmer had told him he could stay as long as he wanted.

No matter what it took, he would find somewhere else to sleep. If he absolutely had no other choice, he figured he would reveal his misdeeds to his mother. He would have to suffer her wrath, but at least he'd have a warm bed and a hot meal.

What's the worst she could do to him? No punishment could be worse than the past two nights had been.

Leslie turned his attention to the rumbling in his stomach.

He decided he would take another shot at enlisting the aid of Mary, who no doubt had access to more food than she could possibly eat.

Knowing the family was boarding at the Ives House, that's where he headed after rising from the straw and brushing himself off. He had no real plan, other than trying to find and speak to Mary. Preferably without their mother finding out.

Leslie hunched against the cold atop his gelding as they ambled into town, a trek of less than a half mile that seemed to take a half day. Upon reaching the Ives House, he strategically positioned himself in a corner of the hotel lobby.

There were no signs of Mary or any other family member, but at least his body was thawing out. After about ten minutes, Leslie no longer felt numb. However, he was hungrier than he could ever remember being.

The aroma of biscuits and gravy and bacon wafting from the dining room didn't help his condition.

Finally, Leslie saw a sight that made his heart leap. Down the stairs connecting to the lobby walked his sister Sallie. He was hoping for Mary, but Sallie would do just fine.

Without saying a word, he sauntered right up to her as she descended. Sallie stopped on the bottom step and glared at Leslie from head to toe. Frowning, she turned and looked back up the stairs, returned her glance to Leslie, let loose a sigh, and hugged him.

"Leslie Warner, what on earth are you doing here?" Sallie asked. "If Mother saw you now, we would have two parents on trial for murder."

"You aren't gonna tell her I'm here, are you?"

"No. For one thing, I'm not supposed to be here, either. Mother wanted the entire family to eat together this morning, but I've got other plans."

"What might they be?" Leslie asked.

"Do you remember the young lawyer who visited our house, Mr. Botsford?"

"Why, sure. He was sweet on you, as I recall. But I guess half the men in Carroll County are sweet on the Widow Nutter."

"Oh, Leslie, stop it. You know how I hate that name. I have half a mind to go upstairs and get Mother right now and let her have her way with you."

"All right, all right, Sallie, I won't call you that anymore," Leslie promised. "So, what does the lawyer Botsford have to do with this?"

"Well, I'm meeting him for breakfast this morning. He lives in Sedalia, and he's invited me to eat with him before the trial today. Of course, he's no longer involved in the trial, having just this week been named the United States attorney for the Western District of Missouri by President Ulysses S. Grant himself."

"Well, good for him . . . and for you, too, I guess," Leslie said. "And maybe for me, too. You know, Sallie, you are one of my very favorite sisters, and I haven't had anything to eat in almost two days. Do you think Mr. Botsford would mind me as company for breakfast?"

"I'm not sure about Mr. Botsford, but I most certainly would mind."

"You mean you would deny food to your favorite brother, starving though he may be?" Leslie pinched up his face, trying to look as pitiful as possible.

"First of all, you're my only brother, and even so I'm still not sure you're my favorite brother," Sallie said. "Furthermore, I planned a private meal with Mr. Botsford. In any case, as I recall, he instructed you to stay away from the trial."

"It's too late now. I was there for the proceedings yesterday, and I expect to be there again today. If I don't starve to death first."

"Well, I suppose I could sneak some food away from the table for you. But I don't want Mr. Botsford seeing you. I'm to meet him presently at a dining room over on Main Street. If you wait here, I'll be back within the hour with some vittles."

Leslie wasn't sure he could wait that long and frankly didn't see the need.

"That will be fine," he said, as his mind formulated an alternate plan.

"Then I'll see you later," Sallie said.

She pulled a dark wool scarf tightly over her head and continued through the lobby and out the door. Leslie wasn't far behind, though he stopped just outside the hotel and watched Sallie walk across the railroad tracks and turn left onto Main Street, heading in the direction of Ohio Avenue.

Leslie returned to his corner of the lobby.

He still wanted to talk to Mary, but he figured he shouldn't spend too much longer waiting. His mother would no doubt be coming down for breakfast before long. Mary probably would be with her.

He could try to get a message to Mary—maybe through Sallie. Or he could see what developed when he just happened upon Sallie and Mr. Botsford having breakfast in their dining room on Main Street.

The second plan of action would perhaps garner some food, and Leslie was almost to the point of no return when it came to his hunger. If he didn't eat soon, he thought, he almost certainly would perish.

So across the railroad tracks he went.

He turned left on Main Street and peered through the front window of the first eating establishment he found. Leslie saw Sallie and Mr. Botsford sitting at a table on the far side of the room.

They weren't eating yet. They were mostly giggling.

Leslie walked past the restaurant and continued up the street. He preferred there be food on the table when he happened upon Sallie and Mr. Botsford, so it would be harder for them to resist his grumbles about hunger.

It was still cold, but the wind was not so biting as when Leslie had ridden from the barn into town. He figured he needed to kill five minutes to make sure the food had arrived. He could survive that long in the cold, he thought, no problem.

This part of Sedalia included a handful of businesses but nothing of much interest to Leslie. The main part of downtown was in the other direction, on Main Street toward Kentucky Avenue, and much of that area consisted of the charred remains of buildings.

Leslie decided to duck into a farming supply store, mainly to find some warmth. Inside, he saw Benjamin Fish, the Lexington stable operator, so he quickly retreated to the boardwalk and continued up Main Street. No sooner had he taken ten steps than William J. Pigott, owner of the Lexington bookstore, came walking down the street toward him. Leslie swore under his breath; Pigott would undoubtedly recognize him and likely assault him with greetings and questions.

Leslie did another about-face. No more waiting; he was going into that dining room.

Returning to the restaurant, he marched to the table where Sallie and Mr. Botsford sat talking.

Mr. Botsford had his back to Leslie, but he turned when he glimpsed a look of exasperation on Sallie's face. Leslie thought Mr. Botsford was distinguished looking, with his dark hair parted down the middle to accentuate a long, pointed nose and deep-set eyes.

"Well, if it isn't the Widow Warner and the lawyer Botsford," Leslie said.

He immediately regretted his words.

Leslie was trying to be clever, but all he accomplished was angering Sallie, which promptly turned the lawyer Botsford sour toward him, as well.

"When you're trying to get food from somebody, it isn't a good idea to insult them," Sallie said.

"I'm sorry, Sallie," Leslie replied. "You know I was just funnin' ya. I'm just so happy to see the two of you, especially together."

"I didn't know you were in Sedalia, Leslie," Mr. Botsford said. "Sallie, it sounds as though you knew he was here. Do you think this is a good idea?"

"Good idea or not, he's here," Sallie said. "I didn't know about it myself until ten minutes ago. He showed up at the hotel and said he was hungry. I planned to take him some scraps, but I suppose he had other ideas."

"I was just too hungry to wait, Sallie," Leslie said.

"Well, sit down and join us, Leslie," Mr. Botsford said. "We'll order you a meal. Or better, you can have mine and I'll order another. You look like you need it more than I do. So, what brings you to Sedalia?"

Mr. Botsford laughed, and so did Sallie and Leslie after a slight pause to make sure Mr. Botsford was in fact joking.

"You remember, Leslie, I said it wasn't part of the defense strategy for you to be here for the trial. Since I'm no longer working on your father's defense, I no longer have an official interest in your presence. But I still don't think it's a good idea. I presume you've been keeping a low profile?"

"Sure have," Leslie said. "You and Sallie are the only ones who know I'm here. I've been sleeping in a barn, and I stood in the back of the courtroom yesterday to make sure nobody saw me. Plan to do the same today."

"You're staying for the entirety of the trial, then?" Mr. Botsford asked.

"Yes, sir."

"And you're planning on staying in that barn for the duration?"

"Truth be known, I was hoping to find better accommodations," Leslie said. "I hoped to talk to Sallie about that."

"You're not staying in the hotel room with Mary and me, if that's what you had in mind," Sallie said. "I recommend you make your presence known to Mother and take your medicine."

"She'd send me home, for sure," Leslie said. "I'm not goin' home and missin' Pa's murder trial. I'll just have to figure out something else."

None of the three spoke for several seconds, until Mr. Botsford broke the silence.

"Sallie, do you think it would be proper for Leslie to stay with me?" he asked. "I would enjoy the company. I'm not terribly busy right now, just waiting to begin my appointment as U.S. attorney. Leslie might even be useful in preparing for the move."

"I'm not thrilled with the idea, but I won't stand in your way," Sallie said. "If my folks find out, they will *not* be pleased with you."

"I guess I can take that chance," Mr. Botsford said. "Besides, I think their minds are on other matters. What do you think of staying with me, Leslie?"

"Your place has got to be better than a barn, I reckon," Leslie said. "What about my horse?"

"He can stay in the stable with my mount," Mr. Botsford said. "Of course, if you'd prefer, you can stay there, as well."

"No thanks," Leslie said. "I'd just as soon never sleep on straw again as long as I live."

The Trial

James Slaughter was first to take the witness stand on the morning of January 26. We don't know much about him except what we can surmise from what he said under oath, and based on that we know he was quite observant.

He provided intricate details of the killing more than two years earlier, recalling things that none of the other witnesses did.

Slaughter said he had known Sam Nutter for eight years and frequently saw William A. Warner in Lexington, where Slaughter lived. This is his account of the killing:

"About 4 o'clock on the 22nd of October 1868, as I was passing west near the bank, I heard someone say, 'Look out,' and then waved his hand. This person was Phares Hammond, and Hammond said, at the same time, 'Get back.'

"We were about four doors apart. Hammond was near the corner of Main and Laurel streets. As I looked eastward, I saw Warner near Pigott's bookstore with a gun in his hand. Warner was looking towards me.

"I was going west, and just then the deceased passed out at my rear near Mitchell's Bank. We were so near that we could have touched each other. Just as Nutter stepped off the curbstone, this calling took place.

"At second noise, Nutter had gotten about eight or ten feet from the curbstone and then turned his head eastwardly. Then Nutter turned his hand up and his head forward. At that time, Warner fired and Nutter dropped immediately.

"Warner stood in front of Pigott's bookstore when he fired. Nutter was going to his buggy when he was shot and was about ten feet from the curbstone.

". . . After Warner shot, he held his gun in a horizontal position. Nutter's sister was then standing near Nutter. Hammond then pushed Warner back into the bookstore.

"I saw Nutter after he fell. He was brought to the pavement. I did not go to where Nutter first fell. When he was brought to the pavement, Nutter was dead. I saw holes in his coat, and I saw blood. I saw no arms on Nutter's person. I saw a watch and pocketbook taken from his person. As Nutter passed out, Nutter's right side was towards Warner. I did not hear Nutter say anything as he passed out."

Upon cross-examination, Slaughter provided even more details: "It was neither cold nor hot that day. I cannot recollect whether Nutter had on a cloak or not. . . . I did not hear Warner say anything before he shot. . . . After the shooting, Hammond put his hand on Warner and also took the gun from Warner. . . . After the shooting, Nutter's sister jumped out of the buggy. . . . Warner had time to fire a second time."

The defense asked Slaughter whether he saw a pistol, prompting the prosecution to object. After some discussion, Judge Townsley overruled the objection.

"I saw a pistol in the hand of Nutter's sister," Slaughter said. "She was holding the pistol in almost every way and seemed almost frantic."

That last testimony prompted the prosecution to seek clarification.

"I saw no pistol in Miss Nutter's possession until after she came to the pavement," Slaughter said. "I saw no pistol when she stood over her brother."

***

Next to testify was William J. Pigott, owner of the bookstore where Warner was taken after he shot Nutter. He indicated that quite a crowd gathered there after the shooting.

Pigott testified that Warner "seemed in an abstracted state of mind" and that he said only one thing: "Goddamn him, he shan't talk so about me."

***

The defense recalled Benjamin Fish, the livery operator, with the *Democrat* article saying, "An effort was here made to impeach the witness."

George Vest asked him whether he ever had been indicted for a felony. Fish said no, but he added that an indictment for grand larceny had been "squashed" and that it had been a malicious prosecution.

Fish also testified that he could not recollect whether he had ever been tried or indicted on perjury charges, prompting the *Democrat* to say, "His memory was of the most non-retentive and facile character."

***

At this point in the proceedings, the prosecution had pretty much proved its case against William A. Warner. Of course, this was no whodunit. Warner had done it—shot and killed an unarmed man in broad daylight in front of multiple witnesses.

The prosecution had even made it fairly clear that Warner's act was premeditated, although that was an area the defense would challenge in coming days.

What an observer might have expected from the prosecution now was testimony from friends and family of the victim, saying what a horrible tragedy his killing had been, what a great and terrible loss.

That didn't happen, however.

Lizzie Nutter Callahan was the prosecution's only other witness, and her testimony on that Thursday in 1871 focused solely on the shooting of her brother.

Nothing was said about the shenanigans that led up to it, which likely disappointed the townsfolk gathered in the courtroom.

Lizzie had married James M. Callahan on May 20, 1869, less than seven months after her brother's death. Callahan was twenty-two at the time of the marriage; Lizzie was thirty-one, or thereabouts. Callahan was studying to be a lawyer under Tilton Davis, a member of the bar in Lexington and one of that town's most prominent citizens.

Davis, you'll recall, made the opening statement for the prosecution in the case against Colonel Warner.

Callahan would become a minor character during later days of the trial, but on the trial's second day it was his wife's turn. It appears she didn't make much of an impact.

Lizzie admitted she was carrying a small pistol at the time Colonel Warner shot Sam Nutter, but she said she didn't know how to use it. She said her brother "was in the habit of carrying arms" but was not armed on October 22, 1868.

"That day, my brother's pistols were at home on the bureau," she testified. "They were navy revolvers."

The defense cross-examined Lizzie briefly about the pistols, and that was it for her, according to the newspaper accounts.

She left the witness stand, and the prosecution rested its case.

It evidently was not too late in the day, because the defense was then allowed to proceed.

* * *

The defense's first witness was John Cather, who owned and ran the City Hotel in Lexington. The defendant had been staying at the City Hotel during the fair, and Sam Nutter was taken there after the shooting.

Cather said that Nutter, whom he described as "a fleshy man," was still breathing when he was brought to the hotel and that he ordered the mortally wounded man to be carried upstairs because a crowd had started gathering.

He said, "I stripped Nutter," and discovered twelve buckshot wounds.

"I should judge Nutter must have had his arm up. . . . The wounds were angling, for the buckshot passed in that way through his body and were seen on the other side of his body where they came out."

At this point, the defense lawyers showed Cather a bloody paper, and he identified it as an item he'd found in Nutter's right-hand pocket. He said he had found four of the rolled-up papers in total. These were copies of the pamphlet castigating the Warners, which Nutter had printed a few weeks before his demise.

The defense moved on, asking the witness about threats Nutter had made against the defendant. That brought an objection by the prosecution and led to Judge Townsley ordering the jury to leave the room so the issue could be argued.

The lawyers' arguments lasted more than seven hours, according to the *Democrat*.

"The Court overruled the objection," the *Democrat* article said, "and the case proceeded."

But not until the next day.

Evening

The second day of his father's murder trial had dragged on well into the evening, and Leslie frankly was bored by most of the legal proceedings.

"Things will get more interesting tomorrow," Mr. Botsford told him.

They were sitting at a table in Mr. Botsford's room, which was in a boardinghouse on Osage Avenue, between the Ives House and the courthouse. The room was on the second floor, and Leslie thought it was kind of pitiful. It was hardly bigger than his room at home, although it had amenities such as the table and a few somewhat comfortable chairs.

Leslie had lived in large houses his entire life. He hoped a boardinghouse didn't feature prominently in his adult future.

Because of the lateness of the trial, Mr. Botsford and Leslie had missed the evening meal. But Leslie was more tired than he was hungry. Two nights in a frigid barn loft had deprived him of his usual nine hours of sleep. In fact, he had gotten almost no sleep.

So, even a blanket spread out on a hardwood floor looked inviting to him at this point.

He plopped down on the blanket, expecting to fall immediately into a much-needed slumber. He closed his eyes, took a deep breath, and lay still. Sleep beckoned, but Leslie's mind quickly returned to the Junction Hotel and its inhabitants. Try as he might, he couldn't get rid of the thoughts.

Finally, just as he started drifting off, Leslie was distracted by muffled noises coming through the room's walls.

Music. Laughter. Hollering. Occasional screeches of joy.

And then . . .

"You're either the luckiest sonofabitch alive, or you're cheatin'."

The loud man's voice seemed to be coming from right next door. Leslie figured it couldn't be from one of the neighboring rooms in the boardinghouse, but he had no idea what kind of people might live in the adjoining buildings.

"I ain't cheatin'," another voice said. "I'm just a better poker player than you are."

"Shut up, the both of you," a third voice said. "We can't have the whole street hearin' you. I can't afford another twenty-dollar fine from the city."

The voices then became more indistinct, though Leslie could still hear much of what was being said. He identified at least five voices, all men. As he listened, they became more businesslike in tone, talking about raises and pots and straights and flushes and such.

Leslie had never played poker, and it intrigued him. He thought he might have to check it out while he was in Sedalia.

He wanted to ask Mr. Botsford about what was going on, but his host was asleep in his bed.

Leslie covered his head with the top of his blanket, trying to block out the noise. Within a few minutes, he was fast asleep.

January 27, 1871

Morning

L eslie awoke feeling refreshed but a bit woozy. He figured he must have slept soundly, because he didn't remember having any dreams or being awakened by the street noises.

It was quiet now.

Mr. Botsford was already awake and moving about.

"Do you drink coffee, Leslie?" he asked.

"Nope, though I do like the smell."

"Just as well. I make terrible coffee. At least that's what I've been told. How'd you sleep?"

"Like a newborn pup. It took me a bit to fall asleep, though. Lots of noises around here. Do you know anything about the gamblin' that goes on next door?"

"That's new," Mr. Botsford said with a half-smile. "Those games tend to move around to stay ahead of the law. It likely will be gone within a week or so. Why? Do you want to join in?"

"It just piqued my interest, is all."

"I imagine you'll run across a lot of things in Sedalia that you haven't seen in Lexington or Carrollton. Most of them bad."

"Bad is OK with me," Leslie said. "At least this seems like an interesting place to live."

"Maybe so, but neither of us is going to be here much longer. I'll be moving to Jefferson City for my new job, and you'll be going home to Carroll County once the trial is over. Hopefully with your father."

"Do you think that's likely?"

"You'll have a better answer after today's testimony," Mr. Botsford said. "Now, we should get down for breakfast. I don't suppose you're hungry, are you?"

"I could eat a horse," Leslie said. "Course, I'd never do that."

Once downstairs and seated at the dining room table, Leslie gave up on talking, instead focusing on stuffing as much food as possible into his mouth. He also ignored the jabbering at the table, where he and Mr. Botsford were joined by three men, all of whom Leslie imagined to be accountants, shopkeepers, and the like.

But then a voice nabbed his attention.

"Do you think this Union colonel will be convicted, Mr. Botsford?"

Mr. Botsford hadn't told anyone in the boardinghouse who Leslie was, having described him only as the son of a friend.

Leslie looked expectantly at Mr. Botsford, toes curling inside his shoes. He waited anxiously for the lawyer's answer.

"Well, I don't know for sure," Mr. Botsford said. "He killed an unarmed man in cold blood, with plenty of witnesses. That sounds like murder. But the man he killed had been making threats and had conducted himself despicably against the colonel's family. Also, Colonel Warner has the best lawyers in Missouri on his side, and I wouldn't bet against them."

Leslie was happy to hear that, because nobody in his family had discussed the likelihood of his father's exoneration. His mother had merely said, "The good Lord will see to it that justice is served."

That's what Leslie was afraid of.

The Trial

CIRCUIT COURT
Important Murder Case
Third Day

The court met at the usual hour and the attendance was unusually large. The prisoner came into the court room attended by his wife and daughters. Col. Warner took his seat at the table in the court room between Col. Philips and Mr. Vest.

He appeared to be in excellent health, and his dress betokened that of a neat business man. He appeared somewhat restless as he cast his dark eagle eyes over the crowd assembled and upon the jurors who were sitting in judgement upon his case. Col. Warner is the last man that would be selected from all that crowd to be an assassin.

—Daily Bazoo, January 27, 1871

There was a reason for the unusually large crowd.

The third day of the trial featured testimony from eight witnesses, according to coverage in both the *Bazoo* and the *Democrat*. Amid that coverage, with no more than a few lines committed to him in either newspaper, was the testimony of General Joseph O. "Jo" Shelby.

After showing his support for William A. Warner with a letter to the Lexington newspapers shortly after the killing of Sam Nutter, the Confederate hero appeared in court more than two years later to help in Warner's defense. Shelby's presence no doubt created quite a buzz in Sedalia. He was one of the best-known men in Missouri, and members of his Iron Brigade had participated in the capture of Sedalia in October 1864.

In any case, it must have been quite a coup for George Vest and John Philips to get Shelby to testify on behalf of Colonel Warner.

We know Shelby had a relationship with Warner, but he also was friends with Vest, the former Confederate congressman. Vest, in fact, later in life told a story about his 1874 visit to Shelby's farm, where he was surprised to meet the two James brothers and three Younger brothers. Vest said they all spent the night under the same roof, although he indicated his sleep was far from sound.

It's doubtful Shelby was on friendly terms with Philips, Warner's other lead lawyer. As a Union colonel, Philips had confronted Shelby and his men at the Battle of Westport and chased Shelby across several western Missouri counties.

This murder trial was certainly making for some strange bedfellows.

* * *

Five people testified before Shelby that Friday morning. First was hotel owner John Cather, who returned to the witness stand as the jury finally began to hear testimony concerning Warner's motivation for killing his son-in-law.

Cather told of an incident in May 1868 when Warner, Georgia, and their daughter Sallie were staying at Cather's hotel. This would have been only a month or so after Sallie had left Nutter and filed for divorce.

A man arrived at the City Hotel and handed Cather a message. Assuming it was for him, Cather opened it. He saw that the note was from Sam Nutter, however, and that it was intended for Warner.

Cather allowed the man to deliver it upstairs to Warner, then visited Warner himself.

"I went and told Colonel Warner that he must stay upstairs for I do not want any fuss in my house," Cather testified.

Soon thereafter, Nutter arrived, and he wasn't alone. It was about 8 p.m., Cather said.

"There were four of the men, some of them very dangerous men," Cather testified. "Two of the men showed pistols, six-inch navy revolvers. The two that showed their pistols were the least dangerous."

Cather said Nutter demanded to see Warner.

"He said he wanted to kill him or make him take back something he had said. I told him he could not see him in my house. I told him I was prepared to defend Warner as long as he was in my house. They said if they could not get him they would find him."

At that point, Cather said, Nutter and his associates went to the hotel's bar, where they downed some drinks, made a few more threats, and left.

Cather said the Warners, at his request, changed rooms, moving from the front of the hotel to the rear.

He continued with his testimony, discussing other meetings he had with Nutter:

"Nutter said Warner was trying to ruin him, and he was going to kill him. Nutter made these threats all summer. Nutter was generally armed—six-inch navies—and generally showed them.

"I communicated the fact of Nutter's making these threats to Warner. . . . Nutter was at my hotel often, twice a week, and continually made these threats; he made them every week. He never made threats but what he displayed his arms.

"Nutter showed me a pamphlet about September 8, and I said to Nutter not to circulate them as Colonel Warner would kill him certainly. Nutter then pulled open his coat, showed his pistols, and said that Warner would never get the drop on him. . . . I had often told Warner of Nutter's threats and that Nutter was armed."

During cross-examination by the prosecution, Cather pointed out that the Warners and Nutter had stayed at his hotel regularly—even after the divorce proceedings had begun.

"Warner and his wife and Mrs. Nutter were there most of a month," Cather said. "Nutter was also there. . . . The last conversation I had with Nutter on this subject was during the middle of October, the time, I think, of the Carrollton fair."

* * *

Cather testified that Nutter and his friends had shown up at his hotel in search of Colonel Warner in the middle of May.

Perhaps it was just a coincidence, but on May 17, the Warners discovered their cistern had been poisoned. That was according to testimony by Sallie Nutter, who followed Cather on the witness stand. She said the cistern must have been poisoned on that Saturday night because the family discovered the problem Sunday morning before breakfast.

"My mother was cleaning her teeth," she said. "The water looked dirty. We all tasted it; it made all sick who tasted it for several hours. The cistern was nailed up, and no water used out of it during the summer, except washing."

She did not accuse her late husband of the cistern poisoning, nor did she accuse him of another incident that occurred on the family farm after she moved there and started divorce proceedings.

Not directly, anyhow.

Sallie testified that two of the family's horses had been killed June 27, 1868: A gray colt having been thrown into a well and a gray mare having been poisoned. She couldn't have been sure that Sam Nutter had committed these foul deeds, but she surely had strong suspicions.

Of the next incident, she had no doubt, however.

She said Sam Nutter paid her and her family a late-night visit July 5, 1868.

The Warners, she said, had lived in a two-story house about two hundred yards from the road, with no trees in the yard but with woods about forty yards to the east. She said it was a very bright night.

"My room was upstairs. I had my nurse girl to get up so that I could look out to see who was about the house as I was in the habit of doing after the cistern was poisoned in May. We were living in constant dread at the time.

"I discovered two men about thirty yards from my window. They ran so soon as the shutter was thrown open. I sent down for my father. As soon as my father came up, they were out of sight in a little piece of woods. Father and I stood at the window about fifteen minutes, and we saw one man return to the same place that both men had ran from.

"I recognized the one that returned to be Mr. Nutter, for he stood there about ten minutes. I went down to procure a stick to put under the window, and when I returned, Mr. Nutter was leaving. My father called to him and told him to stop, as he knew who he was.

"Father called twice. The second time Nutter stopped and fired three times toward the house. After the firing, Nutter ran to the woods. Father fired three shots at Nutter also.

"When father and I were at the window, we stood back, and when Nutter fired, I ran behind the chimney and left my father at the window. One shot took effect under the window we were standing at. He used a pistol.

"I examined the footsteps the next morning and recognized Mr. Nutter's as he had a very small foot, turned his heel in, and had a high instep. There had been a heavy shower that evening just before sunset. The other footstep was very large.

"Four saddles and a carriage harness were taken to the woods and cut up. One carriage wheel was taken away that night. Some tools were carried off that night. I recognized the track about the tool and carriage house as Mr. Nutter's.

"The family were all in dread, after this shooting, of Mr. Nutter. We watched nights, and our neighbors watched."

Sallie said it was because of this dread that Colonel Warner moved the family to near Carrollton in Carroll County on September 2, saying the move was "to avoid and get rid of Mr. Nutter, in whom we stood in great fear."

The move would have been a short one; Carroll County is just north of Dover. But a trip there requires crossing the Missouri River.

In Carroll County, the Warners became neighbors to Georgia's sister Margaret Combs Downing and her family, as well as to Georgia's brother, Howard Tilford Combs, and his family.

The 1870 census shows that the Warners lived in Carroll County and that William A. Warner owned 1,010 acres there. They still lived there during the 1871 murder trial.

When she was cross-examined, Sallie confirmed a few things she already had testified to and emphasized that she had no doubt one of the men who stalked the Warners' house that night had been Sam Nutter.

"It was a clear night after 10 o'clock. I could not tell the features of the man that was there, but I knew it was Mr. Nutter from his appearance as well as if I had been by his side."

***

The next witnesses, Frank Allison and Captain William H. Littlejohn, provided details that supported Sallie's testimony, making it clear that Sam Nutter likely was the culprit in at least two of the incidents at the Warners' house.

Allison lived on a farm adjoining the Warners' near Dover. He said he twice saw two men ride past his place; the first time they were coming from the direction of the Warners' farm late on a Saturday night in June 1868, the second heading toward the Warners' farm late on a Sunday night in July.

He said one of the men he saw on the June night was a Negro.

"The white man I saw each time was fleshy. His general appearance was that of a large man, about the size of the deceased," Allison testified. "On the occasion of my meeting the men both times, they were riding tolerably fast."

Allison said that after the incidents the Warners "expressed fear of Nutter" and asked him to stay at their house, which he said he did on two occasions.

When cross-examined, he admitted, "I suppose there are other fleshy men that live in that neighborhood."

Captain Littlejohn provided an interesting perspective. He had served under Warner with the Eighteenth Kentucky during the war and, like

Warner, had moved to Lafayette County. But he had been a neighbor of Nutter's near Wellington.

He recounted that he was riding on the Independence Road at about 6:15 a.m. Sunday, May 17, 1868—the morning the Warners discovered their cistern had been poisoned—when he encountered Nutter:

"Mr. Nutter and myself met, and I shook hands with him. He wore a dark blue overcoat with the collar turned up and a red handkerchief around his neck. He had on a broad-brimmed hat, with his coat buttoned up.

"'Halloo, old fel,' said I, 'you must have laid out last night.'

"Says he, 'Oh no, I've just been across the country,' and inquired after our family.

"We then parted, he going toward home and I in an opposite direction. As I passed on near a burial ground, I saw a lady coming towards me on horseback. She was dressed in dark clothes and had on a riding hat. The most direct road from Warner's to Nutter's was through Lexington. This road was a sort of lone one. One had to open a number of gates, but still one could go from Warner's to Nutter's on this road.

"The lady was Miss Lizzie Nutter. I raised my hat and said, 'Good morning, Miss Lizzie,' and she returned the salutation.

"After this time, I saw Nutter and his sister. It was about the last of May or the first of June. They came to my house in a carriage. Mr. Nutter and I met between my stable and house and shook hands. He told me that he had bad news. He said he was in Lexington that day and heard that I had charged him with poisoning Warner's cistern.

"I told him it was a grave charge and asked him to give his informant.

"He answered, 'I am not at liberty to tell.'

"I asked him how he expected I should answer such a charge unless he told me who informed him.

"Then I said to him, 'If you do not acknowledge about your being out the morning I met you before two or three persons, I will believe you guilty of the charge.'

"Nutter denied any recollection of meeting me on the morning in question. I then ordered him out of my yard, and we never spoke after that. Up to the morning Nutter and his sister came to my house, I saw Nutter frequently. We were near neighbors."

Upon cross-examination by the prosecution, Captain Littlejohn stated that he was "on most friendly terms with Warner" but that he "knew of no conspiracy to kill Nutter the week of the fair."

***

Mary Warner corroborated much of her sister's testimony about the poisoning of the family's cistern and about the move to Carroll County. But she was also asked about her brother's whereabouts on the day of the shooting.

Mary said Leslie had driven her and Mary Downing (likely a cousin) in a wagon to the Lexington fair on October 22, 1868. She said they ate at the fairgrounds, which were about two miles outside of Lexington, between 1 and 2 p.m. and didn't leave the grounds until about sundown.

They then went into Lexington, where they learned of the fatal shooting.

"My brother was with me all day," Mary testified. "He was with me so much that he could not have gone to Lexington and back without my knowing it on that day."

And, finally, this little nugget:

"My brother is now in his seventeenth year. He's very tall for his age. I think he is taller than my father. He was very tall at this time in 1868."

What Leslie's height had to do with anything is hard to figure. It's also somewhat strange that he apparently wasn't in court. Mary said under cross-examination that he was "at home today in Carrollton."

What sixteen-year-old boy (going on seventeen) would miss the chance to be at a murder trial, especially when his own father was being tried, the jurors must have wondered.

Might Leslie have known something the defense didn't want coming out during the trial?

***

Finally, it was time for General Jo Shelby.

Based on his testimony, Shelby was familiar with Nutter. He said he saw Nutter at the City Hotel in September 1868:

"He asked me to take a drink, which I did. After drinking, he took me to one side and asked me, 'Have you seen anything of that damned scoundrel Warner?' I told him, no, I had not for several days.

"He said, 'I'll kill him on sight,' and we had some conversation about the family feud, and I left. This was after the pamphlet was published.

"Some two weeks after, I saw Warner and told him to be on the *qui vive* as Nutter intended to shoot him on sight. This was shortly before the Lexington fair, some two or three weeks, I think."

The general said he had no other communication with Nutter on the subject.

That was the extent of Shelby's testimony, according to the reports in the *Bazoo* and *Democrat*, although he also was in court the next day, creating a bit of a stir when he was recalled to the stand by the defense.

For now, though, the defense turned its attention to the pamphlet so many of the witnesses had mentioned.

It must have been late in the day by this point, because the two witnesses who followed Shelby on the stand appear to have been questioned only briefly. Most of the pamphlet testimony would wait until Saturday.

* * *

In 1868, Henry Flint was identified only as a Lexington resident, although he also was a grand captain general of the Masonic Order, according to the *Encyclopedia of the History of Missouri*, published in 1901. George M. Mountjoy, also a Lexington resident in 1868, was to become the Lafayette County sheriff and later the county collector.

In other words, both likely had good reputations, which would have made them worthy witnesses for the defense.

Both said they had known Nutter. Flint said he didn't know Warner, but Mountjoy did.

Flint's testimony included the following:

"In the middle of September 1868, in Lexington, I met Nutter. He had a handful of pamphlets which he seemed to be distributing. He handed me one of them and said, 'Read it, and next time you see me give me your opinion of it.'

"About four days after, I met him in the City Hotel, and he asked me, 'Have you perused that pamphlet?' I said, 'I have,' in reply.

"He displayed his pistols to me and said, 'Damn him, if he can shoot before I can he is welcome.' He displayed a couple of medium-sized Colt revolvers. He was speaking of Colonel W. A. Warner."

Mountjoy testified:

"In the fall of '68, I saw Nutter in Lexington. He said he had circulated the pamphlets in Carroll County under the nose of Colonel Warner. He said Colonel Warner was too damned a coward, that he was ready for him at any time. He said he saw Warner in Carrollton when he circulated them.

"I was frequently in Nutter's company, all along from the time of the separation until his death, and never saw him without his revolvers. I do not recollect hearing Nutter at any other time making threats against Warner."

When he was cross-examined, Mountjoy said that "it was the habit of a great many in Lafayette County, in 1868, to carry pistols." So Nutter would not have stood out in that regard, but it certainly sounds as if he liked to show them off.

All of which begs the question: Why wasn't he wearing them the day he was killed?

Evening

Leslie was tempted to leave the courthouse while his sister Mary was testifying about him. He was afraid to make eye contact with anybody. He felt as if people were staring at him, as if they suspected who he was.

However, he figured leaving would only attract attention, which might lead to somebody actually recognizing him. Instead, Leslie bent at his knees a bit and stooped at his waist in an attempt to appear shorter, and he stared at the floor a lot. He felt uneasy and more self-conscious than ever in his life.

It was worth the risk to see General Jo Shelby, not to mention Frank Allison and Captain Littlejohn. Their testimonies enthralled Leslie, almost making him forget his fear of being recognized.

Leslie slid out the courtroom door as soon as the final witness left the stand. He planned to return to the boardinghouse room of Mr. Botsford.

This morning, Mr. Botsford had told Leslie that he was welcome to come and go as he pleased. He also mentioned that he would be out this evening with Sallie, dining and enjoying an evening of music at the Ilgenfritz Opera House.

Leslie ate quickly and quietly at the boardinghouse before venturing onto the chilled and muddy streets of Sedalia. He planned on exploring the town until he either found something interesting to do or became so cold he was compelled to return to Mr. Botsford's room for the evening.

If he was forced into that second option, he thought, he might have to figure out a way to visit the gambling den next door. Of course, he didn't know how to play poker, and even if he did he reckoned the 25 cents in his pocket wouldn't cut the mustard with the other players. Still, Leslie thought the poker players might let him sit in and watch.

For now, though, he had other ideas.

Most of the action in Sedalia was on Ohio or Main, so Leslie plotted a course that would take him down Ohio to Main, then west on Main to the liveliest part of town. It was no coincidence that he would also be heading in the direction of the Junction Hotel and its painted inhabitants.

He passed the Ginter Restaurant and Hoffman's Grocer and the Peterfish Millinery and Sicher's Hotel and finally the Ilgenfritz Opera House. He saw lots of folks engaged in various activities but nothing that interested him much.

When Leslie reached Main, he saw that a train had just pulled into the station, which was housed in the Ives House a block to the north. After a moment's hesitation, he wandered in that direction. His parents were staying at the Ives House, but he figured they would have no reason to be at the rail station. They more than likely were having a meal in the hotel or (even better) someplace across town.

Still, Leslie tried to keep himself obscured behind posts or around corners as he watched passengers disembark from the train while a handful of others anxiously waited to board.

Leslie had ridden on trains only twice, but they intrigued him. It fascinated him that a person could step on a train here in Sedalia and, within a few days, step off in some faraway place like New York or Boston.

The flurry of passengers who disembarked included a couple of cowboys, an elderly couple who appeared to be a husband and wife, and a young family of four. At least, Leslie assumed it was a family of four, because there was a man, a woman, and two children—a boy who looked to be eight or nine and a girl who was a few years older.

The man, woman, and boy walked briskly into the Ives House, but the girl simply stood beside the train as the outgoing passengers boarded. Leslie figured whoever was supposed to meet her was late.

She stood motionless, holding a small canvas bag, even as the train began to pull away.

The girl was perhaps fifteen or sixteen, Leslie thought, and she was almost as pretty as his sister Mary, although the girl's tattered coat and soiled clothes didn't do her figure any favors.

She also wore a dingy, brown wool cap that covered most of her hair and hid some of her face.

Still, Leslie was enamored.

Finally, the girl trudged toward the hotel entrance. As she did, Leslie adjusted his position from one side of a post to the other, so he could keep an eye on her.

Before taking five steps, she stopped. She dropped her bag. She slumped onto the wood planks. And she started to cry.

No one seemed to notice except Leslie.

He left his post and hurried to her side.

"You shouldn't cry," he said, bending so his face was level with the girl's. "You're too pretty to cry."

"Who are you?" the girl asked, sniffling.

When she turned her face toward Leslie, he felt his heart stop for just a second. Her eyes were large and pale blue, and her lips, though chapped, were full and lovely and turned down slightly at the corners. Her face was filled with freckles.

"Leslie Combs Warner," he said. "You can call me Leslie. What's your name?"

"Susie."

"Susie who?"

"Susie Willis."

"Well, hello Susie Willis. What has brought you to Sedalia?" Leslie asked, trying to sound as adult as possible.

"That train, of course."

Leslie laughed.

"I know that," he said. "I saw you get off. I mean, why have you come to Sedalia? Are you returning home after a trip, or are you from somewhere else?"

The girl had stopped crying and had risen to her feet by now, and Leslie was standing close to her. He was nearly a foot taller, so he was looking down at her. She was studiously avoiding eye contact.

"I come from Warrensburg."

Leslie knew Warrensburg was a small town not far west of Sedalia, but he didn't know much else about it.

"You live there, then?" he asked.

"I did until today."

"So you're moving to Sedalia?"

"It appears so."

"What is there here for you? A job? Family?"

"You sure ask a lot of questions," the girl said uneasily.

"That's just my nature," Leslie said. "I'm naturally inquisitive."

"Maybe you should inquisitate somewheres else."

Leslie laughed again.

"But I only inquisitate people I find interesting," he said. "You should take it as a compliment that I'm asking you questions."

Susie finally looked up directly at Leslie's face. He was smiling. She wasn't. She was glaring.

"You ain't scared of me, are ya?" he said, abandoning proper grammar so he might, he thought, seem more approachable.

"I don't guess so," she said. "But I'm scared of this place. I ain't never been here before, and I don't know nobody."

"Well, you must know *somebody*. You got somebody to stay with, don't ya?"

"Not really."

Leslie was beginning to get the picture, and he didn't much care for it.

"Let's go inside and get out of the cold," he said, reaching to take Susie's arm.

She pulled away.

"OK," she said. "But please, don't handle me. Ma told me I ought be careful around men in this town."

Leslie was glad she considered him a man, even if she didn't want him to touch her.

He walked toward the door to the Ives House, turning after two steps to make sure Susie was following him.

She was.

The hotel lobby was bustling with people; in the heat of the moment, Leslie had forgotten about hiding from his parents. Catching himself, he motioned Susie to follow him around a corner.

"What are you plannin' to do, now that you're here?" he asked.

"I don't know," she said, eyes again fixed on the floor. "I ain't got a plan. Ma gave me the name of a lady to seek out here, but I don't know her, and she ain't expectin' me."

"Well, that ain't much good," Leslie said. "I thought I was in a bad state. You got me beat by a long ways. I at least got a place to sleep, even if it is on a floor. I spent my first two nights here in a barn. Nearly froze to death."

"So you're new to this town, too?"

"I'm just here for a little while. I live up north of here, in Carroll County."

Leslie didn't want to get into the specifics of why he was in Sedalia, so he changed the subject before Susie could do any more inquisitating of her own.

"How old are you, anyway?"

"How old do you think I am?"

"Sixteen?" he said hopefully.

"I guess that must mean *you're* sixteen, then," she said.

"You're smarter than you look," Leslie said, and laughed, hoping Susie didn't take him seriously.

"Why, thanks," Susie said. For the first time, her lips split in a smile. "I like you, Leslie. You're different from the boys I know in Warrensburg."

"Maybe that's 'cause I come from Kentucky. Or maybe it's 'cause I ain't no boy. I'm almost seventeen."

"I'm sorry if I offended you," Susie said. "I was tryin' to compliment you."

"I ain't offended. I like you, too. I think maybe we should figure out what you're gonna do next. Do you wanna go find that woman your mother told you to look up?"

"No. But I don't have no other ideas, neither."

"Well, I have an idea," Leslie said. "Come with me."

Leslie again reached for Susie's arm. This time, she allowed him to take it.

***

"Mr. Botsford is at the theater with my sister Sallie," Leslie said as he opened the door to Mr. Botsford's room. "He's sweet on her. I don't think he'll be back till late tonight. He'll know what you should do. He's a lawyer."

Susie walked hesitantly into the room. She dropped her bag on the floor and sat in a wooden chair at the table.

"I guess I should thank you," she said. "But to tell the truth, I'm still scared as can be."

Leslie shut the door, walked to the table, and pulled up a chair across from Susie.

"Can I ask you something?" he said.

She nodded.

"Why did your mother send you to Sedalia if you ain't got any relations or friends here?"

"She said she can't take care of me no more," Susie said. "My pa left a few months ago. It's been just Ma and me since. Now she says she ain't got no way to take care of me 'cause she ain't got no job nor no prospects. She said she'll send for me if she gets back on her feet."

"But how did she expect you to manage here?" Leslie asked.

"She said Sedalia is a boomin' town compared to Warrensburg, and that I'll be able to manage here. She said her lady friend can help me get a job."

"You never did tell me how old you are."

"I'm fourteen, but folks say I look older."

"That's the truth," Leslie said, looking into her eyes. "Maybe you can tell folks you're sixteen when you're lookin' for a job."

Susie had removed her wool cap and her coat and scarf, so Leslie saw her face fully revealed in the glow of the lantern on the table. Her hair was reddish orange, wavy, and fell just below her shoulder blades. She had creamy skin, with her freckled cheeks still pink from the cold.

"I'd hire you, for sure," Leslie said, smiling.

Susie's cheeks flushed a bright red. "What would you hire me to do?" she asked.

"Well, my family has a farm. You any good at plowin' fields?"

"I reckon I could do it if you provide the horse and the plow. The horse does all the work, don't it?"

"I can tell you've never plowed a field," Leslie said.

He and Susie both laughed.

"Your family has a farm? What else?" Susie asked.

"Well, I've got a mother and a pa, as you might suspect, along with five sisters, but only four of them live at home. I'm the only boy."

"That must be interestin'."

"That's true enough. But I don't mind."

"How many sisters are older than you?"

"All but two. I had some brothers, but they died before I was old enough to know them. Some other sisters, too. And I had a brother-in-law who got killed, too."

Leslie immediately wished he hadn't mentioned the dead brother-in-law, but it was too late.

"Oh? What happened to him?" Susie asked.

"Umm . . . well . . . I guess if I can't trust you, I can't trust anybody. It's not a big secret or anything. It's just that . . ."

"I'm beginnin' to think you killed him yourself," Susie interrupted.

"No, but almost," Leslie said. "Fact is, Sam was my friend, and I was his. I didn't want him to get killed, but I think I coulda done more to stop it."

"Who killed him then?" Susie asked, scooting her chair closer to the table.

"It was . . . it was Pa," Leslie said. "Shot him dead in cold blood in Lexington."

Susie gasped, but she didn't say anything.

"He's on trial for murder now. That's why I'm in Sedalia, to see the trial. Only nobody is supposed to know I'm here. That's why I was sleepin' in the barn."

"Gosh, a murder trial. That's excitin'," Susie said. "Shame it's your pa's, though."

"Here, you can read all about it," Leslie said.

He grabbed a copy of that day's *Daily Bazoo* newspaper, which was folded on the table, and handed it to Susie. He turned it to the page with details of the trial.

Susie stared at it.

"I ain't a very good reader," she said. "Can you read it to me?"

"I guess so."

Leslie took the newspaper and began to read:

"The court met at the usual hour, and the attendance was unusually large. The prisoner came into the courtroom attended by his wife and daughters. Colonel Warner took his seat at the table in the courtroom between Colonel Philips and Mr. Vest. . . .

"They're his lawyers.

". . . He appeared to be in excellent health, and his dress betokened that of a neat businessman. He appeared somewhat restless as he cast his dark eagle eyes over the crowd assembled and upon the jurors who were sitting in judgement upon his case. Colonel Warner is the last man that would be selected from all that crowd to be an assassin.

"The wife and daughters of the prisoner are seated in the courtroom on one of the rude benches, watching with eager interest every word dropped by the witness and studying each sentence as to its meaning when coming from the mouth of the counsel."

Leslie stopped.

"You want me to keep reading? It's a long story."

"Yes. Definitely."

"Mrs. Warner is a lady perhaps forty years old and dressed in a very becoming way. She wears the face of one who was weighed down with care and brokenhearted with trouble. Her countenance evinces intellectuality and refinement of a high order.

"Mrs. Nutter, the widow of the deceased S.W. Nutter, is seated next to her mother, rather richly dressed in black and has the mien of one not altogether free from trouble. She appears about twenty-five years old and, like her mother, has a matronly appearance.

"Miss Mary Warner, a young lady of twenty, perhaps, the very picture of health and carries a very pretty face with head tastefully dressed, surmounted by a neat becoming hat and feather. The ladies wear their veils drawn down and very appropriately so, too, to avoid the gaze of the assemblage. . . ."

Leslie hesitated.

"The Mrs. Nutter mentioned is Sallie, my sister. Mary's my sister, too," Leslie said as he scanned down the page. "The rest of the article is about the testimony. I really don't want to read anymore."

He laid the newspaper on the table.

"I guess it's less excitin' when it happens to your own family," Susie said. "I'm sure you're worried about your pa. The trial ain't over yet, I guess?"

"It began Wednesday," Leslie said. "Actually, it took two days before that to pick the jury. The lawyers said it will go into next week before they do their closing arguments and get a verdict. Mr. Botsford, whose room this is, was one of Pa's lawyers until just before the trial began."

Leslie's voice had grown softer as he spoke about the trial, and now it became altogether silent. Susie remained quiet, as well.

"Would you be agreeable to talkin' about somethin' else?" Leslie finally asked.

"Why, sure," Susie said. "You said you come from Kentucky. Maybe you can tell me about that. I ain't never been to Kentucky. Shoot, this is as far from home as I've ever been."

"Kentucky was nice," Leslie said. "My favorite thing was to ride horses. We rode everywhere, over the hills and through the trees and down by the river. Kentucky is the prettiest place I've ever seen, certainly prettier than Missouri. You'd like it there."

"I bet I would," Susie said.

"When the war came," Leslie continued, "that ruined everything. Pa got shot through the chest and almost got killed. We left for here a few months after the war ended. Well, not here. We moved to Lafayette County, not too far from Lexington. Sallie married Sam Nutter almost as soon as we got here, and . . ."

Leslie heard footsteps in the hallway, approaching the room. The door clicked open.

Mr. Botsford walked in. He saw Leslie and Susie sitting at the table, blinked, then looked sternly into Leslie's eyes.

"I presume you have something to tell me, Leslie?" he said without anger. But he wasn't smiling, either.

It was nearly 10 o'clock, and Leslie had lost track of the time. He'd been so involved in talking to Susie that he hadn't even thought about what he would tell Mr. Botsford.

So he opted for the truth.

"Mr. Botsford, this is Susie," he said. "She arrived here this evening on the train from Warrensburg, and she doesn't know anybody in Sedalia, so I brought her here."

"Pleased to meet you, Susie," Mr. Botsford said. "Do you have a last name?"

"Willis," Susie said. "Susie Willis."

"What brings you to Sedalia?"

"Uh, well," Susie said warily, "my mom said she couldn't take care of me no more, and she put me on the train."

"Do you have any family here?" Mr. Botsford asked, frowning.

"No."

"How does your mother expect you to subsist here?"

"Subsist?"

"I'm sorry. What does your mother expect you to do to survive?"

"She said I should find a job."

"Are you trained in anything?"

"No, not really."

"I must say, that sounds ominous. But we have a more pressing issue. Do you have a place to lay your head for the night? Or do you have the means to pay for a bed somewhere?"

"I ain't got but a few dollars. I was hoping to use that on food."

"On that subject, Leslie, have you offered Susie anything? She must be hungry and thirsty after her trip."

"Oh, drat, we were so busy talkin' I didn't even think of food or drink," Leslie said. "I'm sorry. Do we . . . you . . . have anything we can give her?"

"Of course," Mr. Botsford said.

He dispatched Leslie downstairs to fetch some water while he cut slices of bread, which Susie devoured in seconds.

"I guess I was hungry," she said, as Leslie arrived with the water.

"Now, we still must resolve the issue of your lodging," Mr. Botsford said. "Do you have any ideas, Leslie? Never mind, I know what you likely are thinking, and, no, Susie can't sleep here. A young woman can't spend the night in the same room with two men to whom she isn't related. It isn't proper."

"But Mr. Botsford, she's more a girl than a young woman," Leslie said.

"It doesn't matter. Unless she's a toddler, it just isn't proper," Mr. Botsford insisted.

"The only other thing I can think of," Leslie said, "is the woman Susie's mom told her to look up when she got here. But she's not expectin' Susie."

"I ain't sure she even knows of my existence," Susie said.

Mr. Botsford shook his head. "No, no, that won't do. In any case, it's too late in the evening to show up on an unsuspecting woman's front porch with a young girl. There are women at my church who I think would be willing to help us, but, again, it's too late to knock on their doors. I believe we have only one option, and it's not one I relish."

"What's that?" Leslie asked.

"Sallie," Mr. Botsford said. "Susie could stay in Sallie's hotel room for the night. But, Leslie, I'm afraid you must be the one who approaches Sallie. I can't be seen going up to her hotel room, especially late at night."

"That's fine with me," Leslie said.

***

Leslie knew Mary and Sallie were lodging together at the Ives House, but he didn't know whether Sallie had told Mary of his presence in Sedalia.

Mary opened the door when Leslie knocked. Her face lacked the look of surprise and shock that Leslie expected.

"Sallie told me you were in town," Mary said. She wore a linen nightgown and a heavy woolen robe. "But I didn't expect you to come calling at this hour. I wish I could say it was good to see you, but it isn't. Mother would scald you alive if she knew you were here."

"Well, let's not tell her," Leslie said. He then turned to his left, waving Susie to join them from down the hall where he had stationed her.

Now came the look of surprise and shock.

"Mary, this is Susie," Leslie said. "I met her tonight at the train station. She came from Warrensburg."

"Pleased to meet you, Susie."

"The pleasure is mine," Susie replied.

Leslie saw that Sallie was standing a few feet behind Mary, peering over her sister's shoulder. Like Mary, she wore a nightgown and robe. She also wore a stern look similar to the one Mr. Botsford had flashed a bit earlier.

"Sallie, I guess you're wondering what's going on," Leslie said as he maneuvered around Mary. "Well, it was Mr. Botsford's idea. He thought you might could help."

"Help how?"

"Susie needs a place to sleep."

"And Mr. Botsford thought our room might be a good place?" Sallie sounded incredulous.

"He did," Leslie said. "He said it was too late to call on any proper women in Sedalia."

"Was he suggesting that we're not proper?" Mary interjected.

"Not hardly," Leslie said. "I think he knows Sallie is sweet on him and would be willing to do him this favor. Of course, it's not really a favor for Mr. Botsford. It's a favor for Susie."

"I surely would appreciate it," Susie said.

"Mr. Botsford was just being nice," Leslie said. "Like you, he didn't know Susie until this evening. Whadya think?"

Leslie, Susie, and Mary all looked at Sallie, who still wore a serious schoolmistress-like look on her face. After about ten seconds of silence, she looked Susie in the eyes and smiled.

"I think we all know who is sweet on whom here," she said. "Leslie's never had a girlfriend before. I certainly will not stand in the way of true love."

Leslie's face turned red as he tried in vain to come up with a response.

Sallie and Mary laughed. Then, so did Susie.

"There are two beds," Sallie said. "Mary and I will share one. You can have the other, Susie."

"That's awful generous," Susie said. "I'd be more than comfortable on the floor."

"I wouldn't even think of such a thing," Sallie said. "Now, Leslie, you get back to Mr. Botsford's room. We'll take care of Susie, all right?"

"But . . ." Leslie started, "when will I see you again?"

He was looking at Sallie, but everybody in the room knew he was talking about Susie.

She was looking at Sallie, too.

"We'll worry about that tomorrow," Sallie said.

January 28, 1871

Morning

"Is this Saturday?" Leslie asked, as he rose and wiped the sleep out of his eyes. "It's been a long week, but I think it's Saturday."

"Yes, it is," Mr. Botsford said. He was seated at the table, drinking coffee and examining the *Daily Bazoo*. "And tomorrow will be Sunday."

Leslie's imagination had been racing all night with thoughts of Susie, so he didn't sleep much. But he didn't mind.

"From my experience of the past few days, you usually aren't so chipper in the morning," Mr. Botsford observed. "I guess Susie put that smile on your face."

"I guess so," Leslie said. "I sure do like her. I've never met anybody like her, nobody I can talk to as easy as I can talk to her. I want to spend more time with her."

"Do you know what Sallie and Mary plan to do with Susie today?" Mr. Botsford asked, laying aside his newspaper.

"They said last night they might take her shopping for clothes," Leslie said. "But with the trial going on, they weren't sure that was gonna be possible. Mother wants them both in the courtroom behind Pa for every minute of the proceedings."

"What about you?" Mr. Botsford asked. "Are you planning to attend court today?"

"I want to spend time with Susie," Leslie said. "But I want to be at the trial, too. I guess I could take Susie to the trial, but I don't reckon that's a good idea."

"No, I don't reckon it is. You'll have to make a choice. I can tell you that today likely is the final day of testimony. The closing arguments should be Monday, and you most definitely don't want to miss those."

"Are there any interesting witnesses scheduled for today?"

"Albert Keller the shopkeeper and a few others," Mr. Botsford said. "From what I understand, General Shelby might be recalled, as well. That could definitely be interesting."

"Shoot, I guess I don't know that Susie even wants anything more to do with me," Leslie said. "She might have other plans."

"She might," Mr. Botsford said. "But considering she doesn't know anybody else in Sedalia, that seems unlikely. The fact is, it appears you are the only person she can turn to for companionship in this town. I'd almost say she's your responsibility. What's more, she seems to be as fond of you as you are of her."

"Well, you've talked me into it," Leslie said. "I guess I'll be going over to the hotel presently. Right after breakfast."

"You aren't one to miss a meal, are you?" Mr. Botsford said with a chuckle.

***

Leslie still faced the challenge of avoiding his parents, so he had to be careful maneuvering through the halls of the Ives House. They were staying in the room adjoining the room of Sallie and Mary (and now Susie), so he couldn't just walk up and knock on his sisters' door as he had the previous night, when he was almost certain his parents would be asleep.

He decided to lurk down the hallway a bit, where he could duck around a corner if needed.

It wasn't long before he saw his mother and pa leave their room and head downstairs. He knew there was no chance his sisters had completed their preparations to face the world. It was barely 8 o'clock.

Sallie and Mary had developed a routine for the trial by which they were the last people to enter the courtroom (other than the judge, of course). They made a grand entrance each day, with the townsfolk in the room falling silent and staring as they walked solemnly to their seats behind their father.

They were still preparing for today's big entrance.

Leslie approached the hotel room and knocked quietly on the door.

"Who is it?" Leslie recognized Mary's voice.

"Leslie, your favorite brother."

"We don't have a brother. Sorry."

"C'mon, Mary, let me in."

"Leslie, go away." This time it was Sallie's voice. "We're not dressed yet."

"I'm dressed." Now the voice was Susie's. "Can I go on out?"

After a few seconds, the door opened several inches, and Susie slid through. She was wearing the same soiled, ill-fitting clothes as the previous night.

She smiled at Leslie, and he smiled back.

"How have Sallie and Mary been treating you?" Leslie asked.

"Just fine. I had the best night's sleep I've had in ages. What are you doin' here?"

"I wanted to check on you," Leslie said, his smile broadening. "I thought maybe we could spend the day together."

"What about the trial? You don't want to miss that, do ya?"

"Well, no. But I don't want to miss a chance to be with you, either."

"The fact is, Leslie, I have some things I need to do today," Susie said. "Maybe you should go on to the trial. We can meet up after it's over, if you'd like."

She was still smiling, but Leslie's smile had disappeared. He dropped his gaze to the floor.

"It's just that I thought we could take a ride on my horse," he said. "There's a pretty spot north of town where a cliff overlooks a creek and the road from Lexington. I saw it on my ride down here."

"Maybe some other time," Susie said.

"Tomorrow?"

"Maybe."

Leslie nodded, but he wondered if Susie was keeping something from him. Clearly there was more to her story than she had told him; otherwise, what "things" could she possibly have to do today?

"I'll see you after the trial this evening, then," Leslie said. "Will you be back here by then?"

"Likely as not," Susie said.

Leslie said good-bye, turned, and walked back down the hallway. He had a hollow feeling in his stomach, and it wasn't because he was hungry.

The Trial

The fourth day of Colonel William A. Warner's first-degree murder trial came on a Saturday, and it turned out to be the last day of testimony.

It is worth remembering that, although the proceedings were conducted in Sedalia, this was very much a Lexington trial. Or at least a Lafayette County trial.

Most of the leading characters (other than Judge Townsley and defense lawyers Vest and Philips) had traveled the fifty-five miles or more south for the big event. Virtually all the witnesses were Lafayette County residents.

And, although not as out of control as it had been just after the Civil War, when the bushwhackers roamed freely, Lafayette County remained a combustible blend of political and ethnic adversaries.

The end of slavery and the war had resulted in an influx of former slaves from the surrounding areas into Lexington, a situation that didn't sit well with many white folks. The Ku Klux Klan operated fairly openly, calling for the killing of the "coloreds."

The black residents weren't alone in being treated like outsiders.

A large number of Germans had settled parts of Lafayette County in the 1840s and 1850s. They had been staunchly anti-slavery, and many of the men fought for the Union during the Civil War.After the war, the European immigrants were objects of antagonism and derision in Lafayette County, where most folks were still smarting from the demise of the Confederacy. Not only had the Germans opposed slavery and the Confederacy but they also talked funny—if they spoke English at all.

The common term for the outsiders was "Dutch," which evolved from "Deutsch," the German word for "German." It was not a term of endearment.

***

Albert Keller, the first witness on the fourth day of the trial, was one of those objects of derision. The 1870 census listed him as a clothing dealer who had been born in Prussia, which was the dominant German kingdom until the unification of Germany in 1871.

As a parenthetical aside in its coverage of Keller's testimony, the *Daily Bazoo* wrote: "This witness is a regular Teuton and talks very broken.

His testimony provoked much merriment in court, which the Judge very promptly rebuked, threatening to inflict a heavy fine on the first person he heard or saw laugh."

Keller evidently got along well with Sam Nutter.

He said Nutter came into his Lexington store in September 1868 to buy a pair of pants.

"He seemed somewhat excited," Keller said. "I showed him a pair of pants. He went into the back room to try them on. He took off his own pants and took a pistol out of the pocket and laid it on the bed.

"He tried the pants on and at the same time commenced cursing. I said, 'Sam, what is the matter?' He replied, 'I am going to kill the damned son of a bitch on sight.' I asked him who he meant, for I was a little afraid myself. He replied, 'I mean my father-in-law.'

"I tried to have him leave his pistol with me, saying that then he would have no trouble. He would not leave it. I could not suit him in the pants. He seemed to be drinking."

Keller said that soon after his meeting with Nutter he went to New York to buy goods for his business, remaining there about three weeks.

Upon his return, Colonel Warner paid him a visit—with Nutter's pamphlet in hand.

"He interrogated me as to a part of the contents of the pamphlet. My name was in it. I replied that it was the first I had seen or heard of it. I further said that Nutter must have inserted my name on his own responsibility, but I would see Nutter about it.

"I saw Nutter two days after. I said, 'Sam, you have slandered me. You have put something in that pamphlet that I did not utter, and you will have to give me a satisfactory paper or go with me to Colonel Warner.' He replied, 'I will settle that myself. I'll kill him on first sight, anyhow.' He then went away without giving me any satisfaction.

"I went to Colonel Warner and told him what Sam had told me and tried to vindicate myself as well as I could. I told Colonel Warner about the matter either on the first day of or the day before the fair. I communicated to Colonel Warner all that Nutter said in both conversations. I think the fair commenced on the twentieth day of October, in 1868."

Warner, of course, killed Nutter on October 22, so Keller would have told him of Nutter's threats only a day or two earlier.

When cross-examined by the prosecution, Keller said he saw Nutter in Lexington on the Saturday or Monday before the fair and that Nutter was wearing a dark coat with a cape and "slouch hat" and was carrying a revolver. He added that he saw Colonel Warner on the same day.

Keller said he didn't see Warner shoot Nutter, but the prosecution had reason to believe otherwise.

State's attorney: "Did you not, in the St. James Hotel, at Kansas City, on Monday of this week, state to James Callahan (the husband of Nutter's sister Elizabeth) that you did see Nutter shot and that you called out to Warner not to shoot him?"

Keller: "No, I did not."

State's attorney: "Did you not say to James M. Callahan, at the St. James Hotel, in Kansas City, Missouri, on Monday of this week, that you knew a great deal that would be of benefit to the state, and that he ought to get the lawyers to draw it from you, and that Sam Nutter was your particular friend?"

Keller: "No, sir. When I conversed with Callahan at the St. James Hotel, we talked of ordinary topics."

***

Like Keller, Thomas R. Rudd told the court Nutter had expressed contempt for Warner while promising to do him harm.

He said he saw Nutter in Lexington in the spring of 1868, shortly after the divorce proceedings began and just before the Warners' cistern was poisoned.

"I said that he and Warner were having a heavenly time. I said this by way of a joke. Nutter then said, 'I'll be damned if I don't intend to have his heart's blood.' I said, 'That is a dangerous way to settle business.' Nutter then said, 'I'll get the slip on him.' I then started off and said I did not want to hear any more of such talk. Nutter then said, 'I'll be damned if I don't poison the whole outfit.'

"The next day, I saw Warner and told him of this danger from Nutter."

***

Robert Sandifer described himself in court as a cementer of cisterns and was not a wealthy man. But he was stylish for this occasion. The Bazoo said he "was dressed in a good velvet suit throughout, evidently nearly new, with his pants in his boots—boots new, with blue fronts."

Sandifer must have been on friendly terms with Nutter, because he described two conversations the two had in the final month of Nutter's life.

"About last of September or first of October 1868, in front of Fish's livery stable, in Lexington, I saw Nutter," he said. "He ordered his team. In a few moments, Warner passed by and went into the Post Office. Nutter said, 'There goes that damned scoundrel now.' Warner repassed the stable in a few moments, and Nutter said, 'Damn him, he'd rather see his coffin than meet me.'"

About three weeks later, on the Monday before the Lexington fair, Sandifer was returning home from a job when he again saw Nutter.

"I met Nutter on a bridge in the road. We conversed on ordinary topics. Nutter threw his leg over his horse and pulled out a small pistol either from his pantaloons or coat pocket. He held up the pistol and said, 'Bob, do you think I could kill a man across the street with that?' I told him that would depend on how it was loaded and where he hit the man. He threw back his leg and then pulled out a navy revolver and said, 'Damn him, I can kill him with that, though.' Nutter further said, 'I would have killed the damned rascal the other day, but I could not get him to meet me. Whenever he'd see me, he'd dodge and get in the crowd. I could not shoot at him because he'd get in a crowd, and I was afraid I'd hit someone else.' He was speaking of ol' Colonel Warner."

The prosecution then asked Sandifer a strange question.

State's attorney: "Where did you get that suit of clothes you have on?"

Sandifer: "I don't know that is any of your business. Where did you get your clothes?"

State's attorney: "I submit to the court whether the witness will answer the question."

Judge: "Answer the question."

Sandifer: "I got them at General Shelby's."

The witness went on to say that he had come from Lafayette County to Sedalia only as company for General Shelby.

"I met General Shelby in the street just in my working clothes. I did not expect to go any further than his house. Then General Shelby wanted me to go to Knob Noster with him, and when we were there he said I might as well go on to Sedalia.

"I told him I did not want to be subpoenaed and that I certainly would be if I came to Sedalia. . . . I was not subpoenaed until this morning. I always try and avoid courts."

Sandifer's testimony prompted the defense to recall General Shelby, who admitted he had "induced" Sandifer to come to Sedalia.

"I knew that Sandifer was an important witness," he said. "I brought him to Knob Noster, thence to this place. He knew nothing of my object. I took him to my house under the pretext of seeing some work. He is a poor man and a man of family. His clothes were not suitable to appear in a strange community, and I loaned him that suit, and, gentlemen, he is before you."

That line, according to the *Bazoo,* created a sensation in the courtroom.

It seems General Shelby was doing all he could to aid the defense of Colonel Warner.

His testimony continued: "I have been acquainted with the defendant, Colonel Warner, a long time—since I was a boy. For two years prior to the shooting, I knew Warner's reputation; he lived near me for that time. His reputation as a peaceable man in Missouri and Kentucky is good."

General Shelby was then asked about Benjamin Fish, the livery operator who had testified on the first day of the trial that he had seen William A. Warner and his son, Leslie, shortly before Warner killed Nutter, and that Warner had said, "I'll kill them both."

Shelby said Fish's "reputation for truth and veracity . . . is bad."

Three more witnesses—William Hall, John Cather (the hotel owner who had testified earlier), and Henry Flint—said essentially the same thing about Fish. Hall also said that he knew Colonel Warner in Kentucky and that "his reputation as a citizen and as a peaceable man was good."

Captain William H. Littlejohn was recalled and also defended Warner's reputation.

Littlejohn added a new bit of information: "Nutter had a couple of Negroes working for him in 1868; one was named John and lived on

Nutter's farm. John resided with Nutter until the time the pamphlet came out, and then he left."

That supported the testimony of Frank Allison, the neighbor of the Warners who had said he saw a Negro and a "fleshy" man (presumably Nutter) ride past his place late on a Saturday night in June 1868, when the Warners' horses had been killed.

At this point, the defense said it wanted to enter into evidence a copy of the notorious pamphlet Nutter had published, several of which were found on Nutter's body.

Circuit attorney J. D. Hines said he was willing to let the judge decide whether the pamphlet was proper evidence, and Judge Townsley decided it wasn't.

The defense lawyers then read several supportive depositions from reputable men who knew Warner in Kentucky, including General Leslie Combs, Warner's father-in-law.

They then rested their case.

The prosecution lawyers recalled Phares Hammond, the former deputy sheriff in Lafayette County. He testified that in 1868 he had been given a writ to arrest a man named Tom Belt on charges of stealing William A. Warner's horses.

"I do not know who got out the writ, only know that I had a writ against Belt," Hammond said. "Warner did not tell me he swore out the writ."

And that was that. Circuit attorney Hines said the state rested its case, and the court adjourned.

On Monday, the lawyers would take center stage for closing arguments.

Evening

Leslie enjoyed watching and hearing General Shelby in court again, but he had been distracted for most of the other testimony. He kept thinking about Susie.

Specifically, he kept thinking that Susie might not be as fond of him as he was of her. He wondered whether there was somebody else. He even began to doubt her story that her mother had sent her away and that she didn't know anybody in Sedalia.

And what about the mysterious woman Susie's mother had supposedly told her to look up? Was that where Susie was planning to go today? If so, why hadn't she gone straight there when she arrived on the train?

All in all, Leslie was a far cry from the chipper sixteen-year-old he had been at the start of the day.

As the sun sank near the horizon, he raced out of the courtroom and hurried toward the Ives House to make sure he got there before Sallie and Mary and (most importantly) his parents.

When he arrived at Sallie and Mary's room, he felt a sense of dread as he knocked. Leslie was afraid Susie wouldn't be there, that she had moved on and he would never see her again. Almost as bad, he feared that perhaps she would be there but no longer wanted to spend time with him.

But the pretty young girl opened the door with a smile that eased most of Leslie's worries.

"Hello, Leslie," she said. "How'd it go in court today?"

"Good, I think," Leslie said. "The testimony ended, just as Mr. Botsford said it would. Now all that's left are the closing arguments. Those will be on Monday."

"You look tired," Susie said, brow creasing with worry. "Aren't you feelin' well?"

"I'm fine. It's been a long week is all."

"Of course," Susie said. "I guess it wouldn't be proper for me to invite you in. Want to proceed to the lobby?"

"Fine."

Leslie had been fretting so much about Susie all day that he hadn't considered what they might do this evening. Eating dinner would be a logical activity, but he didn't have the funds to buy one meal, much less two.

He figured he'd think of something.

When Leslie and Susie reached the lobby, she walked directly to a nice silk-upholstered chair and sat. There was no other chair close by, so Leslie stood in front of her.

"I guess you're wonderin' what I did today," she said.

Leslie nodded.

"Fact is, I had a real good talk with your sisters last night. They said I was too young to be on my own in a strange town and that I was lucky you found me last night rather than some man with ill intentions.

"But, Leslie, I can't rely solely on your good nature to survive. You'll be going back home in a few days. Then I'll be right back in the same sorry state I was in when I got off that train. So, I decided to visit the woman whose name Ma gave me. I didn't tell you everything I knew about her. I guess I was ashamed."

"What do you mean?" Leslie asked.

"Ma used to work with the woman. They worked in a bawdy house. My mother was a whore for a long time, which she never told me until yesterday, right before she put me on the train. She also told me her and my pa weren't never married.

"In any case, now the woman runs a bawdy house here in Sedalia. Her name is Lizzie Cook."

Leslie gulped, and his knees grew so wobbly he nearly sank to the floor. He felt blood rush to his face.

Susie didn't seem to notice, however. She kept talking.

"Miss Lizzie is real nice," she said. "Ma said she would take care of me, and Miss Lizzie said she would help me, though I told her I didn't want to sell my body. She said that was fine with her, though she mentioned how pretty I am and how the men are gonna like me a lot.

"I must say most of the men I saw there reminded me of my pa, and I wouldn't want nothin' to do with 'em. But Miss Lizzie said some of the fellas who come to her place ain't so bad. She said she would figure somethin' out, and that I should come back tomorrow so we could talk again."

"Do you have any idea what she has in mind?" Leslie asked.

"I think she knows people who might take me in."

"What if my family would take you in?" Leslie blurted out. "I could ask my parents. Maybe you could come back to Carrollton with us after the trial."

"That's nice of you, Leslie. But I ain't sure that would work out. Your folks don't seem to be the kind of people who'd want a whore's daughter livin' in their home."

"But if they got to know you . . ."

"I'd still be a whore's daughter."

Both Leslie and Susie were silent for nearly a minute. Finally, Leslie worked up the courage to speak. He went down on one knee in front of Susie.

"All I know is, I like you more than any person I ever met," he said. "I thought about you every minute I wasn't with you since last night, and I want to keep spendin' time with you. I'm afraid I'll go back to Carrollton and never see you again."

"If I'm here in Sedalia, you can always come visit."

"Oh, oh," Leslie interrupted. "Look."

Sallie and Mary had entered the Ives House lobby, and they were walking toward Leslie and Susie. Leslie figured his mother and pa likely weren't far behind.

"How are Romeo and Juliet?" Mary asked, smiling. "Leslie, you best be moving along unless you want Mother to discover you here."

"I wouldn't recommend that," Sallie said. "You perhaps should return to Mr. Botsford's room, anyway. He wants to talk to you. Susie, you come up to the room with us."

"But we were talkin'," Leslie said.

"You'll have to finish your talk tomorrow," Sallie said. "Mr. Botsford hopes Susie will accompany us to his church tomorrow morning. We'll meet up with you after that."

"But I wanted to spend time with Susie this evening."

"No, you need to leave before Mother and Pa arrive," Sallie said. "And we need to ensconce Susie in our room as soon as possible."

"Fine," Leslie said, pouting a bit.

The three favorite females in Leslie's life then bid their farewells and drifted off up the stairs.

January 29, 1871

Morning

Leslie didn't much care for church.

It wasn't that he didn't believe in God and Jesus and the Golden Rule and such. He did, though he didn't like the lack of wiggle room—no room for doubt, no questions allowed.

And he didn't mind attending church on Sundays. He actually enjoyed it, but he always felt guilty because, instead of paying attention to the preacher and his words from on high, he let his mind wander. He let his eyes wander, too, usually in the direction of pretty girls.

No, it was getting forcibly dragged to church by his parents in Kentucky and Lexington and now in Carrollton that had caused Leslie to grow resentful of the Christian experience. He didn't like to be forced to do anything, especially something that was supposed to be good for him but which produced no immediate benefits that he could see.

He figured if he had been allowed to discover the whole Christian thing on his own, it might have been different.

As it was, he was fairly certain he would stop going to church as soon as he moved out of his parents' house.

On this day, however, he didn't want to be anywhere other than the Old School Presbyterian Church at Second and Lamine in Sedalia, Missouri. That was because Susie was there.

Leslie couldn't recall a word the preacher said, but he knew exactly how many times Susie had turned, looked at him, and smiled.

Six.

She had been sitting near the front with Sallie, Mary, and Mr. Botsford. Leslie had slipped into the back of the church and stayed there. He was still being careful about being spotted by his parents.

As it turned out, they weren't in this church on this Sunday. Leslie suspected they were attending services elsewhere. What with his father's fate to be decided the following day and the possibility of a hangman's noose facing him, Leslie couldn't imagine his mother and Pa choosing this Sunday to skip church.

As the service ended, Leslie kept an eye on Susie, his two sisters, and Mr. Botsford. He saw Mr. Botsford introduce what Leslie assumed were a young husband and wife—they appeared about the same age as Sallie—to Susie, and then to Sallie and Mary. The group chatted for several minutes, with Mr. Botsford and the other man doing most of the talking. Then Mr. Botsford shook hands with the man, and the young couple departed.

Leslie waited until Susie, his sisters, and Mr. Botsford walked toward the church exit, where he awaited.

"Hello, Leslie," Susie said. She had enthusiastically charged ahead of Mr. Botsford, Sallie, and Mary. "I'm pleased to see you here. What did you think of the service?"

"It was inspiring," Leslie said. "I wouldn't have missed it for the world."

Susie was face to face with Leslie now, with Sallie, Mary, and Mr. Botsford coming up just behind her. Sallie interrupted the two teenagers.

"We're going back to the hotel," she said. "You two can do what you please."

"I'll make sure Susie returns safe," Leslie said. "Maybe we'll take that ride I mentioned."

"I think I would enjoy that," Susie said, "though it's a bit cold."

"It's not so bad. The snow's almost all melted, and the sun's shining. Mr. Botsford will no doubt loan me his carriage for the afternoon."

"I wasn't planning on using it," the lawyer said. "Just be sure to return it in the condition you find it."

"Let's go, Susie," Leslie said, suppressing a whoop of joy. "Time's a wastin'."

***

By the time Leslie got the harness on his horse, the horse hooked to the carriage, and the carriage out of the stable and on the road, the weather had turned positively pleasant. He felt a sense of satisfaction driving the carriage with Susie at his side, almost as if they were a married couple.

The spot Leslie had in mind was several miles north of town, and the trip took more than an hour. The road was muddy and heavily rutted. To reach his destination, Leslie had to guide the carriage off the road, across some soft ground, and then up a somewhat rocky incline.

The two didn't talk much on the way, but after Leslie helped her out of the carriage, Susie let out a gasp.

"Oh, my Lord, it's a gorgeous place," she said.

From the top of a ridge running north and south, they could see for miles to the west. It was a vertical drop of perhaps one hundred feet to the valley floor below, where a creek meandered through mostly open terrain.

The two were standing side by side in front of the carriage, gazing toward the west horizon.

"If I was to live in this part of the country, this is where I'd want to build a house," Leslie said. "Ain't it wonderful?"

"Yes," Susie said. "But you ain't plannin' on livin' in this part of the country, are you?"

"Oh, I don't know. I could be persuaded."

Leslie raised his right arm and draped it around Susie's shoulder, pulling her close to his side.

"You ain't thinkin' of movin' here because of me, are you?" Susie asked.

"As a matter of fact, the thought had crossed my mind. I've been thinking I might want to study to become a lawyer, like Mr. Botsford. I could talk to Mr. Vest and Mr. Philips about studying with them."

"What about your plans for today? Did you bring me out here thinkin' we'd make love?"

"No, Susie," he said. "I most honestly didn't. I like you too much for that. Besides, you're too young. Maybe in a few years. Not now."

"Whadya think you'll be doin' in a few years?" Susie asked, her eyes returning to the horizon.

"I don't know. I suppose it depends on what happens tomorrow. If Pa winds up gettin' hung, I'll have to take over the farm. Otherwise,

I guess I want a family with kids, just like other folks. You want to have kids, don't you?"

"I ain't for sure. I don't know if some people just ain't cut out to be parents. Take my ma and pa. They shouldn't have had no kids. They ain't no good at takin' care of another human bein'. They can't even take care of theirselves."

"If they didn't have kids, you wouldn't be standing here, you know," Leslie said. "But I get what you're saying. Sam Nutter shouldn't oughtta been a parent."

"Anyway, I can't think about what might happen in a few years," Susie said. "I'm still tryin' to survive the next few days. Fortunately, with Mr. Botsford's help, I think I've found a place to stay here in Sedalia."

"Where might that be?"

"With the couple we met after the church service today. They said I am welcome to live with them."

Leslie recalled Mr. Botsford's chat with the couple, and he had feared just such a development. He was selfishly hoping that Susie would be unable to find a place to stay in Sedalia, that he could somehow persuade her to come to Carrollton.

Of course, he would also have to persuade his parents to either let Susie live with the family or to help find her some other place to stay, either of which would be a tall order. Especially considering they didn't know Susie existed, or even that Leslie was in Sedalia. And if they learned Leslie *was* in Sedalia, they likely wouldn't be in the mood to do him any favors.

But Leslie could dream.

"Do you even know these people?" he asked.

"They are acquaintances of Mr. Botsford's, from church."

"Hmm. I don't trust people who go to church voluntarily."

"They seem nice," Susie said. "Though, truth be told, I'm fairly certain I saw that same young man yesterday at Lizzie Cook's establishment. I saw several other men from that church there, as well."

"Did the man you saw at Lizzie Cook's house see you there?" Leslie asked, alarmed.

"I don't know. What difference would it make if he did?"

"His motivation for taking you under his roof might be less than Christian if he knows you are acquainted with Miss Lizzie."

"Well, I don't see as I have much choice at this point," Susie said forlornly. "It ain't like I got other options."

"But I was thinkin' you could wind up coming to Carrollton. We have a big house, and . . ."

"Leslie, we've talked about that. I just ain't sure it would work out. Once your parents found out about my family, I'm fairly certain they would disapprove. Your sisters said your mother is very strict and old fashioned. How do you think she would like me, a whore's daughter, born to nothing?"

"Mother doesn't like much of anybody," Leslie said.

"No, Leslie, you and your sisters and Mr. Botsford have already done more than I could have expected. I'm just gonna have to figure things out on my own now. I'll manage to get by somehow."

"So, you've made up your mind?"

"Yes. I hope to move in with them tomorrow."

Leslie shuffled a few feet away, with his back to Susie. After several seconds, he turned to face her.

"I was just hoping somehow to keep seeing you, either here or at home," he said. "Will you at least write to let me know how you're doing?"

"I promise," Susie said.

She then stood on her toes and kissed Leslie full on the mouth.

Late Afternoon

Leslie helped Susie out of the carriage in front of the Ives House and watched her walk inside. He sat in the carriage for several long minutes, his mind still racing with thoughts of Susie and their afternoon together.

He wasn't sure what conclusions to draw.

"You best be moving on, Leslie."

It was Mary, whom Leslie hadn't seen approach from the hotel. He couldn't think of anybody he'd rather see at this moment.

"Hi, Mary," he said. "What are you up to? I have something I want to talk with you about."

"I can't imagine what it might be," Mary said, smiling. "We probably should go inside. It's cold, and I assume you still don't want Mother or Pa to see you."

Leslie climbed down from the carriage, and the brother and sister walked together into the Ives House. They found a private spot between the lobby and the depot.

Leslie took his time getting to the point.

"You know, Mary, I thought I wanted to marry you when I was a little boy," he said. "As I got older I outgrew that stage, but I've been comparing girls to you ever since. Now I've finally found a girl who seems perfect, and I don't know what to do. Susie says she's gonna stay here in Sedalia. I'm afraid I'll never see her again. What do you think I should do?"

"About all you can do is try to remain in contact with her. You can write letters and maybe visit. In a couple years, if you still feel the same, maybe you can move here and pursue her properly."

"I don't know if I can wait that long," Leslie said. "I think about her all day long, even when I'm at Pa's trial, and then I can't get to sleep because I'm thinking about her when I'm lying in bed. Do you think it's possible I'm in love?"

"I suppose so. I've thought I was in love a few times, though I know now I wasn't. But I don't think I was ever as fond of anybody as you are of Susie."

"You've talked to Susie. Do you think she feels the same way as me?"

"Yes, I think so, but she's also afraid. She's just a girl, and she's all by herself in a strange place. She wants to get her feet on the ground before she does anything else. I think she's being smart."

"You'd do the same thing in her place?"

"Yes," Mary said. "It seems to me you have two choices. You can be patient and see what happens in the next couple of years, or you can move out of the house and down here to Sedalia to be near Susie. I don't know how you'd live, but I suppose you might manage somehow."

"Do you think Mother and Pa would approve of that?"

"No, I'm sure you'd be on your own. But if you really are in love . . ."

After dispensing her counsel, Mary went upstairs in the Ives House. Leslie was just as confused as he had been ten minutes earlier.

***

Leslie climbed back into the carriage, intent on returning the horse and rig to the stable. As he started to pull away from the Ives House, he looked left down the street.

"Oh, drat," he said under his breath.

He saw his father walking toward him.

And his father saw him.

"Why, hello, Leslie," Colonel William A. Warner said matter-of-factly as he approached.

"Uh, hello to you, too, Pa," Leslie said, stopping the horse in its tracks. "I guess you might be wondering what I'm doing here."

"Not really," Colonel Warner said. "Sallie and Mr. Botsford have kept me apprised of your situation."

"So you've known I was here? When did they tell you?"

"Several days ago. They thought it best I knew what was transpiring with my own family. We haven't shared the information with your mother, however."

Leslie exhaled and smiled.

"That's probably for the best," he said.

"For your best, at any rate," Colonel Warner said.

"Oh, Pa, you must have known I'd try to come down here. It ain't every day a boy's father is on trial for murder. I wasn't about to miss out on it."

"I understand, but that doesn't mean I approve. What's done is done. Now all that matters is that we remain together as a family."

"What about Mother? She'll be fuming when she learns I'm here."

"Don't worry about your mother. I can handle her when the need arises. In any case, we have more pressing matters on our minds than our insubordinate son."

Leslie smiled again. He was still seated in the carriage, and Colonel Warner was standing just off the boardwalk beside him.

"What are you doing out and about by yourself, anyway?" Leslie asked.

He still wasn't quite sure why a man who was on trial for murder—and could be sentenced to hang—wasn't in jail.

"I needed to clear my head," Colonel Warner said, "and I didn't want your mother or any lawyers around. Tomorrow is a mighty important day. I must confess I'm more than a little anxious about it."

He climbed into the carriage and sat beside his son.

"I understand you've met a nice young girl here."

"Yes, sir. Her name is Susie."

"Well, I'm happy for you. I'm sure she's a fine girl."

Sallie and Mr. Botsford evidently hadn't told him everything about Susie, and Leslie saw no reason to do so now.

"Yes, sir," he said. "I just hope I get to see her again. She's found a place to live here in Sedalia."

"Perhaps you'll find a way. As the poet said, 'Love conquers all.' I suppose you've just returned from a ride with Susie? I recognize your horse, but where did you get the carriage?"

"This is Mr. Botsford's. I was just returning it to the stable."

"Let's go for a ride," Colonel Warner said. "I have some things to discuss with you."

"Do you have any place in mind?"

"No, just out of town somewhere."

Leslie snapped the reins, and his horse commenced trotting. They headed east at a lively pace, and it was only a few minutes until they reached open country.

Leslie slowed the horse to a walk.

"I'd like to know more about you and Susie," Colonel Warner said, "but first we need to talk about something I've been putting off, something very important."

Leslie supposed the subject was sex, and he didn't need that talk. But he also didn't want his father to know he didn't need that talk.

"Oh?" he said.

"Yes. It's about the future of our family. My lawyers say they don't expect it, but I could be convicted. If I am, they think I would go to prison rather than be hanged. But in either case, I would be gone from the family. You need to be prepared for that."

"I've avoided thinking about it these last months," Leslie said.

He kept the horse at a slow walk.

"Well, it's time to think about it," Colonel Warner said. "You might become the man of the house before you turn seventeen years of age, forced to take care of your mother and your sisters. Do you think you are ready for that kind of responsibility?"

"Mother and Sallie can take care of themselves and then some."

Colonel Warner smiled.

"True enough," he said. "But there are many things only a man can do. They'll need you to be that man. Besides, I don't think Sallie will be in the house much longer. She and Mr. Botsford appear to be smitten. I expect a marriage will be in their future. That would leave only your mother, Mary, and the younger girls in the house."

"Pa, I think I can handle it," Leslie said. "I don't think it will come to that, though. I'm pretty sure the jury will find you innocent."

"Why do you think that?"

"I've been watching them. They like your lawyers better than the other lawyers."

"I'm afraid there is more to a trial than that," Colonel Warner said with a chuckle. "But I agree that Mr. Vest and Mr. Philips have been most impressive."

"They've been so impressive they've got me thinking about becoming a lawyer," Leslie said, smiling. He then tugged the reins sharply, and the horse stopped. He turned and looked directly into his father's eyes.

"Pa, why didn't they have you testify so you could give the jury your side of the story?" he asked.

"They thought it unwise," Colonel Warner said. "They suggested that my side of the story might get me hanged."

"What do you mean?"

"Well, Leslie, I shot an unarmed man in cold blood. You know I expected Sam Nutter to be armed, but the fact is he was not armed.

Even you don't know the whole story. Nobody does, because I have told no one. Mr. Vest and Mr. Philips didn't want me to tell it on the witness stand. They wanted to keep our side of the case to the simple story of a family man protecting his home from a madman."

"Sam wasn't a madman," Leslie said. "At the end there, he was trying to apologize."

"So you said at the time. But you weren't certain how serious he was. In any case, in my mind it was too late by then. He had done too much damage to our family and had said too many things about me personally."

"You didn't have to kill him."

"I thought I did. At least I had to try. I had to protect my honor as well as my family. Leslie, I thought it far more likely that any encounter with Sam Nutter would end with Sam killing me, rather than the other way around. I expected I would die and that Sam would go to prison. The family would be safe from him then, regardless of the outcome."

"Weren't you afraid of dyin'?"

"Not terribly. I was on death's doorstep after I was shot through the chest during the war, and I have been ready to walk through the gates ever since. I didn't expect to live as long as I have. I am neither a young man nor a strong man. I doubt I would last long in prison. Even if I'm found innocent and return home a free man, I don't expect to live much longer to enjoy that freedom."

"If you thought you were gonna die, why did you move the family away from Kentucky?" Leslie asked.

"Sam Nutter," Colonel Warner said. "It seems foolish now, but, at the time, your mother and I thought he could help take care of the family, financially and otherwise. It didn't take long for him to dispel that notion. By the time we moved to Lafayette County and Sallie married Sam, it was too late.

"But all of this is beside the point now, Leslie. All that matters is that you are ready to take over as the man of this family."

"I reckon so, Pa."

"I suppose you wish you were free to pursue Miss Susie instead of worrying about such serious things."

"Well, I guess I never would have met her if you hadn't killed Sam and been on trial in Sedalia," Leslie said. He looked his father in the eyes.

"No, I suppose not," Colonel Warner said. "You seem very fond of this girl."

"More than any other girl I've ever known. I've never had anybody I could talk to as easy as her."

"What about your sisters?"

"Ah, they don't count."

"What are your designs for the future where Susie is concerned?"

"Well, she said today she planned to move in with a family here in Sedalia," Leslie said. "Mr. Botsford introduced her to them this morning at church. If I had my druthers, she'd move to Carrollton and live with us. But I doubt Mother would approve of that idea."

"I doubt it, as well," Colonel Warner said. "In any case, we can't make a decision like that until after the verdict in my trial."

By this time, the trail had narrowed and the horse, carriage, and passengers were enveloped by darkness. Leslie had no idea where they were, but that didn't concern him now. His mind was racing with the things his father had said and the unknown fate that awaited him and the entire family.

"We best be heading back," Colonel Warner said.

Leslie pulled on the reins and turned the horse and carriage around. The father and son returned to Sedalia in silence.

January 30, 1871

The Trial

WAITING FOR THE VERDICT

. . . The Court House was densely thronged during the entire trial, especially so on the last night of the trial, every foot of available space being occupied. . . .

Col. Davis, of Lexington, opened the case for the State, and was followed by G. G. Vest, Esq., and Amos Green, Esq., of Lexington for the defense. The court then adjourned until 6 1/2 o'clock, P.M.

Long before that hour, men, women and children were there; window sills, aisles, platforms and the hall were filled to their utmost capacity, and an intense excitement everywhere pervaded the vast throng.

Col. Jno. F. Philips closed the case for the defense in an elaborate and most exhaustive argument. As an advocate he has few equals— no superiors in this State—as all who are competent to judge will fully attest.

. . . What was it to be? Was the popular pulse beating in sympathy with the prisoner's own? Were the twelve men, just retired, to return him to the bosom of his family—or to a felon's grave, or perhaps consign him to an ignominious servitude? Alas! Alas! How many in life are waiting for a verdict which cannot restore the dead to life and may add one more to the mortuary list.

—*Democrat*, February 2, 1871
A. Y. Hull, editor

The four days of testimony had concluded on a Saturday, giving all involved in the murder trial of Colonel William A. Warner a day off on Sunday. The lawyers apparently put the time to good use, working on their closing arguments.

Monday was all about the lawyers, and the folks of Sedalia couldn't get enough of them. It was a time in American history when orators were held in high esteem, and two of Missouri's best—George Graham Vest and John F. Philips—were to take center stage.

It must have been quite a scene, the lawyers standing in front of Judge Chan Townsley, addressing the twelve men of the jury and a courtroom packed with spectators, including reporters attempting to transcribe their every word. This was before official court reporters were commonplace, after all, so newspapers provided the only record of most details of the trial.

The Lexington *Caucasian* didn't have a reporter at the scene (it relied on the Sedalia *Bazoo's* account), but it still generated the following colorful description of the final day in Sedalia:

No case ever came off in Sedalia that excited so deep and universal an interest. The court room was crowded almost to suffocation. The attorneys could scarcely find room to stand while they delivered their speeches. Every available inch of space was occupied. Scores of ladies were scattered here and there amid the throng.
—Weekly Caucasian, February 4, 1871

The *Bazoo* provided extensive coverage only of Philips's closing speech; the *Democrat* reported on both Vest and Philips.

Of prosecutor Tilton Davis, the *Bazoo* said he spoke for an hour and a half and "well sustained the flattering reputation he has won as an attorney. His review of the testimony was good and he was listened to with careful attention by the jury and a large audience."

The *Bazoo* wasn't as flattering of defense attorney Amos Green of Lexington, describing his closing argument as "a labored yet excellent legal effort. While it wearied the jury, it abounded in well arranged legal points, evincing a carefully stored legal mind, and a careful study of the case."

Green also had the misfortune of speaking after Vest and before the court took a dinner break.

Philips would be the main attraction in the evening. Vest likely was the man most spectators had wanted to hear during the day. Remember, he had delivered what has become one of America's most famous closing arguments only a few months before.

In that case, he won the day by arguing that Old Drum the foxhound did not deserve to be shot dead. In this case, he would argue that Sam Nutter deserved exactly that.

What follows are highlights from the Sedalia *Democrat's* reporting of Vest's speech, which the newspaper said "occupied one hour and forty-one minutes":

"Gentlemen of the jury, I think I can afford you no better proof of my intense and earnest sincerity in the conduct of this case than by saying that if I had been placed in the same position that the defendant, William A. Warner, was when this unfortunate tragedy was enacted, I should have *done* just as he did. I do not desire to be misunderstood nor my language misinterpreted by this jury—but I say it boldly, holding myself *only* responsible for the avowal that had I been pursued as was he, that had I been threatened with instantaneous death as was he, and that had my family been maligned, traduced and vilified as was his—I would have shot down as the defendant did, the pursuer, the villain, the traducer. I would have sat in the same place as does Warner today, had I been surrounded by the same circumstances and subjected to the same terrible pressure. . . .

"And here, too, corroborative of what you already find before you, is the testimony of General Jo Shelby, who, like myself, was an advocate of the *lost cause*. He is a brave, true man, and, moreover, entirely disinterested. The defendant during the war was a Federal officer—but here we find Shelby standing by Warner through all the various phases of this tragedy, forgetful alike of previous political differences and personal prejudices. I say then most emphatically, he is a *disinterested* witness, and you must per force give his testimony the most complete credence. And you will remember that the general's evidence was most positive and specific. . . .

"I desire to 'tread lightly on the ashes of the dead.' The prosecutor requested me to do so, and I desire to do so. But I cannot ignore the facts in this case. I cannot but believe that the deceased poisoned the cistern of the defendant. And why do I arrive at this conclusion? I will explain that to you, gentlemen, in a very few moments.

"You remember the testimony of Captain Littlejohn. I submit to you that he was a fair and candid witness. On reviewing his statements you will remember that he testified that on a Sunday morning at about a quarter past six o'clock, he met Nutter near his—the witness'—house, and a few moments after he met Nutter's sister, the present Mrs. Callahan. Now this was coincident with the poisoning. And *now* I will pass home to you a point in this case which cannot have escaped your notice, and which unexplained as it is, speaks volumes against the deceased and his sister.

"If Capt. Littlejohn's statements be untrue, why do they remain *uncontradicted*? Ah, gentlemen, that is a question which none of you can answer. Mrs. Callahan is here—the person of all others who *could* solve this mystery—but her lips are sealed. Distinguished counsel represent the state—we cannot suppose for a moment that so *important* a point in the establishment of their case has been forgotten. No, they *dare* not explain and hence have not explained. . . .

"I desire to refer for a moment to the evidence we have implicating Nutter in the destruction of the defendant's stock and tending to show that Nutter was present on the night the shots were fired near the defendant's door. One or two witnesses distinctly remember meeting two men (the one colored, and the other resembling Nutter) at the times in question. This is uncontradicted, and I believe one of the parties was the deceased. And then we have the testimony of Mrs. Nutter, establishing undisputably the identity of her husband on the night of the shooting. She says she saw his footprint the next day, that there had been a hard shower the previous afternoon, making any impression upon the surface of the ground perceptible; that she is so positive because Nutter turned in his heel when walking; and that by these marks she identified the track beyond any question. Now this is perfectly natural—a wife ought, above all others, to know the shape of her husband's foot.

"Why, gentlemen of the jury in my sad experience, I have found that my wife not only knew my *footsteps*, but frequently on my arrival at home, could tell exactly where I had been and what I had been doing."

(Great laughter.)

"Now, gentlemen, this case resolves itself into this and nothing more—that the defendant killed Nutter because he feared death himself at Nutter's hands, and because the deceased had ruthlessly destroyed his domestic peace.

"The late Edwin M. Stanton uttered no nobler sentiment in his life than that expressed in the recent Sickles case in Washington, when he said, 'I hold that a man has as much right to protect his own honor as a woman her own virtue.'

"But, gentlemen, I must bring this argument to a close, but before doing so desire to reiterate what I have before said. I repeat that had I been placed in circumstances similar to those of the deceased, I would have acted just as did he. I shoulder the responsibility of saying this. When a man ruins my family, he deserves death. I am their natural protector—God has given them to me that I may shield and protect them from harm—and were I to see their peace destroyed and not avenge it, I were an arrant coward, a recreant to my manhood, my dear ones and my God. I say this in all sincerity and truth.

"The case is with you, and if I have failed to point out to you the line of your duty, I pray that God may help you do it."

On that point, Vest concluded. Green addressed the jury, and then the court took a break.

The *Bazoo* said John F. Philips began his closing argument at 7:30 p.m. and described the scene in detail:

> . . . *Men grouped together on the floor, packed close together, to hear the finale of this all absorbing case, and see the keystone of the arch properly placed. Eager, anxious faces, densely packed together, could be seen in the dim light of that apology for a court room.*
>
> *In front of the judge's seat, and inside the rail, sat the prisoner, Col. Warner, with that wearied countenance of his alight with those keen eyes now resting on the jury in whose hands rested his life, then glancing over that sea of faces, and then resting on the floor. By his side was Vest, the Demosthenes of the bar. On the right sat the twelve men with whom was this one man's life, tired and wearied, yet all attention.*
>
> *When Col. P commenced, the scene was a splendid subject for the pencil of an artist. Col. Philips commenced his address for the defense slowly and calmly and amid complete silence.*
>
> —*Bazoo*, January 31, 1871

The *Bazoo* said Philips spoke for an hour and a half, as opposed to the *Democrat's* estimate of two hours.

The newspapers' accounts contain substantial differences, so the summary that follows contains pieces of both:

"We find arraigned at this bar a man who has reached that mature life from which point, not far ahead, he may see the setting sun. A man occupying a high position in society, surrounded by all that makes life happy and pleasant, across whose pathway no serpent had ever crossed, until, in the sere and yellow leaf, we find him now here on trial for his life.

"Now, the question with us, and with you, gentlemen of the jury, is to inquire what motive has impelled him to commit such a deed as that with which he is charged. He has gone outside of the law to accomplish his object, and he stands before the public as a murderer.

"He came from Kentucky to Missouri, where, in the beloved state, he might acquire a competence for himself and family. He finds a home in Lafayette County. A man who never harmed a human being before, who had lived a life of happiness, and whose every attribute of character had made him the embodiment of the noble man.

"But the serpent came to his Eden—came to the happy household to blast and wither it. My friend Captain Davis said it was a sad day that the deceased ever met him. It was, indeed, truly so. But the question with us is, with whom did the great fault lie? We have not been permitted to inquire particularly into the cause of these troubles—troubles which sprang up between the wedded pair. She—the wife of the deceased—found that she was not happy with him—could not live with him—and when she found that the longer she so lived the unhappier she became, she took that demure resort, and went to the home of her father and her mother. . . .

"Gentlemen of the jury, my object is to show that the prisoner was in great danger of his life and that the deceased meant just what he said when he threatened his life. . . .

"The person who poisoned that well sought to grasp in its deadly effect father, mother, daughter, wife—all of that loved household—to hurt them, in his malice, into eternity. Who could have sought this but the man who had been heard to say, 'I'll poison the whole outfit'? . . .

"Poison, the bullet, threats, and the destruction of property had failed to accomplish in full the work of this man, Nutter; and then he turns author, puts his scandal and venomous slanders into print, and publishes a pamphlet filled with words of foul import. What that pamphlet says, you, gentlemen of the jury, are not permitted to see. . . .

"One witness states that he told Nutter, 'Sam, if you publish that pamphlet, Warner will kill you, certain.' No man of any principle would have published it. It was signing Nutter's death warrant when he issued it. We desired and expected it to go to the jury in evidence, but it was not allowed. . . .

"Now, gentlemen of the jury, Warner was cognizant of all the threats of the deceased—this is an unquestionable and irrefutable conclusion from the evidence. And the *law* being as I have stated, was he not justified under the law in striking the enemy just when he did? . . .

"Gentlemen of the jury, our newly fledged prosecuting attorney desires a conviction in this case. He seeks the blood of a victim to paint a feather in his cap and to establish his reputation in his new career. But, gentlemen, I would rather have him practice on someone else than my client. He complains of the terrible increase of crime, that it stalks abroad in the community with no one to molest or make it afraid, and then assigns this as a reason for the conviction of this gray-haired man.

"I am reminded forcibly of the man who became restive under the seeming progress of the women's rights movement and concluded to do his share in smothering this dangerous element of discord. So acting on the reflections, he went home and whipped his wife severely, alleging as his reason, therefore, that he'd teach those women to keep in their places. (Laughter.) And so the prosecutor would sacrifice my client, because crime is rampant, and the immolation of the guiltless will tend to deter the guilty from wrong. Oh! Mighty Caesar, hast thou indeed fallen so low?

"Gentlemen, I have trodden as lightly on the ashes of the dead as duty to the living would permit, and in mercy to and respect for her sex I have spared the sister of the deceased, although her testimony is so remarkable and her conduct so unnatural.

"My task is done. Our cause is in your hands—life, honor, hope, sorrow, family are all at issue—the life of a good citizen, a true friend, a gallant soldier—the honor and happiness of a household proud in the dignity of merited worth and unsullied virtue.

"Do the dignity and peace of the state demand such a victim as a sacrifice? There he sits before you. Look you into his face, and answer by your verdict whether it mirrors the heart of a murderer?

"Yonder, too, are his wife and daughters. They are not here for effect, to sway you away from your path of duty. As the dove when the hawk spreads wing over her young, nestles near to protect and aid, so these loved and loving ones are here, just where you will always find such, to encourage with their presence—to bless with their prayers and whisper in the husband's and father's ear sweet and tender words of hope in this most trying hour of life.

"Let these matters not sway your judgments but ensure your careful consideration of the law and the evidence. May he who delighteth more in mercy than judgment so guide your deliberations, that the majesty of the law may be vindicated and the prisoner acquitted."

Circuit attorney J. D. Hines closed the final arguments with an address that the *Bazoo* reported lasted about one hour, saying, "It was able, argumentative and logical. He closed with an appeal to maintain the dignity of the law." The *Democrat* said Hines "showed himself a master at the bar. Col. Hines acquitted himself very creditably indeed." Neither newspaper provided any further details on the prosecution's closing arguments.

The case was then put in the hands of the twelve men of the jury.

It was about ten o'clock when the jury was taken charge of by the Sheriff, and with some effort, a passage way was cleared through the mass of people for their egress to the jury room. Most of the audience awaited the result, standing, caucusing, conjecturing, talking over the all-absorbing topic. Col. Warner, quiet, pale and anxious, kept his seat.

—Bazoo, January 31, 1871

With the final arguments in Colonel William A. Warner's first-degree murder trial ending so late in the day, you might have expected the jury to wait until the next morning to convene to consider the evidence and reach a verdict, or at least require the next day to conclude its job. Jury deliberations at murder trials these days can drag on for days.

Of course, this was the nineteenth century, not the twenty-first century.

Defense lawyers George Vest and John Philips must have been confident in their case. They argued that the jury shouldn't consider any lesser charges, and they wanted no part of "moral insanity," a nebulous ailment that was an accepted mid-nineteenth-century defense. (It most often was used with female defendants and frequently was associated with their menstrual cycles.)

No, Vest and Philips were gambling they could sway the jury with their claim of justifiable homicide.

As part of that, Philips suggested in his closing argument that Nutter's hand position indicated Colonel Warner might have thought Nutter had a gun. But, for the most part, the lawyers simply claimed that Colonel Warner was justified in killing Nutter because Nutter had tormented his family and was a believable threat to kill Colonel Warner.

The jury didn't know what was in Colonel Warner's mind when he killed Sam Nutter, however, because he didn't testify. You wonder whether jury members read anything into that fact.

They had heard the eloquent arguments of Vest and Philips, and wasted no time in making up their collective mind. The Sedalia newspaper reporters disagreed on just how little time the jury took to render a verdict, but it was quick by any standard.

The *Democrat* said the jury returned with its verdict "in the unprecedentedly short space of ten minutes."

The *Bazoo's* account:

Fifteen minutes passed when a bustle was heard at the entrance and words were whispered through the audience, "Here comes the jury." Crowding through, led by the gray-haired Sheriff, they quietly filed into their accustomed place. All eyes were on those twelve quiet men. Judge Townsley broke the strange silence with:

"Gentlemen of the jury, have you agreed upon your verdict?"

Mr. Chas. Taylor, foreman of the jury, half-rising with the indictment in his hand, responded, "We have."

"Pass it to the Clerk!" quietly yet firmly spoke the Judge.

Sheriff [William] Paff handed it up to the deputy clerk, who tremblingly handled it, and after taking a moment, nervously read it to himself, then in a clear distinct voice read aloud, "We the jury find the defendant not guilty as found in the indictment."

For a moment more that strange silence lasted, then someone commenced a faint tapping of a bootheel on the floor, evidently in dread of a judicial reprimand; none came, and louder and yet louder came these cheers, until swelling into wild yells the very courthouse shook with the wild clamor.

Above the waving of hats, ladies' handkerchiefs waved in token of joy. Out upon the streets rang the wild huzzas, windows were raised, doors were opened, pedestrians stopped in the slippery street, for a moment wondering at the noise but in next they guessed it all.

During the wild enthusiasm which prevailed, the tall form of Col. Warner could be seen erect, free again, surrounded by his friends, with great teardrops in his eyes; both hands engaged in grasping welcomes; first among them came his true and talented lawyers; then Judge Townsley in the kindness of his heart came with an outstretched hand and a cheery word of welcome; then the jury and all.

There was joy in the house, and the light of freedom came glistening through the teardrops of Col. Warner's eye. But happiest of all that happy crowd were the wife, daughters, and lady friends of the prisoner present; tears and joyous laughter were merrily mingled, with interchanging kisses. . . .

—Bazoo, January 31, 1871

There you have it. After more than two years of legal gymnastics, four days of testimony, and a very long day of closing arguments, the jury needed only ten or fifteen minutes to resolve the entire issue. Seems almost too easy.

Evening

As Colonel Warner and his wife led the celebratory march down Ohio Avenue, Leslie bounced along arm in arm with his sister Mary. Sallie and Mr. Botsford were just in front of them. All were smiling and laughing.

Friends and acquaintances followed, as did Colonel Warner's lawyers and most members of the jury. Dozens of curious townsfolk watched from windows and sidewalks, some even joining in the procession.

It seemed like a late-night Independence Day parade, but without the horses and fireworks.

To Leslie, his father suddenly appeared years younger, having shed the weight of more than two years of legal wranglings compounded by an impossible-to-know fate that might well have included a noose around his neck.

"Ain't this grand?" Leslie said to Mary.

Before Mary could respond, Leslie had reason to be even happier. He spotted Susie standing in front of a store, dressed in fine new clothing. She was smiling.

Leslie, without saying a word, let go of Mary and leaped onto the boardwalk, throwing his arms around Susie. He pulled her close and held on for a good five seconds.

"Come with me," he finally said.

Leslie grabbed Susie's left hand with his right and tugged her into the street, angling back to his spot in the family hierarchy next to Mary, who grabbed Susie's right hand.

The parade continued down Ohio, crossed the railroad tracks, and turned left to reach the Ives House, where Colonel Warner stopped to address the gathering.

"Thanks to all of you," he said, raising his hands victoriously. "This is a wonderful occasion that I shall remember for the rest of my life. I am a free man at last."

With that, he embraced and kissed his wife of twenty-five years, then hugged Sallie and shook the right hand of Mr. Botsford. Looking beyond Sallie, he spotted Leslie, still clutching the hands of Susie and Mary.

Colonel Warner took three steps forward and stopped in front of Leslie.

"I presume this pretty young woman is Susie," he said. "It's my honor to make your acquaintance."

At this point, Leslie realized his mother, who stood just behind her husband, was looking at him queerly. Hers was a look that combined disbelief, consternation, anger, and curiosity. She didn't say a word; she simply looked—at Leslie, then at Susie, then at Leslie again.

His mother's burning eyes usually turned Leslie into a trembling bowl of mush. And, given that he had just perpetrated the greatest act of disobedience of his life, he might have expected to virtually disintegrate before her glare.

But he didn't.

"Mother," Leslie said, "this is Susie Willis."

And he kissed Susie on the lips—a quick, affectionate peck.

"I hope to marry her someday."

"We'll talk about this later," Georgia Warner said, without a smile.

Leslie turned to Susie, whose hand he was still holding. Mary had moved a few steps away with Colonel Warner, who was now busily shaking hands with members of the assembled crowd.

"Susie, you know I'll do whatever it takes to see you again," he said.

"I promise to write," Susie said with a wan smile. "But now I have to go."

"Be careful. OK?" Leslie said. "You don't know these folks you're movin' in with. I just hope they have your best interests at heart."

Susie smiled again.

"Oh, Leslie, you worry too much. I'll be just fine. I'm sure of it."

She backed away, turned, and walked to the boardwalk, where Leslie saw someone waiting for her. It was Lizzie Cook.

Georgie Nutter Botsford

EPILOGUE

William A. Warner lived more than thirty years after his acquittal in the killing of Sam Nutter. As far as can be surmised, he was involved in no more homicides—or anything else terribly exciting.

The *Wakenda Record* of Carrollton, Missouri, did mention Warner in its pages a few times in the 1870s, the most notable instance being August 27, 1875, when it said he "hooked a fine pike . . . about 14 inches in length."

By the 1880 census, Warner and his family had returned to Kentucky. He was listed as a "distillery storekeeper" living in Lexington, Kentucky, with his wife, Georgia, and children Ella, sixteen, and Joe. Shelby, fourteen.

The couple lived in Kenton County, Kentucky, for the 1900 census, and the former Union colonel died there May 15, 1902, at the age of eighty-four years, six months, eight days, according to his death certificate.

Georgia then moved to Kansas City, where she lived with her daughter Sallie until her death in 1916 at the age of eighty-nine.

Both William A. and Georgia Warner are buried in Lexington Cemetery in Kentucky.

On November 16, 1871, barely nine months after her father's acquittal, Sallie Warner Nutter married James Botsford in Carrollton. The *Wakenda Record* described the nuptials thusly:

"It is said that a woman is most elegantly and tastefully dressed when a person cannot tell how she is dressed. If this be so the bride, Mrs. Sallie W. Nutter, the daughter of our fellow townsman, Colonel W. A. Warner, was perfect in her toilet, for I do not now remember what she wore; and therefore must disappoint my lady readers, who, doubtless, expect a description of that part of the ceremony. I know that the beautiful bride, and her not less beautiful sister, were the most elegantly and richly dressed, very nearly alike, and that the whole affair was marked with perfect good taste."

The newlyweds, with Sallie's daughter, Georgie, lived in Jefferson City while Botsford served as the U.S. attorney for the Western District of Missouri, a position he held for seven years. Botsford adopted Georgie after he married Sallie, but the couple had no other children.

The family relocated in 1879 to Kansas City, where he established the legal firm of Botsford, Deatherage & Young. It was very much a family affair.

One partner (Marcus Tullius Cicero Williams) had married Sallie's sister Mary in 1875; another (Buckner F. Deatherage) married Sallie's daughter, Georgie, in 1888.

Marcus and Mary Williams had six children, including a daughter named Georgie Warner Williams. Buckner and Georgie Deatherage had two daughters, Dorothy and Sallie Deatherage.

The Botsfords became a prominent family in Kansas City, where wife and husband remained until their deaths, James Botsford in 1915 and Sallie Warner Nutter Botsford in 1923. Both are buried in Kansas City's Elmwood Cemetery.

Sallie's nemesis, Lizzie Nutter, had also married a lawyer, James Callahan. They remained in Lafayette County through the 1880 census but were living in Independence, Missouri, as of the 1900 census. The union produced a daughter, Bessie, in 1873.

The Callahans, mother, father, and daughter, are buried in Machpelah Cemetery in Lexington, Missouri, as are Lizzie and Sam Nutter's parents.

Sam Nutter is not buried in the family plot, however, and his burial place doesn't show up on any grave-search websites.

It is worth noting that the lawsuit Sallie had filed against Lizzie just after Sam's death over the bulk of his estate—for which Lizzie supposedly paid $17,000—was finally settled in October 1873. The verdict favored Sallie.

The other female in our story, Susie Willis, probably never met Leslie Warner, but she was a real person, and she did live in Sedalia.

What we know of her comes from a December 3, 1874, article in the Sedalia *Democrat*:

ANOTHER VICTIM.
DEATH OF SUSIE WILLIS, A PROSTITUTE.

For nearly two years Susie Willis has been living in Sedalia, making her home in Lizzie Cook's house of prostitution.

About a year ago she went to her mother's home in Warrensburg, and gave birth to a child, which her mother took to keep, and as soon as her health would permit Susie returned to Sedalia to resume her life of shame.

When she first entered on the glittering stage, in this city, she was only about 14 years old—her cheek was rosy, and her form though delicate, finely moulded.

For some time she has been fast losing her healthful appearance, her eyes becoming lusterless, and her cheeks growing pail [sic] and wan. A few days ago she was attacked with a violent fever, and the Madame called a physician, who gave her all the attention in his power, but soon ascertained that she must die.

When told of this fact she at once declared that she must be taken to her mother and the little waif Eddie, her baby boy, there to breathe her last.

No persuasions could produce a change of her mind. So yesterday morning she was carried to the depot, and tenderly placed on the cars, and sent to her mother's home in Warrensburg. Her limbs were growing cold at the time, and she was probably dying. At four o'clock yesterday evening Lizzie Cook received a telegram stating that Susie had just breathed her last, and went to Warrensburg on the first train to see that she was decently buried, her mother being a poor widow.

Of all the prominent characters in the Warner–Nutter episode, Leslie Warner became the biggest mystery. All we know is that he died in 1891 and is buried in the family plot in the Lexington Cemetery in Kentucky.

One possible detail about Leslie appears in the Kansas City, Missouri, directory of 1872, which lists a Leslie Warner as a student boarding at 907 McGee.

A Leslie Warner also appears in the 1880 census as a dry goods clerk in Louisville, Kentucky, and in several Louisville city directories of that period. However, the directory listings were for "Leslie S."

rather than "Leslie C.," and the census indicates Leslie's age as twenty-four. Our Leslie Warner would have been twenty-six.

It makes one wonder what became of the boy born into wealth who lived through the violent times of Civil War Kentucky and post-Civil War Missouri. He doesn't show up in any marriage records or military listings, and the county clerk's office in Fayette County, Kentucky, where he is buried, has no will or probate records on file for Leslie Warner.

In any case, Leslie Warner died young. He would have been thirty-seven years old.

July 14, 2012

Georgette Stanley Page opened the door, and her daughter Sallie stood just behind her.

After more than a year of digging through digital records, microfilm, and barely legible court records, I finally had come face to face with my story.

It had been nearly 150 years earlier that the Warners—with mother Georgia (or Georgette), daughter Sallie, and all the others—had moved to Missouri from Kentucky and set the events of this story into motion. Now their descendants were standing before me, still in Missouri, even if it was mere blocks from the Kansas state line.

Georgette had a direct tie to the family I had been researching all those months. Her grandmother—Georgie—was the only child of Sallie Warner Nutter Botsford. Georgette was born in 1925 and Georgie died in 1940, so Georgette had grown up around her grandmother and remembered her very well.

"She told me to stand up straight," Georgette said.

Georgette said Georgie never talked to her about a killing in the family. In fact, Georgette knew nothing about it. She had done some genealogical research and had discovered a few pieces of the family puzzle, but nothing about a killing.

Although a bit apprehensive at first, I was happy to fill her in on the details. She was happy to hear them. And she had no problem with me making them public.

"My grandmother would have died if people knew these things," she said. "But those were different times. I think people should know."